Possess the Land

By the same author

As Alan White

DEATH FINDS THE DAY
THE WHEEL
THE LONG NIGHT'S WALK
THE LONG DROP

As James Fraser

THE EVERGREEN DEATH
A COCK-PIT OF ROSES
DEADLY NIGHTSHADE

Possess the Land

ALAN WHITE

Originally published in England
under the title *Kibbutz*

Harcourt Brace Jovanovich, Inc.
New York

First American edition

ISBN 0-15-146910-5

Library of Congress Catalog Card Number: 70-124828

Printed in the United States of America

for Anthony Samuel

and Julian Muller

"... that ye may live, and multiply, and go in and possess the land which the Lord sware unto your fathers."

—Deuteronomy 8:1

AUTHOR'S NOTE

This is not a historical novel. It is certainly not a history of any part of the journey of people to the land now called Israel, nor is it a description of their lives once they've arrived. The people and places I write about are entirely of my own creation; to the best of my knowledge there never has been a Kibbutz Eli-Dov, or a Kibbutz Guvena.

I am not qualified to take sides or express opinions for or against the Israelis, some of whom are Moslems, or the Arabs, some of whom are Jewish, in the conflict which now ensues in the lands of the Eastern Mediterranean.

BOOK ONE

SEED IN THE DESERT

Abraham counted seven fedayeen stepping slowly down the banks of the wadi round clustered boulders, each nearer the others than was necessary or safe. Arabs are afraid of the night. One moment the wadi was empty, its stream sucked dry by earth and sand since Biblical times, its boulders cracked by incessant hot day sun and cold night winds; the next moment seven men in line moved over the lip of stone down the eroded banks into the wadi bed.

"They never learn," Abraham muttered.

When the Arabs reached the bed of the wadi they turned south at first, then followed the wadi as it turned to the west. Their faces froze in the cold moonlight; skin tanned dark as saddle-leather, yellowed malarial eyes, dark wiry moustaches; they were a long way from home, these Arab guerilla mercenaries, paid in coin to raid and destroy the Jewish farmers of the border lands.

Abraham, Dov and Eli sat still on the promontory halfway up the wadi. Dov had a stiletto and was experienced in its use; Abraham, the oldest of the trio, had the rifle and the five rounds of ammunition; Eli made do with a skinning knife his father had brought from Omsk and four iron canisters loaded that afternoon with gunpowder and blue granite chips. The canisters had originally been covers for oxygen cylinders in the British-controlled docks at Haifa; they would explode with the fury of a grenade when packed with gunpowder and blue granite.

Eli too had seen the fedayeen; nervous, he touched Dov's arm. Abraham heard Dov swallow as he counted. Seven, in one party, the most ever.

The cucumber for supper had been bitter, and Dov had complained he couldn't digest it. Even Abraham, with his stomach of leather, could taste cucumber on the back of his tongue. Dov burped silently. Next year they'd find out why the cucumber they grew was always bitter, why the newly planted apricot trees had leaf curl, the potatoes blight. Next year, if the fedayeen gave them time! The three of them had come over the edge of the wadi under the shelter of a group of cleft rocks. They could return the same way without being seen. The fedayeen below them moved slowly in line up the bed of the wadi. The man in the lead held his unusually long arms wide of his body as he picked his way through the boulders. On his back he carried a long rifle, and in his right hand a knife's curving blade gleamed gold in the tired light of the old moon. He was chewing; Abraham was so close he could discern the flash of teeth. The second fedayeen was carrying his rifle pointed forward, left hand along the barrel, right hand on the stock, finger in the trigger guard. The third man wore the long robes and head-dress of a bedouin, with several coiled halters around his shoulder. All the others were wearing trousers and dark woollen shirts, and all save the bedouin were bare-headed, nothing between them and Allah above. They made no sound and looked neither right nor left.

Abraham touched the shoulders of Eli and Dov and they withdrew through the cleft in the rocks, out of the wadi, as planned.

The kibbutz was less than half a mile away, on the plain where this wadi joined another from the north. There were five stone buildings and a long row of tents. Next year, despite the fedayeen, they'd erect stone buildings to sleep in, one room to a building, with a toilet, a kitchen and a bathroom on the back. Already they had the plan and had marked out the sites, one for each of the families of the kibbutz. Each plot would have its own kitchen garden. All the plots were laid out so that no house would overlook any other, because Abraham believed that lack of privacy

10

had driven more people from the kibbutz than hard work and primitive conditions. This year with 200 dunams of land to clear, stones to move, crops to plant, animals to tend, houses would have been a luxury. "If you want luxury," Abraham had told them when they asked for houses, "go to Tel Aviv and walk down the Dizengoff!" Three couples had taken him at his word. He'd consented to a bathhouse, a communal dining room with kitchens, a store for the weapons they would steal from the British and the Arabs, a covered beast-yard, and an office, which he seldom used. Offices grow paper more easily than a field of barley grows weeds, and Abraham didn't object when they called him a hard primitive man. "Our nation," he said, "will be built by the hard men, not by the Karaites, or Samaritans and such like, or even the rabbis!" Abraham didn't have much time for religion. "I'm a Palestinian," he'd say, "and if you want to know my religion I'll tell you it's none of your business!" And when they'd press him, and say everybody must believe in something, he'd clench his right hand, or pick up a handful of soil, and bellow, "That's what I believe in, our country, and our strength to make it fertile." The men of the kibbutz would smile tolerantly at one another, and at Abraham, and at Sarah, who had reached an age of thirty-six years without bearing him a child, and the women would pat their bellies complacently as women will, and nod their heads at their proud menfolk.

Abraham, Eli and Dov ran swiftly across the plain to the place where the wadis joined. Here the boulders ended; here the wadi bed was flat as a burial ground, littered with stones the size of a man's skull. Eli jumped over the crest, and quickly placed his canisters at six-pace intervals among the stones. They had rubbed them with mud, shaping them like wadi stones, and now they lay indistinguishable. The fuse cords had already been prepared; he cut the estimated lengths with his skinner's knife, inserted the ends carefully into the holes in the caps of the canisters. The cut-off ends he coiled and put into his pocket for future use. Then he

11

unwound the main fuse cord behind him and climbed up the steep wadi walls. Dov placed himself on the other side of the wadi, his knife in his hand. Eli ran the fuse behind a rock where Abraham sat invisible in the pallid moonlight. Eli was sweating, though the night air was cold. Abraham smiled at him from the depths of the shadow; this was Eli's first night job, a *bar mitzvah* gift from all the men of the kibbutz, a *mazel tov* to his manhood.

Eli took out the box of big-headed fuse matches and licked one the way Ya'akov had shown him, to prevent the dust from flaring. An unlicked match can shine a light for fifty paces; one delicately licked, so Ya'akov had explained, would splutter dully with intense heat and no light. Only three matches remained in the box and who knows when they'd get more. The nagging doubts of youth: "What shall we do," he thought, "when we run out of matches and fuse cords and bullets and chemicals to make the explosive canisters; and still the fedayeen come?" Youth is a worrisome time; age gives confidence in an unknown future, faith to face the unknown. Age has hope; youth needs the details. But then Eli remembered how Abraham had answered these questions before they left the kibbutz. "If we worry about that today," Abraham had said, "what shall we have to worry about tomorrow?"

Abraham hissed. The line of fedayeen had entered their branch of the wadi. Seven of them, still at the close three-pace interval that revealed their fear, spanning eighteen paces. Four canisters had been placed at six-pace intervals, spanning eighteen paces. The first Arab would travel six paces while the fuse cord, lit by Eli, was burning its way to the canisters. The next hiss would come when the leader was opposite the last canister but one.

As always, Abraham hoped the Arabs would not see the snake line of fuse cord stretching out of the wadi from the rock-like canisters. Fuse cord is stiff and bends to the landscape only when it wishes. It has a tendency to reassert its independence and spring upward, visible in the moonlight, after it is laid. Eli had been told to twist it continuously as he laid it; Abraham hoped he had remembered his instructions. So much for a boy to learn. Of course he had the excitement and enthusiasm, but those qualities can never replace skilled experience.

Slowly the fedayeen moved along the unseen line of canisters. Abraham watched them, every step, cradling his rifle in his hands. He preferred to shoot sitting down, balancing the barrel of the rifle on his knee for better aim. The rifle had no sling; some of the men wound string through the sling swivels, but Abraham preferred to use it without encumbrances. Firing at twenty yards, if fire he must, Abraham would get a price for each of his bullets; one bullet, one Arab, a fair rate of exchange when you considered the bullets had come all the way from Jaffa, smuggled in under the eyes of the British who thought their Mandate gave them the right to deny the Jews self-protection.

"*Shalom*," Abraham muttered, and pushed forward the safety catch of his rifle; four canisters, five bullets, two knives, seven fedayeen; they needed barbed wire, machine-guns, sentry posts, searchlights, to preserve the peace.

Dov had seen them come into the branch of the wadi. What he would give for a Vickers gun just now! Seven in a line, start one end, traverse along over open sights the way he'd watched the British. What could they do with one rifle and five rounds, two knives, Abraham good as two men granted, but Eli a boy fresh from the *schule*. One two three four five of the fedayeen had rifles, and two of them had bandoliers of ammunition in addition to what was in the magazines already. Trust the Arabs to have rifles and ammunition, though they often had no training in how to use them and no discipline. "We Jews are good at improvisation," Dov thought. Take the canisters. Hand grenades, or even mines, would have been much better. "One of these days," he thought, "we won't need to improvise. We'll have the right stuff. One of these days."

Two paces to go, one, then Abraham hissed. He heard the scrape of the fuse match on the board, hoping Eli had remembered to lick it. He felt, rather than saw, the dull red flare,

13

knew Eli'd press it to the spliced ends of the fuse cord. Eli was a good lad! Sometimes fuse cord had a break in it and sputtered to a futile death somewhere along its length. Five paces, four, three paces, two, and now the leader of the fedayeen is on the first canister. Abraham felt Eli slither round the rock next to him, heard his prayer.

Then, in sequence, front to back, each of the canisters neatly exploded, one two three four. The line of fedayeen stood outlined in the flashes for a brief moment. Then the blast came, screams, and gouts of blood. The leader and the man behind him, numbers four, five and six, all were blown sideways by the shock of the explosion. All were dead, of that there could be no doubt. Each was drenched in blood as if the heavens had suddenly rained paint. Three, the bedouin, was still erect, falling slowly to his knees, his face a mask of blood. As he fell, he tried to speak, but no words came. He raised his knife; lifting his arm to shoulder height took desperate strength. Seven, no doubt feeling the extra fear of being last, must have hurried forward a couple of paces. The sixth man had protected him from the blast in front; the explosion behind was too far away to reach him with full force.

Dov came racing down the side of the wadi. "Leave the bedouin," Abraham shouted, but Dov, in post-concussive deafness, appeared not to hear. Eli also headed for the kneeling figure. "Leave the bedouin," Abraham shouted again, but Eli, caught in the euphoria of action, ignored him.

Neither had seen the last man dart to the shelter of a rock at the side of the wadi. Abraham could see the barrel of a rifle poke forward. He skittered on hands and knees along the wadi top, his heart pounding in his chest. Eli and Dov arrived at the bedouin at the same moment. The bedouin was not dead. His arm made an ineffectual thrust with the knife, which Dov parried easily. Dov looked at Eli. First time, first kill. The boy's face shone pale beneath his sunburn.

"Kill him," Dov said. The boy blinked, swallowed. "Kill him!"

The boy thrust his knife forward towards the folds of the bedouin's robe, but the point stopped there. The boy pulled

14

back his arm and pushed the blade forward again, and again it failed to penetrate. Now tears were rolling down his cheeks. "I can't get it in, Dov," he cried. Dov drew back his own arm, plunged it forward carrying the knife which pierced the bedouin's clothing, through his chest to his heart. Blood welled from the bedouin's mouth as he died.

At that moment the seventh Arab fired his rifle; Eli took the bullet in the back of his head and half his face spattered the bedouin's robes.

Dov went to ground instantly, trying to hide behind the bodies. Abraham stopped, moved cautiously round the rock, saw the Arab behind a rock on the other side of the wadi bed. Twenty yards. He steadied his hand along the barrel, took aim just as the Arab fired his second shot. It entered the top of Dov's head, killing him instantly. The Arab jerked his head round, ducked as Abraham squeezed his trigger. The bullet flattened itself on the rock beside his head, slivers of stone lacerating his ear. He pulled his rifle back from the rock and without aiming it, fired across the wadi. The shot went wide, but when Abraham lifted his head again the Arab was nowhere to be seen. A ridge of rock extended eastwards in the direction the Arab would be certain to take. Think man, think! The Arab won't dare climb since the moon is still up and he could not cross the lip of the wadi without silhouetting himself against the sky. He'll stay in the wadi bed, move from boulder to boulder towards the border. Abraham knew every inch of the ground. He ran a quarter of a kilometre doubled over, completely hidden from the wadi bed, without bothering to look behind him. He ran fifty metres past the place at which the fedayeen had entered the wadi. Last year archaeologists had dug in a barrow behind the promontory. Abraham vaulted lightly over the wall of the tomb from the Age of the Patriarchs they had uncovered, dropped to his hands and knees and crawled along the narrow passage way, one metre high and one metre wide. Towards the end it opened into a chamber two metres by two metres, its vaulted arch three metres above his head. In the far wall of the chamber was a narrow hole through which Abraham wriggled.

15

There, beyond the diggings, the wadi stretched away beneath him. He placed his rifle along a rock, and waited.

The wadi was shaped like the vessel of an ancient lamp. In the centre, a group of boulders massed together, two tamarisk bushes growing on the top like a lamp wick. Left side, right side—which way would the Arab come? Would he come at all? Would he risk climbing out of the wadi despite the danger of silhouette? Would he come east, or strike west, nearer to the kibbutz, hoping his pursuer would anticipate his direction as east? Abraham tasted the cucumber again, its juice bitter in his throat. Slowly he searched the wadi bed with his eyes, looking round, beneath, above each boulder, each rock, each stone. Once he thought he saw him, even pointed his rifle ready to fire, but the shadow was no more than a moon myth, a trick of tired eyes. Then he saw him. The Arab was in the shadow at the near side of a rock. He rose to his feet, looking westwards for his pursuer, not realising he had already been outflanked. The range was seventy metres; Abraham held his fire for a closer shot. He watched the Arab go to ground, saw him move slowly from rock to rock, drawing ever closer. When he reached the place where he had entered the wadi, he paused, then decided against climbing there. Abraham followed his progress through the sights of his rifle. Now he was forty metres away. This time there'd be no chance for him to duck. He must have seen something along the wadi; he dropped into firing position and jammed his rifle into a cleft. Instinct, however, ran high in him, for no sooner had he settled himself than he turned his head quickly, looked directly at the place where Abraham was hidden, and saw the rifle pointed at him. He tried desperately to swing his own rifle round but it was caught in the cleft in the rock. Abraham held his breath, then gently squeezed the trigger the way he'd been taught at Kfar Elihu. The hammer clacked forward, the round exploded, and the butt of the rifle kicked back into his shoulder, momentarily destroying his sight. When he recovered from the kick-back, he saw the Arab slumped to the rock. Abraham ejected the spent cartridge from the breach

16

of the rifle, put it into his pocket for refilling, and walked down into the wadi.

He collected a total of five rifles, one pistol, and eighty-five rounds of ammunition from the fedayeen. The rifles were identical to his own, a long-barrelled Lee Enfield, made in Britain. The ammunition had also been made in Britain. The pistol, a six-cylinder Webley, had been stolen from a police officer. There were eight notches on the butt.

Profit and loss: seven dead fedayeen, plus rifles, pistol, ammunition, against two dead men, or rather one dead man and one dead boy. And, of course, two rounds expended.

Abraham climbed from the wadi. Later they'd come from the kibbutz to bury the fedayeen beneath stones to keep away the jackals. It was the least they could do.

The people of the kibbutz would be waiting, as always, under his strict orders not to move out when they heard explosions and rifle fire. Sometimes Arabs used that trick to draw the men out of a kibbutz before going in to slaughter the women and children and set fire to the buildings.

Sarah would also be waiting, dry-eyed, a quotation on her lips: "Whoso sheddeth man's blood, by man shall his blood be shed." She'd watch him arrive, her eyes making the inventory of his limbs; once she counted him sound, she'd go to cook a meal.

As always when he'd killed a man, he turned aside from the track and vomited, his body racked by the convulsions that emptied him, his mouth soured by the bitter taste of cucumber.

They brought Eli and Dov from the wadi before dawn, wrapped in winding sheets of fertiliser sacking; Misha, Chaim, Chochem and Reuven carried Dov; Noam, Yigal, Shlomo and Ya'akov, who cried all the way, carried Eli. Leiyla, mother of Eli, walked before the cortege; Hagar, betrothed to Dov, supervised the digging of the grave in the

17

centre of the open patch that one day would be the recreation area. Alexander, Eli's father, stayed in his tent. He'd been injured by the tractor and could not rise, stand or walk. Eli had taken his place on patrol. Now his injury was nothing to him in the face of his bitter sorrow. He turned his face to the tent wall and grieved. While the men carried home the dead, the women dug a hole two metres long, two metres deep, and one metre wide, in the hard rocky earth. As such things are when women do them, the walls of the hole were neat and straight for a tomb. Despite Sarah's protests, by common consent there were no obsequies. The two bodies were placed on the ground side by side, each wrapped in its winding sheet; the earth was shovelled back into the hole and levelled.

Then each member of the kibbutz went to the orchard field and brought large stones; they constructed a cairn one metre round and three metres high above the grave. When it was completed, Abraham climbed to the top and planted a wooden stake with a sharpened point rising upwards. Then he stood silent, facing it, Leiyla and Hagar beside him, Ya'akov who had loved Eli crying quietly, squatting on the ground at his feet. "He was a good boy," Ya'akov said, "a good boy." Leiyla knelt beside Ya'akov, cradling his head to her chest, wiping the tears from his face. Abraham turned towards them and looked round the ring of faces. What makes a man a leader? Why is it that, at moments of crisis, all men look to one man for a sign? "We've wanted a name for the kibbutz," Abraham said. Several of them nodded. It had been known as Abraham's kibbutz, because Abraham had gathered them together in the lush comfort of the north and inspired them to come to the cruel arid wastes of the Negev to fight the dry soil and rock, to irrigate and fertilise the land. How many of them would have returned to the Galilee had it not been for Abraham? How many would have tired of the back-breaking work, the constant sand-flies, the hard brackish water and, most of all, the constant fear of the fedayeen who came by night, captured the incautious, and put them to death in
18

horrible lingering ways? "Now we call this Kibbutz Eli-Dov!"
he said. In that one stroke the deaths were justified, the
sacrifice exalted.

"Eli-Dov," they said, and it came easily from their mouths.
"Eli-Dov," "Eli-Dov," and the name was good. They went
from the towering cairn to their own tents and tried the name
in privacy as they prepared to go into the fields. Abraham
went first to his office; there were papers to complete, official
documents for a kibbutz record. In the office was a desk
made of two planks of wood on trestles, and a chair with a
rush seat and back. A shelf ran along the wall above the
unglazed window. The green metal filing cabinet in which
he kept the official papers had been bought in Be'ersheva
when the kibbutz was started in January 1935, two years ago.
Abraham sat at the desk and opened the register of the
kibbutz. On the title page, using ink and a steel-nibbed pen,
he wrote the name in capitals, ELI-DOV. He'd have to get
Misha, who was clever with a brush and a chisel, to carve
and paint a sign for the entrance gate. He turned to Dov's
page. Little was recorded there, since Dov had not been a
man to proclaim his antecedents. Born in El Arish overlooking the Mediterranean, educated an engineer at the
Hebrew University, Jerusalem. Mother dead, father and sister
killed fighting the British. In case of death notify . . . the
space was blank. Leiyla herself had completed the page for
Alexander's family, tracing them back to Omsk. There were
brothers all over Palestine, sisters in America, Spain and
Australia. One son in England, and Eli, born a sabra, *bar
mitzvah*'d in the kibbutz, killed in a wadi in the Negev. Leiyla
had a beautiful hand and wrote Hebrew as few can clearly,
her '*beth*' and '*kaph*' quite clearly differentiated. How like
the woman, Abraham thought, neat, precise, carefully controlled. She'd sob for Eli on the citrus plantation, her hoe
in her hand.

The door of the office opened, and Sarah appeared.

"Will you eat now, or at breakfast time?" she asked.

"Not now," he said, and continued writing.

She stood in the doorway, uncertain, while he finished the

19

page. When he put down the pen and stretched his back, she came into the office, stepping hesitantly up to his desk. "Are you all right?" she asked.

"A bit tired, that's all."

"They've gone out to bury the fedayeen."

"Good, good."

"It's the least we can do."

"I know."

She put out her hand quickly, touched his wrist where he had caught it on a rock during the night. She brushed away the dust that covered the skin wound. "You want to clean that," she said, "and rub it with iodine. You don't want to let it get infected."

He smiled at her. "Were you worried?" he asked her.

She shook her head. "I've learned not to worry about you, ever," she said. He turned his hand over, gripped her hand, rough as was his own, dry, hard, calloused.

"They won't come back for a long time now," he said. "They lost seven in one night. That'll teach them a lesson. They won't come back for a long time," he said, to reassure her.

"Do we always have to kill them?" she asked. "Couldn't we take them prisoner to the British?"

"At Be'ersheva? It's a long way."

"So is hell, and they won't go anywhere else."

"We can't take prisoners," he said. It was an old argument. Once it became known they took prisoners and turned them over to the British, who let them go after a farce of a hearing, the flood-gates would open and the fedayeen pour through. Only the fear of death could keep the numbers down, and then, not for long. Mercenaries were always prepared to risk their lives for a coin or two. Sarah couldn't accept this.

"You're a hard man," she said, and let go his hand. He reached out to grip her again, but she put both hands beneath her apron. "I've asked Leiyla to take my place this morning," she said.

He nodded. They had three cows, two goats, a ram and

20

four sheep which grazed wherever fodder could be found. Taking duty with the animals was a lonely job that lasted all day on the remote scrub. Leiyla could do her crying alone. "You're soft-hearted," he said, "Leiyla was due for weeding!"

Weeding was a back-breaking, hot, dusty job. Of course the hoe helped, but Abraham insisted each weed be dragged out by its roots. Weeds chopped at ground level by the sharp blade of the hoe will always grow again, three and four times each season. Pulling them out by the roots was the only way to eradicate them. Already in the citrus plantation they had grass growing sparsely between the trees, and weeds could choke it. Pulling weeds was reckoned the worst job on the kibbutz; it was one they all took in rotation. "If it had been you who hadn't come back," Sarah said, "Leiyla would have pulled weeds for me."

He got up from his chair, came round the desk, and put his arm clumsily along her shoulder. She turned her face up to him, and he kissed her. Her kiss was dry at first, but as he ground his lips into her, her mouth became moist. He placed his hand on her breast, full and round, firm for a woman nearing forty, but then, no child had ever sucked it down.

"After breakfast?" he asked.

"After breakfast," she promised, "if you'll shave!"

When they left the office the heat struck him instantly, opening his pores and dampening his shirt. He took his conical hat from his pocket and put it on his head, eyes squinting in the bright sunlight. Chochem was waiting behind the tractor, which he'd already started with petrol. The smell of exhaust filled the air; Abraham switched the fuel to paraffin, and the engine raced. He kicked the wood block from the accelerator pedal, climbed on to the driving seat, let in the gear, and slowly drove forward. Chochem walked after him, then as Abraham accelerated leaped on to the back. They'd left the scuffler and the trailer by the corner of the twenty-dunam field they were breaking open. Reuven was there, with Chaim and Shlomo; Shula, Shlomo's wife,

21

stood against the trailer with Miriam and Hagar. No one talked. When Abraham stopped, the men attached the scuffler and the trailer. At the edge of the field, Chochem dropped the handle that lowered the scuffler on to the ground; its prongs bit in as the tractor moved forward, tearing their way through the earth. The men and women worked beside the scuffler and behind the trailer, picking up each stone as the prongs prised it from the ground, tossing the stones on to the back of the trailer. Abraham had traversed the field only once when the trailer was filled; Chochem lifted the scuffler prongs, and Abraham drove his load to the edge of the kibbutz. Men and women threw down the stones, then arranged them in a neat pile before going back to the field on the trailer.

It was Sarah's idea to arrange the stones neatly. Left to himself, Abraham would have preferred to keep everyone working in the field until the land was cleared. But Sarah, looking at the untidy heaps of stone one day, decided they gave the kibbutz a forlorn air. "Let's keep the place neat and tidy," she said in the committee meeting, "since it's our home." Some of the others had grumbled. "We're going to have to move them all again when we start building," they said. "Why move them all twice?" But Sarah had her way.

They had cleared three furrows by the nine o'clock breakfast time. Hepsibah, Chochem's wife, and Rebecca were on kitchen duty; Abraham groaned when the sliced cucumbers were brought out, but helped himself liberally to the sliced cabbage, green and black olives, eggplant, and tomatoes. All but the olives had been grown on the kibbutz; last season they'd had a glut of cabbage and had bartered their surplus in Be'ersheva for olives and olive oil. It would be five years before their own olive trees bore fruit. To drink they had shredded carrot juice, sour cream, and milk from their own herd. Chochem saw Abraham take only a small helping of the cucumber. "We're trying too soon with the cucumbers," he said. "We ought to green manure that dunam for at least two years before we try them. There's no nitrogen in the
22

soil, Abraham, and cucumbers need nitrogen to sweeten them!"

"Already you're a professor of soil chemistry?" Abraham asked, smiling.

Chochem blushed.

"One book I give you to read on agriculture, and already you're a professor?"

"Let's spend a little money," Chochem said, "just a little, on lupin seeds. They make their own nitrates, Abraham, trap the nitrogen in the air, turn it to nitrates, and fix it in the soil. Pull up a lupin and what will you find, Abraham?"

"Don't *ask* me, Chochem, *tell* me!"

"You'll find nodules, Abraham, on the root. Nodules of nitrates. You plant the lupins, take out the seed to plant more next season, but then you dig in the roots and the stems, and that puts nitrates in the soil. And the green matter puts in humus, and sweetens the soil. We'd only need to buy the seed once, and then we could grow our own seed each year, and plant the soil in rotation!"

Green manuring was new to Chochem, and like all young people he considered new things his own inventions, truths that he alone had found. "We'll discuss it tonight after supper," Abraham said. "But I warn you, if it means spending money, you'll have to convince Chaim and Yigal, and you won't do that by talking chemistry to them!"

Chochem said, "*You* could convince them, Abraham, and you wouldn't need to talk chemistry. They'd do anything you suggested."

Abraham pushed his plate to one side. "Chochem," he said, softly, "I don't want them to do things just because I say so. I want everyone to take his place in committee; every voice, every point of view must be raised and discussed."

"You're the leader, Abraham, whether you like it or not! It's what *you* say that counts."

It's easy enough to start a dictatorship; men willingly abrogate small responsibilities and decisions. Men who are built lazy don't want responsibility, especially Jewish men, Abraham thought. That's why so many of them go to the

Torah seeking the ultimate responsibility. But how do you build a democracy? How do you compel men to lift their voices, put their opinions forward in the face of opposition, and hold fast to convictions?

"Look, Chochem," he said. "The lupins are your idea and they could be a good one. . . ."

"You think so," Chochem said eagerly; "you'll support me tonight?"

"Listen! . . . the lupins are your idea, taken from a book. If you believe in the idea, stand up tonight and speak for it, give us all the arguments for and against, and let's discuss it in the committee."

"You won't support it?" Chochem said, despondent.

"See what happens tonight," Abraham said, "but don't rely on me! We have only limited money, and I may have ideas of my own as to how it should be spent. . . . Now, will you drive the tractor for me after breakfast?"

"We'll clear that field by midday," Chochem said.

Misha's wife Ya'el had returned from the tent where she'd taken breakfast with Alexander in Leiyla's absence. "How is Alexander?" Abraham asked. Ya'el shook her head. "I'll take my dinner with him," Abraham promised.

He caught Sarah's eye, and together they walked to their tent. "Maybe this time?" he said as he lay with her.

"I'm too old," Sarah said.

"But you enjoy it?" he asked.

"What do you think?"

They were silent while she moved beneath him, hungrily. "I think you enjoy it," he said.

The pleasure ended, and the need to give and receive, plant and make fertile, impregnate and be impregnated by his seed, took over. When it was over he lay still inside her, and looked into her eyes. "This time," he promised.

"God's will be done," she said.

"You have a wonderful body."

"It's old, and too hard."

"Nonsense. You have breasts like a young girl."

"My skin's too rough. Too much sun. Too much work."

24

"Beauty is in the eye of the beholder."

"You're blind as a bat, then!" She released him, reluctantly. "I have weeding to do," she said.

In the committee meeting that night Hepsibah announced she was pregnant again. Every one slapped Chochem on the back, called him a randy devil, and of course voted to let him have his lupins as an experiment.

After the meeting, Miriam brought the children to their parents for one hour: to Misha and Ya'el, young Abram, aged five; to Chaim and Rebecca, Yashka, aged six; to Chochem and Hepsibah, Mordecai, aged three; to Shlomo and Shula, Rachel, aged two, and Givona, aged four. The parents and their children played together in the corners of the mess hall, while the others, the single or the childless ones, went to their tents. The children kept looking about the mess hall to where the others played, but they were accustomed to these evening sessions, and they tried to be interested in what their fathers and mothers were saying.

Ya'akov walked to the cairn, squatted on his heels before it smoking a black tobacco cigarette. With seven killed last night, and two of their own, they felt safe not to put out sentries, other than Reuven, who sat in the shelter of the covered beast-yard, a rifle at his side.

Ya'akov was born in Austria, and named Jacob Shernhaus. His father owned a baker's shop in Mayrhofen in the Zillertal, and was comfortably bourgeois. Jacob's mother, a blonde Germanic peasant who cared for home and family, cooked and cleaned and sewed, and left thinking to the menfolk, was in her twenties when she bore him. She adored Jacob, his black crinkled hair like his father's; his small button nose. He was her first-born fulfillment. Jacob enjoyed a pleasant boyhood in the Zillertal, climbing the mountains in summer, skiing in winter, avoiding school whenever possible, being adored, rebuked, spoiled, and chastised by his parents. It was a carefree inconsequential existence, a life of activity with the exhilaration of physical endeavour in the air like wine.

In 1933, after thirteen years of vilification of the Jews,

25

the Nazis came to power in Germany. The following day, Nazis of the Zillertal Political Office, anticipating the Anschluss by five years, burned the baker's shop to the ground, killed Jacob's father, violated and then killed his mother, a 'Jew-lover'.

Jacob narrowly escaped death at the hands of the Nazis; only his fleetness up the mountain saved him. In a hut they kept on the mountain, Jacob's father had left a box. All his life, Jacob could remember his father saying, "If anything should happen to me, anything at all, and I die, one of you must open this box." It was after dark when he reached the hut; he went immediately to the place where the box was hidden. Surprisingly, it was quite clean, as if it had been in constant use. Inside, wrapped in green oilcloth to protect them from rats, were a bundle of paper money and a small black book. Jacob opened the book, and began to read in the dark light of the small lamp he had cautiously lit.

"We are Jews," the writing of Jacob's father said, *"not like other people . . ."* Jacob missed the significance of the words at first. His father had often said, *"we are not like other people"*. It had been his father's reply when Jacob had asked, shortly after he started in the village school, why his penis was different from the other boys'; it had been his reply when Jacob asked why his grandmother never came from Innsbruck to see them, as other boys' grandmothers did. What did it matter if they were Jewish? Was it a catastrophe, to be concealed and denied? He had attended the same school as the other boys in the village, the same church. He had been baptised with the other boys, had run away from Sunday School with the other boys to play on the mountains; but now he was *Jewish*, and different? He stayed in the hut for two days. Over and over again he read his father's words in the black book. *"We are Jews, not like other people."* His father's talk had seemed like father's talk to him in the past. "The straight route down the Penken is dangerous. Ski down the side route." All fathers spoke that way, and all boys said, "yes, Father", and took the straight route when fathers were out of sight. "You must always climb in pairs roped

26

together," fathers said. "Yes, Father," the boys said, and left the rope behind the nearest rock, since carrying a rope is tedious for boys with the climbing abilities of mountain goats.

In those days of reading the black book, Jacob realised that he was a *Jew* and he was *different*. Although his father had denied his Jewishness all his life, had even pretended to the religion of the Christians, inside, he and his family were *different*. His father had known that, just as he had known that one day the *goyim* would come to destroy him. In the box were the money to get any surviving members of the family out of the country and the addresses of men who would help.

At night Jacob crossed the mountains into Italy. Following the instructions of his prudent father, he went to an antique shop in Vecchia Roma, where a man changed his money into silver American dollars, good anywhere in the world. To a boy's eyes, they seemed few silver dollars for such a large packet of money, but he relied on the little black book, which said, "Trust no man, believe no man, follow no man, put your faith in no man, unless that man, like you, is a *Jew*".

When he landed illegally at Haifa, Jacob changed his name to Ya'akov and volunteered to work on the remote kibbutzim springing up along the borders. He went first to the Kadoury Agricultural School, then joined the Haganah, to train for defence. It was at Kfar Elihu, where the young men of Haganah held secret drills and target practice, that Ya'akov met Abraham.

Ya'akov walked slowly round the kibbutz, Eli-Dov. All was quiet save the soft murmur of voices from the mess hall. He walked past the office, by the store, and on to the line of tents. His own tent was at the extreme end. He lifted the flap, went in and stretched out on the bunk he had made from canvas and saplings. There was a sudden whisper in the tent as the flap was pulled back again.

"Ya'akov?" a voice said.

"Yes, I'm here."

She came and knelt beside his bed in the dark. He reached

27

out and put his arm around her shoulders, then drew her head down on to his bare chest, where his shirt buttons were unfastened. Her face was wet with tears. He ran his fingers softly into her thick hair.

"I really loved him, Ya'akov," she said.

"I know. I know."

"Can I stay with you? I don't want to be on my own."

"You can stay if you want."

He moved to the side of the narrow bed. She lay along the bed beside him, his arm about her shoulder, as she cried quietly on his chest.

"I really loved him, Ya'akov," she said.

"I know, Hagar," he said, "I know."

The camp was dark when Abraham walked across to Alexander and Leiyla's tent. The grass sprang thick and coarse beneath his feet. "We'll be cutting that grass in a week or two," he thought, his mind never far from day-to-day problems of the kibbutz. The grass seed had been a luxury, bought in Be'ersheva after Sarah had swayed the committee. Abraham diluted the seed with five times its volume of sand to make it go further; it took well and spread into a thick carpet. Abraham had to admit that it gave the kibbutz a focal point, a look of homey comfort amid the arid rocks of its surroundings. It held the members of the kibbutz together by giving them somewhere to sit and talk. Sitting and talking, and sometimes singing and dancing to the music of the harmonica and drums of goatskin, was their only relaxation, their only entertainment.

Leiyla was sitting outside the tent on a bench Alexander had made from three pieces of split trunk. Alexander trained as a carpenter, and the bench was firm. During free after-supper time, Misha, who didn't share the others' enthusiasm for talk, had carved the name Leiyla, surmounting an animal like a gazelle in bas-relief, into the back of the bench. Give

Misha a flat wooden surface and he would use the odd-shaped chisels he invariably carried. All around the kibbutz were examples of his art. Name boards, bas-relief carvings on the lintels of the buildings, decorated salad bowls for the communal dining room. He also carried a flat piece of Jerusalem stone for sharpening his chisels; half his free time was spent carving, half sharpening, and the whole time dreaming of the day he would be free to do nothing but carve wood. Then he'd live in Nazareth where the old olive trees grew wood smooth as marble, thick veined in siennas and ochres.

"Alexander's not asleep," Leiyla said. A day in the open air makes hot canvas interiors intolerable; Abraham had come to see Alexander, but like Leiyla, he did not fancy going inside.

"Did you see anyone where you grazed?" he asked her.

"No one. I imagine last night scared them off." Leiyla had washed the dust of the day from her face and body and combed her hair, setting the tresses in a carved olive-wood comb. There were no traces of the long day of tears. She was wearing the hard cotton kibbutz work clothes. On some the rough cloth hung like sacking without shape or dignity. Some of the women however, unable to forget femininity, took a stitch here and there and fashioned the garments to fit their bodies, revealing womanhood. Such tailoring was not approved by the die-hards. "Who needs to show she's a woman," they asked with contempt, "when there's the work of men to be done, and nothing to be gained by pretending otherwise!" They were hard-limbed, muscular women, who could milk a goat or bring a man to orgasm with equal purpose. Their lips cracked in the sun and tasted of salt, the skin of their breasts was abrasive to the touch, the rhythm of their love-making thrust for thrust a necessary procreative task.

Abraham held Leiyla's hand; it was coarsened and roughened by work as was Sarah's, but somehow, the skin had not been air-tanned to leather, had lost none of its human texture. He drew his thumb along the vein in the centre of

29

the back of her hand, smoothing the down of coarsened hair. She followed the direction of his gaze, felt his thumb caressing her. "Scraps of soap. I boil them in water; I don't take much oil with my meals since it gives me stomach trouble. I warm it, and mix it with the soap and water. I could give Sarah the recipe."

"I'll shoot you if you do," he said laughing. "The next thing would be someone wanting us to build a beauty parlour!" He let go her hand and looked into the tent. Alexander's eyes were closed and he appeared to be sleeping, breathing with the irregular shallow breath of a sick man.

"I won't wake him if he's sleeping," he said, but made no attempt to leave her. She moved to the end of the bench and he sat beside her, his hands in his lap. Then, without thinking, he took her hand again, and stroked it again along the back.

"I'm sorry about Eli," he said. "It wasn't anybody's fault. He did what he had to, bravely and well. It was three against seven; there had to be risk. One got away, at first. We couldn't have predicted it, or avoided it. The same man killed Eli and Dov. It was quick, that's a blessing."

"People always say it's a blessing, but I'm not so sure. I sometimes wonder if there isn't a lot to do in the moment before you die."

"Perhaps I ought to have sent back for more men," he said.

She squeezed his hand. "You must never blame yourself," she said. "This is no time for blame."

"There's no time to grow old either, and that's what I regret more than anything—the young people who are dying when we have so few to take their place."

"I'll have another child, to replace Eli. Of course, no child can take the place of your first, but I'll try."

"And if that child too is killed?"

"Then I'll have another, and another, and go on having them as long as I'm able. Leave it to the women; we'll make the people. You make your plans and dream your dreams, however impractical they may seem. Women cannot dream as men do; we dream of being chased naked through fields

30

of burning wheat; we dream of trying to pack suitcases of impossible clothes with children running about our legs. We have no vision, as the men have, to dream a farm where once there was only rock. We don't grow cities in the desert, Abraham. We work in the fields and make the children." He would have interrupted her, but she stopped him. "I don't believe in all this 'equality of the sexes'," she said vehemently. "Men have the skill and the vision, faith in themselves and their abilities. Women, well what are we? Workers and comforters, a shoulder to cry on, a belly to lie in, a reservoir of the never-ending blood-line!"

Abraham looked to where Alexander was lying. Alexander had been a dreamer, a visionary. "We'll go to the desert, Abraham," he had said, the first time they met in Rehovot. "We'll go south of Be'ersheva, into the wilderness, and there we'll carve a life for ourselves. We'll sink a well, till what soil we can find, and build a city." Abraham had listened, since Alexander's words only strengthened his own desire to leave the lush Samarian plain, the land of the bigots who curled hair behind their ears and trembled at British and Arabs alike.

When the tractor accelerator jammed, Alexander had been dragged across dry land and sharp stones into a wadi; there, as if to emphasise its power and contempt, the tractor rolled back on him, burning his already lacerated flesh with its overheated engine. Reuven had trained as a doctor; he tended Alexander as best he could. "He should be in hospital in Be'ersheva," Reuven said, but Alexander would not permit them to move him at first, and then as his temperature soared the risk of moving him became too great.

"Alexander is dying," Reuven said to the committee.

"If we take him to Be'ersheva, will you guarantee he will live?" Leiyla had asked, an equal voting member.

Reuven shook his head. Leiyla went from the committee meeting and sat beside Alexander, waiting for his one moment of lucidity. Then she had told him what Reuven the doctor had said.

"If I shall die," Alexander pleaded, "let me die here!"

31

Recently, however, Reuven had changed his medical opinion. There seemed to be some force holding Alexander to life, some slender inner thread that refused to snap. At the last committee meeting, Reuven had reported that, if asked again for his opinion, he would no longer be certain Alexander was going to die. Sarah, who had never ceased to pray, smiled wisely. Abraham, who knew something of the human potential, also smiled.

"It'll be a long time before Alexander recovers," he said to Leiyla, sitting there on the bench, "and even then he may not be able to give you more children."

"I will have more. There's Misha," she said quietly, looking down at the ground, reluctant to take his eye, "there's Chaim and Chochem and Shlomo." She looked up, forcing herself to look directly at him. "There would be you, too, if you had proved yourself. They have all made children in their wives; they could make one in me."

"And their wives? What about them?"

"When Chaim was sent to Kfar Elihu for training last year," Leiyla said, "Rebecca didn't sleep in her own tent. When Miriam has her child, it cannot be from Yigal, can it?" No, indeed it could not, Abraham thought. Yigal had been taken by fedayeen fourteen months ago, shortly after they had set up the kibbutz; it took three hours for Abraham and three men to rescue him. During those three hours the Arabs, questioning Yigal to find out how many men were on the new kibbutz, and how many rifles they had, crushed each of his testicles slowly between heavy stones. The three men of the rescue party fled back to Tel Aviv the next day, with their wives. Yigal would not let Reuven examine him at first, and lived and worked with the pain. Only when the pain had gone did he expose himself to Reuven's care. There was nothing to be done; the organs had been crushed, they would wither and die, and in all respects save one, Yigal would be a healthy man. The battle for Yigal's mind, however, had taken longer to fight, and oddly enough, it was Abraham who began to despair. Miriam, with an understanding of Yigal that Abraham could never achieve,

32

arbitrarily solved the problem by becoming pregnant. "It's a miracle," the members of the kibbutz all said in a conspiracy of silence, none more delighted than Yigal himself.

Of course Abraham had known the life of the kibbutz inevitably must slacken marriage bonds. Men and women worked together, ate together, washed together, fought the Arabs together in intimacy. Many in the cities condemned the kibbutzim as hotbeds of free love and immorality, and Abraham knew that a number of people had joined for that very reason, hoping to uncover some sort of bacchanalia. Two or three months of the rigorous work routine had shown them the freedom the kibbutzniks enjoyed must be after and as a result of hard toil; few had the energy for debauchery after a day spent beneath the blazing sun in the fields.

"There were other reasons why Miriam should conceive," Abraham said to Leiyla. "One of the factors in Yigal's slow recovery was his constant thought he had let the kibbutz down by being taken prisoner. Of course, I talked with him, and was able to convince him he had committed no military error; but the guilt was deeper. Yigal felt that he would be failing the kibbutz if he could not produce children to continue its work. Be fruitful and multiply! He was seriously thinking of leaving for that reason. Miriam has shown him the continuity of the kibbutz line can be assured in other ways. She knew, as I now know, that Yigal is not a proud man, and does not believe as so many men do, that only by creating a child can they fulfil themselves."

Abraham was silent; Leiyla looked at him. Did Abraham himself believe that "only by creating a child could he fulfil himself"? Did he believe with Yigal that by failing to produce children he was, in fact, failing the kibbutz itself?

"Men have an awesome arrogance about procreation," she said, "and make such a grand gesture of it. Think about it! *Woman* takes the seed of man and nourishes it to a baby. Man casts his seed as we cast grain; some takes, some doesn't. But when a man has cast his seed that man is not emptied, as a woman is filled when she takes it; man has seed and more seed, and being man, the need, to cast it from him.

33

Mark my words. I'll take the seed of Misha and Chaim, of Chochem and Shlomo, and make a baby, and none shall know whose seed has grown inside me, not even myself who will nourish it, and make it grow. And there will be no wrong in this, no pleasure, no sinfulness."

"Leiyla, Leiyla," he said, "we're not ready for this yet. The women will turn you out as a whore, the men will despise you as men will when a woman's knees can easily be parted. You'd make us a nation of bastards. The children will come; people will come when we have built places for them, Jews, Moslems, Christians, who knows. We'll get the people we need, and the laws of nature will see that we have the children to start a nation and perpetuate ourselves. But not as bastards."

"You're a damned arrogant male," she said, smiling to take away the insult. "You want to know who your father is, and who was your father's father. Son of my seed and the unbroken line, women used as vessels and objects of pleasure. What a typically male point of view. When I have a baby at my breast, how much do I care whose seed has fertilised me? A Jew is a Jew if his mother is a Jew, not because of his father. Nazis raped Jewish girls in Germany and gave them Jews. Jewish men, wherever they may be, will take a girl, it's human nature; but will a Jew give a Gentile girl a Jewish bastard? Never! It's not in the suckle, it's not even in the blood. *Man*, that was of *woman* born . . . !"

"You don't care much for us, do you, Leiyla?" Abraham asked, smiling.

"I care for you as *men*," she said. "It's when you set yourselves up as *gods* that I begin to doubt you."

He got up to go.

"Have I offended you, Abraham, son of Terah?" she asked. He put his hand on her head, twisting his fingers into her thick hair.

"No, you haven't offended me," he said. Her eyes were bright; he knew that all her tears had not been shed in the grazing grounds. "You made one good son, in Eli. You could be proud of him. You'll make other good sons," he said, "here in Eretz Israel!"

She turned her eyes from him when the tears started.

"The land of milk and honey," she said.

". . . and blood, and tears," he added quietly, as he left her.

Fourteen nights later the fedayeen came again. The guards from Eli-Dov had been out each night since the tenth night, on roster. On the fourteenth night, Misha, Noam and Ya'akov were on duty, with Abraham, Reuven and Chaim standing by in the kibbutz itself, sleeping dressed, each with a rifle by his side. Misha and Ya'akov were crouched beneath a tamarisk where they could see the wadi and the hill above it. Noam was fifty metres behind them, in a small observation post they had constructed with stones blended into the landscape.

Three fedayeen slipped quickly over the hill crest. Ya'akov saw them first and hissed to Misha by his side. The fedayeen were crouched together, their silhouette one indistinguishable blur against the lighter sky. Ya'akov looked at them, puzzled. They were too close together, and it was hard to distinguish their numbers. Were they three, or four? And if they were four, was the fourth man already injured? The others seemed to be carrying him between them. There was also a purposefulness about their movement. They could have surveyed the terrain from good cover, but they seemed to have abandoned prudence, and moved in a straight line as if to some specific objective. Few men crossing ground at night travel straight. They move from shadow to shadow, keep to the same height, skirt small hillocks and undulations. A small wadi about three metres wide stretched across the ground. They could have avoided it by making a fifty-metre detour to the right; but they climbed over the lip of the wadi, down into it, and up the other side. They still seemed to be carrying the fourth man among them. Ya'akov looked along

35

the direction they travelled, puzzled. They appeared to be making a bee-line for the kibbutz; but along that line the kibbutz was unassailable. The last quarter-kilometre they'd be on open ground within sight of buildings all the way. The speed at which they were travelling was abnormal too, as if they'd abandoned caution and were making a suicide dash into kibbutz territory. Ya'akov watched them draw closer.

"When they get here," he said to Misha, "I'll take the front one, you take the one at the back." Misha nodded. A group of rocks some distance to the left formed a natural defensive position. Misha had wanted them to occupy it, but Ya'akov said no. "They'll *think* we're in there," he said, "and protect themselves from that position." Who would cast a second glance at a tamarisk, isolated and exposed? Or at a group of rocks with no apparent access?

The Arabs ran crouched across the landscape, hidden from the position Misha had wished to occupy. Ya'akov grinned. The fedayeen had not looked twice at the tamarisk and Noam's cairn. Misha and Ya'akov eased safety catches forward. Ya'akov had pushed a stick in the ground with a Y-shape at the top; he cradled his rifle in it the better to aim. Now the fedayeen were 200 metres away, and coming diagonally closer with every move. Noam would have them in his sights, but at 250 metres. Ya'akov calculated they'd be in his range at 150 and the same distance from the cairn. He'd arranged a plan with Noam; he, Ya'akov, would go for the leader, then switch his fire to the rest of the patrol from the front; Misha would go for the last man, then switch along the patrol from the rear; and Noam would start in the centre. At 175 metres, the patrol stopped, grouped together. Ya'akov smiled. "Bunch up, you sods," he muttered. Then suddenly he cursed; now he could see why the fedayeen had been running almost doubled, and knew there was no fourth man. They'd advanced on a sight bearing, a fixed number of paces. The third man had been carrying the base plate next to his body, the second the tripod already set for the distance, and the first and second between them the barrel of a three-inch mortar. Whoever had trained them knew his job. Within seconds of stopping at the predetermined location, the three fedayeen erected a three-inch mortar on the hard-baked soil above the wadi. Ya'akov flipped down his sights and took rapid aim at the man behind the mortar. He fired just as the man's arms reached up with the bomb. The shot missed. Misha saw what was happening, and he too fired. His shot hit the man crouched beside the mortar barrel. The man was pushed forward by the impact, but the wound must have been superficial since he grabbed the second bomb to give to the loader. The loader had the bomb clasped at the mouth of the mortar as Ya'akov fired again; the shot hit the loader in the throat, and he went over sideways, screaming, knocking the bomb out of the barrel. The bomb must have fallen on its side or it would have blown them all to smithereens; Ya'akov had no time to see it. Already he had sighted at the second man, and shot again. The shot hit him as he was lifting the second bomb; his face slammed against the barrel and Ya'akov heard the ring of what must have been a gold tooth against the metal, so hard had he banged forward. Now Noam was firing too. "Don't let us hit a bomb," Ya'akov said. "We could use a mortar and bombs." The second man had his face against the barrel of the mortar; the third was flat on the ground with another bomb. Ya'akov saw Noam's shot hit the ground two metres in front of the third man then ricochet screaming away. Misha was firing at the second man and missing. The arms of the second man, holding the mortar bomb, climbed the barrel slowly, pushing the bomb before them, in an agony of effort. So many things to be done to a rifle between shots, snap the bolt up, pull it back, eject the cartridge. Push the bolt forward again, snap the knob of the bolt down against the stock of the rifle, place a hand back on the stock, adjust the rifle into the shoulder, take aim. Now the bomb was level with the top of the mortar. Ya'akov, Misha and Noam all fired together. Three shots whammed into the second man's head. As if in slow motion, his arms started to slide away from the bomb poised over the mouth of the barrel. It slipped slowly inside the barrel and out of sight.

"Aim for the mortar barrel," Ya'akov shouted, changing his shot, but already they were too late. The third fedayeen had the end of the lanyard in his hand; he jerked it, releasing the firing pin on its spring-loaded mechanism. The propulsive charge behind the mortar bomb fired and there was a contained crump explosion; the bomb hurtled from the barrel with a whine just as their shots pushed the barrel over.

The next three shots thumped into the lanyard jerker. He died at the very second the mortar bomb exploded in Kibbutz Eli-Dov.

The bomb landed on the grass before the cairn they had built for Eli and Dov, its steel fragments spread by the explosion like angry armour-plated bees. Fortunately the bomb had buried itself half a metre into the soft earth before the explosion came, and most of the fragmentation was contained by the soil. The cairn took the brunt of the explosion above ground. The spike Abraham had planted in its top was never seen again. The fuse ring and tail of the mortar bomb whirled into the air, came spiralling lazily down, whirring in the night air like cicadas.

Miraculously, or so it seemed next morning when they examined the entire kibbutz, no one was hurt, and there was no material damage save that to the cairn.

Alexander died during the night. Reuven gave it as his opinion, impossible to confirm, that he died of the sudden shock of the awesome explosion within the confines of the kibbutz, and the realisation of the desperate character of men who could launch such a thing on women and children.

No one went out to the fields next morning. After breakfast they held a meeting of everyone in the kibbutz except the children and Hepsibah, who was on nursery duty. Breakfast had been silent. Even the rattle of tin plates was suppressed; everyone ate, looking neither right nor left, chewing slowly, like actors in a house of the insane. When he had finished
38

eating, each person rinsed his dishes in the warmed water Sarah on kitchen duty had provided. By chance, Abraham was sitting half-way along the rough wood table; they all sat down again, looking inward at him. He finished eating last, washed his plate and utensils which Sarah silently took from him, then came back to the table and sat down. Ya'akov flipped a cigarette to him, and Abraham puffed at it with the inexpertness of a man unused to smoking. He knew that unless he spoke soon, a clamour would break out that none could stifle. Reuven, Noam, Ya'akov and Hagar, and now Leiyla, the ones without dependants, they'd stick. Sarah would stick, but only because of Abraham. She would have preferred to be with one of the orthodox religious kibbutzim, but she'd stick. Yigal would stick, with Miriam, even though Miriam was expecting a baby. But the others—Chaim and Rebecca, with Yashka to think of, Shlomo and Shula with Rachel and Givona, Chochem and Hepsibah with Mordecai, aged three —was it fair to ask them to live under the threat of sudden, unpredictable bombardment by mortar? Abraham looked round the circle; he knew he could influence them all to stick, but was this the right way? Shouldn't the desire come from within them? Dammit, the kibbutz movement had been in existence for over thirty years, since it was started as the *kvutsa* by a handful of settlers near Lake Kinneret, at what came to be known as Degania. The rules now were the same as the rules then; the group responsible for everything, including individual needs; no money; no use of outside labour; no private property or trading; all profits to be ploughed back for the benefit of the community of socialist Zionists. The *kvutsa* faced hunger, hard work, danger. Often men quit; men had quit this kibbutz now called Eli-Dov; men, women and children had been killed. Hadn't each person present, man or woman, the right to make up his own mind without dialectic, without persuasion?

"Tell us how it happened, Ya'akov," Abraham finally said. Ya'akov described how they had seen the fedayeen, his voice flat and unemotional. Like Abraham, Ya'akov knew the danger they faced was this morning's, not the previous night's.

They were down to seventeen adults and five children, ridiculously small for a kibbutz, many of which had hundreds of members. If all the married ones went with their children, Kibbutz Eli-Dov would cease to exist.

When he had described how the mortar had been fired, he looked for the first time at Noam and Misha for confirmation. Misha nodded his head. "Why didn't you shoot the man with the lanyard first?" asked Chaim, who'd been to the weapons training school.

"There was a man with a bomb, trying to put the bomb down the barrel. It seemed natural to get him first."

"But the bomb couldn't have exploded, if the man hadn't jerked the lanyard," Chaim persisted. "These large mortars are pin-fired, you know, and unless the pin is freed by a pull on the lanyard . . ."

"I know," Ya'akov said, "I was firing mortars before you were born!"

Abraham stepped in, quickly. "You must realise, Chaim, that at that distance it'd be impossible to know for sure, especially at night, just who was holding the lanyard. They did right to go for the man with the bombs. I would have done the same."

"Well, I wouldn't," Chaim said, flatly.

Miriam raised her hand to speak, nervous as ever. Abraham nodded to her; she could be relied upon to talk sense, though she was slow to grasp technicalities. "These mortars, can they be fired in any direction? Does the new use of mortars mean we have to guard the kibbutz all the way round?" In the past the fedayeen had always come to the kibbutz via the wadi; last night they'd avoided the wadi for the first time. Certainly the fedayeen could circumvent the kibbutz, come in from the other side.

"We haven't the manpower for a perimeter defence," Noam said.

"And even if we had," Yigal added, "if we used what men we have, our output in the fields would be cut to ridiculous levels. You can't expect people to stand guard all night and work in the fields all day, every day."

"How many men would it take to defend all round the kibbutz?" Miriam asked.

"You could manage with three, if they stayed still," Yigal said, "but they'd need a change every four hours." Sentries go black blind staring into darkness.

"If we used four, letting one man walk for an hour, they could all stay out longer," Reuven said. "It's sitting still that tires a man during the night. If each one of the four could spend an hour walking, they'd survive all night. That way only costs four men against the six you'd need for the static defence."

"What are we then, farmers or tin-pot soldiers?" Shlomo asked, irritated by the calm way everyone was discussing techniques of guarding what to him had been a lost cause since the mortar bomb landed. First they must discuss *if* the kibbutz were to be defended, not *how*. "I came here to work the land," he said, "to build a life for us all, not to be a soldier. It seems to me some of you are losing sight of what we all came here for; what we came to this country for. When we came the place was a mess; the villages the Zionists had started were a mess; agricultural production was almost laughable, and they were using cheap labour to do jobs they could have tackled themselves, just like everywhere else in the world. I came here to help build a *community*, not to kill Arabs."

"So what would you do?" Ya'akov asked him, angry. These damned socialists . . . "Stand there and let them shoot and drop bombs on us?" There was an angry murmuring around the table. Reason soon drowns in emotion; half of them lost their fear of the mortars in the anger of being the victims of bombardment.

"You're like a gang of boys," Shlomo said, not losing his temper. That was never his way. "You want to go out every time someone hits you, and lash out at him. You want revenge, an eye for an eye. Let's get back to our purpose," he insisted. "We're here to build a new country, and a new way of life. We want to raise the ethical value of labour so that men can work in the fields and not be despised; so that

41

a man can work for the benefit of himself and the *community*. If we can't do that here, we ought to admit our mistake, and go somewhere else to do it. We ought to leave Kibbutz Eli-Dov, and start somewhere safer."

That got them. Half of them were thumping on the table, shouting. "Eli gave his life for this place!" "Dov died defending this place!" as if the blood of the two who were dead had sanctified the ground and made it a hallowed possession.

Abraham held up his hand, and gradually the shouting ceased. Shlomo sat on his chair, his lips pursed, his resolve firm against the onslaught that he considered childish. When they were silent, Abraham looked at Shlomo, and at Shula, bracketing them with his eyes. "You both knew when we decided on this location that there'd be special difficulties. The British don't approve of us being so far south in the Negev, and certainly the Arabs don't. The Gdud Ha'avoda won't send its labour battalions down here to help us construct our buildings and develop our methods. I told you myself that we'd have danger, and be outcasts. We all wanted to go 'into the wilderness'. We didn't approve of the kibbutzim founded by the Zionist revolutionaries from Russia and Poland and Czechoslovakia."

"We had a bellyful of the Zionists," Yigal said. Sarah said nothing, as different in her religious beliefs as she had always been in this community.

"Yes, I knew all that, we accepted all that," Shlomo said impatiently, "but I might as well be in the Galilee working for the Haganah as doing sentry duty down here. I can't seem to make you understand that I'm tired of fighting. I don't want to kill anybody. I want to make things grow, not cut them down. Shula and I, we're both fed up with all this killing, no matter who's killing whom!" he said.

Abraham knew that what he was about to say would be dangerous, but in fairness he had to say it. Many of the kibbutzniks were obviously as fed up with the killing, with the danger and the deaths, as Shlomo and Shula were. "What do you suggest, Shlomo?" he asked. All bent forward eagerly.

"I knew it wouldn't be easy," Shlomo said, "but I thought

42

that here we'd be able to do some farming, make things grow, find a market. It's my opinion, for what it's worth, that we've chosen the wrong place. In our desire to get away from the revolutionaries, the Zionists, the zealots, and all that crowd, we've come too far into the wilderness. Let's face it, there's no defence against mortars. First it was knives, then it was rifles, now it's mortars. The Arabs have plenty of backing. What'll it be next?" he asked, his quiet voice impassioned. He looked around the table. Now he had the attention of everyone. "Will they start on us with artillery?"

Each round the table looked at his neighbour. All knew it was a possibility. It was true, the Arabs had backing. Many said the British, despite the Mandate and the Balfour Declaration, were readying the Arabs to push the Jews into the sea. Certainly the Jordanians had open British support and training. Would artillery come next? Bombardment from the air? Poison gas? The weapons of war offered limitless destruction and death.

"I say we should acknowledge our mistake," he went on in his quiet voice, "we should move out of here and go further north. I don't mind where. We could try the borders of the Dead Sea; we could stay somewhere near Be'ersheva, or even go up into the Galilee."

"Like lap-dogs," Ya'akov said with contempt, "with the British all round us, with the other kibbutzim to protect us? Maybe we should try to get a loan from the Zionist Organisation, or the Jewish National Fund, and build ourselves houses, with bedrooms. Shall we have a *seder* at Passover, get out the *menorah* at Hanukah, wear *yarmulkas*?"

"If you had been brought up as a Jewish boy should be, you wouldn't commit these blasphemies," Sarah said, white with rage.

"Sarah!" Abraham said. It was a command. The meeting had broken into factions; there'd be no more rational discussion that morning. "As I see it," Abraham said, "we have alternatives as usual. I think it would be a mistake to make decisions instantly. I think we would be better advised to end this meeting, and let these matters soak in our minds for a day

43

or two. Shlomo thinks we should leave this place, Ya'akov, I imagine, thinks we should stay." He held up his hand to stop Ya'akov's interruption. "We all know why we came, and we all know what our life here has become. Miriam has asked how we may defend ourselves; Reuven has suggested a method. We will meet again in a few days, and we will discuss these matters. Until then, I hope we can all work and think; and if such a thing is possible, keep our talk on this subject to a minimum."

They all smiled at his attempted humour save Shlomo and Shula, who stood up. "If anyone can give me an infallible method of protecting two babies from mortar bombs that drop unexpectedly from the sky," Shula said, "there might be grounds for discussion. Otherwise I don't think there's anything to talk about." She and Shlomo left the dining hall together.

The bell-tent of Chaim and Rebecca was first in the line; like the others it was just over two metres in diameter, with 'walls' of a half-metre, and a pole in the centre three metres high. The two beds, constructed of wood with canvas strips and a palliasse of soft tamarisk foliage, stood across the centre of the tent on either side of the pole. An olive-oil lamp provided illumination; it was used, by kibbutz custom, for only a half an hour each evening. Chaim and Rebecca shared the lamp, in weekly turns, with Yigal and Miriam in the next tent, since there were not enough lamps to go round.

Rebecca, who could build almost anything from almost anything, had woven pliant rods into a cupboard unit shaped like a long thin basket with shelves. Inside the basket were the few clothes they possessed, the spare shirt for each of them, the spare trousers for Chaim—Rebecca, as a woman, was not given a ration of spare trousers—the woollen sweater each was allowed for cold evenings, and the thonged sandals

44

Rebecca had made to put on after work. During the day, they all wore British army boots from World War One. On the shelves were two borrowed books neither had yet started, an unread newspaper Ya'akov had bought in Be'ersheva, an old tin alarm clock, and Rebecca's collection of unusual minerals, the stones of green and blue, pink and red, she had gathered in the field and polished until the original colour shone through.

When Chaim and Rebecca returned from the breakfast meeting, they went into the bell-tent, despite the heat, and sat on the beds. Chaim had not yet rolled up the walls of the tent as they usually did during the day, but the canvas door was open. It overlooked no other tent; each had been sited as an island of privacy. Chaim and Yigal were joint treasurers of the kibbutz; Chaim had the books of account and the right to take time off manual work to see them. He opened the book beside him, but didn't look at its pages. He sat there with Rebecca looking through the triangle of the tent flap, out into the space behind the covered beast-yard, seeing nothing.

"What do you think, Chaim?" Rebecca finally said.

Chaim remained silent. He was a slow man; thoughts lumbered about the darkness of his mind before finding their way to speech. Rebecca was swift, resolute, daring, as women often are.

"It's not for ourselves, of course; it's for Yashka, and all the other kids! We the old ones are expendable; the kids deserve a good start."

"They ought to have shot at the man with the lanyard," Chaim finally said; "that's what I would have done!" That thought was now buried, and he could proceed to the next one. "It seems a waste to give up so much; all the money we've spent on seed and plant, all the work we've put in."

"Do you think we ought to move to a new place? Somewhere a bit further from the border, out of the Negev?"

"It just seems such a waste to me." The kibbutz had been started with the money of the kibbutzniks, without outside help from anyone. Loans were available, of course, but that

45

meant you had to get official approval for the site, and you had to follow the rules of the Kibbutz Federation or the Jewish National Fund. You also had to follow the principles of a particular political party, to be socialist—or even further to the left, almost communist—in aim and outlook. A smaller group, the Hakibbutz Hadati, required its members to be orthodox Jews. Abraham and his followers wanted none of this. Attracted by the idea of community without political or religious strings, they clubbed together all their available resources. Abraham provided money and the lorry, Ya'akov used what was left of his father's money to buy a second-hand tractor and a trailer; Chaim paid for the scuffler and plough and a few other pieces of farm equipment; Noam, Chochem, and Reuven together paid for the tents. But already the origins of everything had been forgotten. Chaim flicked the pages of the account book, though he knew the sums and the totals by heart. "What we have left wouldn't buy more than one year's seed," he said; "it seems such a waste to throw away everything we've worked for."

"You keep on saying that," Rebecca said, though kindly. She was used to his slow ways. "What I'm asking is, what do you *want* to do? In your heart, Chaim. Do you want to stay here and risk it, or do you think the danger's too great that one day Yashka might be standing near one of those mortars when it lands?"

He stood up, rolled up his trousers leg to the top of his thick woollen socks, and scratched his leg. Then he sat down again, half twisted on the bed so that he could look at her. "We have a good life here, you and me, Rebecca. And Yashka's coming along very nicely, isn't she, with the other kids. We can have more kids. It's not like your mother, is it? Every kid she had was another burden to her, and she worked herself into the grave looking after you all. But look at you; you've got as much freedom as the rest of us; you could have a dozen kids if you wanted. . . ."

"God forbid!"

". . . if you wanted!"

"Which I don't. Especially not to carry them in this heat!"

46

". . . if you *wanted*, you could *have* 'em."

"All right, all right! I could have a dozen kids, if I wanted. Does that make you feel any better? But meanwhile, since we only have one kid, what's your decision? You're still the head of the family! Shlomo wants to go, Ya'akov wants to stay, what do *you* want to do?"

"I wonder what Abraham wants to do?" he asked, thinking of the meeting. Strange, wasn't it? He and Yigal were joint leaders of the kibbutz during their one-month term of office; two treasurers, one in charge of personnel and accounts, the other of production and defence. Of course, they were responsible to the committee, but everyone in the kibbutz had an equal voice, and for practical purposes, the committee included everyone who had anything to say. How was it, then, that no matter who the treasurers were, everyone automatically referred to Abraham? Theoretically, he and Yigal were in charge of that meeting after breakfast, but neither he nor Yigal had thought to express any kind of authority. If Abraham had said what he wanted to do, you could guarantee that all the ones who had not yet made up their minds would have agreed with Abraham.

"This time," Rebecca said, "I get the feeling Abraham won't tell us what he wants until it comes to the vote, and then his hand will be the last to go up. Which is as it should be!" Hero worship is for men, not women! "Anyway, make up your own mind. Tell me what in your heart you really want to do."

"I want to do my accounts," he said, "and it's time you were working!" He pulled a worn book from his pocket, turned its pages, ran his finger down the list of names. "Rebecca," he said, "there you are. Hoeing all morning; so you've no time to waste, have you?"

"You bastard," she said, as she stood up. "Wait until it's my turn to be treasurer! I'll have you hoeing every day!"

"See you tonight," he said, and winked.

"You'll be lucky! My back'll be broken as it is, without you ramming me into the palliasse!"

*   *   *

The rainfall of the southern Negev is approximately fifty millimetres a year, the lowest annual average in the whole of Palestine. In early times, wells were sunk below the brackish salt pans, but supplied only a trickle of water for the immediate vicinity. From the third to the seventh centuries however, the Nabataeans straddling the trade routes made the land fertile by a system of irrigation which stored what little rainwater there was. Grasses were planted to hold the sands of the desert at bay; the loess was mixed with the subsoil to hold water trapped in irrigation ditches, and cisterns were carved out of solid rock to hold the rainwater for dry times. Figs and pomegranates were planted because they tolerate the salt, and produce was grown to sell to the caravans of rich traders on their way to and from the lucrative Far East. It was a green and fertile land. But centuries of neglect destroyed the irrigation systems. The grasses withered and died, and the sand went on the move again. Sun baked the loess hard and cracked its surface; hot wind and what little rain there was formed flash floods, ran the top soil off the hills into the sea, and left behind only the dead rock meal which would support no life since it could not hold water. A few scrub bushes tried to survive, but the undisciplined herds of the nomadic bedouin sought them out, and with voracious appetites the goats nibbled new shoots, while sheep cleared everything that grew above the ground. For hundreds of years the ground baked and the desert took over. What loess remained rose to the surface where it set hard and cracked wide in the heat of the unshaded sun. The ground was rent by cavernous splits and rainwater that could have given life vanished without trace into the torn earth.

Even the few wells disappeared; some were vandalised by feuding bedouin who found, in the destruction of a well, the simplest method of driving enemies from the land; others collapsed or were gradually choked by the sifting ubiquitous sand.

Abraham, Ya'akov and Alexander travelled far south into the Negev, far from the internecine squabbles of the political parties, the religious and non-religious factions, the oppressive-seeming rules of the new order. They had no idea what they were looking for, and no one to guide them. They crossed the coastal strip, the plateau, and descended into the Arava Valley. That initial journey took them five days, by lorry, by hired bedouin camel, and on foot. The night they arrived in the valley of the Arava they camped, unknowing, within three kilometres of where Solomon had worked his mines. What is the instinct that takes men through a wilderness along a route travelled hundreds of years before? Who will ever know; since time began, men have made tracks in the tracks of their forefathers, and some would say that God has shown the way. But Abraham, Ya'akov and Alexander did not walk in the paths of the righteous; they wanted no part of being Jews, and would not have heeded the word of God, even had they been able to discern it.

When they awoke on the first morning in the Arava, Abraham told the bedouin to take the camels and return with them in five days, when the rest of the money would be paid to them. The bedouin thought for a moment of killing them, to take the money and save another journey, but one look at Ya'akov's face as idly he played with his knife dissuaded them. Abraham, Ya'akov and Alexander stood beneath the sun of the Arava, watching the bedouin ride across the flat land, up the hills to the plateau above. Then they folded their tents and strapped them to their packs.

"Which way," Alexander asked, "south, east, or north?"

Abraham said nothing, looking slowly around at the bare land. There was little to choose. The plain of the Arava stretched north and south; ahead of them rose the hills of Jordan, and between, one desolate plain, broken by wadis and parched cracks. There was no sign of people or animals, no wild life. There'd be lizards, and snakes, and sand insects, among the rocks at night, but all had sense to hide from the fierce glare of day. Finally, he beckoned towards the hills, purple in the heat haze of morning. "East," he said, and they started to walk. All morning they walked eastwards. When midday came they stopped and sat beside a rock. "You

49

all right?" Abraham asked Alexander and Ya'akov. Both nodded. There was no shelter; each took a sip from his water bottle to lubricate his cracked lips.

"We must be mad!" Ya'akov said.

Abraham was sitting very still, staring at the rocks about fifty metres ahead of them; he stood up, and a shiver of excitement ran through him. "What is it?" Ya'akov said. Abraham didn't answer. Ya'akov looked at Alexander, but he had seen nothing, heard nothing. All about them was the silence men hear only on mountain tops or in the wilderness; all round them the sun, unshielded by clouds, beat down. "What is it, Abraham?" Ya'akov repeated.

Abraham walked to the formation of rock. Ya'akov followed him. They stood there, looking at the rock. They were at the edge of a crevice, but Abraham wasn't interested in it; he was looking at the rock formation. It was two metres in diameter, saucered in the middle, filled with sand. The rock was cracked all round its circumference, or could those have been individual stones, shaped round a circle? If so, who had put them there, how long had they been there, and what were they for? Abraham beckoned to Ya'akov, and together they brushed away the sand piled against the outside of the rim. The rim turned into a collar, which stood about twenty centimetres above the surrounding rock plate. It was impossible to tell if this were one circular piece of rock, thrust from the rock below and then polished by centuries of sandblasting and sun erosion to an almost perfect tube, or if the cracks were spaces between individual stones which had been piled together as a tube, before time had polished their outer edges. Placed above the ring at some time or other, by divine geological or human means, had been a large slab of rock.

"See it," Abraham said. "That slab must have been twenty-five centimetres thick, about two metres square!"

"A lid? It'd take some lifting . . ."

"Yes, but it could be done. That slab was on the top of this ring, but over the years, the sun and wind and rain on the slab have cracked it, then worn it down. See how these two pieces once fitted, side by side?" Abraham lifted two

50

large pieces of the rock, and held them together. When he pulled them apart again, the line of the fissure could clearly be seen. "That slab was on the top, and then it cracked," he said, "but what I noticed was this circular shape."

"If there had been a circular shape with a slab on it for hundreds of years, the slab would have protected the shape beneath it, wouldn't it?" Ya'akov asked.

Abraham nodded, took his knife from its sheath, and picked at the rock. Ya'akov saw what he was doing, and he picked away on his side with his knife. It took them an hour to remove the top ring of rock, while Alexander sat watching. No one spoke, but they all knew the unspoken hope of the others. When they had removed the top rim, they scooped out the centre. Beneath the surface of sand, the cracked rock powder had settled into a crust about eight centimetres thick. They dug slowly through it, cutting carefully away at the sides near the rock, levering out chunks in the centre. Beneath it was pure fine silted sand which ran through their fingers like salt. The stones were again set in a ring. Still none dared to hope as they slowly removed the second ring. "Only one sign, only one," Abraham thought. After an hour they had removed about fifteen inches of fine sand from the centre and two stone rings from the outer edge.

Abraham flung a large handful of sand on to the pile behind him.

"Look," Alexander said, pointing to it. They looked at the sand.

"Look," Ya'akov said, showing them the stone he had just prised loose. The sand was a shade darker than the rest of the pile. The stone bore the unmistakable mark of an ancient carving tool. A key had been chipped, to lock it into the next stone. Abraham held up his hand. Grains of sand were stuck to it, where previously the sand had sifted through his fingers.

They had found the site of an ancient well.

They dug into the well for three days. Into its walls, some two thousand years ago, footholds had been carved, a spiralling ladder down which a man could easily descend. Since they had no ropes, they filled their shirts with sand and passed up a human ladder. In three days they cleared the well to a depth of five metres. It was back-breaking, slow work, because the man at the top had to climb up and back with each shirtful of sand. As they got further down, the sand grew more moist. At three metres, it held together, at four metres could be moulded into sand balls, at five metres, by squeezing hard, a drop of moisture could be separated.

On the morning of the fourth day, they woke at dawn as usual, rolled up their blankets, ate a breakfast of oat cakes washed down with a sip of water from their canteens. Abraham looked at the other two; they looked like scarecrows. Ya'akov's face was normally lean and tanned; now his cheeks were sunk hollow, his lips brown and purple and cracked. Alexander was little better, though he had started with more flesh than Ya'akov had.

"Do you think we could live here, Ya'akov?" Abraham asked.

"With a well we could live anywhere."

"The well may be seasonal," Alexander cautioned him.

Ya'akov shook his head, grinning. "This is the middle of the dry season, the water's at its lowest ebb, right, but only five metres down we've got to it."

"How far do you think we'll have to go," Abraham asked, "to drop a bucket in it?"

"Fifteen metres maximum. If that was a seasonal well, they'd never have gone to the bother of lining it that way. In the dry season, like now, the level will be fifteen metres, mark my words. In the rainy season, it'll come up to the top!"

"Why was there water near the top?" Alexander asked.

"How does the water get to the top of a tree?" Ya'akov replied. "They say water runs only downwards, but somehow it gets up to the tree-tops, doesn't it?"

"Do *you* think we could live here?" Abraham asked Alexander, who looked about him as they had all looked about during their brief spells out of the well for the past three days.

52

"Somebody must have lived here once," he said, "or why would they have bothered with a well? We'd need shade, of course, but that wouldn't be difficult. Mark you, the Federation would never back us, not to come down here!"

"Bugger the Federation," Ya'akov said, "we'll come on our own. We've got water, and that's what counts. Nobody's going to lay claim to desert land; we'll cultivate it and the land will belong to us by right of settlement! We'll bring women and children down here, and put down roots of human beings as well as trees . . ." Already, in his excitement, Ya'akov could see a settlement, a village, a small town, shaded by trees, self-sufficient and satisfying.

"Hang on, Ya'akov," Abraham said, laughing, "all that from one well that may not give us more than a bucket of water a day . . ."

"Good for a thousand gallons a day, that well is," Ya'akov said, "and there'll be other wells hereabouts. All we have to do is find 'em."

"All we have to do with this one, at the moment, is to fill it in again," Abraham said. "If the nomads find it while we're back in the north, they'll start a colony here, and we'll never get rid of them." They compromised by jamming one large boulder into the neck of the well, and filling it with stones to a depth of a metre. Then they covered the stones with sand, sifting it carefully into the cracks. Alexander built four cairns of stones at a distance from the well; where the diagonal lines between the cairns would have intersected, there was the well. When Ya'akov and Abraham had spread the sand they had excavated from the shaft, no evidence of their find could be seen.

Abraham walked across to the eastern cairn and looked down the line between that cairn and the one opposite. "Let's be clever," he said, "and move one cairn to the side!"

Alexander laughed. "Abraham," he said, "seed of thy father! Thou didst rightly come from Ur of the Chaldees, and art verily a wise man! And a sly tricky bastard!"

Abraham punched him lightly on the chest. "It takes one to know one, grave robber!"

For the next half hour, the three of them chased each other like excited boys, there in the heat of the sun. Now they knew *where* to add to the *why*; *how* would follow, and *when* was as soon as possible, and each felt the euphoria of the lifting of a tremendous burden of indecision and care.

The bedouin arrived before high sun at the rendezvous point ten kilometres to the west. They showed no curiosity; the Jews had paid them well and it was in the natural order of things that questions would be answered by lies. Abraham, Alexander and Ya'akov climbed to the camels the bedouin had brought, fast racing camels that would cover distance at speed. A tap on the snout by the bedouin camel-handler, and the three camels rose on their forelegs, climbing awkwardly to their feet, swaying under their load. Abraham turned his head to the east. The sun had risen behind the hills of Jordan, blazing its path across the sky from the east. At that moment, or so it seemed to Abraham, the sun seemed to hover over the floor of the Arava Valley. In his mind's eye, as if in a mirage, he suddenly saw the land fertile, with date and pomegranate, cool buildings, trees, and, miracle upon miracle, green grass and water pools.

"*Le shana, habe be Ha'arava.*" He muttered so that only Ya'akov and Alexander could hear him. Both smiled.

"Yes, and there we'll build our own Jerusalem," Alexander added, as his camel started to walk northwards towards the fertile lands, out of the wilderness.

Ya'akov had trained at the Kadoury Agricultural School, but he had no head for plants, and remembered only the use of machinery and implements.

Reuven the doctor remembered the botany classes he had taken as a student in Amsterdam and became the agricultural expert of the kibbutz.

"One thing is certain," Reuven had insisted at an early committee meeting, "we must make up our minds to grow each year fifty per cent of crops for our own consumption, and fifty per cent for selling." The town of Be'ersheva had few shops but one of them bought and sold agricultural produce. The bedouin were of course not farmers, and earned such money as they had from the sale of the young of their herds, or by selling the old ones for meat. They were the best customers for the agricultural produce of the kibbutz. Later, when the amount became sufficient to warrant it, the produce could go further north into the markets of the co-operatives.

"We must grow cucumber, and tomatoes, green vegetables, peppers, grain for flour, oats for oatmeal, almonds and olives mostly for the markets, citrus trees if we can get them to root, for ourselves and for the market. We must plant grasses to hold the land stable against the wind, and trees for wind-breaks, the Jerusalem pine they call the aleppo, brutia, the canary pine, tamarisk, and cypresses."

"That's all very well," Yigal said, "but where will we get the stock? Fancy going into Be'ersheva to ask for aleppo pine seedlings, and cypresses. . . ."

Eventually Chochem was given the money, the lorry and a list of their requirements. The lorry broke down half-way to Be'ersheva, and Chochem stood beside the road and gave himself a lesson in auto mechanics; not even he knew how he got the carburettor to work, but work it did, and took him all the way to the nurseries in the Judean Hills.

He brought back a lorry laden with bags and packets of seeds, rooted cuttings and seedlings. He'd been stopped twice by the British, who insisted on searching everything, and run the gauntlet of a nomadic bedouin marauding gang, armed with rifles, who appeared to have been waiting for him south of Be'ersheva. He routed them by shooting through the side window and sounding his hooter loudly. The shooting scared the bedouin; the hooting scared the camels who reared and raced away. One of them ran in front of his lorry; the impact killed both the camel and the bedouin riding it. Chochem left the bedouin by the road for the jackals to pick clean. He made an improvised hoist by jacking the back axle of the lorry off the ground, removing the wheel, and winding a rope round the brake drum. He passed the rope through a stanchion behind the roof of the cab, and revved the engine with the truck in gear. The axle slowly revolved, winding up the rope, winching the body of the camel which must have weighed a couple of thousand kilos, on to the back of the lorry.

"Why didn't you simply strip the flesh off the camel, and bring as much as you could that way?" Ya'akov asked him, laughing as Chochem gave his account of the meeting with the bedouin.

Chochem looked shame-faced. "I never thought of that," he said. They took all the meat off the camel's bones, gave Chochem the skin to air dry as a rug for his tent, and ground the bones and sprinkled them over the soil.

"Work for us now, you bastard," Ya'akov said, as he spread the fine bone meal, the first fertiliser they'd ever used.

The day after the mortar bombardment, Reuven took Abraham to the long shed built beside the beast-yard, a lean-to, constructed of timber lathes and draped with thin white paper. The paper seemed to have a million stars in it, though the light within the 'paper house' was diffused. After the paper had been fixed to the lathes, three of the women had slowly worked over its entire surface, pricking needle-fine holes a centimetre apart. Then they'd gone over the paper with olive oil, making it translucent. Thus the paper house had light, and air, but was shielded from the blazing heat and light of the direct sun. Stones had been laid along one side to form a trough, and at one end, the trough's sides had been cemented to make a water vessel. Smaller stones and soil had been laid in this trough, and water constantly flowed into it from the cement water vessel, which was filled each day by bucket from the well. All along the trough, plants grew to a height of a metre and a half, and from each plant hung a dozen or more green tomatoes.

"They've set well," Abraham said, as Reuven took him along the row.

"Wait until you see this," Reuven said, unable to conceal

56

his excitement. For the last three metres of the trough, the texture of the growing medium was different from that in the rest of the trough.

Abraham examined the growing medium, poked into it with his finger. "There's no soil," he said astounded.

"That's right. No soil. It's something I read about as a student, experiments they were trying in California, or maybe it was Florida. I forgot the details, but then, I started working it out again, for myself. Plants don't need soil, really; they take all their nutrition from the *water*. The water dissolves the chemicals in the soil, and the roots of the plants take that water and its chemicals. All this business about humus is just to make the chemicals more soluble in the water. Well, I reckoned that all that was probably happening in the rest of the bed anyway, so I'd try down here to do away with soil. If you take those stones out, and that's all small stones they're growing in, you'll find the roots curling about among 'em, quite naturally. But since the roots don't have to fight their way through the soil, they grow longer and bigger; so they can take in more nutrition, and look . . ." He pointed to the branches of the plant. "Same plant, same water as all the rest, but thirty per cent more tomatoes, and each tomato is at least twenty per cent bigger, and in some cases a good fifty per cent."

Amazed, Abraham looked at the plants. "Plants without soil. It doesn't seem possible."

"Well, it is, and there's the proof." Reuven looked at Abraham, seeking his approval. "Come across here," he said. On the other side of the paper house cucumbers were planted in soil enriched with the manure of their beasts. One section, however, contained no soil, and the cucumbers were lying on sheets of paper on the stones. The stones appeared to be dry, but Abraham knew the roots would be embedded in the water. These cucumbers were one and a half times the thickness and almost twice the length of the ones in the soil.

Abraham twisted one of the cucumbers; it was ripe, and separated from the plant. He picked it up, firm and heavy. "Now that's what I'd call a cucumber," he said.

Reuven wiped his pruning knife on the seat of his trousers and cut the cucumber a quarter way down its length; juice flowed out. He could not conceal his joy. "Taste it," he said, "taste it!"

Abraham bit into the cucumber, though he remembered their bitterness apprehensively. He chewed, swallowed, and immediately bit again. "Well, I'll be damned," he said, "you've cured the bitterness. The cucumber's sweet!"

"They're all sweet," Reuven said, "every single one grown by the new method!"

They left the paper house together. "It's a miracle," Abraham kept saying, but without thought of the Almighty. When they had gone about ten paces, Reuven suddenly stopped. The joy had gone from his face.

"I showed you the cucumbers, Abraham, for a reason."

Abraham nodded. "I guessed you had," he said. "You were trying to show me that all things are possible, to persuade me to influence the others to stay . . . ?"

"I wish it were that," Reuven said, "but it's not quite so easy. I want us to stay here—desperately! I even want us to sink some of our pride and get in touch with the Federation, to see if they'll help us financially, and send more people. I wouldn't mind sacrificing our principles and taking in a few religious members, to live and worship in their own way. I wanted you to see what I myself could do to help, in a personal and positive way. But what I have to say now is negative, weak and cowardly, when I should be strong and brave."

"What is it, Reuven?" Abraham asked. The younger man was sweating with nervousness and the strain of exposing himself.

"When the bombs start to fall," Reuven said, "believe me, no matter how brave I might try to be, I couldn't guarantee to stand . . . I might run. I don't think I can stand for bombs, Abraham," he said. "I wanted you to see the tomatoes, and the cucumbers, so that if I run when the time comes, you won't think too badly of me. I mean, it's a bad thing to run, and I know that, and we've put so much into this, and I don't mean the money . . ."

"I know what you mean, Reuven," Abraham said, "but there's nothing I can say that will help you. Not one of us knows what will happen when the bombs start to fall. The brave might run, the ones who think they are cowards stand fast. Eli was a case in point; he was a brash kid, swaggering about the kibbutz, nagging us all to let him stand guard. Remember? 'Let me get at them', he used to say; but on the night I took him out with me, he was as scared as all the rest of us. But he did what he had to do, Reuven. Fear can show itself quite easily, but just because a man's afraid, it doesn't mean he's useless. This country's been built so far by people who could be afraid and achieve something at the same time. Even the *bilium* who landed at Jaffa in 1882; just think, fourteen young men and women who came here with nothing and started the first *aliyah*; don't you think they were afraid? They didn't know if they'd stick or run any more than we know now!"

"But they had 'If I forget thee, O Jerusalem'."

"Most of us have that!"

"Except Ya'akov, and he wasn't brought up a Jew."

"He was brought up in a land of so-called Christians, and didn't even know it was Passover when his father said *le shana habe be Yerushalayim*."

"I'm still afraid of when the bombs come, Abraham."

"Like most of us here, you've been brought up to think of yourself as part of a Jewish minority, persecuted not because of the shape of your nose, but because of the strangeness of your religion, simply because you are a Jew. You've always been afraid, Reuven. That's why we've come here, to get away from being Jewish. Now that the people of this country are at home, they think that because they're a majority, they no longer need to be afraid. That's where we differ. You know that. We've come here because we want to be in the homeland without feeling the need to be Jews, whether in a minority or a majority. Perhaps some of us will go back to religion. Perhaps when we prosper and take in new people, and they have a *seder* for Passover, some of

59

us will be converted back to religion; but we'll be Palestinian citizens who worship in the Jewish way, as distinct from Christians, or Mohammedans, or any other religion each individual may choose. The important thing, however, is that by converting ourselves from Jews into Palestinians, we shall have lost the inborn, natural, timeless fear the Jews cannot escape. That's what's been wrong, Reuven. All through the Diaspora, Jews have lived in other lands, but they've always been Jews, they've always practised Judaism as if it were a nationality, not a religion; they should have concentrated, as far as they could, on being Germans, or French, or British first, and Jews as a permissible method of religion. They'd have been persecuted, certainly, in the same way that all religions have been persecuted at one time or another. The flow of mankind across the face of the earth has often been to escape religious discrimination; but other religious travellers, like the Huguenots who went into England, or the Quakers in America, have allowed themselves to be absorbed by the country that's given them a home. Jews have always fought that. They've had a fierce pride in the blood of Judaism, and they've resisted absorption. I suppose the nearest they've ever come to it is in America. How many American Jews have come here, Reuven, how many?"

"Not many, I grant you, though they've been generous with money and help."

"That's as it should be! But have you ever thought why they haven't come? It's because in America they've learned to live without fear of being Jewish, at least the ones who don't make a parade of their Jewishness have. There are hundreds of thousands of people of Jewish blood who don't believe in 'If I forget thee, O Jerusalem'. They're good *Americans* first, and Jews second. They don't want to be afraid any more than we do. We want to be good *citizens* first, and let them who want to be good Jews second."

"And if I stop thinking like a Jew, and learn to think like a Palestinian, I'll lose my fear?"

"I can't promise that. Everyone's afraid of bombs. But it might give you the justification for staying here, and defend-
60

ing our little bit of land against the Arabs."

They started to walk again, through the kibbutz. Abraham took Reuven's arm. "The death of Eli and Dov was a tragedy," he said, "a stupid tragedy. But if we run away from here, it becomes a waste."

The boat sailed along the north coast of the Mediterranean, out of sight of harbours but near enough to run for land should the British appear. Hagar lived on the after-deck in a space about one metre square. Immigration into Palestine was strictly controlled by the British and the annual quota filled within a month of each new year. The volunteers, undeterred, bought boats all over the world with funds provided by Jewish sympathisers and ran illegally into Palestine under the noses of the British.

When the boat had been sailing for nine days and nights and food and drinking water were running low, the captain, a burly American who never shaved and spent his time aboard in a sweat shirt, canvas twill trousers and tennis shoes, announced over a loud-hailer that he was "ready to make a run for it". "This is it," he shouted. "From here on in there's no turning back, and the only land we can run for is Eretz Israel!" The cheer that greeted him was ragged; sea-sickness, the monotonous food and cramped conditions had all taken their toll. The touch-down point on deserted sand dunes north of Tel Aviv had been arranged long in advance; the captain would run in as close as possible and lower the twelve lifeboats; all the old and infirm in the boats, younger people and men of any age dumped into the water with lines to the lifeboats; a desperate landing if ever it had been made. The British caught them two kilometres from the coast, called them to 'halt and be taken under tow to Cyprus'. The captain refused to halt; the British fired a shot meant no doubt to go across the bow. The gunner must have lacked accuracy or the ship rolled; the shot landed amidships below the water-line. The boat cracked and sank immediately; only five people survived. Hagar held on to a spar of wood from the sinking boat, surprisingly uninjured. Her youth and natural vitality helped her paddle three kilometres in to the coastline. There she was immediately seized by young men and spirited inland to what later she learned was a kibbutz.

During the first few months of her new life Hagar attended classes in Hebrew and soon became proficient. Her pale skin tanned brown in the unaccustomed sun of the new land; she worked long hours in the fields, studied hard, danced the native folk dances and sang their songs. She lived the life and intimate ritual of these strange people called the Jews and was instructed in their religion. Now she learned those things which her father had dared only to whisper for fear of persecution, the sophisticated ideals too profound for a flighty young mind. As she grew into the ways of the kibbutz-niks, she absorbed their seriousness, and religious teachings. All her life her father had tried to tell her these things against her mother's objections. "Don't bring her up to be a Jew!" her mother had pleaded; since the ideas her father expressed were difficult and incomprehensible to her, Hagar had remained immune to them. When she came, however, to this strange and barren land and saw the burgeoning of everything about her, she was infected by the earnest sincerity of those she lived with. Here, being a Jew was natural; it was the way of life and of purpose and she became absorbed in its natural rhythm. Once a year at Passover when the sun went down, all work at the kibbutz would stop. The tables of the communal dining room were joined together and laid with special care using tablecloths reserved for the purpose and immaculately laundered. On them were candles, bowls of field flowers, wine from the vines they grew. When the sun went down the youngest male present would read from the *Haggadah* the words immortal to the Jews, "Why is this night different from all the other nights of the year?" And they would celebrate their going forth in triumph from slavery into freedom, and Hagar remembered her mother and her father in a distant land, who thought themselves too old to start a new life in Israel.

Hagar was in the fields with the grazing cows when she saw him approach. She'd heard about him from Shulamit, her 'best friend', though strong relationships in the kibbutz were discouraged as tending to break down the community feeling into cliques and factions. He had been away from the kibbutz for three years, studying engineering at the Hebrew University at Jerusalem. Hagar and Shulamit signed up for a Jerusalem visit three months ago merely in the hope they'd catch a glimpse of him. "You'll like him," Shulamit promised. Now he had finished his course, qualified as an engineer, and soon would be leaving the kibbutz completely to go to Haifa to work in his profession.

She sat on a wooden fence, pretending not to see him. Normally she wore trousers when she was on grazing duty, but this day she had decided her trousers needed washing, and had been compelled to wear a skirt. And wearing a skirt, of course, she had needed to iron her shirt, and brush her hair. Hagar had long black hair and though Moshe the kibbutz secretary had often indicated that she ought to get it cut short, Hagar was proud of her long locks. He was as tall as Shulamit had said he would be; and slender. His face was only lightly tanned, but taking an engineering course, slaving over books and drawings, especially in the final year, must be an inside matter. Hagar suddenly felt sorry for him for his last lost year, though proud of his achievement.

"Hagar?" he asked, enquiring. She nodded. "Shul told me you'd be here!"

"You could have found that from the work office," she said to tease him. Don't let him think being Shulamit's brother gave special privileges! He stood silent, appraising her. She looked boldly at him, appraising him. If he wanted maidenly modesty and the lowering of eyes, let him look elsewhere. Plenty of girls in the kibbutz would give him lots of that and giggling too.

"You ought to get the cows in," he said finally.

"What on earth for? I don't start in until just before sunset."

"That's late, isn't it?"

"Scared I might be out after dark?"

"No," he said, "but it is a little late to get back on *shabbat*!"

She'd forgotten it was *shabbat*. She always had difficulty remembering it. It wasn't that she didn't enjoy *shabbat* more than any other day, the way they all did, but she seemed to lack that inner instinctive feeling that said, 'today is *shabbat*, different from all other days'.

"You hadn't forgotten?" he asked smiling.

"Forgotten? Forgotten *shabbat*? How could I?" She climbed down from the railing, and started to call the cows. They knew the sound of each voice in the kibbutz, knew it was time to go home. Hagar went to Seppa, the lead cow, and caught her by the scruff of hair behind her long ears. "Come on, Seppa," she said. "Time to go home . . ." Seppa made for the gate in the railing that would lead them to the kibbutz and the covered yard. Milking would be early that day, the bag less heavy to carry.

He fell into step beside her, and walked with her across the field. When they got there, he opened the gate and held it while the cows wandered through. Then he shut the gate, and ran up the line of cows to where Hagar was walking beside Seppa.

"I wouldn't be surprised if you had forgotten *shabbat*," he said, "I often forget it myself."

"Why keep going on about it? What does it matter?"

"Only this," he said, "I was going to ask you if you'd take a walk with me, after supper. It's been a long time since I've walked round the kibbutz, and I want to see all the new things you've done while I've been away." It had been seven months since he had been to the kibbutz; during the last university holidays, he'd worked on the city projects in Tel

Aviv—one day, Tel Aviv would be a fine big city; in thirty years it had already grown enormously. Now there were docks, and a fishing port. One day it would be the largest city in Palestine, larger even than Jerusalem!

"Won't your father want to talk to you after supper? He and the rabbi and the men always talk together on *shabbat*, late in the night. They'll want you there with them, I should think!"

He looked at her as they walked along. "Shulamit tells me you're not a very religious person," he said shyly.

"Shulamit has no right to say such a thing about me," she said. "Wait until I see her! I'm just as religious as she is anyway!"

He took his *yarmulka* from his pocket. "I haven't been wearing this much in Jerusalem," he said. "In fact, few of the students wear them at all, even for meals!"

"What are they, Bolsheviks?"

"Why does everyone call you a Bolshevik, just because you don't want to wear a *yarmulka*? Everybody's talking about the Bolsheviks, when they ought to be doing something about the Nazis. There's going to be a war, Hagar, you mark my words!"

"Is that the only news you've brought back from Jerusalem, that everybody calls you a Bolshevik, and that there's going to be a war? Well, perhaps I'd better not bother with that walk, because I don't know any of that smart talk about Bolsheviks and wars, and I really don't think I'd be able to say anything to interest such a worldly person as yourself," she said, as she led the cows into the beast-yard. She waited until the last cow was through the gate, then shut it firmly, he on the outside, she on the inside.

That night, he sat between two visitors who'd come to see him at the kibbutz, men he'd been introduced to in Jerusalem, and had met once in Tel Aviv. Both seemed cordial, and talked with the people on the other side of the table, but one could hardly fail to notice that their *yarmulkas* were either new or had been freshly laundered.

After supper Hagar walked alone out of the communal

dining room. He was waiting outside, with the two men.

"What about that walk? You never gave me an answer."

She looked at the two men. "You're busy now, aren't you?"

"They'd like to come, too."

"I mustn't be long."

"By the way," he said, "this is Abraham, and this Ya'akov, and this is Hagar." She shook hands with them. "If I can stop her from being so aggressive, I shall probably marry her one day," he said.

They started walking down the path. Ya'akov looked at the couple walking in front of them. He nudged Abraham and winked at the sight of their linked hands.

By the time Abraham and Ya'akov had found the well and were ready for the services of an engineer, Hagar had stopped being aggressive towards Dov, the only man she had ever loved.

Some days go badly, some go well. Some mornings a man would be smart to turn over, pull the blankets over his ears, and sleep the day away. The day started badly for Noam when he put his foot into his trousers leg, caught his toe in a small hole at the knee, and ripped the trousers leg down to the bottom. Putting on his boot, he broke a lace in the most awkward place, leaving two pieces each too short to tie. On his way out of the tent, his foot caught a tent peg and he went sprawling to the ground; and as if that were not enough, when he put his hand out to save himself, his finger bent almost double beneath him, and the resulting sprain brought tears to his eyes. Reuven examined the finger. "Nothing broken," he diagnosed, "but it'll give you hell for a day or two!"

"Anything I can do to stop the pain?"

"You could stick your finger in a bucket of ice . . ." Big joke; the air temperature was already ninety-seven, and even the water from the well would be warm. Reuven tied a bandage round the finger, binding it to the next. "One will support the other," he said, and that was the best he could do.

Noam had been on weeding duty. "You can't handle a hoe with two fingers missing," Yigal said. "Do you think you could drive the tractor?" That day it had been Miriam's turn to drive, an easy assignment that meant sitting down; she changed with Noam, took the hoe, and set off for the orchard field. Noam climbed aboard the tractor, the scuffler and the trailer were connected, and away they went.

The soil of the new field was breaking up very well. When they started to scuffle it, the field had been a mass of rocks and stones, perfectly flat, though criss-crossed by deep fissures. They had dumped the first stones in the bottom of the crevices; and repeated passing with the scuffler worked the surface soil loose and obliterated all traces of the cracks. Now the field was flat as a table top and the surface loam, granular and friable, was at least twenty-five centimetres deep. The dust had settled beneath the granules, and most of the stones had been removed. Today would be the final scuffling; then the field would be ridged to prevent the top soil from washing away when the rain came, and trees would be planted around the north and the east sides to break the prevailing winds. Ya'el, Misha, Rebecca, Chochem and Sarah were on stone-picking duty; it was a hot dusty morning for a hot dusty job. "Roll on breakfast time!" Ya'el said, catching Noam's eye as he turned the tractor round at the end of a row. The stones were small, and the trailer took a lot of filling, a lot of bending and picking, scrambling in the soil for stones whose tips only were showing. Nails worn down by work soon split even further, yesterday's blisters burst, and dust got into the chapped cracks between fingers. But worst of all was the constant bending. At the end of each row, all stood erect, stretching fully, easing tired shoulders. Misha was the only one with a watch, an old tin hunter he carried on a short leather strap in his shirt pocket. "Isn't it breakfast time yet?" they asked him constantly. Finally he stopped putting it back in his pocket and left it dangling for all to see.

67

Noam had a pipe; he had no tobacco, and smoked dried cabbage leaves mixed with thyme herb from the kitchen garden. When they came upon a large pile of stones, he drew the tractor to a halt, to give the pickers time to get them on to the trailer. Usually the driver would leap down to help the pickers when the tractor stopped, pleased of an excuse to stretch his legs. Noam sat on the seat of the stationary tractor, filled his pipe with the cabbage/thyme mixture, and lit it. The cabbage leaf had not been properly cured, or he'd over-damped it, or maybe it just wasn't his day, but it took some time to get it alight. The others had been picking stones at the usual rate, throwing them on to the back of the trailer. Misha looked at his watch; still fifteen minutes till breakfast. He straightened his body to relieve the pain in the small of his back and suddenly inhaled a lungful of the acrid smoke from Noam's pipe. They were all aware that Noam sat while they worked. Misha strode to the tractor. "Bloody stuff," he shouted, "what the hell are you smoking, anyway?"

Noam made the mistake of smiling, insensitive to the nearness of flash-point. He puffed on the pipe again; "Eli-Dov mixture," he said, "I think I'll patent it . . ."

Misha reached up, snatched the pipe, and threw it as far as he could across the field. Inadvertently, he caught Noam's bad finger. With a roar, Noam leaped from the tractor. "What are you doing? That was my pipe you threw away," he shouted, and struck out at Misha's shoulder.

"Well, at least it got you down off that tractor seat; perhaps now you'll join in the work, instead of sitting on your back-side like a chauffeur . . ."

Sarah had walked across the field to retrieve Noam's pipe. She dusted it and handed it to him. Rather, she took his arm, drew him gently back, and forced him to take the pipe in his hand, knowing he would not strike Misha with it. " 'Can two walk together, except they be agreed'," she said.

Noam looked at Misha, then at Sarah. "Always ready with a quotation, eh, Sarah?"

Misha took a half-pace forward, offered his hand. "I'm sorry," he said, "it's been one of those mornings . . . !"

68

" 'When the wicked man turneth away from his wicked-ness, and does that which is right, he shall save his soul alive'," Sarah said quietly.

"Forget it, Misha," Noam said. "I was sitting up there feeling sorry for myself, and that's not good for a man." He took Misha's watch and turned it so that he could read the hands. "It'll be breakfast in a few minutes," he said, "let's take this load over there and we can dump it afterwards." They all scrambled on to the back of the trailer, except Misha, who lifted the scuffler clear of the ground and stood on the tractor beside Noam. The old tractor puffed a little under the increased weight, and blew out a stinking cloud of paraffin smoke which set them all coughing.

"I tell you," Noam said, "it's just one of those days for all of us. We'd have done better to stay in bed!"

There were to have been griddled oat cakes for breakfast, and all were looking forward to them as a change from the constant diet of tomatoes, cucumbers and chopped cabbage. The smell of burning that greeted them as they went into the communal dining hall told them the oat-cake tasting would be delayed. "What happened, Hepsibah?" Noam asked.

"Don't speak to me, it's been . . ."

". . . I know, one of those mornings!"

Strength comes from adversity, Sarah would have said, finding an appropriate quotation from the Bible; for the first time since the bomb fell, the conversation round the break-fast table was gay as they discussed the evil things that had happened to them all. Miriam had broken a hoe, Reuven had fallen through part of the roof of the paper house, Abraham had hit his thumb with a hammer, even Ya'akov, with skin like leather, had raised a gash along his cheek when a hinge he was making had sprung from the anvil. Soon each was recounting his misfortunes, often with a touch of exaggera-tion that added hilarity to the simple account. "Where's Leiyla! What's happened to Leiyla?" Shlomo suddenly asked. Leiyla had a gift and could recount any tale with side-splitting humour. Yigal mentally flipped down the work

69

page; no, Leiyla wasn't on grazing today; Shula was on grazing and sure enough absent from the table.

"Anyone seen Leiyla today?" They all looked around, but nobody could remember seeing her. Yigal took out his book; a copy of the day's page was clipped to the wall of the dining room, and while Yigal was finding the right place, Abraham got up and looked at the wall sheet. "According to this, Leiyla was on General this morning."

Yigal confirmed, "Yes, I've got Leiyla down for General all morning. Then she takes over from Sarah."

General was their name for dogsbody duty. It meant going all around the camp, checking everything, clearing up, tightening guy ropes, looking at canvas to see where mending was needed. People with clothes to repair left them hanging on their tent, and whoever was on General usually did the repairs sometime during the day. "She must know it's breakfast time; she must have seen us come," Sarah said. "I'll go and look for her."

Some premonition settled on the dining hall, however, and they all got up and went out to look for Leiyla. They searched all round the camp. Abraham found a guy rope on his tent that had not been secured; the first task of the General was always to check all guy ropes. Yigal's shirt left for repair at the pocket had not been touched. Noam checked the tent Leiyla had shared with Alexander, but Leiyla was not in the tent. Soon all were shouting, "Leiyla, Leiyla", but there was no reply. "Can she have gone out to the grazing with Shula?" they asked, but they could see Shula in the field of alfalfa and she was alone. "Have—you—seen—Leiyla?" they shouted, but Shula couldn't make out the words.

"I think I know where she might be," Hagar said, "at least, I know where I might be if I were Leiyla!" Abraham and Hagar went together down into the wadis, following the route he had taken on the night they had met the seven fedayeen. The ground on which they found her was stained with the blood of her son. A knife was sticking from just below her left breast and her hand was firm on the handle. She had been dead only a short time, an hour at most.
70

"Why did she do it?" Abraham asked Hagar.

"You should know, Abraham; you are the wise one."

"Only a few days ago, she spoke of having another child."

"Alexander wouldn't have been able to make children for her."

"She didn't seem to mind that; she spoke of Miriam."

Hagar was silent for a long moment, looking down at Leiyla. "It's one thing to have a child by other fathers, knowing your husband will be with you to protect you from slanderous tongues; it's another thing entirely to have a child in that way without a husband, with no one to protect you. We think we've emancipated ourselves in this matter of children by having our children brought up communally. Lots of people think this makes a woman free to have children as she wants, with whom she wants; but that isn't the case," Hagar said. "In the small communities we've created, a bad word is heard like thunder, and a look can turn in you like a knife. Leiyla knew she couldn't have any more children once Alexander was dead. Not unless she left the kibbutz to find herself a husband. She'd have none of our men for a husband."

"Why not?"

"Who could compare, for her, with Alexander?"

He stood there, silent. Alive, Alexander had been a giant-hearted, giant-bodied man, a physical brute with an extremely sensitive intellect. Ya'akov had all the physical attributes, but not even Abraham, who had known Ya'akov longer than anyone else in the kibbutz, would have said he had an intellect. "And Leiyla chose to die here, rather than leave the kibbutz to look for a husband?"

"That's right," Hagar said. "Leiyla was trying to tell us all something; to tell us to stay here, even if it meant the sacrifice of personal intentions, even if it meant the loss of life itself."

Abraham picked up the body of Leiyla and carried her back to the kibbutz. He put her on the bench Misha had carved with her name, outside her tent, and they wrapped her body in the sheet that had been on her bed. Noam,

71

Ya'akov and Yigal dug a hole in the ground for her next to Alexander; Misha carved her initials beneath a Star of David; they placed her body in the ground, returned the soil, and planted the headboard. Then they all left the cemetery save Sarah, who knelt by the grave.

Shlomo and Shula were working together after breakfast, sorting the stones into sizes for building. Shlomo took the heaviest, erecting a wall that soon hid Shula from his view. They did not talk as they worked; they thought of Leiyla and Alexander, Eli and Dov.

After a while, however, Shlomo noticed the clink of stones on Shula's side had stopped. He went round the wall to find her sitting on the pile of stones, tears running down her face. He sat beside her without speaking, his arm around her waist.

When Shula stopped crying he gave her the piece of cloth he kept in his pocket as a handkerchief.

"I'm sorry," she said.

"No need to be sorry. Tears are good for you, they say, though I've never understood why."

"Wash your eyes out, I suppose?"

"Something like that."

"Anyway, I've stopped now. It was the thought of Leiyla down there on her own. Alone! Alexander and Eli gone; Leiyla, down there, on her own . . ."

"All of us here, but nobody she wanted."

Supper was eaten in silence again that evening. Nothing is more eloquent than silence, nothing provokes impetuous speech more than the absence of sound. The human animal was not designed for silence. After they had eaten, they sat

72

in the dining hall; and the meeting started of its own volition.

"Why did she kill herself?" Ya'el asked, voicing the thoughts of them all. Abraham forbore to answer; his look enjoined Hagar to silence. "Why did she kill herself *in that place*?" Ya'el persisted.

"The blood of Eli was on the ground, and the ground was unclean; the blood of Leiyla fell on to the ground, and cleansed the ground, according to God's will," Sarah said. If any heard her, not one would give a sign.

"Do you believe that if two people die in the same place, they join each other in the life hereafter?" Hepsibah asked, but no one answered.

"She can't have had much to live for," Reuven said, "with Eli and Alexander gone!" Of the three postulations, this was the least credible. In the community they had established, the individual had a total existence, and wives were freed from the slavery of a husband's domination, equal in the work of the kibbutz, equal in the meetings of the committee, equal in the kibbutz prosperity. Granted, some wives may wish, for subjective emotional purposes, to subordinate themselves to their husbands, but this was of no more account than the position on the marriage bed.

"My mind is quite made up," Shlomo said, "and, if anything, Leiyla killing herself that way has added to my conviction." This was the moment Abraham had dreaded. He looked quickly at Ya'akov, saw his concern. "I intend to leave the kibbutz," Shlomo said, "and Shula intends to come with me and bring our two children. I hope you'll all be sensible, and agree to come with us. Let's face it, life is too dangerous here. If we stay we're merely sitting targets for the fedayeen; it may take one month, it may take twelve, but eventually, they'll have us all, one by one."

He looked around the hall. He was confident of the support of Chaim and Rebecca; Chochem and Hepsibah looked as if they might also agree. Misha and Ya'el, well, he couldn't tell—Misha had a mystic streak in him, and Ya'el was unintelligent. "We all get on very well," he said, "we've worked together very well. Why can't we write this off as an un-

73

successful experiment, and go back north where at least we'll be safe?" Still no voices were raised in support. "I don't give a damn how successful we make the kibbutz," he said, exasperated by their silence. "What's the use of making the land productive, if not one of us is alive to see it?"

"We could get more people to help us with the fighting," Yigal proposed.

"The Haganah?" Noam asked. "They'd never spare anyone from Haganah; they're too busy along the other borders."

"Newly arrived immigrants, possibly," Reuven suggested, "illegals?"

"You'd be taking a chance!" Chaim said. Not all the illegals were themselves legal; many criminals saw illegal immigration into Palestine as a means of evading the law in their own country.

"The university?" Hagar suggested, remembering Dov.

"The university's a fine idea," Misha said; "we were certainly lucky with . . ." He looked at Hagar, suddenly tongue-tied.

"With Dov?" she said. "Yes, we were lucky there. Having an engineering degree, and laying everything out the way it should be. We'd have had a much harder job with the buildings if it hadn't been for Dov. He put his whole heart into those buildings, and the plans for the homes we'll start next year, and the water schemes when we find other wells . . . He put his whole heart into it. . . ." There were tears in her eyes, but she shook them away. "I think we've had enough talking about this issue," she said. "Why don't we take a vote? I propose that we honour the memory of Dov, and Eli, and Leiyla, and Alexander, and that we stay here with a determination to complete the work they started, the work for which they gave their lives!"

Before Shlomo could speak, Miriam said, "I second that proposal."

"I've never heard such a blatantly emotional appeal as that one," Shlomo said amid the uproar. "Let's cut out all this sentimental female claptrap and get back to the case in point!" That was where Shlomo lost all the support he
74

could have won. Rebecca and Hepsibah were offended by *female*, Chaim and Chochem by *sentimental*, and the whole room by his use of the word *claptrap*. Still he ploughed on. "Let's appeal to reason. I propose we recognise this kibbutz is indefensible. We cannot defend it, therefore we must leave it, or stay here and be killed. I say, let's get out of it while we still can."

"We have a proposal before the meeting," Yigal said, asserting his half-treasurership. "Hagar's proposal has been seconded by Miriam; let us proceed to a vote. I can't see any reason for a secret ballot, though I'm quite prepared to arrange one if anyone wants it." He looked round; there were no takers.

"Right then, show of hands. Will all those in favour of the proposal please raise their hands?"

Abraham had hardly dared look during the previous exchange. Now he stared at Ya'akov, seeking to read the result on his face. His eyes opened incredulously, his face a mask of surprise. Then his eyes half closed, and a smile came to his lips. Abraham looked round the room. Everyone had an arm raised except Shlomo. Even Shula, defying her husband, had stuck up her arm.

"No need to count," Yigal said. Shlomo got up, and stalked out of the hall. When he got to the door, Shula called after him.

"You've forgotten to wash your plate, Shlomo," she said, "and you'll need it for breakfast in the morning!"

Abraham and Ya'akov walked out of the hall together. "Marvellous," Abraham said, "they did it all by themselves."

"You're a fox," Ya'akov said, "you knew damned well you couldn't pull it off, so you primed Hagar to do it for you. What did he call it—sentimental female claptrap? The sad thing, Abraham, is that he was right, you know. Considered impartially, as a sample of debating strategy, it was deplorable. It was *sentimental female claptrap*!"

"But think where you'd have been with rational masculine logic!"

"Where we'd all have been, on the road to Be'ersheva."

They could see a figure sitting on the stone wall of the covered beast-yard. When they drew near, Shlomo got to his feet. "You think you're smart, don't you?" Shlomo said to Ya'akov. His words, of course, were meant for Abraham, and all three knew that, but Shlomo was not the man to tackle Abraham head on. Ya'akov didn't reply. He went to the wall and stood with his arms on it, looking into the beast-yard.

"If it's any consolation to you," Abraham said, "we both think you were right; it was sentimental female claptrap."

"Then why didn't you stop it? They'd have listened to you. Why didn't you help me? I wouldn't have tried to sway them by that sort of cheap trick, you know that. I'd have put the matter to them rationally, and logically, and they could have made up their own minds on the basis of what was said."

"Ah, Shlomo, you're too good for this world, or you're too simple. The world's never been swayed by logic. This whole business was not started on logic; there's no logic in our laying claim to a land that doesn't belong to us; there's no logic in pretending to ourselves we're here by God-given right. We're here because of the sort of emotional claptrap you've been listening to in there. The only difference is that this is on a small local scale, and the other is larger and international."

"I won't go into the Biblical aspects, Abraham, because I know how completely you've turned your back on the Scripture, but may I remind you that the League of Nations confirmed the claim we have to this land in the Mandate."

"The League of Nations? What God-given right has the League of Nations to confirm anything, Shlomo? The League of Nations, like our entire existence, is based on expediency. Men get together and decide what will cause the least international trouble for their own nationalistic aims and vested interests. A war in Spain, but what the hell is the League of Nations able to do about that? Italian murderers in Ethiopia! People are being persecuted in Russia, in Poland, and now in Germany simply because of their religion, but
76

how could any League of Nations stop the butchers? Logic, Shlomo, logically and ultimately, is the weapon of the assassin. It was logic that killed Caesar, when emotional debate kept him alive incompetent. How many men have we assassinated since we came here, Shlomo? That's logic. Emotion would sit down before them and beg."

"I never wanted the killing."

"But you were prepared to do it. You stood guard with the rifle in your hand, and one of our five bullets up the breech. You helped make the bombs we placed in the wadis, so don't talk to me, Shlomo, about what you wanted. Look inside yourself, man, and admit, as the rest of us have admitted, that we're just plain scared, we're afraid, Shlomo, every one of us. But the difference between us and you—and I admit there is an *us* and a *you* as that vote showed tonight—is that *we're* scared and admit it, *you're* scared and try to cover it up with, guess what, Shlomo, a load of emotional claptrap."

"If you want to go back to Tel Aviv, I'll take you in the lorry," Ya'akov offered. "I could use the trip to get more saplings for the wind break."

"Don't do me any favours." Shlomo pushed past them. "When I go, I'll make my own way," he said.

"Why does he hate me so?" Ya'akov asked, laughing quietly. "I never did him a kindness!"

"Come on, you Jew, let's take a walk," Abraham said.

Two fedayeen, trained by the Arab Legion but drummed out for lack of discipline, crawled behind Shula. Chaim and Chochem were on guard, forward; Shula and Miriam were between them and the kibbutz. Shula was set behind a rock, amidst other low rocks, with a wide arc of vision. She was crouching forward, resting her weight on the rock in front of her, staring out into the semi-dark. There was little moonlight, and no stars. The rifle was resting on the rock beside her, with nine rounds in the magazine, one in the breech. The gun was cocked, the safety catch off. She raised her hand to brush the hair from her ears. The Arab behind her froze, still. He was breathing slowly to avoid making a sound. He wore no shoes, and the bottoms of his trousers were bound to his ankles with British army puttees. In his right hand he carried a short length of oiled cord with a knot at each end; his left hand was drawn back in front of his face, the knuckles bent and held hard in position for the killer jab. His eyes were yellow, but whether from recurrent malaria or *kif* it would be impossible to say. Shula bent forward again, her breasts heavy on the rock. Boredom was the worst part of night sentry duty, boredom, and the inescapable feeling you were wasting sleeping time. How many times she had waited and they had not come. Miriam was across the wadi, in a nest of rocks. Shula could not see her, but would hear her moo like a cow in warning. Neither could she see Chaim and Chochem, up forward, but it was arranged that Chochem would come out behind his cairn of stones should any approaching fedayeen be sighted.

The Arab moved a step forward. Now he was in position, ready for the strike. His companion was behind the rock only three metres to the side.

Shula heard the sound behind the rock to her left, the faint rap of a rifle butt on stone. Slowly she swung her rifle round to point in that direction. The Arab behind her leaped forward, a brown blur, but before she could scream he had whipped the rope round her throat, caught the end knot with his left hand, doubled the rope behind her neck, pulled her back on to his bent knee, and garotted her. She tried

78

vainly to chop backwards into his groin, but hit only the hard portions of his leg. Then fear took over and her hands reached through the red mist of death for the cord around her throat. When her hands fell slowly away, the Arab took his knees from her back, placed his thumbs against the base of her skull without loosening the pressure of the cord, and snapped backwards, breaking her neck. He let go of the cord, and she fell lifeless to the ground.

Two fedayeen killed Chochem in exactly the same way.

Two went after Miriam. She was kneeling when the man with the cord pounced. Miriam had trained in judo at another kibbutz and her reactions were automatic. She threw him over her shoulder into a rock. Then, for Yigal, she kicked his testicles with her army boots. When the second fedayeen came round the rock she shot her rifle at him, low. The bullet caught him in the lower body, smashed him back round the rock. The sound of the rifle shot woke everyone in the kibbutz. Chaim turned towards the direction of the firing; a bedouin leaped from behind a rock at his side, and sank his long curved knife in Chaim's belly.

Miriam could hear the fedayeen behind the rock. She backed quickly and scrambled out of the cairn of rocks. The bastard was in there, somewhere, but now she had the advantage. She knew where he was; he couldn't tell where she had jumped. She heard him moaning, softly, and then the moaning stopped. There was silence for several seconds. Then the moaning started again.

"Moan, you bastard," she said to herself. Moaning Arabs! You stayed still, stuck it as long as you could, then went forward in sympathy to put a shot through the poor bastard's brain and give him a speedy death. It was an old trick. When you got there, expecting to find a helpless Arab lying on the ground clutching his stomach, you found him smiling, his rifle or his knife or his garotte cord ready to receive you. Miriam was too experienced to be caught like that. She circled the rocks slowly to the left, not making the slightest sound.

Chaim felt the shock as the knife went into him. His

hands clasped over the knife, holding it in. He staggered forward, but the Arab stepped back, still holding the handle of the knife, his hands touching Chaim's hands, through which the blood was seeping. The Arab looked at Chaim without emotion. Chaim's eyes held his in shock as if to ask why have you done this? The Arab nodded, and the second fedayeen leaped out of cover, threw his garotting cord round Chaim's throat, put his knee in the small of Chaim's back, and tightened the cord. The Arab ripped upwards with his knife through Chaim's stomach and breastbone, killing him instantly; Chaim sagged down, suspended on the garotte cord, hanging lifeless in the Arab's arms. The Arab threw the corpse from him in disgust.

When Abraham heard the shot, he leaped off his bed and out of his tent. Sarah was immediately behind him. "Get the children," he said, "and into the dining hall."

At that moment, the positioned mortars started. The first shot blew the roof off the covered beast-yard, showering fragments of the corrugated iron down on the animals, which started to bellow. Everyone in the kibbutz was rushing out of the tents. The second mortar bomb fell on the green by the cairn, blowing a funnel of earth up into the sky but doing no apparent damage. "Ya'akov?" Abraham shouted, above the noise of the beasts bellowing and the explosions.

"Here," Ya'akov shouted as he dashed from his tent, already fully dressed.

"North," Abraham shouted, "they'll come in after the mortar attack." Ya'akov grabbed the rifle and the ammunition from his tent and raced out of the kibbutz. "Go with him, Hagar," Abraham shouted. She grabbed the rifle from Leiyla's tent, a bandolier of ammunition, and ran after Ya'akov.

"Misha, you go south, and try to spot the mortars. I think they're using two, both south. Shlomo, you go east, and find out what's happened to the sentries." The next bomb came, whistling down through the sky. Abraham stood still, marking its progress, then dropped at the last minute. It had come from the south. The bomb hit the tractor by the beast-yard, flung jagged shards of metal in all directions; Abraham heard them whistle above him, and when he got to his feet blood was running down his leg.

"Reuven, where the hell are you," Abraham shouted, "and Noam?"

"We're both here," they said quietly. They were standing behind him, waiting for his instructions.

"West," Abraham said, "both of you. And for God's sake watch it. I imagine they'll come in from the west, and if they do, don't try to take 'em on single-handed. Withdraw back here into the kibbutz. We'll defend the dining hall, as long as the bastards don't blow it up." Noam and Reuven ran. All perimeters covered. Down came another mortar bomb, then another, two together, straddling the kibbutz. Damn it, one from the south, one from the west; down on the ground, flat. One bomb wasted, overshot, the other from the south—God, they'd got the range damned quickly— plastered into the office building and scattered stones and papers.

Abraham crouched and ran into the dining hall. Sarah had got the kids in there, and had piled all the chairs and tables to make a cave in the centre of the floor. The kids were sitting in the cave bawling their heads off. The dining hall was stone, and would survive anything save a direct hit from the mortars. Ya'el was crouched beside the window, her rifle pointing out. "They won't come yet, Ya'el," he said, "not while the mortars are firing." Sarah and Hepsibah were sitting on the floor.

"It could be the same as last time," Hepsibah said, hope-fully.

"No," Abraham said, "this time it's the real thing, a big attack. This is what we do. We've got men out on every compass direction, and whichever one spots them first will fire, or will get back here to tell us; then we'll know which direction to go. As soon as I say go, we all get moving."

He opened the door; went outside rapidly, watching the sky for mortars. He crossed the yard outside the dining hall to where the lorry was parked, on a slight incline. Sometimes when the lorry had been standing, the magneto didn't work as it should, and they had to coast the lorry down the incline to start it. He went round the lorry, and climbed into the driver's seat. Then he took off the handbrake, and climbed out again, leaving the door open. Yigal was standing beside the lorry.

"You all right?" Abraham asked.

"Miriam's out there!"

"I know that. Give a push!" The two of them bent their shoulders against the side of the lorry, and heaved. It wouldn't move at first. "Rock it," Abraham said. They pulled backwards then pushed forward, alternately. The lorry moved one centimetre, then two. "It should go this time," Abraham said, as they pulled and heaved. The lorry started to roll forward. Abraham leaped into the cab, Yigal on to the running board as the lorry coasted down the slight incline towards the newly broken field. Without lights, and very little moon, Abraham couldn't see the path. He knew that even a small boulder would stop them dead. Once or twice he saw the boulders just in time, trying desperately to remember from the day time where they had left them.

When the lorry finally came to rest, it was nearly a kilometre north-east of the kibbutz buildings. "Now we'll go and see what's happened to our sentries," Abraham said, striking off on a route that would take them into the area of the wadis. Two more mortar bombs had dropped on the kibbutz. Abraham saw the first land on the tent area; the second flash seemed to come from the paper house. They ran and crawled into the wadis, following a familiar route. At the end of the first wadi, they found Chaim. Abraham looked about him; Yigal was standing with his face against a rock. "At least they killed him," Abraham said, as he slid swiftly down the wadi side. The second sentry, he knew, should have been directly across the wadi from the first; he didn't know who it would be, didn't know how they'd decided to place themselves. It was Chochem. The Arab had left the garotte tied round Chochem's neck, his face had swollen and his tongue was protruding. His eyes were open. Abraham cut

82

the cord from Chochem's throat, closed his eyes, pushed his tongue back into his mouth.

"These are professionals," he said.

"How do you know?" Yigal asked him.

Abraham looked at him. "I just know."

"You mean, because they don't mutilate the way they mutilated me?" Abraham nodded. "Damn you," Yigal said, "if you'd spoken out today, we'd have been thirty kilometres up the road to Be'ersheva." It wasn't true, of course; it would have taken them a week to strip as much as they could from the kibbutz; and then it would have required three or four journeys with the lorry and trailer; it helped Yigal to curse, since they had not yet found Miriam. They found Shula next; her clothing had been cut open. "Professionals," Abraham said, "they like to look but don't waste time touching."

"Except with a cord round the neck, damn you!"

Another bomb fell on the kibbutz and they heard the death bellows of beasts in the yard. "Either they are having trouble with the mortar, or weren't properly in position when that rifle was fired." Both had the same unspoken question. Had Miriam fired the rifle, and if so had it saved her life?

They recrossed the wadi. "Take it easy from here," Yigal said. "If it was Miriam who fired, she's a crack shot, and she doesn't panic or ask questions before she shoots." Abraham nodded then started to crawl forward seeking the cover of every stone. When they had gone about seven or eight metres, suddenly they heard the moaning sound in front of them. "Oh God," Yigal said. He got to his feet and started to run forward. Abraham grabbed at his leg but missed.

"Come back, Yigal," he shouted, abandoning caution. There was a sudden crack from the rocks ahead of him; Yigal spun round, and then dropped. From the rocks a little to the left came three shots rapidly fired. An Arab rose out of the rocks ahead of them, screaming, blood streaming from his head. Then came a fourth shot, which dropped the Arab cold. "Miriam?" Abraham called softly.

"Abraham?"

"Yes." Abraham was crawling forward. When he reached Yigal, lying on his face, he lifted him up and turned him over. Yigal was still breathing.

"Stay down," Miriam said. "I think there was only one, but stay down just in case. Is Yigal all right?"

"Yes, I think so." Abraham felt at Yigal's shirt. There seemed to be a hole under his arm just by his rib cage, and another hole at the back where the bullet had gone straight through. Abraham tore off a piece of Yigal's sleeve and stuffed it into the hole. There was a risk of infection, he knew, but at least it would staunch the flow of blood. "Cover for me, Miriam, I have to get back to the kibbutz. The lorry's down by the new field. See if you can get Yigal down to it; but for God's sake, be careful."

"I'll be careful, for my sake," she said.

Abraham got quickly to his feet, and started to run crisscross, darting from side to side to make a difficult target of himself. There were no shots. He hadn't expected there to be. The Arabs always used two sets of men for an operation like this. First they sent in the assassins, whose sole job was to knock out the sentries, and then retreat. Often they carried no weapon but the garotte cord and the knife, and usually they were hopped up on *kif* or heroin. They were trackers, cold-blooded murderers; they went in, knocked out sentries, came out again and took their money. After them came the troops with rifles, the poorly paid battle fodder. Running zig-zag all the way, he got out of the area of the wadis, then up the slight incline to the kibbutz. The bombs had destroyed all the buildings save, miraculously, the dining hall, though the corner of the wall by the cooking area had been punched in by falling stones. Sarah and the kids were intact; Ya'el had been hit by a stone and had a lump on her forehead the size of a hen's egg, and Hepsibah was nursing a slashed arm.

"She went out to find Rebecca. She's dead," Sarah said. Sarah believed that God controlled everything on earth and visited his wrath on the transgressors. The Arabs were a manifestation of the wrath of God, no more, no less.

84

Ya'el had been watching out of the window; there had been no bombs for a couple of minutes. "I'm not doing much good here," she said; "could I go out to Misha?"

Abraham shook his head. "When we leave here we'll need all the help we can get to carry the kids." Abram was sitting in the improvised cave quite happily, but Yashka, one year older and able to understand a little of the terror of what was going on, was shouting with fear. Rachel and Mordecai were sitting as if stunned by concussion; Givona was crying, but making no noise.

"What did you find, out there?" Hepsibah asked. "Did you see Chochem?"

"No," Abraham lied, "I didn't go down there. I've run the lorry down to the new field. If the Arabs come they might miss it, and we can use it to get away."

"I wish I could go to look for Chochem," she said.

"And leave Mordecai on his own?"

"Well, it isn't as if Mordecai needs me."

"Chochem doesn't need you. It's better for you to stay here, in case."

"In case what?"

"How do I know, woman?" Abraham said, her listless apathy jarring on him. If only he knew! If only any of them could know what was happening.

Ya'akov knew. He and Hagar were lying side by side in a stone outcrop, facing north. This was the way they would come, Ya'akov had told himself, as he and Hagar took position. They'd cross the border north of the kibbutz in the range of low foothills, and make their way down the cleft in the ground. Ya'akov and Hagar had placed themselves to one side, to give them a line of retreat.

They'd need it. Ya'akov counted one hundred men, with camels and horses, crossing the ridge about a kilometre to the north, where he had supposed they would come.

"This is it, Hagar," he said. "This time, they mean to destroy us. Get back to the kibbutz and tell Abraham. If Abraham is dead, look for the lorry; he'll have moved it somewhere out of the kibbutz. Get everybody to the lorry,

85

and I'll come out there."

"Where are you going?"

"To warn the others, if I can."

They skittered away, back towards the kibbutz, back through the stones and the fields they had cultivated. At the bend in the track, Ya'akov slapped her rump, and made for the west, to where he knew Noam would be watching. Hagar raced towards the kibbutz buildings, shocked when she saw the damage the mortar bombs had done. Not one of the tents was usable. All the buildings had been destroyed except the dining hall.

"Abraham," she shouted, "Abraham, Sarah . . . ?"

The door to the dining hall was flung open, and Abraham stood there. "They're coming," she said, "at least a hundred of them. Camels and horses. Ya'akov's gone to bring in the sentries. He told me to make for the lorry." Hagar was looking wildly about her at the debris; suddenly she screamed. "Rebecca," she said, cradling what was left of Rebecca's bloody head on her knee.

"Leave her," Abraham shouted. Hagar didn't move. He ran across to where she was crouched on the ground, seized her by the arm and shoulder, and dragged her away. "Leave her," he said. "She's dead, and there are living people to look after."

Sarah came out of the dining hall, carrying Rachel and Givona. She set off, running down the slope towards the lorry. Hepsibah followed, with her own Mordecai and Rebecca's Yashka. Ya'el ran out with Abram.

"Get a couple of cans of water," Abraham commanded her, "and take them down to the lorry."

Hagar went round to the back of the dining hall, got several cans, and took them to the well. Parts of the coping around the well had been destroyed, but the windlass Ya'akov had put in still worked. Abraham ran from the ruins of the office with the tin box in which the kibbutz money was kept and four bandoliers of ammunition. One of the water cans was filled; he grabbed that, and raced towards the truck with it. He could see the other three, with the children, running before him, bunched together.

"Spread out," he shouted, but they didn't hear.

The bomb came then, the last of the mortar bombs. He heard its whistling before he could see it. He stopped and yelled, as loud as he could, "Get down!" They heard him shout and stopped running. "Get down," he shouted, as he fell to the ground, but already it was too late.

The bomb landed, as if guided, in the very centre of the group. The explosion of it sounded louder to Abraham than all the other bombs, and when the dust and debris settled there was a crater in the ground and no sign of any living person.

Abraham lifted his face to the skies, tears running down his dust-streaked face. "Damn you," he shouted. "Damn you to all eternity!"

He picked up the bandoliers of ammunition, the box with all that was left of the kibbutz money, his rifle, and the can of water and ran to the lorry as if in a dream. There was no time for grief, none for recrimination. He flung the things he carried on to the back of the lorry and ran back up the incline towards the kibbutz. Now they had only minutes; once the mortars ended, the Arabs would come. Their only hope was that Miriam's rifle shot had alerted them before the Arabs were properly in position. On the way up the slope he passed Hagar. "Stay by the lorry," he said, "but hide yourself if you can. Keep an eye open for Miriam; she'll be bringing in Yigal. He's wounded in the chest."

Ya'akov ran in from the south, panting like a racehorse, Misha behind him.

"Hagar told you?"

"Yes, about a hundred . . ."

"On camels and horses."

"Did you find Reuven, Shlomo and Noam?"

"Yes."

"Dead?" Ya'akov nodded.

"Garotted?" Abraham asked.

"What does that matter, Abraham? They are dead, and that's all. Where did you put the lorry?"

"Down the slope."

"Anybody left, down there?"

"Like you said, what does it matter? You'll see when you get down there . . ."

"Bad as that, eh?"

Hagar had filled four more water cans. "I've got the money," Abraham said, "and three cans of water. Take a couple of cans each, and get down there. There's nothing left to do up here."

Misha started to crawl through the tattered canvas of his tent. "Come on, Misha," Abraham shouted, "we only have a few minutes before the bastards get here."

Misha reappeared carrying his carving tools. "Is Ya'el down there," he asked, "and Abram?"

"They're both down there. Now get going," Abraham said, looking at Ya'akov. Suddenly Ya'akov knew the extent of their loss. He handed two cans to Misha. "Go on, get going," he said. Misha raced away, down the slope.

Ya'akov stood beside Abraham and together they looked over the kibbutz. They saw it as they had seen it the day they had found the well. Then it had been scorched brown; now the green had spread its tracery over the ground. "Next time," Ya'akov said, "we'll build a bloody great wall, all around us."

"Walls don't help, Ya'akov," Abraham said. "Walls didn't help 'em at Masada. We've got to tear down the walls between us and the Arabs, us and the Jews, and the British, and the zealots, and the rest of the whole stinking world."

The two of them ran down the slope, taking a detour around the bomb crater. Suddenly Abraham heard a whimpering sound. "Get on down to the lorry," he said and ran towards the noise. Among the rocks, he found Sarah. Miraculously, she was in one piece. Bombs do that, sometimes, when they explode. The seam splits along its length, and the blast leaves a wedge in which there are no flying fragments, only air. A man right next to an exploding bomb can have the clothing stripped from his back but walk away unhurt. Sarah was in a blast wedge, and had been blown

88

off her feet and concussed when she landed against the cluster of stones. Abraham left her where she was, quickly ran round the blast area. No one else had escaped.

He picked her up in his arms and took her to the lorry. They were all grouped around the back. Miriam had arrived, carrying Yigal, who was conscious again. Miriam and Yigal, Abraham and Sarah, Misha, Hagar, and Ya'akov. They all looked around, looked at each other. "Where are the others?" Misha asked. "Ya'el, and Abram. You said they were down here. You told me . . ."

"They were coming here," Abraham said, quietly, "down the path ahead of me. There was a mortar bomb. . . ." Misha turned away from Abraham; Miriam held him in her arms as he sobbed.

"We'd better get on board," Ya'akov said, and climbed into the cab. Abraham took the starting handle, inserted it into the cog, and waited for Ya'akov's signal. Ya'akov advanced the ignition and the mixture, pumped petrol into the carburettor, and nodded. The remaining few were lying down in the back of the lorry. Miriam had her rifle aimed over the tailboard, but her left arm cradled Yigal's neck to protect him when the lorry started to bounce.

Ya'akov nodded, and Abraham swung the starting handle. The engine coughed once, spit back vigorously with a force that could have broken a man's arm; but Abraham knew the engine, waited, and then swung again. It started immediately, running high and fast the way Ya'akov liked it. Abraham ran round the cab and climbed in beside him. He held his rifle half out of the window space, ready.

Ya'akov let in the clutch. "Don't stall, baby," he said, nursing it along. The lorry moved forward. Once the engine had taken the strain of moving them, when the revs had picked up after that first sickening drop, he pressed the accelerator firmly to the floor of the cab. The lorry took off like a three-year-old racehorse.

The Arabs started to fire as soon as they heard the noise of the engine, but the shooting was erratic, and the lorry was heading away from them. One group, riding to the flank of the main attacking force, swooped down on them over the crest of a small hill, but the combined fire of Abraham and Miriam and Misha, who picked up a rifle as soon as the shooting started, drove them away.

Ya'akov drove north, then west, following the route they had taken when they had discovered the well. When they reached the crest of the hill, half-way up to the plateau, he stopped the lorry to cool the engine. All save Sarah and Yigal climbed down and looked back to the east. The sun was starting to rise behind the hills of Jordan, its rays meeting the plume of smoke that soared into the calm air over what, for a very short time, had been Kibbutz Eli-Dov.

BOOK TWO

THE BELIEVERS

Abraham was waiting as instructed.

At the far end of the wooden hut the reception clerk wrote laboriously in a large book the particulars of three Jews standing at his desk. Two had blood on their hands and faces; the third appeared to have a broken leg. It had been strapped to a plank of wood with a brown bandage.

"Do you think I could sit down?" he asked the clerk.

They were no more than sixteen years old; the clerk spoke to them as if they were recalcitrant schoolboys. "In a minute," he said crossly, "when I've got it all written in the book." It was apparent that he regarded the book with reverence and that writing and Hebrew were recently acquired talents. Abraham grabbed three chairs and banged them down behind the three boys.

"Take a seat," he said, exasperated. "He can take details whether you're sitting or standing, the bureaucratic bastard."

The clerk looked sourly at him. "You again, already?"

Abraham ignored him. "What happened?"

The one with the injured leg spoke for them all. "We were building and a wall collapsed on us. Broke my leg, we think, and did something to his arm."

"When did it happen?"

"About an hour ago . . ."

Abraham looked at them, then at the clerk. "Take a walk," he said to the clerk.

"Who are you talking to?" he asked, spluttering with outrage. Abraham seized him by the top of his shirt and lifted him from the chair.

"Go have a piss."

91

The clerk got out rapidly, without glancing back, his mincing walk a ballet of outraged virtue. The three boys grinned.

"You must be mad," Abraham said, "coming in here with a story like that. Don't you know the British check hospitals? Especially after a raid. 'Injured,' you say, 'doing a bit of building when a wall collapsed, and only an hour ago.' You're lucky that clerk isn't sharper or the British would be on their way right now."

"You don't fall for that story, eh?" the leader of the trio said.

"Firstly," Abraham said, "there's no dust on your clothes, and there'd be a hell of a lot if a wall had fallen on you. Secondly, you say it happened only an hour ago, and yet the blood's already caked. You wouldn't have been on the Jerusalem road when the British army lorry was ambushed about two o'clock this morning, would you?"

The leader smiled. "Who wants to know?"

"It's nothing to do with me," Abraham said, "but all these bloody bureaucrats are in with the British, and they'd turn you in as soon as look at you; so either get out of here, or change your story."

"Know a good one?"

"Tell 'em you were knocked down by a hit-and-run driver on the Haifa road; when they ask you for the number, tell 'em you didn't get it, but it was a British Army Staff car, you'd recognise the major and he had an Arab bird sitting with him! That'll hold 'em. They'll have to believe you; they wouldn't want a thing like that to get any further, would they? The murdering swine . . ."

Abraham had seen the doctor come in at the front of the hut. "What's this my receptionist tells me about violence?" the doctor asked, frowning at Abraham.

"It wasn't him," the leader of the trio said quickly, "it was me. I think I must have a touch of concussion. We were knocked down by a British Army Staff car on the Haifa road; a major sitting in the back with an Arab girl just drove on. . . ."

92

"Did you get the number?" the doctor asked. "I'll report that . . ."

"We couldn't quite catch it," one of them said.

"I'd recognise that major again," another put in.

The clerk had come back. "Get Doctor Simon to attend to this man's leg at once," the doctor said.

"I haven't finished taking the particulars!"

"That can wait until later."

The hospital—if such it could be called—on the outskirts of Tel Aviv had been donated by a textile magnate from Leeds in Yorkshire, England. Humble beginnings. Five wooden huts, three filled with beds; one reception hut which also served as a casualty, out-patients department and dispensary; another that combined treatment room and operating theatre. Three doctors were on the staff: a surgeon, a general practitioner, a consultant neurologist, cum ear-nose-and-throat man, cum jack-of-all-trades.

"My name's Walters," the neurologist said to Abraham, "and I'm looking after your wife."

"How is she, Doctor?"

"That's what I want to talk to you about," Dr Walters said. "I've examined her completely, and apart from one or two bruises on her back caused when the bomb blew her into the rock, I can't find signs of physical damage. Her pulse is right, her heartbeat's fine, she has perfect co-ordination and balance."

"But something is wrong with her?"

"She wants to come out with you and I'm satisfied that physically she's capable of doing so. But I'd like you to persuade her to stay a while. I don't mean in bed. They're short of staff on the wards, and an extra pair of hands will be useful. Meanwhile I can keep an eye on her, and we'll have her here if anything goes wrong."

"What do you mean, Doctor, if anything goes wrong?"

Dr Walters thought a while before answering. "I'm a neurologist," he said, "or rather I was before I came here. Nowadays I do a bit of everything. I've seen lots of people like your wife. It's very hard to explain. They almost seem to be waiting for something to happen. It's like, oh dear how can I put it? I don't suppose you've ever seen it, but when a man is cruel to a dog, and kicks it, the dog comes licking back at him. The dog is expecting another kick. In a sense, he's waiting for it, almost willing it to happen. I'm not suggesting you beat your wife," he said, with an attempt at humour, "but there is something of that quality about her. It may be physical, in which case the symptoms will show themselves and I can treat them; it may even be neurological, and there'll be no difficulty once we can establish the cause."

"But it may be neither of them, eh? It may be in her mind? Are you suggesting that she might be going out of her mind?"

"Is your wife a devout woman?"

"Is she religious? Orthodox? Yes, she is . . . but we don't live orthodox lives."

The doctor sat back on his chair, thinking. "That *could* be it. That could be the thing we're looking for. Your wife thinks the bomb was an act of God. A dog doesn't question a kick from its master. And now, your wife is crawling back, just as the dog crawls back, expecting another kick." He rose to his feet. "Yes, I think we might be on the right track with that. What do you think, Abraham? Will you ask her to stay? I gather there are no family complications."

"No, we have no family."

"I believe you have no settled home at the moment?"

"We've just left one kibbutz; we shall go to another as soon as Sarah is well again."

"Take my advice," Dr Walters said, "leave your wife with us; she'll be looked after, we'll give her a job to keep her busy and take her mind off the past, and I'll treat her like any other patient. Meanwhile you make a home for her to come to."

"Have you somewhere she and I can talk in private?"

"Use my office."

* * *

Physically, as Dr Walters had said, there was nothing wrong with Sarah. She came into the office smiling, kissed Abraham and held his arm. "Good news, isn't it?"

He hugged her, then held her back so he could see her face. "I've had a talk with the doctor," he said.

"He told me there's nothing wrong. I've been so worried."

"So have I," Abraham said. "Since we left Eli-Dov you've not been yourself, Sarah." A cloud crossed her face the moment he mentioned the kibbutz.

"I don't want to think about that place," she said, carefully not naming it. "Let's put all that behind us."

He drew her to a horse-hair couch across one side of the office. He sat with a knee beneath him to look at her.

"You and I have always been straightforward with each other, haven't we, Sarah?" he said. She looked away from him. "Haven't we, Sarah?" he insisted.

"You're being serious. You always say something unpleasant when you're like that."

"The doctor wants you to stay here," Abraham said.

She turned and looked at him again, her eyes filling with tears. "Oh, I feel so strange here, Abraham, lying in bed all day when I know there's nothing wrong with me."

"You won't be lying in bed. The doctor says he'll find a job for you in the wards. You know you'll like that. He says there's nothing wrong with you physically."

"Then why can't I come with you?" she asked. "If there's nothing wrong with me, why can't I?"

Abraham reached out his hand, and stroked her neck below her ear. She caught hold of his hand and pressed it to her. He felt her tears run on to his hand as she bent her head to hide her face.

"They're orthodox in this hospital," he said. "You'll be able to observe the *shabbat*."

"What good will that be," she said, "without the head of the house, without you?" She wiped her face on a handkerchief from the pocket of her dress.

"I like your dress," he said; "it's a long time since I've seen you in a dress."

"They took my trousers to be laundered." She put the handkerchief back into her pocket. "See, they even gave me a handkerchief to cry into."

"There's no point in feeling sorry for yourself. They're short of beds; they wouldn't keep you if they didn't think it necessary. If you stay in here under sufferance, that'll be no good to anyone. If you agree to co-operate they can help you, but not if you feel sorry for yourself."

She straightened her shoulders and sat upright. He took his hand away from her neck. She placed her hands in her lap, looked down at them, up again at him. "You're so sure of yourself, Abraham! I'm quite certain you're right about me staying in here, but Abraham, you were wrong about Eli-Dov! You and Ya'akov, and Alexander in the old days, you thought you could do anything. All you needed was the strength, and among the three of you, you had plenty. When God struck down Alexander it was a warning you and Ya'akov ignored. As a result, they're dead, all of them. . . ."

She was going to cry again, but somehow held the tears in check. "Oh, Abraham, I love you so much for the strength you have; there's no man like you, Abraham, but even you, strong as you are, even you need God. We all need God."

He stood up, walked around the office. Then he stopped in front of her and drew her head to him. "If I have so much strength, Sarah, there's enough to share. That doctor thinks something is not quite right; he admits he doesn't know what it is, but he wants you where he can look after you!"

"I want to be where *you* can look after me."

"I want that too, Sarah." He crouched, and put his hand beneath her chin, lifting her face level with his. "But I don't have his knowledge, or his skill. He wouldn't say there was something wrong if there wasn't, would he?"

"But I *feel* perfectly all right."

"It's not the way you feel that's important, Sarah; it's the way you are inside. You've hardly spoken to anyone since we left the kibbutz. You've been wandering about, as if you were in some kind of dream."

"Shell-shocked, wasn't I? You can't expect anyone to

survive that laughing." She put her hand to her face but couldn't blot out the memory of the children.

"Sarah; they're dead. I feel as badly about it as you do; more so, because it was my responsibility. But you must face it."

She took her hand away, her eyes dry. "I *have* faced it, Abraham. A million times I've said to myself, if only I'd run faster, or slower, I wouldn't have been on that exact spot when the bomb came down, and Rachel and Givona wouldn't have been killed, blown out of my arms! The things we do are ordained, Abraham. God wanted me on that place at that time; and let me live to know what He had done. And that's the most awful punishment He can inflict. That's what Hell is, Abraham, to know you're going to live with such a memory for the rest of your life. You won't ever suffer such torment because you don't believe in God; but *I do* and I could never change that!"

"If there's a God," Abraham said, "why has he ordained we have no children?"

It was as if he had slapped her face. "You've always held that against me, haven't you, Abraham?" They'd submitted to tests before they went to the kibbutz and discovered there was no medical reason. Sarah, at thirty-six, was long past the age when most women have their first child. They'd been married sixteen years and had never avoided children. "You've always blamed me, even after the doctors said there was nothing wrong with me!"

"I've never blamed you. Be honest! I wondered before the tests, was it me, or you, but there was no blame."

"It's the will of God, I keep telling you that, Abraham, but you don't listen."

"It's not enough. You may be able to reconcile yourself to it that way, but for me, Sarah, it's not enough! Dammit, I love you, Sarah, and want babies from you!"

"That's why you want me to stay in the hospital."

"Perhaps it's at the back of my mind."

"Can't you be honest?"

"Perhaps it's at the back of my mind. But first of all, I

97

want you to get well again. To be yourself, not necessarily to have babies, but just to be yourself."

"And you think Doctor Walters might be able to help?"

"I don't know. But you should stay in here, as he suggests."

He sat beside her once again, troubled by his inability to help. So much of what she thought was based on a religious instinct. He could understand God would be an inspiration to someone of faint heart but Sarah, a whole woman, shouldn't have such needs. She was competent, warm, loving and yet behaved as if a dark shadow at her shoulder sought her guilt.

"Put all this out of your mind for a while. Do as Doctor Walters says. Stay here, let him keep an eye on you, help you get well. If you'll do that I promise that when you come out I'll listen with a new mind to what you have to say about God. Honestly, I will."

"You have to *want* to believe, not be persuaded."

"Then don't try to persuade me; just talk to me and let's both see if somewhere inside me we can both find the wanting. I won't do it without you, Sarah, and you can't help me unless you're well yourself."

"You're a clever devil. You know me so well. You've hit on the one argument that'd persuade me to stay, a hope that if I get better I might make a good Jew of you. You're a clever devil, Abraham!"

"You'll stay?"

"Yes, I'll stay," she said, "though I get a feeling it might be for a very long time."

Four of them sat in the hot room in the small house off the Dizengoff in Tel Aviv. Abraham recognised three from the underground military school in Kfar Elihu, Ben, David and Moshe. When the fourth one, an American, spoke, his Hebrew was atrocious. "*Shalom*, Abraham, congratulations!"

"Congratulations? For what?" Abraham said, mystified.

98

"With Jews like you around, who needs the British?"

"I don't get it!"

"Eli-Dov! That was stupid, Abraham. Did you really think the Arabs would let you stay? One rifle, and five rounds of ammunition? You must have been out of your mind!"

Ya'akov was sitting behind Abraham, a glass of lemon tea in his hand. He stood up, towering over Abraham. The lemon tea slopped from the glass on to Abraham's shoulder, but neither noticed.

"We don't have to take that kind of talk from you," Ya'akov shouted; "you invited us here. We can open that door and walk out."

"Sit down," Abraham said, "sit down, Ya'akov." He pulled at Ya'akov's shirt, and Ya'akov did as he was told. Not one of the four had spoken. "Kibbutz Eli-Dov," Abraham said, "was our mistake alone. Everybody was a volunteer; we did it with our own money; we never asked for or received any help from anybody!"

"Twenty-four at Eli-Dov," David said, quietly, "including you two! Twenty-four people who could have been working on a settled kibbutz, giving their labour to help all Israel. Seventeen died . . ."

"We can add," Ya'akov growled.

". . . I know you can subtract," David continued patiently. "Seventeen people could have doubled the production of fifty kibbutzim. Alexander was a trained soldier, just as you two are, but that training was wasted, wasn't it? You killed seventeen people just as surely as if you yourself had dropped the bombs, or handled the cords!"

Abraham could feel Ya'akov tensing to spring forward. He gripped his knee hard. "You're right again, David," he said, "and that's one of the troubles. You Jews are always right."

"And you're not a Jew?" Ben asked, bristling.

"I'm not a Jew, I'm a Palestinian," Abraham said wearily, "but anyway, let's get to the root of it. You didn't ask me here to be offensive. Your type of bureaucrat can be offensive anywhere. You want to let us know how wrong we are, how right you are, you want the pleasure of sneering at us. Okay,

99

so you've sneered. Now either tell us why you asked us to come, or let's get out into the fresh air."

David looked at the American, "I told you what it'd be like. I know this devil," he said. "Attack him, and he'll attack back. It's what the psychologists call a conditioned reflex."

Abraham had risen from his chair; Ya'akov stood behind him.

"I don't have time for games," he said as he prepared to leave.

"Won't you sit down," the American asked, his tone conciliatory.

"Get to the point."

"Let's talk like civilised men, for a change, huh?"

Abraham sat down; Ya'akov, growling, sat down behind him.

"We want you back in Haganah," the American said. "With more kibbutzim being formed every day, we need people like you in kibbutz defence, you and Ya'akov both. We'd like you to go to the special three-month officer's course at *moshav* Kfar Vitkin."

"And play toy soldiers?" Ya'akov asked.

"I'm worried you might be a bit old! Abraham, you're thirty-seven, aren't you, and you, Ya'akov, thirty? Average age is twenty-three, and even then, twenty per cent don't make it."

"After the course?" Abraham asked. "Assuming we old men don't die of exhaustion . . ."

"You'd be posted to one of the trouble areas, supervise defence systems for a group of kibbutzim and *moshavim*. Help train young people, teach them to defend themselves, show the *gar'in* how to set up a defensive system, work with *nahal*."

"David made the recommendation," Ben said. "I remembered you both, of course, from Kfar Elihu. You were excellent trainees!"

"Thank you," Abraham said, smiling sardonically.

"I don't know how closely you've kept in touch with

what's going on in the country," Ben continued, unperturbed.

"We could hardly miss it," Ya'akov said. "Arabs on strike everywhere, new guerilla units being formed, Haj Amin el Husseini ranting on Radio Jerusalem . . ."

"What about the findings of the Peel Commission?" Abraham asked.

"They've not yet been published."

"But you have your ear to the ground."

"We do hear things. They're talking about partition. Separate Jewish and Arab states, the Jerusalem area and a corridor to the coast at Jaffa still under international mandate, the British in control of the Negev!"

"Do they know it won't work?"

"The British said the Mandate wouldn't work, and yet they tried to impose it on us. They say kibbutzim can't work and do their best to destroy us by making it impossible to get sufficient weapons to defend ourselves, and outlawing the Haganah!"

"I don't think Abraham and Ya'akov are as interested in these matters as we are," the American said.

"Well, they ought to be. It's the duty of every Jew . . ." Moshe said, his face inflamed by the passion of his convictions.

"But Abraham has told us he's not a Jew. The matter's very simple, Abraham," the American said. "Despite the Arabs and the general strike, tens of thousands of new people are coming in every year, many from Nazi Germany. We can't house them in Tel Aviv, even if we wanted to. We form new settlements every week. We can get all the young ones we want for the Youth Aliyah, a steady stream through the non-commissioned officer's course of Haganah; but we're short of officers. David thinks you could be the type we're looking for. I'm sorry about the psychology. It was Moshe's idea to give you a rough time."

"We wanted to find out, in the fastest possible way, if your experience at Eli-Dov had left any scars. It doesn't appear to have done that. I'm very glad."

"Eli-Dov left scars on everybody who survived. My wife

101

Sarah is in hospital, perfectly fit physically, but the doctor won't let her leave because of what you call 'scars'. Miriam is in hospital. The doctors are scared she'll have the baby prematurely. Yigal her husband is in the next bed with a bullet through his arm, as well as other injuries which aren't your concern. Misha's lost his wife and kid; all he saved from the wreck of Eli-Dov is a set of carving tools. Right now Misha is sitting in a tent out on the coast overlooking the sea between here and Herzliya, and he's carving a Madonna and Child out of wood. He's carved seven since we left Eli-Dov, and every one looks like Ya'el, his wife, and Abram, his kid, killed when he was five years old."

"What are you going to do with the rest of *your* life, Abraham?" David, the quiet one, asked. "How will *you* prepare for the Day of Atonement? It doesn't concern us that you won't admit to being a Jew. We need trained people and you've been trained. We need men of courage and resource, which you are. And we also need men who are not afraid of the Arabs and the British, and don't fear the dark!"

"I don't hate Arabs or British," Abraham said.

"How can you say that," Moshe demanded, "after what they did to Eli-Dov?"

"An eye for an eye? I've no time for revenge. All I ask of any man is that he let me build my own life."

"And you, Ya'akov?" Moshe asked.

"Abraham speaks for both of us."

Abraham looked at the four men facing him. Each was sincere according to his own convictions. Ben would march on a belief that what a man *must* do must be logical; David would dissimulate, even prevaricate, to achieve what he wanted, for the end justified the means. Moshe would let bigotry blind him to the true objective, and never know; doubtless the American had looked at the society about him, found it wanting, and chosen the way of Zionism; his logic was to make his new society work.

"I don't think we'd be much use to you in Haganah. We plan to find a kibbutz where we can live and work. We'll take part in kibbutz defence, as we've always done, but we

102

don't want responsibility for a while. Ya'akov and I, we have a lot of settling down to do, haven't we, Ya'akov?"

Ya'akov nodded. "Get rid of some of the scars Moshe was talking about, eh?"

Both stood up, the interview at an end. Moshe despised them, Abraham knew. Ben was already thinking of the people they would see next. David wondered if it would do any good to talk with them somewhere away from the interview room, over a glass of tea. The American recognised Abraham for a born leader, a natural commander. He knew he'd see him again when the burden of Eli-Dov did not weigh so heavily. He stood up. Abraham held out his hand, tentatively. The American took it, and smiled.

"Naeem luh'hakeer otkhah," he said.

"And I am pleased to meet you," Abraham said. *"Shalom!"*

He went out without looking at the others.

The following day, the doctor examined Miriam again, and pronounced the danger of premature birth passed. Yigal was discharged with her, and they went to join Abraham, Ya'akov and Misha at the tented camp on the dunes between Herzliya and the sea. They still had some of the money they'd brought from the kibbutz, but it was nowhere near sufficient to set them up in a venture of their own. Hagar had taken a temporary job as a ward maid to help with finances. They were about to eat when Yigal and Miriam arrived, shaky after their long walk across the dunes.

Misha had made a fire in a ring of stones. "Dump your stuff in the tent," Ya'akov said, "and come and get some food inside you!" Each had been given a small knapsack of clothing and personal items when he left the hospital. Miriam helped Yigal take the pack from his back, and they rinsed their faces in the bucket of water Misha had put outside the tent. The evening was cool.

103

While they waited for Ya'akov to dish up the food, Yigal picked up the wood Misha had been carving. It was driftwood, sea bleached white and close grained. Misha had cut all the sea-softened wood away; the inside was hard as olive. The figures he had carved were forty centimetres high, a woman wearing a sabra hat like the hat Ya'el used to wear. Her hand was placed on the head of a small boy, who was looking up at her. Both were exact likenesses. "I don't know how you do it," Yigal said. "If I put a knife to wood it turns into a clothes peg."

Misha took the wood, held it. His hands curled round it, caressed it. "You have to know where the grain goes," he said, "and ease your way along it."

Slow and easy, Abraham thought, just like Misha himself. He'd forget Ya'el and Abram of course, but it'd take time. "Give Ya'akov a hand," he suggested. Misha put down the carving, and went to help Ya'akov with the meal; boiled sweet corn, ragout of lamb.

"Canteen food," Ya'akov said in apology.

"When do they think you'll have the baby?" Abraham asked Miriam.

"In about two months."

"Any preference?"

"I have none," she said.

"How about you, Yigal?" Abraham asked. Delicate subject, since the child wasn't his.

"I'd like a boy," he said, "but I don't mind. Just as long as Miriam comes out of it all right."

She grasped his arm. "The doctor told me as long as I keep active, there's no danger at all."

Ya'akov and Misha had washed the plates and the dishes in the sea, and came and sat by the fire. "It's getting colder," Ya'akov said, "must be down to eight degrees."

"It'd be over twenty down there!" All knew where she meant.

After the evening meal, discussion time as always. "I've been to see the Federation, and they can place us all together on a kibbutz," Abraham said, "or a *moshav*, come to that.

104

With what we have, we could set up in a *moshav*; we'd get a loan all right. Then there's a *moshav shitufi*, which I've just heard about. It's like a kibbutz, in that everything is owned collectively, but each family has its own house, does its own cooking, looks after its own kids. The *moshav* pays wages, 'according to circumstances', whatever that may mean."

"We'd get paid more an hour because of the baby," Yigal said.

"I suppose you would."

"What I had in mind," Abraham said, "was that, if we go to a *moshav shitufi*, we could have our own collectivisation within the system. That's if we want to stick together. We could pool our wages, and have a rota each day for who did the cleaning, who did the cooking, who looked after the baby."

"I could do all that," Miriam said. "A couple of houses wouldn't be difficult to look after; it'd give me plenty of time to do the cooking, and to look after the baby, and perhaps a part-time job."

"You'd be tied down," Yigal said, "and you've always said you didn't want that."

"What's wrong with going to a kibbutz?" Ya'akov asked. "If we do that, it's all looked after, isn't it? All the cooking and the cleaning and the laundry. And the kid can go into the kibbutz nursery . . ."

"Miriam might not want that," Abraham suggested.

"I'd have no objection," she said. "I've never thought the ability to make a child automatically gives the parents the skill to bring it up in the best possible way. I've no idea what kind of a mother I'd turn out to be."

"I have no doubts on that score," Yigal said.

"All I have against going to a kibbutz," Abraham said, "is this. No matter how long we stay we leave with nothing to show for our work. That's fine if it's our own kibbutz; I never cared to be a millionaire. But what happens if in a few years time we want to go off again, perhaps back into the Negev to start up on our own? We'll either have to raise

105

a loan from the Federation—and they're not well disposed towards us after Eli-Dov—or start the hard way with no resources."

"We have money left from Eli-Dov?" Yigal asked.

"Yes; but if we go to a kibbutz we'll have to turn that over."

"How can we?" Yigal asked. "That's not our money. Part of it came from Reuven, and Chochem, and Chaim; they have just as much claim as the kibbutz. I mean," he said hurriedly, embarrassed, "I mean their relations."

"Deposit that money in a bank," Misha suggested, "and if we want to move out of the kibbutz, we have that money to start up with. And talking about money," he added, "I could do with some new trousers. I've been sitting cross-legged all evening so's not to bother Miriam."

They all laughed. Abraham got a note from his pocket. "We can't have you giving yourself a chill," he said.

End of meeting; it was always the same. They'd raise a point, discuss it, and need to think. Any time one of them felt he wanted to think before he heard any more, he'd change the subject. *Moshav*, kibbutz, or *moshav shitufi*; these were the alternatives. They could live in the city, of course—plenty of work and high wages. Perhaps they'd discuss that possibility before a final decision was made. One thing, however, had been established. They wanted to stay together.

The darkness creeping over the ocean pulled a canopy of stars behind it. They'd eaten well. Ya'akov threw a cigarette to Abraham, who never seemed to have any. Neither Misha, Yigal nor Miriam smoked. "Take your trousers off, Misha," Miriam said. She brought a blanket to cover him for warmth, not for modesty. He wrapped the blanket round his legs, picked up his piece of wood, and started carving.

Ya'akov took out his harmonica, shook it and started to play. "Remember the words, Yigal?" he asked. Yigal nodded, and started to sing; "*'Fuchs Du hast die Gans gestohlen, gib sie wieder her',*" Abraham joined in, "*'sonst wird ich'n Jaeger holen, mit'm Schiessgewehr, ehr, ehr, sonst wird ich'n Jaeger holen, mit'm Schiessgewehr'.*" Fox you have stolen the goose.

106

Give it back, or I will bring the huntsman with his rifle! A song simple as the occasion. The night was dark; fishermen would be out until two in the morning in the cold wind that blew across the ocean. Miriam finished mending the trousers.

Ya'akov put down the harmonica. "I've a shirt needs looking at, Miriam," he said.

"Give it to me in the morning. Don't forget."

"The doctor told me I'll be able to work in a week," Yigal said.

Abraham frowned. "Take your time; no point in rushing things and giving yourself a permanent damage."

"Listen to what Abraham says," Miriam added. They were all silent for several minutes. "Doesn't it seem strange, without Sarah and Hagar," Miriam said.

Sarah was lying on her bed when Abraham came in.

"We've made up our minds," Abraham said. "You said I could vote on your behalf. We're going to a kibbutz. Northern Galilee, not far from the Syrian border, but there are other kibbutzim about if the Syrians try anything. This time we shan't be alone."

"What's it called? how big is it? how long's it been going?" Questions burst from her, and she swung her legs from the bed as if to start immediately.

"It's called Kibbutz Guvena . . ."

"The cheese kibbutz?"

"Apparently they do well with cheese."

"They must have good grass! How big is it?"

"A hundred people. It's been going three years, and they've really made a good job of it, the Federation told me. They had the Gdud Ha'avoda in the early days to build for them; everybody has a house, and there are buildings for everything."

"Is it near Safad?"

107

"Further north than that . . ."

She was silent for a moment. "That's a long way north, Abraham. Almost as far north as Eli-Dov was south!"

"Yes, but there are lots of others about."

The door of the ward opened, and Hagar looked in. "Have you told her?" she asked Abraham. "Can I come in?" Sarah lifted her legs back on the bed; Hagar came in with a broom and a dustpan, and started to sweep the floor. "You don't mind if I get on, Sarah?" she asked. "If I finish this end, I shall be able to get away to camp with Abraham, when he goes."

Sarah didn't mind. Abraham and she had nothing to say that couldn't be said in front of Hagar.

"I thought you were supposed to be working," Abraham said.

"I am, but every so often they take a test with some new equipment, and I have to be inactive for a half day before it. They'd like me to sleep, but I can't seem to manage to sleep during the day."

"You never could."

"Can't teach an old dog new tricks?"

"Who says you're an old dog?"

She squeezed his hand. "It makes me feel awful, Hagar working when I'm lying in bed feeling so well."

"Ladies' maid, that's what I am!" Hagar said, but there was no complaint in her voice. "You concentrate on passing your tests. We'll soon put you to work. They tell me churning cheese gives you muscles big as breasts." Both laughed; Hagar was far from flat chested, and since she rarely bothered to fasten the top buttons of her shirt, the fact was well known.

"There's a school for the kids at Guvena," Hagar said, unable to get thoughts of the new kibbutz out of her mind.

"And a meeting hall. There's even talk of building a swimming pool."

"Anything else?" Sarah asked, with pretended casualness.

Hagar put the broom in the corner of the ward, and came across to the bed. She grasped Sarah's hand. "There's a

108

small synagogue, Sarah," she said.

When Abraham's visiting time was up, Hagar came back to the ward to collect him and to say goodbye to Sarah. The journey from the kibbutz would be long, and she would see Abraham much less frequently.

Sarah called Hagar to her bedside. "Look after Abraham for me, won't you?" she said.

They came by Caesarea in Samaria along the plain of Sharon, and their eyes glistened when they saw the beauty of it. In Tel Aviv they had sold their lorry and rented an old Citroen which held only the six of them and a driver called Joel, who had come from France in 1901, the year of Abraham's birth. He'd been everywhere in Palestine with his Citroen. The engine sounded like it.

"This road's been here since ancient times," he called back to them. "I shouldn't be taking you up it, by rights!"

"Why not, Joel?" Ya'akov asked.

"Isaiah thirty-five; though I don't suppose you heathens have done much reading of the Bible?"

But Abraham had a good memory. " 'Then shall the eyes of the blind be opened and the ears of the deaf shall be unstopped' . . . ?"

" 'Then shall the lame man leap as a hart'," Miriam continued, looking at Yigal, " 'and the tongue of the dumb shall sing, for in the wilderness shall waters break out, and streams in the desert'."

"Go on," the old man commanded, but they could remember no more. " 'And an highway shall be there'," he said in his thin reedy voice, " 'and a way; and it shall be called the Way of Holiness; the unclean shall not pass over it!' "

"I've got a quotation for you, Joel," Ya'akov said, "but it's not from the Bible. 'If the clean shall accept the money of the unclean, the clean will forever after hold his tongue '."

Joel laughed. "Never a truer word spoken," he said, "but an Englishman put it better when he said, 'Don't bite the hand that feeds you!' "

They rattled along the road through banana groves, past the road leading into Caesarea itself. "Herod the Great, as the idiots used to call him—Herod the mad, I say—built that city. What is it now, fishermen's houses, a wall with marble columns jutting into the sea."

"What's this, Joel, a guided tour?" Ya'akov asked. The old man turned to look at him, one hand off the steering wheel resting on the front of the scoop.

"The past doesn't mean anything to you, eh?"

"Not a thing," Ya'akov said; "it's the present and the future I care about. And if you don't put your hand back on the wheel and look where we're going, we shan't have much of either!"

There was no more talk of the history of Palestine, which pleased everyone except Joel and Misha, who had a feeling the old man could have enlightened them all. They ran steadily along the plain of Sharon, the mountain range to their right becoming steeper. Joel watched the high peak ahead, looked several times at Abraham, bursting to speak. Now the road curved to avoid the swamp which stretched from the foot of the mountain range, almost to the sea on their left. Agricultural settlements stood where the swamp had been drained; the soil was dark, and many banana trees had been replanted. Some had existed since time immemorial; the new plantations were neat and orderly, with wooden and stone houses clustered in the reclaimed fields and courses to drain surplus water. Grain had been planted and sweet corn. "No citrus fruits," Ya'akov said.

"The soil's no good for oranges," Joel said.

Finally, as they turned right into the bay of Haifa, he could contain himself no longer. "That was Mount Carmel back there," he said, "where Elijah called down the fire of the Lord to consume a bullock, and turned the people of Israel away from Baal." Maybe the Lord heard what Joel had said, and decided to sport with him, for at that moment,

110

Ya'akov saw smoke coming from beneath the bonnet of the Citroen.

They stayed the night at the foot of Mount Carmel, in a transit camp built as a hostel for Germans who helped Turks establish a railway between the port of Haifa and the southern end of the Sea of Galilee, to link with the Hedjaz railway from Damascus to Amman. The British wanted Haifa to be a terminal for the oil line from Iraq, and a naval base in the Eastern Mediterranean. They knew the Mufti of Jerusalem would cut the rail link with Haifa if Israel flourished as an independent nation.

During the night, Ya'akov and Joel worked on the Citroen, washing the engine, cleaning the magneto and the electrics, grinding the valves and valve seats. Shortly after first light Ya'akov and Joel went into the canteen together and found Abraham and Miriam already having breakfast. "There're another million miles in that old thing," Ya'akov said, wiping his hands on the clean rag Joel had provided. They collected food from the dispensary, and sat down. Joel put on his *yarmulka*.

"You going to be fit to drive?" Abraham asked. "You must be worn out if you've been working all night."

"I'll be all right," Joel said; "at my age, you don't need much sleep."

"How old are you, Joel?" Miriam asked.

"You won't believe me . . ." He looked at Ya'akov, and at Abraham. "I'm seventy-five," he said, "and never a day's illness."

"That settles it," Ya'akov said. "Abraham and I will drive; you stretch out in the back and sleep."

They carried the old man with them through the pine forests surrounding Haifa and the brilliant wild flowers of the hills of Galilee, orange, golden, and blue, scattered beneath olive groves old in Biblical times. Arab villages and Jewish agricultural settlements, cheek by jowl, were dotted about the hills. Ahead as they climbed they saw the mountains of Golan in Syria; on the left, dangerously close, the border with Lebanon, and behind it peaks dashed with snow.

111

On each side of the road which wound and turned through the hills, Arabs ploughed as they had done throughout history, great wooden ploughs held by one or two Arabs, a bullock or two dragging it slowly through the red soil. Once the hills had been stepped to keep the soil in place; centuries of neglect and surface working destroyed the soil's tackiness, broke it to a fine powder washed down the hills with every rain. In many places the bare rock, limestone and sometimes black basalt, showed through like an elbow through a well-worn jacket. Everywhere, Arabs worked slowly on the land, winter-pruning fruit trees, carrying hay and firewood on donkeys. Little boys tended herds of black goats. Camels wandered beside the road, small boys riding atop the hump with no visible means of support, hands twined into camel hair, eyes grinning, white teeth flashing a welcome. These Arabs had learned to live with the Jews; many sold them land, and worked on the early agricultural settlements as farm labourers, accepting their future as Palestinians just as always they had accepted conquest. At least this time the land had not been taken from them by force. The Jews paid for land or labour; they brought new techniques and showed the Arabs how to use steel ploughs, harrows and rakes. Not many Arabs would change their own primitive methods of tillage; somehow, it seemed right they use the new methods on the lands of the Jews, and stay with history on their own meagre dunams.

The Jewish agricultural settlements were models of precision compared with the Arab villages and homesteads. The farming was planned and deliberate, crops planted according to the quality of the soil. The land was terraced and broken old walls rapidly repaired by hired Arab labour. When walls were completed, the Arabs carried soil in wickerwork back-panniers up the hills again. Lands that had been neglected were soon flourishing; grape vines were sown again in the Vineyard of the Lord.

Ya'akov, Yigal, Miriam and Misha beamed as they drove through this land. Only Hagar and Abraham seemed unenchanted. Some agricultural settlements had not succeeded, and derelict Jewish farm-houses matched Arab villages. They often saw a boundary line ploughed to preserve derelict farms for absent Ottomans.

Most settlements appeared prosperous, life burgeoning, settlers happy. Many waved to the little Citroen. When they stopped for water, a group clustered around the lorry.

"Where are you going?" they asked.

"Guvena."

"Guvena!" they said, and looked at the pioneers in admiration. "That's near the border," they said, "too near for us. . . ."

They pressed food into the hands of the travellers, soured milk, cucumbers and fruit. "And when you've eaten it," they said, "wipe your face with the inside of the skin, and feel how it cools you." Abraham let in the clutch and they drove away. Ya'akov looked back and forth, side to side, gazing in wonder at all they had achieved.

"Dammit, comparing them and the Arab settlements," he said, unable to contain himself, "it makes you glad to be . . ." He had been going to say a Jew!

Joel was now awake, content to sit in the scoop while Abraham and Ya'akov took turns driving over the winding road. "When are you expecting?" he asked Miriam.

"In about two months!"

"Very good, my dear," Joel said; 'the Lord says 'be fruitful and multiply'." He turned to Yigal. "You the fortunate man?"

Miriam, holding Yigal's hand, squeezed it. "I've been the fortunate man ever since I met my wife," Yigal said.

The old man beamed, nodded his head. "To join a man and woman in happiness is as difficult for the Lord as the parting of the Red Sea," he said. "To be unmarried is a terrible thing, to be married without children, the worst thing of all. A man who does not make children, who disobeys the commands of the Lord, 'be fruitful and multiply' . . ."

Ya'akov thought of himself, unmarried; Abraham, married but without a child; Yigal, married but physically unable to

113

make a child; and Misha, who'd made a child and lost it.

"Stop your Talmudic ramblings, old man, and tell us what this place is, up here."

"Kfar Biram. In the olden times the Jews gathered here to read the scroll of Esther during the festival of Purim. Queen Esther was supposed to be buried here."

"And that heap of stones?"

"Watch your tongue, young man! Heap of stones, indeed! That's the remains of a very fine second-century synagogue. If I thought you could appreciate it, I'd suggest we stop, and refresh our spirits with the glory of the past!"

"If we'd stopped everywhere you wanted, Joel, we'd still be on the plain of Sharon." At every bend of the road they could see the Galilee to their right, the hills rolling down to the fertile plain of the Emek. Whenever they turned to the left, they glimpsed the tip of Mount Hermon.

"Charming legend about Mount Hermon over there," the irrepressible Joel said, "but I don't suppose you'd want to hear it." They had all heard it; it was a legend everyone heard at least once a year.

"Go on, old man, tell us the legend," Ya'akov said. Everyone in the lorry, save the old man, was feeling tense. They knew their destination was approaching and they were silent, lost in private thought.

"The legend is," Joel said, "that the Lord gave the Ten Commandments to Moses on Mount Sinai . . ."

"That's not the legend," Miriam said, laughing. "All good Jews believe that part of it."

"I know, I know. I was just coming to it. The legend is that when the mountains of the Holy Land heard that the Lord had honoured Mount Sinai and had passed them by, they all complained bitterly. One small mountain, well, not a mountain really, more of a hill, appeared before the Lord and asked, 'Lord why have you forsaken us?' The hill, Mount Hermon, then burst into tears. And the Lord commanded Hermon to rise up, and it became the highest mountain in the Holy Land, the Lord capped it with snow, and its tears became the source of the River Jordan. Isn't that charming?"

114

They had turned the bend of the frontier and were heading north. A short, low crest beside them suddenly dipped; below and to the right stretched the Hulah Valley. Abraham stopped the lorry; they all dismounted and looked down to the flat green valley below.

"Is this it?" Yigal asked. Abraham nodded. "Forty thousand dunams," he said, "all of it, Eretz Israel."

The Franco-British treaty of 1923 included the Hulah in Palestine. It was a marshy area infested by malaria-carrying insects, papyrus reeds and multi-coloured water lilies. Above the swamp flew cormorants, gulls, wild duck, herons, pelicans and crested grebes. The early settlers began small drainage projects on the sides to reclaim the land for agriculture. Around the rim of the valley, several kibbutzim were already operating, waiting only for more drainage to be completed before they moved to the fertile valley below. One such kibbutz, on the western slopes of the Hulah Valley, was their destination.

They arrived at Guvena on 31 January 1938, just as the Citroen mysteriously failed.

The first things Abraham noticed were the cows; there must have been a hundred, sleek and fat, in pastures that ran around the slope of the hill.

Ya'akov looked at the people, as many of them as there were cows. When they saw them arrive they ran from the fields. Soon the Citroen was propelled by twenty pairs of willing hands; everyone was talking at once, singing work chants, old Russian songs of the Volga boatmen, German songs of maidens from the barges of the Rhine.

Miriam saw the stone nursery school, and the twenty or so children of all ages who came rushing from it when they heard the commotion, leaping and dancing around the swirling whirlpool of humanity surrounding the truck.

Joel saw green lawns with benches where an old man could sit in the cool evening with other men, and pick an intricate path through the dialectic of the Torah, the written and unwritten precepts of the whole body of Jewish teaching, or wander in the runic maze of the Talmud, a thousand years

115

older than the Bible itself. Joel always carried a leather bound copy of the Vilna edition in a box beneath the driving seat of the Citroen. "It's time," he thought, "for me to stop wandering." A man as old as Joel was standing beneath an olive tree near the gated entrance to the kibbutz. Joel caught his eye, and the old man smiled a shy welcome. The Citroen stopped at the gate. Joel reached out, and stroked the *mezuzah* set in it, and the Citroen rolled into the kibbutz.

Kibbutz Guvena had the outline of a six-pointed star built around a central hexagon. The sides of the hexagon were the communal dining hall, the synagogue, the crèche-nursery, the store, and a building containing the office and the hospital. Along the obliquely laid wings of the star, houses had been built for the kibbutzniks, six to a row, with a *mikva* at each of two tips of one triangle, and a less ceremonial bathhouse cum drying room cum lavatory, at the three tips of the other. Where the third *mikva* would have been, an impressive entrance arch had been built spanning two of the blocks of houses. Above it, in letters made of sticks bound together, was the name GUVENA. As one approached the entrance gate, the blocks of houses stretched to the sides behind triangles of lawn, in which young trees had been planted. The houses had small verandahs, and such was the layout that, from the depths of each verandah, no other dwelling could be seen. Inside the archway to the left was the office and hospital building, to the right the store. Beyond the office on the left was the synagogue, beyond the store the dining hall. At the far end of the hexagon were the crèche-nursery and living quarters for the children. The school was set deliberately among the fields where the children could see the adults working.

The kibbutzniks pushed the Citroen beneath the arch and halted it outside the office. Then they fell back to give themselves a chance to look at the newcomers. One man detached himself from the crowd and came towards Joel, the oldest man among the newcomers, with his hand outstretched.

"*Shalom*," he said, "I'm Nimshi and this quarter year it's my turn to be secretary of the Committee." He beckoned to

116

a girl of about twenty-four and a man in his fifties. "Rowena, our treasurer; next quarter she'll be secretary; and Samuel, farm manager; next quarter he'll be treasurer, and then secretary."

Rowena and Samuel shook hands with Joel; all three then walked down the line, as Joel introduced Abraham, Ya'akov, Yigal, Miriam, Misha and Hagar. As Joel announced each name, Nimshi called it out loud so all could hear it. Many of the kibbutzniks answered the call. "*Shalom*, Abraham, I'm Ahab!" "*Shalom*, Ya'akov, I'm Ya'akov too!" There appeared to be a number of Mishas, several Yigals and Miriams, but no other Hagar and, oddly enough, no other Abraham. Nimshi and Rowena identified the buildings for the newcomers. In the centre of the hexagon was a lawn surrounded by trees, and beneath the trees, benches. Abraham had noticed trees and benches all around the kibbutz. "You have a lot of benches here," he said to Nimshi as they walked towards the dining hall.

"We designed this kibbutz from the very beginning," Nimshi said. "Of course, people thought we were mad, that we should get our tents up fast and start planting; but the first committee was wise, and wouldn't permit anything temporary. It's always been our belief," Nimshi said, "that a lot of time and effort is wasted on temporary things. One of the first things we did was mark out this central area. We believe a man is a fool who doesn't give himself time and space for contemplation. We're not a mad rushing community. We built the benches, and set them all around, here, on the approach, in the fields where we work; if anyone feels like sitting to think, well, that's what the benches are for! I'll get you something to eat," Nimshi said as they mounted the steps into the dining hall. The long room was big enough to seat three hundred.

Abraham looked out of the back window. Just behind the dining hall was a triangle of green like the one just inside the archway. This one was full of green vegetables. "We have five plots this size; we grow all our own stuff for the table," Rowena said. On the other sides of the triangle were houses

117

with verandahs overlooking the vegetable plot. "That's one of our two *mikvot*," she said.

"How orthodox are you?"

"Some of us completely, some not. We let everyone here practise religion the way they feel."

"Are *you* orthodox?"

"No, but Nimshi is . . ."

Nimshi came from the kitchen at that moment, with a tray on which he'd heaped plates for each of them. A woman brought orange juice, sour milk, fruit, and tin mugs on another tray. "Eat!" Nimshi said, "eat, you must be starving."

He looked round the group as they sat down. Only Joel produced a *yarmulka*, and said a silent prayer, his head bowed, but Nimshi made no comment. Nimshi produced some sheets of paper while they ate. "We keep records," he said. "I'll give you a page each, and you can complete it at your leisure and give it to me in the office. On these sheets, one for each of you, we've written a few things we think are important." The paper was printed in that blue ink reproduced from a dish of gelatine. "I hope you can read them," Nimshi said, apologetic. "I need to write a new master, but I'm afraid I keep putting it off. Don't read it now, take it with you and study it at leisure. You understand, these are not regulations, just a few notes we've compiled to see that the majority aren't inconvenienced. If you don't want to comply, you're not obliged to."

He showed them their quarters, four houses side by side behind the synagogue. Hagar's house was in the corner nearest the nursery and the synagogue; Abraham next; Ya'akov and Misha sharing; then Miriam and Yigal. "The *mikva* is at one end of this row," Rowena said, "and the bathhouse at the other end."

"If we become overcrowded, you'll have to share," Nimshi said to Abraham and to Hagar.

"I don't know if the Federation told you my wife will come when she gets out of hospital?"

"How long do you expect them to keep her?"

"It could be at least six months."

"Don't worry, we'll arrange accommodation together whenever she feels like coming." He walked along the block of houses, making certain everyone was settled in. "You can draw all your clothing, bedding and utensils from the store. It will be open at five o'clock this afternoon for an hour. Dinner's in the dining hall, six until seven, and after that you're free, except for any personal tasks you may take on. You've all been on a kibbutz before; you know how we go on."

He unlocked the door of each house, and stood back while they went in. Abraham pushed open the shutters of the windows, front and back. The back shutter, three centimetres thick, was solid. There was no glass in the windows; the view extended north as far as Mount Hermon, its top capped with snow. Outside the window a triangular garden; more vegetables. The front shutter was slatted. That window space, also without glass, overlooked the back of the synagogue and the side of the nursery, with the ubiquitous vegetable garden. The window sill was wide, and had hinges. He lifted it towards him to expose a box, about twenty centimetres wide and thirty deep. In it were a Lee Enfield rifle and at least a hundred rounds of ammunition. He leaned out of the window and looked along the row of houses. Each house had a similar rifle store, though those on the other side of the triangle all had flower boxes on top. The flowers were blooming, trailing down almost to the ground.

"That's your first job," Nimshi said from the doorway, "to clean and oil your rifle and load it, and make yourself a window box to conceal it from the British. And the Arabs too for that matter, not that we allow Arabs in here."

"The rifle boxes, too, were part of your design?"

"Close all these outside doors and windows, and we have a fortress; open them, and we have a verandah." Abraham shook his head, wondering at the far-sightedness of men who could plan with such regard to detail. Even the window boxes were ideally suited to their purpose; a man could get at his rifle from inside or outside his house and, as Nimshi said, once the window barriers were in position, the outline of the Star of David occupied a classic strategic position, infinitely variable, perfectly defensible.

"It's not on that list of suggestions," Nimshi said just before he left, "but murder and rape are two of the three crimes for which you can be expelled from the kibbutz."

"What's the third," Abraham asked, "losing your rifle?"

"That's right," Nimshi said as he closed the door.

The orthodox kibbutzniks sat at one table in the dining hall and all the men wore *yarmulkas* and said a prayer. They collected their food, and when they all were seated, ate as a family. At the other tables, some small, some large, people sat and chatted, smoked, ate whatever they wanted from the buffet along the wall outside the kitchen.

"This is a special night," Nimshi said when he joined the newcomers later. "Gabriel has been down to the lake, and we all have fish. Gabriel," he explained quietly, "used to live near the estate of the Count von Hohenlange in Germany, and the count was a keen fisherman, when Gabriel's poaching left him anything to catch."

Gabriel came to their table, shook the men's hands and kissed the women. "Gabriel," he said in a deep baritone, "also doesn't agree with the emancipation of women. Hands I shake with men! For women, well, the cheek was made for kissing . . ."

He sat at the table, pushing his way gently between Miriam and Hagar. "I'm Gabriel," he said, "poet, poacher, sculptor, artist, free-thinker, and lover! Though not necessarily in that order."

"Which are you at the moment?" Hagar asked him.

"Gabriel the gourmet. Take this lovely fish," he said, indicating his plate, "that has been lurking at the bottom of Lake Hulah all his life, where his father lurked before him, *his* father and his father's father's father. This little fellow can teach us all a lesson if we observe him closely.
120

You see how he has skin wrapped around him just as you have a skin wrapped around you, my dear, but his skin"—Gabriel deftly inserted his fork under the skin of the fish and peeled it away from the flesh—"his skin, which you now see, is rough, while your skin is smooth. His skin is meant to repel; yours is designed to attract."

"I hope you're not going to put your fork in me, and start skinning me," Hagar said with mock distress.

"Next we have the bone, hiding beneath the flesh, just as your bones hide beneath your flesh; once again, we insert the point of the fork, so, and move it so, and the flesh comes away, and there we have the bone on one side . . ." He flipped the fish over, inserted his fork under the skin and removed it, inserted it under the flesh, and removed that, leaving the bone in the centre of his plate, clean as if the ants had picked it. "And now we have the bone on the other side. *Schoen, nicht wahr?*" He picked a piece of the flesh in his fork, and ate it. "Delicious," he said, "come along, eat! Eat your fish before it becomes cold." Each tried to emulate him. Some used the fork, some the knife; Abraham tried with the fork and tore the flesh of the fish beneath it. Hagar, realising the trick with the fork was not easy, started with her knife. "You'll never do it with a knife," Gabriel warned her, but still she tried. Miriam tried, failed, finally scraped the skin and the flesh from the bone with the prongs of the fork. Ya'akov cut the fish in two, put one half in his mouth, chewed, and then spat the bones on to his plate. Only Misha could do the job properly. He took his knife, inserted its point at the fat end of the fish in the centre just below its gills, and drew the knife down to the fish's tail. Then he inserted the blade of his knife carefully along the slit, and curled one side of the fish back, so that the flesh was lying on the skin, the bone exposed. He exposed the bone on the other side, then ate the flesh from the skin before he neatly flipped the fish over, and did the same on the other side. "Fascinating," Gabriel said, "absolutely fascinating. Now I'll tell you about yourselves. Ya'akov," he said, "that is your name?" Ya'akov nodded. "Ya'akov is the man of action; he doesn't care what

121

other people do or think! You, Hagar, are like Ya'akov, except that you are prepared to adapt other people's methods to your own ways. You wouldn't try the fork, that was my method, you used the knife but you tried to use it the way I had used the fork. You, Miriam, are persistent. You will try whatever anyone may suggest, and then you grit your teeth and say, 'I will succeed'. Abraham, nothing very clear from Abraham, so I suppose he is a complex character. Nothing very clear from Yigal either, but from Misha, *schoen* Misha . . . !"

"What about Misha," Hagar asked, "what about him?"

"Misha, like me, is an artist! *Nicht wahr?* Misha is creative! He saw the way I did it, but then he did it just as expertly in his own way. Tell me quickly. I can't bear not to know. Is Misha an artist?"

All nodded, except Misha.

Gabriel arose; there is no other way to describe it. He arose, reached his hand across the table to Misha. "Welcome to the Philistines!" He came round the table. "Come on," he said, "let's get away from these vultures, who live off our artists' blood." He and Misha left the hall. When they were at the door Gabriel turned, aware of the need for a curtain line. "By the way, Nimshi," he called, "tonight, for a special treat, I'll let you wash my plate . . ."

It was dark when they came out of the dining hall. Miriam and Yigal excused themselves to get an early night's sleep. Ya'akov and Joel went to have a look at the Citroen, though they both suspected it had breathed its last. Hagar and Abraham were walking on either side of Nimshi; they turned left across the green to the V-shape of houses by the entrance to the kibbutz. A girl aged about eighteen was sitting in a box beside the foot of the arch, a rifle by her side. "We shan't be long, Givona," Nimshi said.

"The gate's always guarded?" Abraham asked.

"Night and day, four-hour shifts. Everyone takes that duty, on roster. It'll be your turn in, let me see, ninety-two times four hours. How's your math?"

"Four o'clock in the morning, fifteen days from now,"

Hagar said. They both looked at her, amazed. "Divide by six," she said, "but that's assuming you work eight to twelve, twelve to four, and so on."

"I wish you'd teach some of our camp treasurers to add as quickly as that," Nimshi said, shaking his head.

Abraham had been looking along the valley. "What are those lights over there?"

"Another kibbutz. You can see it in the daytime. They only have tents, poor devils. I don't think they're going to last very long. They work like hell producing vegetables, and then they sell them all, and have to buy other things to live on. You can't survive on one crop alone."

"You mix?" Hagar asked.

"You'll see tomorrow; we have a bit of everything. We even grow tobacco."

"The soil must be good!"

"What we have! I'm afraid that'll be part of your job. Everybody takes a turn. Carrying soil from the lakeside. This time tomorrow, I can promise, you'll be on your bed with your back feeling as if it's broken. And scratching! The mosquitoes down there like anybody new; they get bored with the taste of old flesh."

"I wondered why we'd been given high-necked shirts, long trousers, and boots."

"Did they give you a veil?"

"Yes, I wondered what it was for."

"You'll learn tomorrow. Wear that hat, and the minute you get beyond a certain point, drop the veil. It won't keep 'em all out, but at least it'll keep the weakest ones away from you."

"And the strongest ones?"

"They just bite through the veil," he said, laughing.

They left the flat plateau on which the kibbutz had been built and turned left, northwards, down a track that descended the slope. "We built this track," Nimshi said, "piled stones in it, then filled it with more stones, and broke them down with a hammer. We built that wall too. It's over a kilometre long and it stops the road from being washed out when the rains come."

"Do you get much rain?"

"Thank God for it, yes we do. This is the first year we've measured it, but we recorded over 700 millimetres. We had sixty-two rainy days . . ." He looked at Hagar.

"Approximately eleven and a half millimetres for each day it rains," she said, smiling.

"How does she do it, Abraham?" he asked, stopping in the roadway.

"That one was easy. Six into seventy, eleven and a half."

Without changing his voice, Nimshi suddenly said to them, "Get down behind the wall!" He had been carrying a rifle slung over his shoulder; now it was in his hands. Abraham and Hagar crouched against the stones. Nimshi walked to the wall further down and looked over. It was only four feet high, made of solid limestone, with no cement binding. Abraham could see Nimshi profiled against the glow of the moon and the light from the valley.

They waited in silence.

Then Nimshi called, the *cooee* of a bird.

There was no reply.

Nimshi dropped below the level of the wall, and crawled back to them. "This is a damned thing," he said, "your first night here. A sentry should be on this wall, about ten metres below that bend, but there's no sign of Martha, who's supposed to be on tonight."

Abraham looked cautiously over the wall. He knew his face would be hidden by the blackness of the hillside behind him. "Where's the actual post?" he asked.

"About sixteen metres below here, on the left. We bent the wall to provide a sentry post. It doesn't show from the other side, just looks flat; we should be able to see the sentry from this side!" While he was talking, his eyes scanned the area just beyond the wall. "To get behind Martha and take her by surprise, they'd either have to come over the hill, where the other sentries should have seen them, or entice her down the path. The sentries have strict orders not to move and to fire at anything suspicious without asking questions."

124

Hagar and Abraham walked cautiously down the hill beside the wall; Nimshi covered them with the rifle for fifteen metres, then he hurried after them. They had reached the bend in the rock wall, the corner in which Martha should have been standing, guarding the kibbutz.

"How old is she?" Hagar asked.

"Thirty."

"Too old to frighten?"

"She's a sabra. Will you stay here with the rifle? I'll organise a search party . . ."

They heard the clunk of a foot on stone.

"It came from over there," Hagar whispered, pointing at the other side of the track further down the slope. They found Martha on the ground tucked tight against the wall. She was still breathing, though with an awkward rhythm. A vile-smelling slime down the front of her shirt showed she had vomited. Hagar felt her hair and the scalp beneath. There seemed no trace of a blow, though her hair was matted wet. Her body also glistened with sweat.

"I think she's ill," Hagar said.

"Can you carry her back to the kibbutz?" Nimshi asked. "I'll take her duty. Please ask Rowena to send out a replacement. If Martha turns out to be wounded, tell Samuel. He'll know what to do . . ."

They held Martha between them, limp, unconscious, breathing in that strange manner. It was too awkward to carry her that way, so Abraham hefted her over his shoulder. He walked swiftly up the hill, Hagar behind him, her eyes fixed on Martha's face.

"Take her to the dispensary," Givona said, as they went through the gate, "first building on the left, where the office is . . ." She started to wind the handle set into the wall of the gate. An alarm wailed. She waggled a shutter to produce an intermittent warbling note that meant medical services were required. If she had held open all the shutters and turned like mad, that would have sent them all digging into window boxes. By the time they got to the dispensary, the duty medical had the door open and the light on. Abraham

125

put Martha gently along the bed. "Is there a doctor?" he asked. "I think this might be poisoning."

The door opened again, and a man of about fifty came in. "I'm a doctor," he said, "at least that's what they told me in Odessa." He opened Martha's mouth with his finger and looked inside, then opened her eyes and looked at them. He turned to the orderly on duty.

"You know what we're going to do?"

The orderly nodded.

"I wouldn't stay if I were you," the doctor said to Abraham and Hagar. "Thank you for bringing her in. Will you mind if I give you a medical tip?" He was rolling up his shirt sleeves as he spoke. "Whenever you can see someone has vomited, don't lay them flat on the back," he said. "Solid left in the mouth could choke them. Always sit them with the head slightly forward to help the mouth to drain."

"What do you think it is?" Abraham asked.

"I hope I'll be able to tell you that when we've finished pumping out her stomach."

Abraham found Rowena, who arranged the relief sentry to take Nimshi's place. "It was lucky Nimshi decided to take that walk with you," she said, "or Martha could have stayed there until midnight. I suppose she felt the pain of food poisoning, didn't know what she was doing, and staggered down the path instead of up it. She must have fallen where you found her. Last October Jeremy fell and broke his ankle. He didn't want to shout for help in case there were Arabs about, and he lay four hours until his relief came; imagine that, four hours with a broken ankle. Martha was very lucky," she said.

Abraham felt his anger rise, but hid it; it was his first day on the kibbutz; there'd be time enough to speak at the meeting.

Hagar had gone straight to her house when she left the

dispensary; with Martha in capable hands there was nothing she could do. Abraham noticed that Ya'akov's light was out; he and Joel must have given up the Citroen as a lost cause. Ya'akov was usually persistent with machinery; there were few things he couldn't get to work given the time, but the Citroen was beyond mortal care! Abraham lit his lamp. He knew he was going to feel uncomfortable here in Guvena for a while, with a stone house and its institution furniture. It was a part of the kibbutz ethos that everyone be treated exactly alike. Whatever one had, the others were entitled to; and where there was not enough to go round, names were drawn from a hat. Abraham knew every other house would contain an exact replica of this bed, three boards with three horsehair-filled palliasses; this chair with its wooden seat; this table of four plain straight legs and plain wood top. Every other house would have a similar carpet of woven sisal. Pattern variations were unlikely; even a different pattern can begin to look more attractive, make an article appear more valuable. The box with a door would serve as a wardrobe; a shelf on the wall would hold any books. Plain curtains, a plain bedspread on each of the two single beds forty centimetres apart—just sufficient for the *separation*, Jewish ritual that forbade a man to sleep with his wife during certain days of the month. "How many of them," he wondered irreverently, "push the beds together?" All his married life, Abraham had lived on one kibbutz or another. His father was a potter who came from Iraq at the turn of the century; because of his looks, he could pass as either a dark-skinned Jew or a hook-nosed Arab. Abraham had two brothers, Nahor and Haran. Nahor, whom he hadn't seen for years, was living somewhere in Samaria. Haran and his father were dead, and his mother had died when he was a baby. With none of the ties so dear to a Jewish heart, Abraham had hoped for a Jewish family life when he married. Perhaps Sarah from the religious kibbutz near to him at Ashdod would give him a family, would give meaning to his life. But gradually the conviction had grown that Jewishness had nothing to give him; and when Sarah failed to bear his children, he lost

127

hope of starting his father's line again, of living with his children about him to a happy old age. Sarah had maintained her religious convictions though she had not forced her beliefs on him. Except in the one particular, the *separation*. He had never insisted and soon he lost physical desire for her; ceased actively to love her in a physical way. During the past few years, their only physical contact had been for the futile business of trying to conceive, and even that had become less frequent than Sarah would have liked. "Be fruitful and multiply," the Bible said, but how can you be fruitful when your seed apparently falls on stony ground? He pushed the two beds together. It was a gesture, no more. He took off his shirt, grabbed a towel, and walked to the bathhouse. Along the outside walk, he met Hagar. She'd taken a shower, and her hair glistened wet. "I thought you'd be asleep by now," he said.

"I wanted a bath to wash away some of that vomit."

"I got some on my shirt. Do you think I could put it in the laundry tomorrow? I've only worn it once."

"Give it to me, and I'll wash it."

"Don't be silly. I'll wear it in the shower." She laughed, and a voice from a nearby house called for quiet. He pulled a wry face, and continued on his way to the bathhouse. It had three showers, three lavatories, drying racks for clothing and two long washing troughs. He turned the tap, and the water splashed down. It was the first kibbutz he'd seen with running water; he'd seen taps, of course, but usually you had to pump water into a heated tank to take a shower. He left his shirt on and let the water pour down over it. He rubbed it with soap, rubbed his short curly black hair, then let the water cleanse the suds from him and the shirt.

He took off the shirt and washed the rest of his body, rubbing every part of himself with soap as a ritual. He hadn't realised he was singing until he saw the naked figure standing in the doorway. "Pack it in, will you?" the man said. "We're trying to get some sleep!" Without waiting for Abraham's apology, he turned round, his hairy white buttocks catching the gleam of the moonlight as he stomped back to
128

the first house on the left.

When Abraham got back to his house, Hagar was there giggling. He was carrying his wet shirt under his arm, wrapped with what had been his dry trousers and underwear —now all were damp! "Turn around!" he commanded, and slipped on clean dry underpants and trousers. "Now you can turn back again."

She was looking at him mystified. "What's all this 'turn around' business?" she said. "This is me, Hagar, remember? We've seen each other stark naked a hundred times."

He sat on the bed next to her. "I know, Hagar," he said, "but don't you feel different here? I can feel it. Somehow, it seemed as if someone was about to walk in and accuse us of immorality."

She put her hand in his. "Abraham, Abraham," she said, "you're like a child. Gabriel was right when he said you were complex; you're like an older child who's never learned how to be babyishly simple again, the way adults can be. You have a feeling in your mind, and then you project it as if it existed in the minds of other people. And then you react to it. Look, you've just had a bath, you're in a new place, you're missing Sarah for a hundred different reasons. I'm a woman, we're alone together, and maybe somewhere inside you is the comfortable feeling of how nice it would be if I were Sarah. We both know I'm *not* Sarah, but instead of recognising that simple fact, you think of what would happen if suddenly I became Sarah in one or more ways."

"What ways?"

"Well, of course, number one, sexual; number two, an armful of reassurance for this first lonely night in a new place; third, possibly . . . I don't know . . . third because you're in a new place and there are things shrieking out at you, and you'd like to be able to talk about them, intimately, the way you would with Sarah."

He was looking at her. "You're a damn sight wiser than I am," he said. "Ya'akov's good with cars, I'm good with— what am I good with, I don't know."

"With people!" she said.

129

"But you're good with minds. I'm not happy here, Hagar, and somehow I feel you're not happy either."

"We've got to give it a chance. We've only been here a few hours; we've got to wait and see."

"Have we really?" he asked. "You walk into a place, and a black cloud hits you, well, not exactly hits you, but surrounds you, seems to be choking you. Do you know what I mean?"

"I often wonder if kids feel that when over-possessive mothers clutch them to their breasts."

"You're changing the subject!"

"They're well organised," she said. "Medical orderly on duty day and night, sirens by the sentry posts, codes to say what type of help's needed, a kibbutz doctor, rifles and ammunition outside everybody's window. They can teach us, Abraham!"

"And we can teach them! Wait until the next committee meeting. I'll speak my piece!" It was understood at Eli-Dov that a matter to be introduced in a committee meeting wasn't discussed in advance except perhaps between husband and wife. That way they avoided cliques trying to get advance support for a possible difficult matter, but most important of all, it kept the kibbutz from dividing into factions.

"Can I ask you something personal?" he said. She nodded. "You and Ya'akov. I thought there was something brewing there."

"Not really," she said. "When Dov went, I was very lonely. Ya'akov let me sleep in his tent to keep me company. I don't know who was keeping who company. He was really grieved about Eli, you know."

"I know," Abraham said. "But nothing came of it? You and Ya'akov, I mean."

"Well, of course something did. But not in the way you mean. Ya'akov and I don't share the same interests most of the time. I'm bored by anything mechanical; Ya'akov adores tinkering with engines, and bits of metal and wood. And then there's a fundamental difference."

"Human beings?"

130

"Yes. Ya'akov is quite happy with people the way they are. I'm not. I have this basic Jewish discontent with the state of things. I think the purpose of human existence is neglected. Ya'akov says, 'let 'em alone, they're only human', and that annoys me beyond belief! So you see we fight all the time."

"I'm sorry," Abraham said.

"Don't be. You and Sarah and Miriam ought to start a matchmakers' union."

"I wasn't trying to influence you."

"I know! You're a great one for clearing the ground in advance, sweeping out the rubbish. You like to pick all the stones off a field so you can plough when the right time comes."

"So I won't damage the ploughshare."

"That's what you think, Abraham."

"It's time you went to bed!"

"It was time I went to bed hours ago."

"Then it's time I went to bed. I'm getting old," he said.

"How funny men can be about their age," she said, smiling. "Suggest a man's weak when he's nearing forty, and he'll flex his muscles at you; suggest he's young and virile, and he'll tell you how old he is." She got up to go, straightening her shirt and trousers. "Turn out the light before you open the door," Abraham said, "in case anybody's still about!"

She laughed. "Abraham, you're the absolute limit!" But she turned off the light before she opened the door, in case anyone was still about.

Abraham stripped off his clothing and got into bed. The sheet was coarse bleached calico cotton, cut from a roll and hemmed top and bottom. It had been a long time since he had slept in cotton sheets, and his body kept slipping against the smooth surface. After a while he got up and stripped the sheets from the bed. Then he got back in beneath the blankets and within minutes was asleep.

*   *   *

The following day they all reported for work, including Joel. "When are you going back to Tel Aviv?" Yigal asked as they waited outside the office.

"I don't know. There's lots of pretty young things about," Joel said impishly. "I might stay here. Get married and settle down!"

The doctor approached them. "I didn't have time to introduce myself last night," he said. "My name's Ari." He shook hands all round, and told them how Martha was. It had been a simple case of berry poisoning. "I've drawn the berry and we'll pass word around for everyone to avoid it. There can't be much of it about; Martha was carrying soil yesterday; she must have eaten some down in the valley. It's really lucky you happened along when you did, though. If you hadn't brought her back so swiftly, she'd have been dead within an hour!"

Abraham was shocked, but again he held his tongue. So many things he had noticed were treated in such a casual way. If they'd found such a berry anywhere near any of the kibbutzim he'd been on, they'd have organised uprooting parties and destroyed as much of it as they could find. They'd had snake-hunting parties at Eli-Dov. Ya'akov said they tasted delicious, but Abraham hadn't tried to eat them.

"They usually post the assignments on the board," Ari said, "but with Nimshi so busy last night it didn't get done." The majority of the kibbutzniks had semi-permanent jobs and didn't need to look at the board. "That's how it works out," Ari explained, "You get the straightforward jobs for a week or even a month at a time. That lets you develop a knowledge of them, and a rhythm. Labouring jobs, like carrying soil and stones for building, are assigned daily. It usually works out you get a month of labouring for every week of a more skilled job."

Abraham, Yigal and Ya'akov were put on soil-carrying; Miriam on clothing store—which meant a day sewing; Hagar was in the kitchen; Misha, no doubt because of Gabriel's influence, was on general repairs; and Joel, who'd never worked on a kibbutz, was on laundry duty.

132

"You'll be sorting out the clothes," Hagar told him, "clean one pile, dirty another, wet out to dry, dry in for mending. It's not much for your first day's work in a kibbutz. They ought to have found you something better!"

" 'Whatsoever thy hand findeth to do, do it with thy might; for there is no work in the grave whither thou goest . . .' " Joel said.

"You and Sarah will be great friends when she gets here!" Hagar said, laughing. She flung her arm around his shoulders. "You're a marvellous man, Joel!"

Abraham and Ya'akov went to their houses to get their rifles and ten rounds of ammunition. The 'Customs of the Kibbutz' leaflet had warned them, "No one shall go through the gate of the kibbutz to work in the fields unless he is carrying his rifle and ten rounds of ammunition."

" 'Every one with one of his hands wrought in the work, and with the other hand held a weapon . . .' " Joel said when he saw them. "I hope I don't have to carry a rifle in the laundry."

"I wouldn't like to be working in there if you did, you old goat," Ya'akov said laughing, as he and Abraham set off with Nimshi. They walked down the road to the fields, all immaculately tended, all contained by stone walls to prevent soil erosion. The kibbutz was laid out in contoured strips along the side of the hill, each strip flat. Each strip was devoted to a different crop: one had been ploughed for grain, another grassed and walled in for cattle, one carried sweet corn, another maize. There were tobacco plants, grape vines, low-lying fruit bushes; orange trees, lemon trees, and esrog.

"When they come into fruit," Nimshi explained, "we shall build our own packing plant, and box the fruit for market."

Near the top of the hill was the chicken run, with a row of nesting boxes like sentries. Already the kibbutz produced more eggs than they could eat; the surplus was used in baking, and to stir into drinks for the children. "We had a job getting the kids to drink the stuff," Nimshi said, "but eventually they realised it was good for them." Abraham

133

pitied the kids; he'd tried but couldn't manage to force it down! Below the chicken run was the herd that produced milk for the cheese from which Guvena got its name; it was the permanent charge of Henk from the flat lands outside Amsterdam, who had spent a life-time making Dutch cheese. "It's good in one way, but bad because it uses so little man-power," Nimshi said. "Henk and one helper, usually Frieda, can manage the herd and the cheese plant between them. We need more concentrated agriculture that uses less land and more people."

It was an old kibbutz problem—finding sufficient land and enough for the people to do. "If it wasn't for all this work on the walls and the soil-carrying, we'd be hard pressed to keep everybody occupied," Nimshi said. Where he came from, ten men had looked after five times as much land as Guvena now occupied.

As they went down the road, the temperature rose with every step. There were no cool breezes here; the air was damp and hot, steamy as a jungle. The fields had not yet been ridged, and swamp trees, bog oaks, mangrove, olive trees gone wild with fertility, grew at random. "Pull your veils down," Nimshi cautioned them. At first Ya'akov seemed inclined to leave his coiled about his hat, but when Abraham pulled his down, Ya'akov followed. Soon the road ended. "We're going to lengthen it half a kilometre next year," Nimshi said. Everything was fixed, everything planned. They knew what was to be done this year, what would be done next. Now the ground was softer and dark brown, almost sepia. Abraham picked up a handful. In the few places it was dry, it was coarse and crumbly, almost like peat, with limit-less ages of leaves rotted into it. It was heavy too, though free from clays; it would hold its moisture long after the rains had ended. Here they divided into diggers, loaders and carriers. The diggers dug the dry soil, the loaders filled the baskets, the carriers slung the baskets on their shoulders and climbed back up the hill. The baskets were woven of wickerwork. "We used to have cloth bags," Nimshi said, "but somehow they seemed heavier."

The contents of the basket weighed at least fifty kilos. Each had to be carried 400 metres, and then dumped behind a newly built wall. Here the rock showed through in places; Simon and Ari were chipping the more outstanding rocks with a large sledge-hammer and a spike. Samuel spread the soil as the carriers tipped it. It was a seemingly endless procession up the hill and down again; ten men carrying, one man filling, one man spreading. Every time Abraham passed Ya'akov, they smiled at each other, but neither wasted energy speaking.

At midday, the klaxon sounded from the kibbutz gate, echoing round the valley. They dumped the baskets and climbed the hill for lunch. At the top, Ya'akov lifted his arms, opened wide, rested them on the top of the stone wall, and pressed his head and back between them, relieving the strain on his back muscles. Yigal beside him helped to press down. Then Yigal positioned himself, and Ya'akov pressed for him. So enthusiastic was his movement that Yigal cried out in pain. "Steady," he said, "you'll have my chest on the ground."

"Call that a chest? I've seen a pigeon with better!"

There was fish soup for lunch, and the usual sliced tomatoes, cucumbers, white cabbage, lettuce. "They don't waste a thing," Hagar said as she sat beside them at the long table. "The soup's made from the leftovers of yesterday's evening meal." Abraham pushed his plate away; Ya'akov reached across and helped himself. Lunch was far more lively than supper. Abraham looked around the huge room. Most of the people seemed to be between twenty-five and forty. There were quite a few young ones, and a few old ones. Joel sat at the orthodox table; most of the people there were aged forty and over, though one or two younger ones with them wore the *yarmulka*. Around that table, everyone was serious, the conversation quiet, reverent in tone.

In contrast, the rest of the room was bedlam, with people calling from table to table. "What do they find to talk about, these people who spend all their lives together?" Abraham wondered, irritated by the noise. All the kibbutzniks were

135

wearing the same 'uniform' of grey trousers and shirts, even the girls and the older women. There were no attempts at personal adornment, nobody wearing a coloured scarf as Leiyla would have done, or a bandana the way Hagar and Hepsibah used to. The klaxon sounded again at ten minutes to one. Within five minutes the dining hall was empty and people were making their way back to the fields.

"You dig this afternoon," Nimshi said, "Ya'akov fill baskets, and Yigal go on the top and spread out the soil."

"I'm fit enough to carry," Abraham said.

"First day we make a rule; anyway, we don't want to break your spirit; we reckon we've a lifetime of soil-moving!"

"You haven't thought of getting a tractor?" Ya'akov asked.

"We think of nothing else. Next year we'll have a tractor," Ari said. Next year the promised land! When there was a break in the line of carriers Ya'akov turned and looked at Abraham. "Smoke?" he asked. Abraham lifted his mosquito veil, and lit the cigarette Ya'akov gave him.

"That money we have in the bank in Tel Aviv. That'd buy a tractor," Ya'akov said.

Abraham thought about it. "Yes, I suppose it would!"

"What do you say?"

"It's not my money; it's not for me to say."

"But the others would do what you tell them!"

"Call a meeting, and put it to them."

Ben, the first of the carriers, returned. "Trying to smoke the mosquitoes away?" he asked. "That smells like a British cigarette." Few kibbutzniks smoked, but when they did, they used their own tobacco, grown and cured in the kibbutz, rolled in thick yellow paper. "It is British," Ya'akov said. He looked at Abraham. "Unfortunately, it's my last or I'd give you one."

Abraham took the cigarette from his mouth. "Smoke this," he said. "I've finished with it." Ben smoked while Ya'akov filled his pannier. Then he nipped off the glowing end, put the butt in his pocket, and set off up the hill.

"You ought not to have done that," Ya'akov said. "Now we'll have all of them asking."

136

"They've a right. Everything shall equally be shared; you know that's how it is!"

Ya'akov snorted. "They can share anything they want," he said, "but they're not having my cigarettes."

When Schmuel dropped his pannier for filling, he looked at Abraham and Ya'akov. "Ben says you've got cigarettes," he said.

What did I tell you, Ya'akov's look seemed to say.

"Sorry, we just smoked the last. Ben's got a butt Abraham gave him." One by one, all the kibbutzniks on carrying duty asked about the British cigarettes. Abraham saw them gather in a knot, near where Yigal was spreading the soil but out of his hearing.

"There'll be trouble, Ya'akov," he said. "If you've got any cigarettes in your house, I'd smoke 'em or hide 'em."

After the impromptu meeting, no one mentioned cigarettes except Ari, who said, "Anyway, smoking's bad for the health."

"First time I've heard that," Ya'akov replied.

The meeting, held after dinner on the day following *shabbat*, was in two parts. First the secretary, the treasurer, the farm manager and seven elected 'elders' discussed the routine running of the kibbutz. Crop yields, capital outlay, the budget, running expenses. This took about an hour. The executive committee had eaten supper early and retired to the secretary's office. Three quarters of the way through supper time, volunteers began to move the tables so that everyone could see the end of the hall. Here a platform of tables was erected for the committee. Throughout supper, Abraham had noticed the atmosphere seemed charged, as on the first night of a new play. Despite the prohibition on pre-discussion, he noticed several groups of kibbutzniks obviously preparing one another for what they would say in the meeting. Abraham's group helped with the arrangement of the hall but didn't talk.

The committee came in to a hush of silence. All the kibbutzniks sat. There was no roll call: those who wanted to be there were there already. The committee sat high on the tables, completely exposed to the body of the hall. Nimshi got to his feet, and in his thin tenor voice, went through the notes of the executive committee discussions. Everything seemed routine. "The number of actual man-hours in the laundry exceeds the number allocated, and it would be appreciated if everyone would try to wear clothing a little longer before turning it in. The man-hours allocated to general maintenance will have to be increased; six chairs have been brought in for repair this week. Please take better care of the furniture, since funds to replace it will not be available for at least another three years. Please try to keep the bathhouses cleaner. General cleaning of the kibbutz site should be a free-hours duty and not an allocated task." Many good-natured groans greeted this. Free time was scarce, and few could relax when they had finished the day's allocated work. Most had 'extra interests': art group, poetry, play reading, adult education, vocational training, political discussion, crafts study and practice, languages, music.

After about ten minutes, Nimshi ended his summary, and the real meeting began. Ari rose to his feet. "Some of us," he said, "have been on the kibbutz for three years and apart from going to Haifa, Nazareth and Tiberias with the lorry, we've never been away. Granted that we get newcomers all the time, and that we look to them for new knowledge and information. But I would like to propose that we start a scheme to let everybody who wants to—and for the sake of our mental health I think we should all want to—go away from the kibbutz for one month to witness some of the life that's going on in other parts of Eretz Israel."

"What about the cost?" someone called out.

"We ought to have a fund, so much a day for living expenses. I think one couple ought to go each month in order of seniority, i.e. how long they've been on the kibbutz.

138

And while they are away, if some of our unmarried young men could contrive to bring a wife back with 'em, so much the better."

"What about the girls?" Rowena asked from the platform. "Shall we 'contrive' to bring back a husband?"

Rowena, current treasurer, confirmed the money could be made available from central funds. The idea was discussed for a half an hour and a vote was taken. The proposition was defeated by a large majority. Ari noticed oddly enough that most of the people who voted against it would have been the first to benefit from it. Five other propositions were raised; three were passed, one turned down, and one delayed for further information.

Then Hagar got to her feet. "Is it in order," she asked Nimshi, "for a new member to raise a point?"

There were general cries of "of course, of course, speak up".

Hagar waited until everyone was silent.

"I was thinking of Martha last night, and the boy who broke his ankle. Every other kibbutz I've ever been on puts out sentries in twos. That's so that they can help one another, and if anything goes wrong one can get back while the other holds the fort, so to speak. I wondered if there was any particular reason why you put out single sentries?"

There was silence, but everyone looked at Aaron, the leader of the six-man defence group. They had been trained by the Haganah, as Abraham, Ya'akov and Yigal had been, and they were responsible not only for the actual defence of the kibbutz but also for training the kibbutzniks in the use of weapons, and fighting. No one on the kibbutz, except the orthodox Jews, was exempt from this military training.

Aaron stood up. "It's part of the training, of course, to post sentries in such a way that one covers the other. The defensive system is arranged so that even if the Arabs by-pass one sentry they will always find others in their path. This kibbutz is more favoured than others in its design. Six men effectively placed at the points of the star could keep an enemy at bay for a long time. As to posting sentries in

139

twos, I've never seriously considered that."

"It'd double our sentry duties," Ben called; there was an immediate storm of agreement, and disapproval.

"I think the point should be made," Ari said, "that but for a pure fluke of Nimshi taking our two new members for a walk last evening, Martha would have died. The double-sentry system Hagar advocates would prevent that. Furthermore, from a medical and psychological point of view"—there were groans from one side of the hall—"it would be a distinct advantage for each sentry to be accompanied. Sentry duty would not cause such a drain on our resources." He was careful not to look round when he said this; he had pronounced four kibbutzniks unfit for sentry duty on medical grounds.

An hour later, they were still discussing this point when Nimshi adjourned the meeting to give them all time to think. If Abraham had been in charge he would have adjourned half an hour before, when the meeting split into two factions, those who agreed with the suggestion, and those who didn't want the doubled sentry duty it would entail.

"You really put the cat among the pigeons with that one," he said to Hagar as they made their way out. In a stone cairn in the centre of the green, a camp fire had been lighted. That night the music group were to give a concert. There were six of them accompanied by a fiddler and a harmonica player.

"You'll have to join the music group," Hagar said to Ya'akov. "They could probably use another harmonica player!" After the group had sung for half an hour, Gabriel came into the centre carrying two drums made of carved wood sections of tree trunks and covered with dried, sun-cured goatskin. He played with the tips of his fingers and the heel of his hands, in the way of the old French tambour, and he sang German songs he had learned in his childhood. With his deep baritone voice, he was obviously the star turn, and he sang for a half an hour without stopping. As the evening grew longer, more and more people drifted in to the circle and seated themselves on the grass. Lithuanians and

Latvians, Czechs and Poles, Serbs and Croats, sitting side by side. Italians, French, Germans, English, Iraqis, Yemenis, a congress of nations meeting free beneath a million stars. When Gabriel stopped, they were silent, lost in evoked moments of happiness snatched in younger terror-ridden days. The mind selects when it remembers. No one moved. Gabriel sat with his hands limp on the drums. Then he beckoned to Hagar, and she went across to him. They spoke quietly together for a minute before she called over to Ya'akov. Ya'akov played, Hagar and Gabriel sang, and Gabriel tapped on his tambour a song from Hagar's childhood in Paris, *"Les perles de mes larmes, étincellante, les perles de mes larmes, qui sait qu'ils sont?"*

When the last notes of song had died, Gabriel kissed her cheek and touched Ya'akov's shoulder, content with what they had just achieved together. The audience did not applaud, but went satisfied to their houses. Soon the fireflies of their lamps danced on the verandahs. The kibbutzniks lay silent on their beds, reluctant to sleep away the euphoric charm of the night. They listened to the sounds of trees they themselves had planted outside their windows; they smelled the odours of fresh life and the rise of the cleansing sap, the force that enveloped and defended them against old evils.

One by one the lamps were extinguished and the camp was left to the slow tread of the night guards, the heavy scent of oleander, esrog, bog roses, and Biblical myrtle and jasmine.

Miriam didn't miss Yigal in the morning. His bed had been rumpled and she thought it strange he had left without waking her, but as she said to Abraham at breakfast, Yigal had been strange ever since they arrived at Guvena. Both assumed he'd risen early and had gone about his work without breakfast. His task for the day was picking stones and wall-building in the lower field. Abraham and Ya'akov had been re-assigned to the upper orchard when Nimshi learned they'd had pruning experience. Prune a tree wrong when it's young and you'll never bring it round, prune it right and you can bring it to fruit a season early. Miriam was still employed in the clothing store, repairing shirts. "If you like that job," Nimshi said, "I'll keep you on it until you have your baby." It suited Miriam well, since she had always liked sewing; now her belly was big she had no desire to martyr herself in the fields.

When lunch time came, Miriam was one of the first in the dining hall, looking for Yigal. She went to the serving table and procured two plates of food. She arranged Yigal's plate in an attractive fashion and placed a petunia in the centre of his plate to brighten the food. She got two mugs of orange juice, two of sour cream, and set them by their places. Abraham came in with Ya'akov, Hagar with Misha and Gabriel, but still no Yigal. When Abraham had finished eating, he beckoned to Ya'akov.

"Where are you going?" Miriam asked.

"I thought we'd wander round a bit before we go back to work."

"If you see Yigal . . ."

"If we do . . ."

"Don't tell him I sent you."

"Of course not. Anyway, you're not sending us, are you?" They walked out together. "Where do you reckon he might be?" Abraham asked.

"No use looking down in the fields. If he was sulking, he'd choose a spot where nobody'd see him. He wouldn't want everybody saying, aren't you coming for dinner?"

Through the main gates of the kibbutz they took the road to the south. They walked for ten minutes but saw no trace of Yigal. They made their way back over the crest of the hill. The kibbutz stretched below them once they crossed the hill but they saw no trace of Yigal.

They found Nimshi carrying soil at the bottom of the hill. "I have this job another four days," Nimshi said. He listened

142

while they told him about Yigal. "You've searched the kibbutz?" he asked.

"No, why should we?"

"He didn't turn up for work this morning. I thought he was taking a morning on the bench. A bit selfish with so much to be done but it wasn't up to me to interfere."

Nimshi, Ari, Abraham and Ya'akov searched the kibbutz and its immediate environs, without finding any trace of Yigal.

"We'll have to tell Miriam," Ya'akov said.

Her face was grave; she sat on her bench in the store, a shirt in her hands, a needle and thimble in her fingers. Then she pinned the needle into her lapel, put the thimble in her pocket, and crossed her hands.

"Have you any idea where he might be?" Abraham asked.

She shook her head.

"Did you have a disagreement?"

She shook her head again, and then she spoke. "He's gone," she said, "and we shan't see him again. It's because of the baby and what Joel said that day we came here. 'Be fruitful and multiply.' You remember!" Nimshi, mystified, glanced at Abraham.

There were tears in Miriam's eyes. "It wasn't Yigal's baby. He couldn't make a baby after what the Arabs did to him."

Ari nodded. "The night you arrived, after I had looked after Martha, your husband came to see me. . . ."

"He told me he was going for a walk."

"He came to see me. I was tired, I suppose. It's an awful job pumping out a stomach. I'd been carrying soil all day and perhaps I wasn't as helpful as I might have been."

"Why did he come to see you," Abraham asked, "or is that a professional secret?"

"He wanted me to verify he had no chance of ever making a child. I can't make that kind of an examination here. It takes apparatus, and it's a very complicated matter even in hospital. I asked him what had happened to him, what the doctors in Be'ersheva had said. From what I was able to gather, it really was quite hopeless. I suppose I ought to have

143

told him I'd make tests, or something, but it would have been . . . well, useless. I ought to have been thinking about his psychological condition, but I didn't know him, you see, I mean, I'd only just met him . . . and . . ."

Abraham took Ari's arm and pulled him to one side. Then they left the building with Nimshi. Ya'akov stayed with Miriam.

"We accept you were hasty, and we understand the reasons for it well enough, even though I've never pumped a stomach on top of a day's work. But you've no right to say anything to Miriam until we know something definite."

"You're right of course," Ari said, wearily. "It's easy to have a guilty conscience after the event."

"You think he's killed himself?" Nimshi asked. Dammit, this quarter he had to run a kibbutz, not a nursing home.

"He's a classic case, now I come to think of it," Ari said, "a depressive. You know him, Abraham. Was he once gay, ebullient?"

"Yes, he was."

"Since his accident, has he become taciturn, going off on his own for long times?"

"Yes, though this is the first time he's stayed away from Miriam all night."

"And this thing Joel said; I suppose it was the usual Jewish philosophy—man is born to beget children, and if he doesn't he's thrice cursed?"

"That's it," Abraham said.

"They make me bloody sick," Ari said, "absolutely bloody sick." He turned round, walked a couple of steps, then turned and walked back to them. "Yigal's case is classic," he said. "His testicles were crushed, he was medically incapable of producing children; his wife, the silly bitch, got herself pregnant by another man, thinking she was doing Yigal a favour; and he had to run across a stupid blabbermouth with idiotic philosophies. Down there's where we'll find Yigal, in the swamp."

"You won't say anything to Miriam."

"I shan't say anything to anybody," Ari said, "I can't even

144

bear to think of it."

He walked with them into the clothing store. "I think you've done enough work for one day," he said to Miriam, resuming his professional manner. "Come over to the hospital, and I'll run a few tests, see how the baby's doing." Nimshi led Miriam from the clothing store; the shock of Yigal's disappearance made it difficult for her to walk. Ari dropped behind, with Abraham and Ya'akov. "I'll keep her in the hospital for a few days," he said, "under mild sedation."

"She's already had trouble with the baby. They thought she was going to deliver prematurely in Tel Aviv," Abraham said.

"Babies have a habit of doing what they like. You don't know who and where the father is, I suppose?"

Abraham looked at Ya'akov. Ya'akov shook his head. "It wasn't me," he said. "I thought it was Chochem."

"I thought it was Shlomo," Abraham said.

"And *we* all thought it was Yigal," Ari said as he hurried away.

Abraham and Ya'akov sat on a bench. "Do *you* think he's killed himself?" Ya'akov asked.

"I wouldn't be surprised now that I come to think about it," Abraham said.

Miriam was kept in the hospital for three weeks and under opium and belladonna sedation for the first week. Hagar, Abraham, Misha and Ya'akov went in to see her every day before supper. Hagar often sat with her for the evening. The clothing store kept a steady supply of shirts at her bedside to give her something to occupy her hands. They could do nothing to occupy her mind.

After three weeks and almost without effort, Miriam gave birth to a boy who weighed three kilos on Ari's primitive scales. The boy looked like Noam, insomuch as he looked like anyone, but she called him Reuven and let them draw their own conclusions. When he was born, her breasts were dry. Rachel, who had come into the next bed three days before Reuven was born and had given birth to a girl within hours of her arrival, had milk enough for two. As soon as

145

she was fit, Miriam discharged herself from the hospital and left the child in Rachel's care. When Rachel was discharged, she took over the nursery as her permanent occupation, and Reuven moved in with her.

Miriam chose to remain in the house assigned to her and Yigal; Hagar offered to move in with her, but Miriam preferred to be on her own as long as the kibbutz had houses to spare. At first no one mentioned Yigal's name, but when it came out innocently in conversation and everyone became embarrassed, she turned on them. "You'd think he was dead or something, the way you avoid mentioning him!" After that they included him in every relevant conversation. Miriam often referred to "when Yigal comes back", and they all maintained the fiction that he was away on a long journey and would return at some unspecified time in the future. A month after she'd had her baby, Miriam's turn to hump soil came up. She did three days before she could go back to the clothing store. Yigal's clothing was always kept in the cupboard in her room, and no one suggested she hand it in. His slippers were kept under her bed, since he had worn his boots when he went, but he had left his hat and his mosquito veil behind. Sometimes during the night, returning from the bathhouse, Ya'akov or Misha would hear a sound and listen outside her door.

Sometimes she was singing, other times laughing to herself, sometimes reading aloud from the books she borrowed from the kibbutz library. But usually, during those long silent bitter hours, she was crying.

Abraham was granted special leave from the kibbutz to see his wife. A lorry had arrived with seed supplies, and Abraham hitched a lift as far as Haifa with the load of cheeses and vegetable produce. In his pocket he had kibbutz money— not actual money but a draft drawn on the Federation—and instructions to buy a lorry. "Get a good one," Ya'akov pleaded. "I wish I were going to be there with you when you buy it." The list of prohibitions and recommendations Ya'akov had given him would have filled an auto manual. Look for oil on the engine casing, check the magneto for burnt contacts, wind the engine by hand and feel for compression on all four cylinders, get someone else to wind the engine and listen to the valves rising and falling, check the tyres, check under the wings for rust, and so on and so on, *ad nauseam*.

In Haifa he hitched a ride to Tel Aviv. When he arrived at the hospital, he asked the same surly clerk for Dr Walters. The clerk kept him waiting ten minutes while he completed an entry in his book, but after coming all that way, Abraham was in no hurry.

"I think we're on to something," the doctor said to Abraham in his tiny office. He shuffled through papers on his desk, until finally he found what he was searching for. "Here's the lab report. You'll be happy to know that your wife's problem is not mental, as I had supposed, but physical. We don't know half enough," he said, "but it looks to me as if there is something wrong with her blood."

"Can it be cured?"

"Oh yes, I'm sure we'll cure it eventually."

"What is it? Would I understand?"

"It's a form of anaemia. Your wife just isn't making all the red corpuscles she should. From a purely medical point of view, of course, it's a fascinating case, since we can't yet find exactly what's doing it. Fascinating, absolutely fascinating!" he said, looking at his notes. "However, you don't want to hear a lecture. You want to know how your wife is, and whether she can go out yet. The answer to the first is, she's very well. The answer to the second is, I don't want her to leave just yet."

Abraham thought for a while. "Tell me, Doctor, do you want to keep my wife because she's a fascinating case for research, or because it's important for her welfare?"

"I wouldn't keep your wife for a second if I believed her fit to leave, no matter how fascinating her case may be. This

147

is a treatment hospital, not a research centre. But there is considerable danger to your wife if we send her out. Normally the blood takes care of wounds quite effectively; your wife's blood couldn't cope with a pinprick. The wound would become septic, her whole body in fact. She could die within days of a simple cut."

"Taking her away is out of the question?"

The doctor nodded. "I'm afraid so."

"You can't give any indication of how long it might be before you can cure her? It's just that I know she'll take it better if she knows how long . . ."

"I've got all sorts of people working on it," the doctor said, "labs and research pathologists and so on, but until they find an answer, I'm stuck. It could be something as simple as an abscess tooth, though I've looked at all her teeth over and over again. It could be, oh, it could be a hundred things. All I can say positively is this. If you let her leave in that condition, you'll be signing her death warrant."

"You happy here?" Abraham asked Sarah.

"I enjoy the work; I don't enjoy the tests. They keep messing about with me; I never know what's coming next. Sometimes they look at my teeth, sometimes scrape a bit off my fingernails; I think they're as confused as I am . . ."

"They think you have anaemia, and they don't know what's causing it. They're trying to find out."

"Why don't they put me on a tonic, and let me get out of here?"

"It would be dangerous." Abraham repeated everything the doctor had told him.

"You don't want me to come out," she said.

"Of course I want you out, but it'd be too dangerous. The doctor's insisting you wear gloves when you work in here, to avoid even the slightest cut. Look at my hands." He showed them to her; they were lacerated by the work he did

148

on the kibbutz. "I took the skin off my elbow the other day when I slipped on a stone; it was a simple accident; but if it happened to you you'd be dead." She was silent; there was no answer.

"Tell me about Guvena," she said, "Ya'akov, Misha, Hagar, Miriam and Yigal; have they had the baby yet?"

Abraham told her about the baby—her face tightened when she learned Miriam had called it Reuven—but he didn't say a word about the disappearance of Yigal. When he told her about the synagogue, Joel, and the orthodox table, she smiled happily. "That's where we'll be eating one of these days," she said. It seemed a threat to Abraham, not a promise. He stayed three hours, and they talked all the time, or rather, she talked to him about her work, patients she helped care for.

"You ought to have been a nurse," he said.

When the time came for him to go, she had resigned herself to remaining. Her face became serious. "One thing I want to say, Abraham, before you go. I meant to put it in a letter, but when I came to writing it, well, I didn't know how. While you're up there on your own, if you get lonely, well, you know what I mean, if you wanted somebody, I wouldn't, I really wouldn't hold it against you."

"I'm *your* husband, Sarah," he said. "There is no one else for me. There never has been and never will be."

Abraham found Kibbutz Guvena in uproar. Syrians had attacked and killed two sentries.

"At least it's made us double the duties," Hagar said bitterly. "If it had been done when I suggested, they might still be alive." The irony was that the two killed had been the most vociferous in opposition to the scheme. "Why, oh, why can't we arrive at decisions quickly?" Hagar said plaintively. "It must have been obvious that doubling the guards

149

was essential, why did we have to have this tragedy to prove it?"

"If the democratic process is long and drawn out," Abraham said, "that's the price we pay for the kibbutz system . . ."

"And if it costs lives? Ben and Elihu are *dead*, Abraham."

"Rather they died than the system itself!"

That night there was a committee meeting with only one subject. Not even Hagar could complain the discussion was long drawn out; within an hour the kibbutz had voted seventy per cent to thirty per cent to launch a counterstrike against the nearest Arab village, and if possible destroy it. The orthodox members voted against it, as did Abraham and Misha. Hagar, Miriam and Ya'akov voted for the resolution. That same night, Ya'akov joined the defence group which probed Arab territory across the Hulah Valley and came back with a plan.

The strike was planned for the following night. "Hit 'em swiftly, hit 'em hard," Ya'akov said. According to their principle of *collectiviut rayonit*, once the decision had been taken in committee, it was binding on all members. Names of everyone, except the old, the orthodox, nursing or pregnant women, and children under sixteen, were put into a hat with a mosquito veil to prevent any glimpse of the contents. Nimshi and Samuel made the draw in the dining hall after dinner. First name out of the hat: Nimshi. A happy augury; everyone cheered. Twenty-five, in five units of five each, were to take part in the strike. Samuel, Gabriel, Abraham, Ya'akov and Hagar were drawn. The final force had twenty males and five females. All were excused work for the afternoon, and told to sleep. Ya'akov slept; so did Hagar. Abraham lay on his bed, awake. It's one thing to defend your home against marauders; even to kill can be justified in those circumstances. But to attack and destroy a village was to Abraham's way of thinking impossible to justify. Two thoughts were in conflict. Collective living depends on collective decisions; he would be obliged to accept any decision the meeting might take by vote of all the members. He intended, at an early
150

meeting, to suggest the woven baskets might be remade to allow the bottom to be dropped out, thus avoiding the need to take the fully-loaded baskets from the carrier's shoulders. He'd hurt the muscles of his back one day letting down a heavy load of soil. If the members decided that the work necessary to adapt all the baskets was not justified, he would abide by that decision, regardless of the temptation to adapt his own pannier. In a collectivisation, there were no degrees of importance; every decision taken by the majority was binding on all members, no matter how unimportant that decision may seem to be. If he agreed to accept their verdict on the baskets, he would be obliged to accept it on the foray against the Arabs.

The orthodox could avoid it on a matter of religious belief. The Book of Isaiah specifically said, "Nation shall not lift up sword against nation, neither shall they learn war. . . ." But the Book of Exodus spoke for the other point of view. "Life for life, eye for eye, tooth for tooth, hand for hand, foot for foot . . . wound for wound . . ." Doubtless Joel and his friends could discuss the merits of those two until the sun came up without arriving at a conclusion. But the words of the *ve-elleh shemoth*, the second book of the Pentateuch commonly called Exodus, were quite specific. "If a man come presumptuously upon his neighbour to slay him with guile; thou shalt take him from mine altar that he may die." Joel would discuss the words *neighbour, presumptuously*, and *guile*. Could an armed assault be termed *by guile*? Was it *presumptuous* to destroy an Arab village, when the Arabs had killed two men and would doubtless destroy Kibbutz Guvena were it not so well defended? And what interpretation would Joel put on *neighbour*? Did it merely mean someone who lived geographically nearby, or did *neighbour* imply *love*? Abraham did not sleep that afternoon. He could refuse to go with the raid, but if he did so, he would be obliged to leave the kibbutz; and though he and Ya'akov and the others were almost like blood brothers, he could not be certain they would leave with him. He missed Sarah more than anyone at that moment; with Sarah he would have been able to

151

discuss this entire matter, and though she would have opposed the raiding party, the heat of her arguments would have helped him forge his own decision.

At five o'clock the raiding party assembled outside the kibbutz to the west. Aaron drew a map in the earth and they clustered around it. "Here's the village," he said. "Unit one will circle left, unit two right. These will be our first attacking units. Unit three will wait at the west and stay on the ground, unless needed. Units four and five will wait until units one and two have cleared the village; then they will go in and destroy it." It was a simple plan. The first attack would come from the direction the Arabs would least expect. Abraham studied the ground and listened to what had been decided by Aaron, the commander. There was no democracy, no discussion. Aaron was in charge; everyone would follow and obey him. "I shall lead unit one," Aaron said, "and you, Nimshi, will lead unit two. Samuel three, Abraham four, and Ya'akov five. Any questions?"

No one questioned the appointed leadership, the method of attack, or Aaron's leadership of the first wave. It was a Haganah maxim that an officer leads from the front, not from the rear. Each man had fifty rounds of ammunition, and each commander had coloured tracers for signals. Finally, when everything was clear to everyone, Abraham spoke. "May I ask a question? It has to do with something I was taught at Haganah school. We know our objective, we know our method, but would you, Aaron, like to state clearly what our intention is to be? Are we going in there to destroy a village or the villagers? To burn down houses, or to kill people?"

"Our intention is to destroy that village, to wipe it completely off the face of the map. If we have to burn houses to the ground to do so, then we shall! If we have to, we shall kill people!"

"But if a man is trying to escape?"

"If he offers no danger to any of our men it is permissible to let him escape."

152

"They killed two of our men. I hope I shall kill at least two of them," Samuel said.

"We're destroying that village because it may have strategic value and to dissuade the Arabs from trying to destroy Kibbutz Guvena. This isn't a pogrom," Abraham said, angry as he had ever been.

"Nobody means it to be," Hagar said, placating him. "We're not murderers, Abraham. You heard what Aaron said. Units one and two will shoot high to frighten the Arabs into leaving, and then they will bring the Arabs out of the houses before units four and five come in and burn them. There'll be no unnecessary killing, Abraham."

At dusk they left the kibbutz. Units one and two took a wide sweep in order to skirt the village. Later, three, four and five headed across the valley, skirted the swamp and lake, and began the long climb up the hill, swinging northwards.

Mokhra village was situated in the south-east foothills of Mount Hebron across the Syrian border. They climbed steadily on a compass bearing; soon the fertile valley gave way to hard limestone rock rent by streams. Here and there patches of coarse broad-leaved grasses supported sheep and goats. They moved away from the grazing herds; Arab shepherds have extraordinary hearing. Tamarisk shrubs flickered in the semi-light and whispering fronds rubbed together. On such a mission men are tuned to the faintest sounds, senses taut as goatskin on a drum.

Abraham led his patrol along the edge of a valley beneath the skyline. His sixth sense heard the clink of goathoofs from enormous distances; several times they crossed the valley to avoid the herds. They met no one, and Abraham brought them safely to the knoll which was to be the rendezvous point for units three, four and five.

Ya'akov's patrol had already arrived. "Hagar all right?" Ya'akov asked. She had marched behind Abraham, keeping step for step. "What kept you," he asked, smiling at Abraham and Hagar; "we've been here for ten minutes!"

"How many shepherds did you avoid?"

"One jumped us," Ya'akov said, "but it's the last time he'll do that."

"You killed him?" Hagar whispered.

Ya'akov nodded.

"You could have gone round him," Abraham said.

"And add another two kilometres?"

Abraham turned away. Unit three arrived ten minutes later.

"You've only got four men?" Abraham noticed the missing man as the section came over the hill.

"Minna stumbled on a rock and twisted her ankle," Samuel said. "We told her to hobble back as best she could."

"You should have sent someone with her," Hagar said, fuming.

"Hey, who's running the section?" Samuel said. "We need people up here, not down there helping silly girls who can't watch where they put their feet!"

"It could have been a silly man!"

"But it wasn't, was it? Don't go feminine on me!" He made feminine a dirty word.

Abraham's watch showed two minutes to go before the attack started. They moved into position below the village, Abraham to the south-west, Ya'akov to the north-west, and Samuel to the west. At this edge the village was built on a slight plateau and there was little danger to the three units from the bullets of units one and two. Mokhra had fifteen houses, half semi-derelict but occupied. Each house had a vegetable patch and milking goats, and the village smell could be detected even beyond the ridge. No one was about. Through the glassless holes in the walls they could see lights from wick-lamps burning cooking oil. Most of the houses were of stone with mud stucco walls. The well in the centre of the village had a one-metre-high stone surround, worn smooth, no windlass, its bucket held by a leather-plaited cord. The meeting-place, which would also serve as a *kif*-smoking centre, was beyond the well; rough-hewn benches stood outside, and the holes in the wall were shuttered. Aaron was in position on the west side of the village. They'd made the journey across the valley without difficulty. But there was no trace of Nimshi's unit, with just one minute left to go. Had Nimshi lost his way in the dark? It didn't seem possible. Five men, fifteen houses—it would be too dangerous without them. What should he do? Postpone the start? That would make it difficult to complete the job and get back over the border before dawn. Should he send a messenger to one of the other detachments to order them to join the attack? He saw how inflexible his plans had been and cursed. They ought to have attacked from the west, over the lip; and he should have been able to communicate easily with at least three units, instead of being locked in here with only five men. At that moment, he saw a shadow approaching. Within two minutes, Nimshi was by his side. "Sorry I'm late," he said, "we had to make a hellish detour; we'd have gone for the shepherds, but there were three of them and they had rifles." One shot would have alerted shepherds for ten kilometres into Syria!

"Better late than never," Aaron said. "Take the left side of this street; we'll take the right. Otherwise we'll stick to the original plan. Understood?" Nimshi nodded, crawled back to his men. They advanced towards the village, two metres between them. Fifteen metres from the nearest house, Aaron checked to see that Nimshi was ready, then fired a red tracer into the air above the village: the attack was on. Each man aimed five rounds high up at the stones of the houses. Within seconds, the village was in uproar. Goats brayed, dogs barked, women screamed, children wailed, and men shouted. When the shooting stopped, the adults within the house became silent. Not a shot had been fired back! Aaron cupped a hand to his mouth and shouted in Arabic. "You have fifteen minutes to come out of your houses and leave the village, and then we shall start shooting again. The village is entirely surrounded, but you can leave if you come out now. No one will be shot, if you leave now." Everyone watched the doors. Suddenly in the centre of the village, a bead curtain was flung aside and an Arab came out in his ceremonial robe, hastily tying the cord around his waist. On

155

his head he wore the rounded cap with its tightly curled decorations. He walked fearlessly into the centre of the street. "Who are you?" he bellowed.

"Cover me," Aaron whispered, then walked down the village street.

"Who are you? What do you want?" the Arab asked. Aaron, his face black, his grey uniform muddied by the trip through the valley, his stockinet cap over his ears, must have seemed an apparition from some dark shade. "I am the leader of this village," the Arab said. "Who are you, and what do you want?"

"I am the leader of the village where last night Arabs killed two men, and tried to drive us away. I wish only peace for your people, but we mean to drive you away from this village. Go from here and tell your people that in the future for every attack on our village, we will destroy one of your villages."

"*Andak!*" the Arab said with contempt. The knife in his sleeve dropped into his hand as he came forward. He swung it upwards, blade driving for Aaron's belly. As he jumped aside Aaron pulled the trigger of his rifle. The knife caught his hip and slashed to the bone. Nine rifles spoke as one, nine shots slammed into the body of the Arab, bowling him over backwards into the dust. There was a howl from within the house and a younger Arab charged out, a rifle in his hands: he ran only two steps before they dropped him. They started to shoot again, but this time they aimed for the black gaping holes in the walls of the houses. As agreed, each man fired five rounds. During the firing Aaron crawled back to his own line on hands and knees.

The firing ceased. Inside one of the houses, a woman wailed. The dogs had run from the village during the shooting, and their barking could be heard to the south. Suddenly the first door opened, and the first Arab came out, carrying a cloth bag with his hastily packed possessions. Behind him came three women, two sons, and five small children. All save the sons carried bundles. The man fussed over the procession like a mother hen. He shut the door, took his place at the head of the family, and walked slowly down the street, away from where the shots had come. When he was a third of the way down the street, another door opened and another family came out; then a third door opened, and a fourth. Within minutes, the stream became a flood, and there were a hundred people walking down the street. Several families untethered their goats and led them away. Horses stabled beside the houses were also led out. One family carried heavily laden wickerwork hampers, and although they bowed beneath the weight, they walked with dignity.

Nimshi looked down the line. Two of his men turned away, unable to look.

"That could be you and your families three nights ago," he said, "marching out of Guvena on your way to nowhere. If the bastards had left any of us alive." They began a house-to-house search. Most of the families had lived, eaten and slept in one room. To their hygiene-accustomed sense of smell, the rooms stank horribly.

Nimshi found an old man lying on a bed, covered in an uncured camel hide which smelled stronger than he did. The man must have been a hundred years old, emaciated, wizened. Only his eyes seemed capable of movement. Beneath the old man's bed Nimshi uncovered a box with twenty-four new hand grenades in it, the grease still on them.

"What are we going to do with him?" Nimshi asked Aaron.

"Anybody else know he's in there?" Aaron asked.

"No; I went in on my own."

Aaron went inside the house; when he came out he said, "No problem. The old man's dead."

The right side of the village was cleared, and the four men of Aaron's unit walked through and made contact with Ya'akov. Aaron stayed behind with Nimshi. There were only two more houses, one at the end of the ragged row, another almost behind it. "I don't remember anyone coming out of this first house," Nimshi said. "I checked all the others in this row."

"Cover me," Aaron said.

Nimshi's unit spread out, running between the buildings until they had the house under cover. Aaron worked his way round the corner, and slid along the space between the two houses below the level of the window opening. Nimshi didn't envy him; a goat had been tethered in that alleyway and its droppings lay everywhere. Aaron flattened himself against the wall of the house, slowly eased his way to the door. He grasped the wooden latch, rifle held at his right side, hand through the trigger guard. He depressed the latch with his left hand, swung in a single jump through the door. As he rushed towards the house, Nimshi heard the shot. In the room he found Aaron laughing. A large mirror, with ornate gold wood framing, stood shattered in the corner of the room. "Their one prized possession," he said, "a looking glass. Imagine lugging that all the way from Damascus or Quneitra. I caught a flash as I bounced in, thought it was somebody about to jump me, and fired."

They came out of the house together, still laughing. Nimshi waved his men forward and explained the shot; big joke, lots of laughter. As they walked across to the last house, still laughing, the Arabs inside began to shoot. Nimshi fell first, Aaron across him, and the four others fell where they walked: Moses, wife and two children in the nursery; Benjamin, single; Yaariv—which means fight—wife, two children, mother and father, all living in Kibbutz Guvena; and Paula, aged twenty, a virgin.

Five Arabs rushed to the corpses. With one slash of his knife, one of them cut open Paula's clothing, then sliced off her breasts. Three went to the men, ripped open their trousers and cut off their genitals. The fifth had just mutilated Aaron, and was about to slash open Nimshi's clothing when Ya'akov's shot caught him in the forehead. A hail of fire followed. Three of the Arabs, who were only wounded, escaped round the back of the house with the shattered mirror.

"Surround the village," Abraham shouted. No one questioned his taking charge. Under cover of the unit Abraham

158

had left in the village entrance, he ran with Ya'akov and Hagar to the corpses. Hagar turned Paula's exposed body over, then walked to the Arab who had mutilated her. The shot had taken him in the chest, and he was bleeding profusely. He looked up as he saw her approach, his eyes pleading, blood in the corner of his mouth. She put the foresight of her rifle into his crotch and fired five bullets into his genitals.

Nimshi was not dead. Abraham dragged Aaron's body off him. "You're a very lucky man," he said.

Nimshi's eyes were open. "With luck like this, who needs misfortune?" he said, and fainted. Abraham beckoned to Hagar to look after him.

The three Arabs had gone to ground in a small stone quarry the other side of the village. They were surrounded. Abraham looked at his watch; half an hour had passed since the red tracer.

He selected six men to burn the village. They ran off, grim-faced but delighted. Then Abraham turned his attention to the quarry.

It was an impossible position to attack, with rocks at odd angles hiding a hundred caves. "Any idea where they are?" he asked Ya'akov.

"They're in there, and that's all I know, the dirty murdering swines, the syphilitic sons of prostitutes."

Abraham put his hand over Ya'akov's mouth. "They can't hear you, Ya'akov, and I can."

Ya'akov shouted into the night. "Your father was a donkey, your mother was a whore." There was only silence in reply. Clouds of oily smoke and roaring flames lit the scene as the fires took hold. The cooking oil burned fiercely once it had caught; heaps of ignited straw burned with pyrotechnic fury, sparks flying. The light from the burning village was cast into the quarry, but still no trace could be seen of the three Arabs. The moment of decision came; the flames would be seen from a long distance and the alerted Arabs would wait for the Jews to return. Abraham fitted a tracer bullet into the breech of his rifle, then pointing skyward he

159

pressed the trigger. A green light whipped from the barrel—
the command to withdraw, to return to Guvena. Even
Ya'akov obeyed. He and Abraham carried Nimshi between
them. Three times during the night, they had to dodge fire
from isolated Arab patrols. Apart from Aaron and the four
members of Nimshi's unit, one other kibbutznik, Elisheva,
died when she lost her footing in the hills of Mount Hebron.
They carried her back to the kibbutz for a decent Jewish
burial. The others they had left in the village, sparing relatives
the knowledge and sight of their mutilation.

The meeting that night discussed the raid. Most people
thought it a success, because its aim had been achieved. The
casualties were a shock, but they had seen a lot of death, and
they almost took pride in mourning. Nimshi looked very
dramatic on the platform, his bandage a laurel of honour.
"They died for all of us," he said, "they died for the kibbutz,
and their death will be a beacon!"

Abraham, reminded of Shlomo, muttered, "Sentimental
claptrap!"

Ya'akov heard him and grinned. "Nimshi's a good rabble
rouser," he said.

For the first time, Abraham felt doubt about the kibbutz
system, the spirit of collectivisation that was supposed to let
a man achieve his potential. Together they had achieved the
lowest common denominator, not the highest common factor.
The rabble rousers were taking over, while the voices of
reason were shouted down in endless rhetoric. Suddenly and
surprisingly, he found himself in sympathy with the orthodox
kibbutzniks, who wanted none of the militancy that flared
like a forest fire with every emotional appeal.

"Why wait for them to come and attack Guvena?" Dody
was saying. "We learned a lesson at Mokhra. Next time we
go in shooting, and if they won't leave, let them lie there
dead when we burn their houses!" Mokhra had given him
160

the taste of success. "Go out," he said, "and empty all the Arab villages within ten kilometres of the border. Teach them that for every raid they launch against us, ten villages will be destroyed, for every kibbutznik who lies dead, ten Arabs will be killed."

There was an immediate outburst from the more moderate people. Ya'akov got up to leave the meeting, but Abraham held his arm. "Stay, Ya'akov," he said, "we may need you later!"

When the vote was taken on a show of hands, twenty were in support of the motion. "They didn't stand a chance," Hagar said, "with that kind of militancy."

But Abraham's worry could not be assuaged. "There were *twenty* hands raised. Twenty people want to turn us into a band of murderers."

"Erect a barricade, and you'll always find the people to die on it; run wild and you'll find people to run with you," Hagar said. "The world has never been short of martyrs."

The meeting broke up in disorder at nine o'clock.

In Tel Aviv Abraham had found a sump on a broken down Citroen and a connecting rod with a big end that seemed serviceable; Ya'akov rushed from the meeting with Joel to work on the old lorry. Misha, Hagar and Abraham walked back to the house together. Miriam had not been at the meeting; she seemed to live in a quiet world of her own, apathetic to anything outside it. Hagar had tried to interest her in several things, but she wanted to sit in her house each evening, carrying on the sewing she worked at all day long, reading books from the kibbutz library. Once Hagar discovered her with a Russian book open on her lap. She knew that Miriam didn't understand a word of Russian. Ari explained that mental shock could take many forms. "The mind suppresses information," he said, "won't accept what it doesn't want to know." He was confident that in time Miriam would recover. When Hagar remembered Yigal had spoken Russian, she shivered with a nameless apprehension.

When they arrived at the houses, Misha opened his door. "If you're not going immediately to bed," he said, "I've

161

something to show you." They went into his house. He had made a drum like Gabriel's tambour of a hollowed section of a tree trunk, about forty centimetres in diameter, with a scraped and dried goatskin at each end. Leather thongs went from one skin to the other down channels carved along the drum barrel. By twisting the pegs set in each channel it was possible to tighten the drum skins to vary the sound. It was an ingenious arrangement. But Misha wanted them to see the sections between the channels, twelve of them, each about twelve centimetres wide and thirty long, where he had carved a bas-relief portrait of each member of Kibbutz Eli-Dov. Hagar squealed with pleasure when she found herself; Abraham and Sarah had a panel; Misha was with Ya'el and Abram—each individual or family had one to themselves. Around the top, just beneath the goatskin, were bas-reliefs of the buildings, the crops they had grown, the tractor, the lorry, even the well. It was a complete record of Kibbutz Eli-Dov, each face a remembered likeness of the original.

Coming after the meeting, the sight of the drum gave Abraham a heart-breaking nostalgia for everything Eli-Dov had meant, for all they had tried so hard to achieve. "It's wonderful, Misha," he said.

Hagar tapped one of the goatskins; it reverberated melodiously at her touch. She put her arm around Misha. "You are clever," she said, and then she kissed him on his forehead.

Misha looked delighted, his face glowing with pleasure. "I'll have to get you to pose for me sometime," he said.

She laughed. "I posed for a sculptor once, in Paris. I won't tell you what happened, but you could almost say it was directly responsible for my coming to Israel." Bad memories die swiftly, fade like night mist in the bright light of day. Misha would forget Ya'el and Abram, just as Hagar had forgotten her life in Paris, just as, in time, she would forget Dov.

When they came to Abraham's house he opened the door and took the protective shutter from the window. She came in and they sat on two chairs by the window space, staring

162

out over the terrain. The hills stretched away from them, rising higher as they approached the border. On them grew the stunted browned remains of oak trees, and young shooted, light green carobs, terebinth and laurels, with the silver-grey twisted olive trees, hundreds of years old. "Legend has it that when God created heaven and earth, he forgot to scatter stones. He tied two sacks containing stones of all sizes round the neck of an eagle, and told the eagle to fly over the earth, scattering the stones everywhere he flew. However, no sooner had the eagle started his flight than both the sacks split, and cast the stones in one single place," Abraham said.

"The northern tip of Eastern Galilee?"

"Right here!"

"Do you think they'll ever get a majority to favour these assaults on Arab villages?" she asked. She knew Abraham well; rarely would he introduce a subject uppermost in his mind.

"We can't be sure. Once these firebrands start, they light the whole place."

"But there are enough moderates; the orthodox have enough power to stop them. Remember *kashrut*?" Many of the kibbutzniks had wanted to end *kashrut*, the observance of orthodox dietary laws. They had wanted to start a piggery, to ignore the old Jewish law that said you shouldn't plant different seeds in the same field. Some wanted to work on *shabbat*, to keep the momentum of the kibbutz going. The output on the days following *shabbat* was higher than the rest of the week, and a move had therefore been started to have a shift system in which everyone worked four days, took a day off, worked four days again. This would have increased production, but the orthodox fought it, just as they fought the ending of *kashrut* and the piggeries and the mixed seeding. Chickens had replaced pigs, fields contained one type of seed only, and *kashrut* remained, with the orthodox eating at their own tables, saying prayers in their own way. And everyone stopped work on *shabbat*. "The orthodox must have won over quite a lot of people on *kashrut*; surely they can influence them again over something as fundamental as this?"

163

"It's not that that worries me," Abraham said. "It's the sight of those hands in the air; the thought that on this kibbutz there are so many people who want to go out and murder Arabs. And don't let's mince words; it is *murder*; an act of aggression that results in killing is *murder*."

The night air had turned chilly; a wind blowing across the high lands waved the tops of the trees. Now the view was dark and sombre, menacing. "Is it the view," she thought, "or the effect of what Abraham is saying?" She got up and went to sit on the bed. "It's draughty over there," she said. "Suddenly I feel quite cold." He closed the shutters and the door. There was no heating in the house, of course. He took the bedspread from the second bed and draped it round her shoulders.

"You'll feel warmer with that round you," he said. "I could go to the canteen and make you a mug of tea if you like." Though they all had the right to use the canteen whenever they wished, few ever did so.

"No," she said, "I'll be all right in a minute."

He put his hand on her neck, moved his fingers underneath her thick black hair, and started to rub. Her shoulders relaxed at his touch. "If you go on doing that, you'll have me purring like a cat!" He continued to rub, and though his skin was rough and abrasive, his touch was comforting.

"I wish I'd seen that sculpture of you," he said.

"You'd have liked it."

"I know I would. You must have been very young when it was made."

"I was fourteen, nearly fifteen." The bedspread had slipped from her shoulders. She unfastened a button on her shirt to allow his hand more freedom of movement. Now he could caress down to her shoulder blades. She hunched her shoulders against the movement of his hands, straining her neck against his strength. His hand moved along her shoulder, under her chin, along the fine bones of her neck, across her throat. The coarseness of his skin was exciting against her smoother skin, exciting and masculine. She un-

164

fastened another button on her shirt, and now his hand moved down and began to caress her breasts, though avoiding her nipples.

"You ought to be in bed," he said.

"I am in bed, almost." She got up, took off her shirt, boots, socks, trousers, and underwear, flipped back the bedspread, and snuggled between his blankets. "I don't sleep in sheets either," she said.

He was standing beside the bed, still dressed.

"Don't be a bastard," she said. "Come to bed."

He undressed slowly, then climbed into bed beside her. "You must understand . . ." he said, but she placed her hand over his lips. "No talk," she said, "no explanations, nothing. I'm here, you're here; neither one of us is a virgin, neither one of us is capable of seducing the other."

He lay beside her a long time, his right arm around her, his hand on her breast. Her hair, soft and long, fell over his shoulder; he could feel the firmness of her other breast pressed against him. Perhaps she went to sleep, perhaps he did; perhaps his consciousness fled the grim truth of the evening's meeting. When he returned to reality he was erect, and she was moist and open to his touch, his mouth was on her mouth, and they were touching along their entire length. She shuddered as he plunged into her, clasped her hands around his back and drew him to her. They made love slowly, as men and women do when not devoured by the hunger of youth. He kissed her, tasting her sweet breath in his mouth; she put her hands on his shoulders and pushed his face from her, her eyes locking his. Her mouth was open, the tip of her tongue protruding; and then, suddenly, her body became rigid, her hands clenched his shoulders as if she would tear away chunks of his flesh. She arched her back, all her muscles stiffened, her eyes opened wider, then suddenly she jerked in an uncontrollable spasm that repeated itself, and went on repeating itself, and gradually was still.

She lay beneath him, as he went into her to satisfy himself, loving him but observing him, serving him as he served himself in her, climbing with him to a height of sexual passion

165

she'd never before experienced, spiralling to a peak of exaltation over which suddenly, he broke. "Hagar," he said, "Hagar!" She brushed the sweat from his forehead and the tip of his nose with her hand. He collapsed on her, body to body, his hands entwined in her hair, his mouth open in the angle of her neck. They lay there together; the seed of his father, and of his father's father, entered into her, was fruitful, and fertilised her.

The following morning Abraham was in the bottom field stone-picking and wall-building with Ya'akov. Hagar was on kitchen duty; Misha was mending broken furniture, a job he'd been given more or less permanently because his mended furniture was often stronger than new. Abraham and Hagar sat together at breakfast as usual, and no one noticed their silence.

The day was already hot when he returned to the fields after breakfast. The wall they were building was thought unnecessary by most kibbutzniks, since its only function was to separate different types of planting. However, the orthodox people said it had to be there, and their commands prevailed. Within an hour, Abraham had stripped to the waist. Ya'akov moved about the field with his kibbutz-made wooden wheelbarrow, tirelessly carting stones and tipping them on to the ground near Abraham.

"Hot, eh?"

Abraham nodded.

"Hot enough to roast a bullock!"

"Get on with it," Abraham said, testily. Ya'akov put out his tongue and went back for more stones.

It was Ya'akov who saw Misha coming down the path, shouting and waving.

"You've got visitors!"

"Who on earth . . . ?"

Abraham was silent when he saw Ben and David from

Tel Aviv. Ya'akov greeted them like old friends, took them into the dining hall and got them food, orange juice, sour milk. Abraham sat at the table while they ate. Nimshi came in to talk to Ben of mutual acquaintances, then left. The dining hall was silent; knowing others were at work gave Abraham a feeling of truancy. Ben finished eating and lit a cigarette.

"You didn't come all this way just to taste our food," Abraham said. Ya'akov was surprised by his surly tone.

"We're trying to round up a few lost sheep! To get them back into the flock."

"*Lost* sheep?" Ya'akov said. "You mean black sheep!"

"Border incidents are increasing all the time and we need more trained men. The British continue to harass us, and we need help with armoury raids. We lost a number of men a month ago, raiding an armoury in Tel Aviv; those men have to be replaced."

"Count me out," Abraham said. "I'm not a raider."

"What about Mokhra? You were there. The way I hear it, you took over when Aaron was killed. Made a good job of it too."

"Anyone could have done that."

"Anyone could have, but you were the one they all looked to, and you're not a *vatikim*, an old-timer. You're new around here, and already you've got them looking to you for leadership. That's the spirit we need."

"I'll let you in on a military secret, Abraham," David said in his soft insidious voice. "The kids we've got in Haganah are very good fighters, but not leaders. They're fine in a group but we need men of authority. Somehow we don't seem to be getting them from the kibbutzim."

"I'm a kibbutznik and I always have been!" Abraham said.

"No, you're not, and neither is Ya'akov. You're rebels!"

Abraham was forced to smile. "You could be right," he said. "What do you want?"

Ben took out a notebook. "There's a course starting to-morrow at Kfar Vitkin. We'll take you as far as Nazareth;

you'll get transport from there."

"Leave today, just like that?" Ya'akov said, looking at Abraham. Abraham was thinking of two things: the attitude of the militant kibbutzniks, and his changed relationship with Hagar.

"All right," he said, "I'll come." The decision was valid for both of them.

Hagar had been listening from inside the kitchen. She came out after Abraham when the others left. "You can love a man for years and never know," she thought as she walked across the dining hall. "Then in one night you realise no feeling for any other person can compare!" She'd loved before—her sculptor, Dov, Ya'akov and Misha and Yigal in a certain way—but for none of them had she felt this intense insupportable pain of love.

"You're going away?"

"You were listening, you should know."

"Why? Because of what happened? It needn't happen again."

"It would. We couldn't help ourselves, but that's not the reason. They're going mad here, taking the offensive with raiding parties. They wouldn't need to raid if we were properly defended. I'm going to Haganah school so that I can come back and teach them to defend the kibbutz. Your idea of doubled sentries is only part of it. I'm going to learn the rest!"

"Look after yourself then," she said, and turned towards the kitchen. He watched her go. "I love Sarah," he said over and over again as he watched Hagar walk away from him.

Ya'akov was standing in the doorway, already packed, all his worldly possessions in a small canvas bag. He watched Abraham for a moment, quickly crossed the dining hall and took Hagar's arm.

"We shan't be gone long, Hagchen," he said; then looking at Abraham over her shoulder, he kissed her on the mouth.

Three days after Abraham and Ya'akov left for Kfar Vitkin, Dr Walters received information that sent him scurrying to Sarah's room. She was lying in bed, taking the afternoon rest he had ordered. He placed his hand on her throat, feeling for the curve of her breastbone. "In there," he said, "a small growth no larger than the head of a match; I never even suspected it." The next day they put Sarah under anaesthetic and operated. It took five minutes, and at the end of it he had removed the source of her trouble. "Now you can go home," he said.

Abraham's letter about Kfar Vitkin arrived the day after she left the hospital, but she was already on her way north in a lorry carrying seeds and saplings from the tree nursery near Tel Aviv. "Now you can go home," the doctor had said, but who knew where home was. Certainly it was not Eli-Dov, nor the several kibbutzim on which she had lived since her marriage to Abraham. It was not Amsterdam, from which her family had brought her, a terrified young girl, just after the turn of the century. Would it perhaps be in Kibbutz Guvena with its orthodox table and its synagogue? Would it be anywhere Abraham was? Abraham was looking for a dream no one had yet found; impatient of human frailty, he sought to eliminate human discord. She knew the religious life of the orthodox was far from perfect. There were petty squabbles among the believers just as there had always been discord in the House of God, for no man born of woman can hope to reach perfection. Her father in Amsterdam had been keen on music; had he not told her many times in her earliest childhood that without overtones even the strings of a Stradivarius violin would sound meagre? The resonance of its imperfections echoed melodious in the ear of man since music began. The Lord made good, but he made evil too; he made light and darkness together. "Shall the clay say to him that fashioneth it, what makest thou?" But how could she make Abraham accept that?

Misha met her when she arrived and told her of Abraham's departure. With her usual stoicism she said nothing; it was the will of God. He introduced her to Nimshi, to Rowena, and to Samuel, and took her to the shed where Joel was working on his Citroen. Joel walked with her round the kibbutz while Misha went back to work. He showed her the synagogue, the store houses, the living quarters, the nursery and the dining hall; and like Abraham, Sarah wondered at the far-sightedness of men who could plan so accurately, so far ahead. Sarah went to the clothing store and saw Miriam, but it wasn't clear that Miriam knew how much time had elapsed since last they met. She greeted Sarah as if they'd broken fast together that same morning, talking of the work to be done on the shirt she was sewing.

Sarah met Hagar in the dining hall. Hagar put down the dish she had been carrying, rushed to Sarah, and hugged her. "Sarah," she said, "Sarah! It *is* good to see you and looking so well."

She took Sarah to the house. All Abraham's linen and clothing had been handed in to the store, and the house was bare. Hagar drew bed linen for her, curtains, towels, clothing, brought a huge armful and set it in the room. She opened all the shutters wide and gathered some gladioli. Then they began to chatter. Sarah told Hagar about the hospital and her miracle cure; Hagar told Sarah about the kibbutz. "You've met Joel, of course. Isn't he marvellous; you'd never believe he was seventy-five. He was going to drive us all the way here. What a pity his truck broke down; but when you come to think of it, what a good thing it was. I get the feeling that even when the Citroen is running again he'll choose to stay. He seems happy working here."

So far, Hagar had not said a sentence that included the word Abraham. Sarah held her hand to make her stop bustling about the small room, pulled her on to the bed, and said, "Tell me about Abraham. Does *he* like it here? How did he get on with everybody?" But on that subject Hagar was strangely tongue-tied.

Later Misha told Sarah of Abraham's distress over the militants. Sarah's eyes shone and she thanked God for helping Abraham.

That evening, at supper, she sat with Joel, and her heart

was lifted when he said the prayers that meant so much to her. After supper, she had a long talk with the rabbi, listening to his deep resonant voice as he talked of their intention, of the Jewish law which had lain dormant for centuries and was now being revitalised here in the land of Israel in the hearts of its people. ". . . thine eyes shall see thy teachers; and thine ears shall hear a word behind thee saying, This is the way, walk ye in it . . ." That night, alone in the house in which Abraham had slept, looking over the Galilean hills where so much of the faith of Judaism had been nurtured, Sarah knew she was at home. Sorrow fell and peace reigned within her. She lay between the cool clean sheets, and the lights of the kibbutz went out one by one.

After three months at Kfar Vitkin, Abraham and Ya'akov were given a week's leave and transport, and ordered to return for the three-month advance course. During the time they'd been away, twenty-five new kibbutzniks joined Guvena, and Sarah took Hagar into her house. Sarah had written to Abraham every week on the eve of *shabbat*, long chatty letters filled with news. Sometimes the letters waited three weeks for a lorry, and some never arrived. The lorries that carried them were destroyed en route. The kibbutz had been attacked twice; on each occasion militants organised a counter-raid and destroyed a village. Once a herdsman had been killed by a Syrian sniper. The militants went out in broad daylight, killed three Syrian shepherds, and slaughtered their flocks, leaving the bones to be picked clean by vultures and jackals, a warning for all to see. Abraham and Ya'akov arrived in Kibbutz Guvena on a Monday morning after travelling all night in the Haganah motor car.

There were two pieces of information Sarah had not told Abraham: Misha had married Miriam in a joyous kibbutz wedding, and Hagar was pregnant. Sarah had taken her into her house as soon as Hagar had told her. She told Abraham

171

and Ya'akov the news together. She looked at Ya'akov as she spoke, for who else could have done this thing? Ya'akov looked down at the table, afraid his eyes might reveal his thoughts. Abraham put his hand on Ya'akov's arm. "Leave us," he asked. Ya'akov went.

"I made Hagar pregnant," Abraham said, "not Ya'akov."

Sarah looked at her husband, a self-confessed adulterer. "Do you love her?" she asked.

He shook his head. "I love you, Sarah," he said.

"You took me at my word, in the hospital. You needed someone. But why, Abraham, why did it have to be Hagar?"

Again he shook his head. "I'm no better than I should be," he said, "I did what I did and I'm sorry for what's happened."

"I can't forgive you," she said, weeping bitterly. "Why did it have to be Hagar? Did you hope to make her pregnant, is that it? Were you afraid that you'd never have a child with me? Was that it, Abraham?"

"I wish I could say it was." He couldn't give her the comfort of a lie. She would forgive him if she thought that he went with Hagar because of her own failure; but he knew that wasn't true, and he refused to hide behind falsehood, no matter how comforting it might be.

"Have you been sleeping together? With Hagar next door it must have been very easy."

"It only happened once, the night they held the meeting about raiding the Syrians. I was upset."

"You must have been, to sleep with someone young enough to be your daughter! Anyway, it's done now, and there's nothing can undo it, except the will of God, and He knows I've prayed enough for that this last few weeks. Oh, Abraham, why did it have to be Hagar? Anyway, she's going to stay here with me and you'd better move into Ya'akov's house. That's if the meeting will let you stay. There *was* some talk about asking Hagar to leave, but I talked to the rabbi, and he managed to persuade them."

"You told the whole kibbutz?" he asked, angry beyond measure.

"They would have found out sooner or later."

172

"Don't you think it was Hagar's place to tell them, or rather since I've admitted to being the father, don't you think it was mine?"

"Would you have done so, Abraham? Either of you?"

Would he have told the kibbutz? It was hard to say. She had probably made certain that Hagar could stay by telling. In the late months, when Hagar's belly could no longer be hidden, they would have known a secret had been kept from them, and they would have resented that. "No, perhaps I wouldn't have told them," he said, "and then there'd have been hell to pay."

He went to Ya'akov's house. "Kicked out, eh?" he said. "Well, it's only what you deserve!"

Abraham lay on the bed, cradling the back of his head in his hands, looking at the ceiling. How many years had he tried with Sarah to make a baby. How many? All that time feeling perhaps his seed was no good! He'd been faithful to Sarah, never so much as looked at another woman. But one night, with Hagar, and suddenly all Abraham's fears were banished. He turned on his bed, and looked at Ya'akov. "I'm a man, Ya'akov!"

"You're a fool; any lad of sixteen without hair on his lip can get a girl pregnant if he's a bloody fool about it."

Abraham shook his head. "You don't know what it feels like to realise you have strength to make a woman pregnant."

Ya'akov had never seen Abraham so self-satisfied. "Spare a thought for Hagar," he said, "you selfish sod! What do you think this has done to her, having to live here with the whole kibbutz knowing she's an adulteress, a fornicator. Isn't that what the Scripture calls it? Think what it's meant for her! And for Sarah, of course. Although Sarah didn't know until today you were the one responsible, she's had to stand by someone she loves—and she does love Hagar, more than you or I ever will—to help her face all that scorn and disapproval. Spare a thought for her, Abraham."

"Well, what do you think I'm doing?" Abraham said. "Hagar's gone off somewhere; you can't find her, so there's no real point in me looking, is there? I could go round making a show of looking, but you know me too well for that. I've told Sarah, I've accepted the blame with Sarah, with no attempt at concealment. Of course I'm sorry," he half shouted, "but at this identical moment there's nothing I can do about either Sarah or Hagar. Unless you'd like to see me on my knees in the synagogue? But in the meantime, I can indulge myself in the thought that for sixteen bloody years I believed I was sterile, and now suddenly I know I'm not. Don't you think it does something to a man to find out a thing like that?" He turned his head away, and looked again at the ceiling, determined not to lose his moment of triumph. It wouldn't be easy, dammit. He knew that trouble for all of them was only just starting. But if the kibbutz didn't accept what had happened, they could always make another life elsewhere. They'd done it before. They didn't have to live in Guvena. He swung his legs off the bed and sat facing Ya'akov. "Try to see things from my point of view, Ya'akov," he pleaded. "I'm not trying to evade responsibility. You know that's never been my way. But I refuse to gnash my teeth and wail. If Hagar had needed me, she'd have written to me; but she didn't. Sarah never mentioned it in a letter, Nimshi never mentioned it that time we saw him in Tel Aviv and spent a whole evening with him. When I see Hagar, obviously there'll be a lot to say, and I'll have to make arrangements for her. If she wants to leave Guvena, I shall leave too, and see her fixed up somewhere."

"That won't be necessary," Ya'akov said. "When *I* see Hagar, I'm going to ask her to marry me; I shall tell the kibbutz I am responsible; it'll be your word against mine."

"Are you trying to tell me you slept with Hagar? That the baby may be yours, not mine?"

"No," Ya'akov said, "I won't take that away from you. The baby's yours, you can be certain of that. Hagar's not promiscuous, and I know she's been in love with you for a long time. But I'll take responsibility for Hagar, starting off by marrying her if she'll have me."

"Do you love her?"

"What's that got to do with it?"

174

"Do you love her? Answer me, damn you!"

"Why? Would you be jealous? Look, old friend. Sarah's yours, not Hagar, and it doesn't matter to you what my feelings may be."

The klaxon sounded for dinner. "Give me a few moments with her, Ya'akov, before you ask her. Please?"

Ya'akov looked at him, trying to assess Abraham's motives. He could see the triumph in him, the new inner strength. If only Abraham could know; but Ya'akov would never tell him. He'd felt everything Abraham was now feeling the night Leiyla had told him she was expecting a child. Alexander had been a wonderful man, but what a dreamer of dreams. He hadn't realised a woman needs not only dreams, but the comfort of a man's arms about her, the closeness of his body. It had never occurred to Ya'akov or Abraham to question the sort of *man* Alexander was. Leiyla had lain in bed waiting, while Alexander talked the nights away with Abraham. The night Leiyla crept into Ya'akov's bed, Alexander had not even noticed she was missing. Ya'akov had mourned Eli because he was his only child.

"All right, Abraham," he said. "I have to go over to the office anyway. See Hagar first, but don't forget that when I see her, I shall ask her to marry me . . ."

Neither saw Hagar. She had left a note with Rowena, who had taken office from Nimshi. "Give that note to Sarah after supper tonight."

"Where will you go?" Rowena asked.

"Tel Aviv."

"It's probably best." Rowena reached into the drawer in her desk, and took out a small packet of money. "I must have made a mistake with the accounts when I was treasurer," she said. "I had this money over, and I've been ashamed of admitting it to the meeting." She gave the money to Hagar. "Take it, I can't bring myself to be strong, as you were, and admit my error."

While Ya'akov was away Joel had repaired the Citroen. When Hagar asked him, he got leave from the kibbutz to go to Tel Aviv and put his affairs in order. He had decided to end his days at Guvena. "Anyway, I'm the best laundry man they've ever had," he boasted to Hagar.

When Sarah got the note after supper tears sprang to her eyes. She showed it to the rabbi, who read it and gave it back without comment. Hagar was not of his flock. She took the note, and gave it to Abraham. "Go find her, Abraham," she said, "find her and ask her to come back. I can't bear to think of her on her own in the city carrying the burden of your child. Bring her back; tell her there's nothing to fear from me; tell her I'll look after her as if the child were my own."

"You're a good woman, Sarah," he said.

The following morning, Abraham ended his leave, and set off for Tel Aviv with Ya'akov.

They came down by the Sea of Galilee, the shorter route to Tel Aviv, to give themselves more time to search for Hagar if she had left Joel with no address. The chance was high that Joel would have arranged accommodation for her, since she had no friends in Tel Aviv. "I wouldn't be surprised," Ya'akov said, "if we find her at that hospital. If she is, it might be better for her to stay, and have the baby there." He had already assumed the proprietorial rights of an intending suitor.

They followed the track past Meiron and Safad, the Sea of Galilee to the left, the heights of Golan shining brown and pink through the afternoon sun. The track was made of stones and rock, stamped flat by centuries of feet. When they turned by Capernaum, the road ran almost at the edge of the lake. Ya'akov was driving as usual, taking every curve on two wheels, cursing the Haganah's Hillman when it would not accelerate fast enough up the hills. He leaned forward on his seat glaring at the road beyond them. Occasionally they met a goat, or a sheep. "Get off the bloody road," Ya'akov shouted as if it could understand. The horn worked

176

only intermittently, and he pounded the button to try to make it sound.

Shortly after they turned along the lake, they passed Tabgha, the Mount of the Beatitudes behind it, trees growing on its fertile slope. Here the rocks pressed down upon the road. The car was going well. "At this rate," he said, "and with luck, we'll make Tel Aviv tonight." Luck deserted them at that moment. They were passing a steep cleft of rock on the right and the ruins of a second-century synagogue on the left, when suddenly from the ruins, a shot came straight through the front wing. Ya'akov braked hard and turned the car into the rock. Abraham grabbed the two rifles between the seat, flung the door open and leaped sideways. Ya'akov did the same, and they rolled to the rocky edge of the road. Abraham gave Ya'akov a rifle, and they started to crawl forward. Bullets whanged into the rockface behind them, ricocheting back fragments of stone. "Move away fast," Abraham said, "or they'll cut us off." They stumbled southwards half bent over, behind the boulders at the side of the road. Where the boulders ended, the rock jutted out into a promontory. They broke cover to round it, one at a time, Ya'akov first. Rifles crackled as he went; Abraham counted at least six. Ya'akov made it unhurt; then Abraham followed, screwing his courage, legs pumping, arms held across him to minimise the target, body bent. The marauders sighted on him. One shot plucked his shirt, burned his waist, one seared past his cheek; one banged into the rock beside him and showered him with stone fragments. But then he was round the promontory.

"Silly sods," Ya'akov said with contempt, "they ought to have put a man here and at the other end of the rock. Then they would have had us whichever way we'd gone."

"They haven't taken the course," Abraham said. They were sitting immobile behind a boulder. "What about the car?"

"Belting it into the rock shouldn't have harmed it too much. Might have banged a bumper, but what the hell . . ."

"Any chance they'll steal it?"

"Only if they know about jumping wires," Ya'akov said,

as he held up the keys he'd snatched from the dashboard. "What do you think? Draw them off?"

"We could do," Ya'akov said. He took two matches from his pocket, broke a piece off the end of one, turned round, and arranged them between his fingers so that only the heads showed. "Short one goes?" Abraham nodded, touched the match on the right. It was the long match. "Right, I'll circle round, come in from the north," Ya'akov said.

"I'd better *die*, I suppose," Abraham said.

He took a rock, and threw it across the top of one of the boulders. There was the sound of rifle fire as several shots were aimed at the stone. Abraham let out a blood-curdling scream and a shouted gasp, enough to convince any marauder of the accuracy of his marksmanship. He settled himself into a crevice between two rocks, and nodded to Ya'akov, who made his way noisily up the hill. There was a salvo across the road, and Ya'akov fired back, his position obvious. He moved and fired again, moved and fired again. "One dead, one taking to the hills," they'd be saying. They came out of concealment. "Amateurs," he thought. All of them had grouped inside the ruins. With no men outside they wouldn't have stood a chance against a larger attack. They crossed the road in a bunch, safe from Ya'akov behind the promontory; Abraham let them come. "Oh for a grenade." One went around the promontory point and another followed. Abraham saw them crouch behind a rock. Ya'akov must have seen them too; he fired a shot that sent them skittering to ground. One man fired in his direction, and Abraham heard Ya'akov howl like an operatic star. "Don't overdo it," Abraham muttered. Then Ya'akov ceased firing. Now the marauders thought they had him, and assembled behind the rocks with little caution. They were seven tall swarthy Syrians, different in type from the Jordanians in the Negev. They gesticulated at each other as they argued in an Arabic dialect Abraham could not understand. Thank God they didn't bother to find out if he was dead. One of them seemed to be urging the rest up the hill; the dissenters wanted to take the car and go. Ya'akov must have been reading their

178

minds for at that moment he fired another shot, as if to reassure them he was still alive. They started up the hill.

Abraham waited until they were equidistant from Ya'akov and himself, took careful aim, and started shooting. It was like being on the target range with the order ten rounds rapid fire. First shot first Arab, second shot second Arab, third shot, pulled a bit and missed, aim and fire again, fourth shot, third Arab. By that time, Ya'akov was also shooting, and the Arabs, caught in the open, were trying to find cover. It took three minutes altogether; then Ya'akov came plunging down the slope. He, of course, took care to check each Arab; all were dead. "You did well," he said to Abraham, "shooting uphill!"

"You didn't do badly, downhill." Together they walked on to the road, back up to the car. Drawing fire is a game two can play. The Arab commander had stayed inside the ruins; his first shot hit Abraham high on the left arm. Ya'akov bellowed from anger and self-disgust at being so easily tricked. Abraham felt himself falling through a red mist of pain. He clasped his hand to his left arm, blood pouring from the torn flesh. Then the ground rose to meet him. Ya'akov bellowed and drove straight forward. The movement upset the Arab who thought he would run for the rocks and had lifted his rifle ready. Ya'akov barrelled round one of the columns. The Arab was big, much bigger than any of his compatriots, and strong. When he saw Ya'akov he yelled *andak*, the acceptance of a challenge. Ya'akov carried his rifle with the barrel pointing upwards in order to get round the pillar more quickly. The Arab was incredibly swift for a big man. He darted forward seized the end of the barrel behind the foresight, pulled it down and to the side. Ya'akov felt himself go forward. The Arab jerked his right hand; the bony heel took Ya'akov on his chin; fingers scrabbled for his eyes. Ya'akov slammed the butt of the rifle against the Arab's hand. He felt the shock as it smashed against the pillar, and the Arab roared with pain. "Knee," Ya'akov thought, "his knee will be coming up." He turned violently to his side, just in time to avoid it. Ya'akov drove his right

179

hand against the Arab's windpipe; the Arab grunted and banged his forehead into Ya'akov's face. Ya'akov felt himself falling backwards. He relaxed his weight and dropped to the ground; the Arab fell on him, rolled to the side. Ya'akov wound his fingers into the Arab's greasy hair and smashed his face on to the mosaic paving. The Arab reached behind him and grasped at Ya'akov's trousers, trying to find his genitals, but Ya'akov moved quickly out of range.

They were both gasping, seeking to restore energy with deep lungfuls of breath. The Arab was heavier than Ya'akov and faster, but Ya'akov was more skilful, more aware of what his opponent was doing. The Arab lifted his head from the floor, a short curved-bladed knife in his hand. Ya'akov grasped the Arab's wrist with one hand. The Arab leered at him through blood-filled eyes. Slowly he bent his arm from the floor. Ya'akov tried to keep the hand down, but he didn't have leverage or strength in that position. He bent his knees, then reached up suddenly and kicked the Arab under the chin. The Arab shook his head, a bull of a man. His other hand came round in an unaimed self-defensive swing that took Ya'akov at the side of the head and made his ear ring. Still the Arab held the knife, his hand rising from the floor; Ya'akov could not hold it down. The Arab started another roundhouse swing. Ya'akov knew that if the blow connected with the side of his head he would not be able to retain consciousness. He saw Abraham crawling through the doorway, flat on the floor, his rifle in his good right hand. He was pushing the rifle in front of him, holding the trigger guard, shaking his head to fight the waves of unconsciousness. Ya'akov raised his hand and blocked the roundhouse punch on his forearm. The shock of the blow made him shudder, but he held his hand steady, reached for the Arab's thumb, and with a quick twisting snap bent it backwards and broke it. The Arab screamed with pain, and he jerked the hand with the knife in pain and anger. Ya'akov then used two hands, not fearing another roundhouse blow, and pressed the hand which gripped the knife down on to the floor. Cunning grows of desperation. The Arab suddenly relaxed his hand as it

180

neared the floor and Ya'akov was thrown off balance. The Arab jerked his hand to the side and Ya'akov lost it. The knife swung under his hands, under his arms, his rib cage, into his chest. Ya'akov went over backwards. Abraham, lying flat on the ground, looking along his rifle, pulled the trigger. The bullet went into the Arab's throat and came out of the back of his neck, shattering his spinal column. Abraham crawled to Ya'akov and tried to lift him forward, but couldn't. The knife was still in Ya'akov's stomach, blood gushing from the wound. Ya'akov clasped his hands round the wound, pinching its edges together. "Don't go, Abraham," he said, "don't go!"

Ya'akov sank back, his shoulders resting on the dead Arab's chest. Pain arched his spine. Abraham shook aside the mists of unconsciousness. "Ya'akov," he said, the word an effort. Ya'akov looked at him, half turning his head. The pain of the knife in his stomach rocked him again.

"Find . . . Hagar," he said, "don't leave her alone in Tel Aviv." Abraham shook his head. Ya'akov was dying rapidly, his face turning paler as blood drained from him. His eyes were sunken into his head, his cheeks hollow. "Call . . . the . . . baby . . . Eli . . . for . . . me . . ." The words took the last of his breath; so faint was his voice that Abraham did not hear him. Ya'akov slid slowly sideways over the chest of the Arab, then died with his head on the mosaic floor of the synagogue.

There was no sound; a fly came buzzing to where they lay, two corpses, and a man near to death from loss of blood. Abraham would have died had he stayed in his stupor. The fly buzzed across his face, irritating his cheek. It settled on his eyelid and he raised his good hand to brush it away. The movement sent a flicker of energy through him. Slowly, a centimetre at a time, he dragged himself from the ruins of the synagogue and over the road. It took him ten minutes to cross the five metres to the car. He groped for his bag. Inside it was his medical kit. He fumbled a bandage from it, then wound the bandage loosely round his arm over and over again, constantly fighting the desire to lie down and rest. Under the seat was a small bar of iron with a key on the end

181

for extracting spark plugs. He inserted the bar into the loose bandage and turned it so he had a twist of bandage caught on the bar. He turned and turned again until the bandage was tight on his arm above the wound. Within minutes the blood stopped flowing, stemmed by the tourniquet. In his bag were food supplies he had brought from the kibbutz; his water bottle had been filled with orange juice, which he drank. Ya'akov's bottle contained sour milk; he lifted the bottle from the satchel and tipped the contents slowly down his throat. The sour milk overflowed his mouth and ran down his shirt but his sole intention was to drink as much of it as possible. He sat by the car waiting for the food to give him a vital spark of energy. Slowly he felt power returning to his limbs; after twenty minutes of inactivity he could lift his arm. Ten minutes later he was able to stagger to his feet. It took him another twenty to get back into the synagogue, lurching forward, resting, lurching forward again, resting again. Abraham wound the Arab's belt round Ya'akov's chest and under his arms. He gripped it with his good hand and leaned backwards against the weight. Little by little he dragged Ya'akov from the synagogue over the road. Getting him into the car was a nightmare but Abraham was determined not to leave him. Eventually he pushed Ya'akov into the passenger seat; when he walked around the car he saw Ya'akov's nose, like that of a little boy, pressed against the window, flattened into a snout. When at last he sat in the driving seat he rearranged the body so the top of Ya'akov's head, not his face, was touching the windscreen. He turned the key. The motor fired first time. He let in the clutch and used his good hand to push the gear lever into the reverse slot; then he slowly worked the accelerator pedal and the clutch, steering with one good hand, and backed out of the boulders. Once on the road he put the car into gear and drove eight kilometres into Tiberias.

They put him into a bed in the dispensary of the agricultural settlement. They buried Ya'akov in Tiberias cemetery beneath a headstone of black basalt, in the birthplace of the Palestinian Talmud, described by rabbis as 'a sea of knowledge in which a student could swim all the days of his life without ever reaching the other shore'.

Abraham discharged himself from the dispensary, and with his arm in a sling, he went into Tel Aviv to search for Hagar. The Arab's bullet had missed an artery by a millimetre; but a large chunk of muscle had been shot away, and the doctor said he wouldn't be able to use his left arm or hand effectively for six months. They had predicted that he wouldn't be able to leave his bed for a month because of the blood he'd lost, and he had proved them wrong.

He found Hagar easily. The man who'd taken Joel's property, a maker of religious trivia in brass, remembered that Joel and a young lady were going to a hospital in Bat Yam. Abraham rode out to the hospital on one of the lorries that served the area as a municipal bus. They brought Hagar from the ward where she was working. Her once shining hair was lank, her complexion had the sallow city look, her eyes sunken. Nor did she brighten when she saw him. "I ought not to have told them where I was going," she said listlessly, "but I couldn't be bothered hiding. I knew you or Ya'akov would find me!"

"Ya'akov's dead, Hagar," he said, without preliminaries.

She looked at him uncomprehending at first; then the flood of tears started. He put his arm round her shoulders, doing nothing to stop the tears. An orderly walked by them, his face impassive. Tears and death were no strangers to him.

Abraham told her what had happened, though he didn't say they had chosen the Capernaum road in order to find her more quickly: it's not good to know a man has died for you. It's good to know a man cares sufficiently to abandon personal caution; that thought would buttress Abraham during the bitter times to come when he would remember Ya'akov had died from carelessness.

Hagar stopped weeping while they talked of Ya'akov. She dried her face on the hospital pinafore.

"You could have written to me," Abraham said. "I could have helped you if only I'd known."

"How? By writing consoling letters? Leaving the course to come to Guvena? I didn't need help; I wanted someone to talk to in a way you wouldn't understand. If only Miriam hadn't, well, you know, gone a bit funny, I could have talked with her. I'd rather have talked with her than with Sarah, but I had no option, in the circumstances."

"I wish you'd talked to me. What are we going to do now?"

"They say I can have the baby here. There's a nursery where the baby can stay after it's born; I can take a job after the confinement. I'll be all right. They pay me wages, but I don't spend them; they provide a room, and my food, and my uniform. I go for a walk in the town sometimes, down the Dizengoff. I go into Old Jaffa, down to the docks to watch the fishing boats leave in the evening. I always liked the sea. I look across the sea and think 'so many lands, so many miles away', and my problems don't seem so pressing. Not that I have any problems."

He held up her hand. She was wearing a wedding ring. "I tell them my husband was killed in a raid on the kibbutz; everyone believes me. The hospital authorities know, of course, but everyone else is sorry for me; they think I'm some kind of a heroine!" she said with a semi-hysterical laugh.

"Before Ya'akov died, he gave me an instruction. 'Find Hagar', he told me, 'and take her back to Guvena'."

She shook her head instantly. "I'll never go back!"

"Why not?"

"A million reasons!"

"The first two are probably the only important ones!"

"Sarah!"

"'Tell Hagar I'll look after her, as if the child were my own'; that's what Sarah said."

"The orthodox?"

"Do you really care what they think? These aren't the
184

important things, Hagar. We both have to face up to the fact that you're going to have a baby."

"Dammit, I can't escape the fact, Abraham."

"We shan't be hurting Sarah if you come back to Guvena. She told me quite specifically, 'bring her back'. She'll be more worried if she thinks of you bringing the baby into the world without friends to help you. Much as she likes Guvena, if you stay here, Sarah will move from the kibbutz to live near you. Sarah truly cares for you, Hagar, as if you were a younger sister. Most important of all, there's the child. Is this the place to bring up a child? These places are built for moles who scurry from tunnel to tunnel, Hagar, not for human beings who work with their hands, who create and build. Tel Aviv is a town of whores, commercial whores, administrative whores, even old-fashioned sexual whores."

"What kind of whore am I, Abraham?"

He shook her shoulder gently. "Not any kind! You feel sorry for yourself. I understand. You didn't want to face me! I understand that. You didn't want to be there when Ya'akov learned you were pregnant, because you knew, as I know now, that Ya'akov had strong feelings for you. Come back to Guvena, Hagar. Ya'akov, and everyone like him, is still alive in Guvena!"

They went together to see Ben and David, who had recently returned from another recruiting tour. They gave Abraham three weeks leave and told him to report to Kfar Vitkin as an instructor. "You won't be the only one-armed instructor down there," Ben said.

"Do you think I might, er, borrow the Hillman again?"

Ben looked at David frowning. "For three weeks? This isn't a hire car service, you know."

"If Abraham had the Hillman in Northern Galilee, he could save us a lot of travelling," David said. "He could do some journeys for us in his spare time!"

"Spare time? You've obviously never lived on a kibbutz!"

"I'm afraid not," David said, "I've been too busy defending 'em in Haganah."

185

He promised to undertake some trips; they promised him the Hillman for three weeks.

The tour of the Galilee was a great success; Abraham's personal interest in kibbutz life rapidly established him with the local units, whereas David's obliqueness, Ben's down-to-earth and often tactless bluntness, and the thought they were representatives of a needless bureaucracy had tended to alienate the fiercely independent kibbutzniks. Abraham talked their language, came from their own background, and they were quick to recognise his qualities. When he completed the tour and reported back to Tel Aviv before going to Kfar Vitkin, the American asked him to undertake similar duties in other parts of the country, co-ordinating the defences of kibbutzim, *moshavim*, and agricultural settlements. "You're a great success, Abraham," the American said. "You should have been doing this years ago, instead of frigging about down in the Negev!"

Abraham's smile was sour.

Hagar was instantly accepted back by Guvena. That she had returned from Tel Aviv seemed somehow to have purged her of sin. She moved into the house with Sarah, and was tolerated by the orthodox. Gabriel became her champion with the non-orthodox kibbutzniks, Joel spoke out for her, and soon her unmarried state was ignored.

When the baby came Abraham was touring the area south of the Judea, on the edges of the Desert of Zin; when he returned to Guvena, the baby was six weeks old, and already named Ishmael. Sarah brought the baby from the nursery after supper. Abraham was ill at ease with the child. When he had been there half an hour, Hagar arrived and put out her finger for the baby to suck. Sarah clucked at the lack of hygiene but Hagar ignored her. She was looking at Abraham. "What do you think?" her eyes seemed to say.

Abraham looked down. "He's a very healthy boy," he said;

186

"you must be very proud!"

"And what about you," Sarah asked, indignantly, "aren't you proud to have made such a baby?"

He put his hand on Hagar's arm. "I'm very proud," he said. After the hour new parents were permitted to spend with children, Sarah took the baby back to the nursery, and Abraham and Hagar were left alone together. "I was sorry not to be here, but there was an attack on a *moshav* while I was there, and I had to stay to reorganise the defensive system."

"I understand," she said. "Gabriel visited me, and Joel, and Misha and Miriam. And Sarah never left me all the time I was in labour. She's been wonderful. You'd have thought it was she having the baby, the way she suffered."

"She's a good woman."

"Ishmael's a good baby. I dried up, I'm afraid. Ari said it was nerves. Luckily there were plenty of other babies about at that time, so he didn't go short."

A baby is usually the third side of a triangle, three people united each by his relationship with the other two; but Ishmael was the point of a wedge that would be driven between her and Abraham. Sarah would be a problem. Since the baby was born she had been obsessed, treating Ishmael as if he were her own. Abraham was her husband, Ishmael his child and therefore a triangle that should have included Hagar included Sarah instead. Sarah would take over the child in time, Hagar knew; she had the fierce possessiveness of a barren woman, and since her own husband was the child's father, it would never occur to her that she was not its parent. Hagar accepted the kibbutz principle that a child belongs to the community; even if she'd wanted to lavish mother-love on it, some other woman, impersonally selected by rota system, would hold the child in her arms to still its crying. It was accepted that although men and women may create children together, the family was no longer dominant. Children were raised without regard for the economic or emotional claims of their parents; all kibbutz children had the same resources, the same dependencies.

187

But what of love? What of the desire to raise children together, to build a life with family all about? Hagar knew she had forfeited those possibilities by taking the seed of a man committed to someone else, and by surrendering her child to the collective upbringing of the kibbutz. Her mind could understand this, but her heart and her breasts longed for the intimate clasp of her own baby.

"He'll be a good kibbutznik," she said, hiding her tears from Abraham.

"A sabra!" Abraham said as he put his arm about her shoulders.

When Britain declared war on Germany Abraham left for Tel Aviv to join the British army. "After all," Ben said, "what better training can you have to fight a war?" Abraham embarked on the first ship out and joined the Royal West Kent Regiment as a private soldier. When they discovered he could shoot a gun he was promoted to the rank of sergeant. He trained with the army and fought in North Africa, Greece and Italy. In 1944, Winston Churchill authorised the formation of a Jewish brigade; surprisingly, Abraham joined it and went into Europe. As he landed on the beaches of France, he thought of Ya'akov and the Nazis of Zillertal. The journey through France and Belgium, Holland and Germany, became a crusade of revenge for Ya'akov's father. Then he saw Dachau, Buchenwald, and Auschwitz, and realised for the first time the true bestiality of the Nazi ethos. "Could any other creed have done this?" he asked himself, and the voice of his conscience answered, "Remember Mokhra, and the Syrian Arabs."

His number was high on the list for demobilisation; he went to Clapham south of London, turned in his khaki, and received a large brown suit, a suitcase, and the trappings of civilian life. His back pay, gratuity, and savings totalled over two thousand English pounds. On his way from the demobilisation centre, he stopped at a pub to celebrate his return to freedom, ordered a half a pint of beer, and stood at the bar. The man standing next to him had a suitcase by his feet, a glass in his hand.

"Just out?" the man asked.

"Yes!"

"Here's to civvie street," the man said. "What mob was you with, what regiment? Hey, maybe you was an officer, though you look a bit like a sergeant major. Just think, at last, Private Hotchkiss at your service, but I can stand next to a sergeant major without fear and trembling. Was you an officer, sir?"

"I've forgotten," Abraham said.

"I'll bet you was an officer, you bleeding yid," the man said. Abraham put down his glass and left the pub.

He caught the next boat home: ex-Major Abraham Chaldean, M.C., of the Jewish Brigade, four times wounded. He'd won his M.C. and his fourth wound when he led a detachment into the headquarters of the Zillertaler Nazi Party, which a group of Jugendherberge fanatics held with their last machine-guns and anti-tank panzerfausts. *"Nicht schiessen,"* they pleaded when they finally left the headquarters. But Major Chaldean, avenging savage that he had become, remembered Ya'akov's father and squeezed the trigger as he had been taught all those years ago at Kfar Elihu in distant Samaria.

Seven of them rode the lorry from Haifa to Guvena. Moshe had lost a leg, Solomon an arm; Misha had been blinded when he trod on a land mine near Brussels. Daniel and Samuel had spent the war in liaison jobs around London. With Abraham, they helped the others down from the lorry outside the kibbutz entrance. The kibbutzniks had arranged a triumphal ceremonial homecoming. A band of flutes, goat-skin drums, harmonicas, a piccolo, and a bugle, was waiting.

189

Chaim, the current secretary of the newly formed secretariat, fussed over the returning soldiers and arranged them in a line. Abraham described the scene for Misha. When the music started, they marched together through the entrance arch decorated with gladioli and petunias. Abraham stared in amazement; there must have been 250 kibbutzniks to greet them. The houses along the edges of the Star of David had increased in height to two, or even three, stories. The nursery building had been enlarged, and in the centre of the kibbutz were a bandstand, a fountain, and a swimming pool. Trees and shrubs had sprouted everywhere, masking the hard lines of the buildings with a profusion of foliage and flowers. The kibbutz looked as if it had been waiting for their return since Biblical times, a green and hallowed home. They marched round the triangle of grass, and on to the bandstand. The crowd pressed in about the base of the stand while the heroes sat. Abraham was describing the changes to Misha when he saw Miriam in the crowd below. She was standing quite still, looking up at Misha. Abraham waved, and she waved back, but she remained where she was. So long, so far . . . she could wait a few more minutes.

Chaim stood at the front of the bandstand and waved his arms for silence.

"Our men are back," he said, "and there are some who will never return but will lie forever in foreign soil. We praise God for bringing our men safely back to us; we recognise His wisdom in taking those who will never return. We thank our men who left the comfort of their homes to seek the foul enemy and destroy him in his lair; on behalf of the millions of our blood who have perished we bless God for our men who did not sleep while still the tyrant roared."

"Gabby bastard," Misha whispered to Abraham, "when's he going to shut up?"

The flight of rhetoric—what Ya'akov would have called rabble rousing—lasted another five minutes. When it ended, the invisible barriers broke and the crowd washed forward, claiming its own. Blind Misha held out his arms to the vast unknown; Miriam came into them, touching his face with
190

familiar hands. Letters had prepared them; hers had warmed with love and eagerness for his return.

Sarah stood below the bandstand beneath Abraham; he was looking for her in the distant crowd when she tugged the legs of his trousers. There was not sufficient room to leap from the bandstand. He crouched, grasped her in his hands, and kissed her where she stood; if ever she had doubted they were one entity, one being, one life, the kiss would have melted the doubts like frost in the morning sun. He put his hands under her arms and lifted her beside him.

"It's been a long time!"

"You've been a long way," she replied, looking into his face. "You're all right. There's nothing you haven't told me about?"

"I hurt my big toe in Tripoli . . ."

"Seriously . . ."

"No, daft one," he said, ruffling her hair, "it's only a joke!"

"You've been to so many places, seen so many people."

"None like you, my old girl . . ."

The crowd started to withdraw, and he was able to climb from the bandstand. He held his arms and she jumped into them. "Let's get away from here," he said.

"There's a meal planned, and a celebration in the dining hall."

"Oh God," he groaned, but for once she didn't mind his blasphemy, "the last thing I want is a meal and a celebration!"

"Aren't you glad to be back?" she said, her eyes sparkling.

"I'm glad to be where you are and that's the total of it for the moment," he said. They had walked across the lawn towards the synagogue.

"You don't want to go inside?" He shook his head. "You will one day," she said as they turned on to the path to their house.

Inside he took off his canvas pack and the jacket of his demob suit.

"I've never seen you in a suit before."

191

"There's a present for you, in my haversack."

"Can I look at it now?"

"No, certainly not!"

"When can I?"

"Later!"

"Afterwards?" she asked.

"Afterwards," he promised.

Six years of separation slipped from them, a catalogue of places and events that no longer existed except in memory; there were new sights to see, old wounds to touch that would not be reopened; there were places to name, and names to list, and the warp of separate existences to stitch with intimate words.

"I was so worried when you were in Africa and I didn't hear from you for three months; but then I got seven letters all at once."

"Misha was a mess when I picked him up; I never thought he'd live."

"A thousand kilos a week, isn't that marvellous?"

"We had a wonderful leave that time. Fancy me, in Cairo . . ."

"There's more Yiddish than Hebrew spoken in the dining hall now."

"Moshe ought never to have lost that leg; if he'd stuck to the road in Holland, the way I told him . . ."

"And then, when the sentries came back, there was Hagar . . ."

"Hagar!" he said, "Hagar, where on earth is Hagar?"

"I thought you were never going to ask," she said. He flung back the blankets and leaped out of bed. "She's on sentry duty in the new tower we've built. She volunteered."

"Where's Ishmael?"

"In the nursery."

"How is she? How is he?"

"They're both very well . . ."

"That's not what I mean. Dammit, he's six now. What's he like? What's he like?"

"You get dressed," she said, "and go up and say hello to

Hagar. It'll be supper time soon . . ."

"Supper time! Where's the afternoon gone?"

"You had a sleep," she said, "afterwards! Get dressed, and go and see Hagar. I know she'd like that!"

Hagar was standing guard in a round tower they had constructed in the hills north of the kibbutz. Its entrance was completely hidden in a fold of the ground. The new Hagar, at thirty-three, was elegant and poised, burned brown by the sun of the Galilee, her skin smooth as dusted silk. "Hello, Abraham," she said, and kissed him on the mouth.

"I've brought you a present," he said to hide his embarrassment. Inside a box was a heavy gold chain and a gold nameplate, thick and solid. The name-plate was engraved with the word HAGAR. On the back, in small fine script was the message 'from Abraham'. "Whatever happens, you'll never be short of money," he said. "It's made of gold, and it'll fetch a price anywhere any time you want to sell it." He clasped it round her wrist and fastened it.

"My, you have changed," she said.

They were two old friends meeting after a long interval. There was no memory of intimacy between them; the feelings they had shared one night of their lives could never return.

Abraham met Ishmael after supper. He was a sturdy boy of six and a half, already articulate. "We've all agreed," Sarah said to Abraham during supper, "that we shan't burden Ishmael by telling him you're his father. He knows Hagar is his mother, but that's all he needs to know at the moment. Perhaps we'll tell him when he's old enough to understand, but until then you'll just be Abraham to him." Ishmael spent most of his two hours in the house with Sarah.

Hagar sat in an easy chair each member of the kibbutz now had. "We made a profit two years ago, and we've made a profit ever since, even with the capital expenditure on new buildings!" Hagar had been elected area agent of the workers' union, the Histadrut, and spent much of her time on the *moshavim* and agricultural settlements in this part of the Galilee. Abraham had noticed many new settlements as

193

they came from Haifa. "We managed to bring in a large number of illegals every month, despite the British and their infernal quota," Hagar said.

With the increased population, the kibbutz now had three times as much land under cultivation, and there was talk of draining the swamp of the Hulah Valley below. "We've had water experts and geologists studying the problem," Hagar said. "Apparently, at some time in the past, a volcanic thrust pushed basalt rock into the outflow of the Jordan like a cork. If they can shift that rock, the whole valley will drain itself quite naturally. They have plans for a pilot scheme if we can acquire the land. But, of course, that's the problem."

"Go to your mother," Sarah said, pushing Ishmael from her. Ishmael stood silent by Hagar's knee.

"Hello, little one," she said. She ruffled his hair while she continued to talk to Abraham. Abraham drew the boy towards him.

"I've brought a couple of toys for the nursery," he said. "Maybe you'd like to play with them." He opened his satchel and took out a jigsaw puzzle and a box of water colour paints. "There weren't many toys in England," he said to Sarah, seeing the look on her face.

"That's not the problem," she said. "You ought to have handed those in to the nursery. You don't want to provoke feelings of ownership, do you?"

"Oh, let him play with them."

Sarah took the puzzle and the paint box and put them away. "In the nursery!" she said. "Anyway, it's time he was getting back."

"Can I carry them?" Ishmael asked.

"No, I'll carry them," she said.

"Can I play with them in the nursery?"

"I suppose you can; why not, when it comes to your turn."

"She takes very good care of him," Hagar said, as Sarah led Ishmael out through the door.

*   *   *

Abraham slipped easily back into kibbutz routine. There were differences, of course, most of them having to do with size. With over 250 people, administration had become a problem, and a secretariat of seven dealt with the day-to-day routine. Being secretary of the secretariat was a full-time job for six months. Each floor of each arm of the kibbutz Star of David elected a representative to the monthly meetings; the 'committee' had twenty-four members. Hagar was the representative for their arm for six months; then the arm would elect someone else. These elections were staggered so that only four members were changed each month and there was never any break in continuity.

In January 1947 the British announced they were handing the Palestine problem over to the United Nations, and that they would take no part in implementing its decisions unless they were equally acceptable to both Jews and Arabs.

Also in January 1947 Sarah, now forty-six years of age, informed Abraham that she was pregnant. "Thanks to Doctor Walters in Tel Aviv," she said, but Abraham laughed and pretended to be insulted. At least she had not said it was God's will.

In August 1947 the United Nations Commission reported the conclusion of a summer of deliberation. British rule, it declared unanimously, must be terminated as soon as possible, and the land of Palestine divided between Arabs and Jews by partition.

On 21 August 1947, in the hospital at Kibbutz Guvena in the Galilee, a son was born to Sarah, wife of Abraham. The boy was named Isaac. He was strong as his father, as healthy as his mother; he had his father's black hair, and his mother's soulful eyes, though he was born, as all babies are, with the complexion of a pink walnut.

Sarah was sitting up in bed when Abraham came to see her. She couldn't restrain her pride. "Fancy me, at forty-six, producing a baby for you," she said.

"What does age matter?" he asked. "This is only the start; we'll have one a year from now on." Ari joined them as he

195

came by on ward rounds. When Sarah saw him her face was solemn.

"I'm afraid not, Abraham," she said. "Ari says this one is the first and the last."

Ari put his hand on Abraham's arm. "You're a very lucky man," he said. "It wasn't an easy birth; I'm afraid there can't be any more."

Abraham held Sarah's hand. "It doesn't matter," he said; "one is enough!"

Hagar and Ishmael, now eight, came in to visit while Abraham was there. Abraham took Ishmael to the crib. Ishmael looked, and then looked at Abraham, Sarah and Hagar. And then, awed by the adult occasion and the need to say something, he started to laugh and said the first thing that came into his head.

"That's a funny-looking thing!" he said, as laughter streamed from him. Soon the laughter choked him and he gulped. "That's . . . a . . . funny-looking . . . thing," he said between gulps, "a funny-looking thing!"

Sarah's lips clamped tight. Hagar snatched Ishmael's hand, and took him hurriedly out of the ward. But the damage was done. "Ishmael's never seen a new baby before," Abraham said. But Sarah turned her head into the pillow and cried.

Ari came rushing to the bed. "Out," he said to Abraham. "Out! She's tired, poor thing!"

Abraham kissed Sarah on her forehead. "He's a beautiful baby," he said, "but what's more important, he belongs to you and me!"

Sarah watched him go, tears in her eyes. The nurse on duty removed Isaac and his crib and Ari took Sarah's pulse and temperature. The birth had been extremely difficult, and another baby was really a physical impossibility now. Abraham had two children, but he had just said he'd like a child every year. Who was to give them to him? During the long years of waiting there had always been a hope that whatever prevented them from having children could be cured and Dr Walters had cured it when he removed the growth from her glands. But now she was too old, the risk too great. There was no more hope. "I wish I were dead," she sobbed into her pillow. Ari could have told her that depression was normal after a birth, but in her postnatal state she realised with awesome clarity that any special claim she might have on Abraham was finished. He had given her a child to justify their relationship; if he wanted other children, might he not turn to the younger and infinitely more desirable Hagar? She and Hagar had been equal contestants for Abraham's love, but now, Sarah felt, her age and her new incapacity had loaded the scale against her.

The kibbutz needed more land. The land to the north was plentiful but too rocky to plough and too far to carry soil. Abraham estimated the maximum time that they could spare the tractor from routine ploughing and other duties, then calculated that it would take over five years to carry sufficient soil from the valley. It would probably be worthwhile in the long run, but they needed a solution soon. Abraham had an idea.

Anyone who wished to introduce a new idea to the committee had two choices: to wait for the semi-annual meeting at which all members of the kibbutz were present; or to convince his own delegate. Abraham had to convince Hagar.

"You've gone a long way, Hagar, since the early days. Now your head is full of big schemes, the workers' union, the federation of kibbutzim, even politics."

"Life isn't bounded by Guvena!"

"It used to be."

"Those were the early days. You did me a great favour when you gave me Ishmael. Being an outcast gave me the perspective to see what we were doing on the kibbutzim and the *moshavim* and the agricultural settlements, and a lot of what I saw worried me! We have to think of larger issues, Abraham; we have to ask ourselves what will happen if ever our dream of a unified country comes true. Shall we be politically mature enough to cope?"

"And you don't find 'political maturity', whatever that may mean, in Guvena? You don't find maturity in having a child to look after?"

"That's part of the fault of the system, Abraham. You've put your finger on it, right there. I have Ishmael and I think, good, that's another child who can be sure of the advantages of the new collectivism, a perfect case. He starts life a bastard, but the kibbutz system is big enough to deal with that. He won't suffer what normal bastards do because he'll be brought up *collectively*. But what do you discover, when you really look into it? Children are reared collectively during the day, but in the evenings they step back fifty years into the heart of a great big mamma complex. These women can't give up their babies, Abraham; they're not mature enough to do it. Take Miriam and Reuven. He's very 'mothered'."

"And Sarah?"

"She's just the same with Ishmael, but it's worse in her case because the child doesn't belong to her. We no longer have ghetto problems, how to allocate the food so that the child doesn't starve, how to keep his body free from lice in a rat-infested hole, how to find clothes to keep him warm. Instead, we have the mamma problem! I'm trying to get the union to sponsor separate camps with trained nurses and first-class children's doctors and psychologists, so that the kids can get away from Mamma and learn what collectivism is all about . . ."

Hagar had a new strength honed by the adversity of being an unwed mother in what was, though no one would admit it, a bourgeois society fumbling with an experimental social method. One weakness of the system had been shown when people refused to give up ownership of houses, and formed *moshavim*, where a man could be as bourgeois as he liked at the end of his day's work, and only the land and the equipment were owned collectively. In some *moshavim*, he knew, women refused to give up their babies at birth and reared them as they would in a town. Imagine creating a bastard in such an environment! But in this new strength, had Hagar lost something? He remembered her as she was when Dov died; the quality she had shown on the way back from the Negev, the warmth and understanding.

"You don't have a special feeling for Ishmael?" he asked.

They were sitting under the window space in Hagar's house. She walked about the room, straightening the covers on the beds, moving the books on the shelves, poking her finger into the soil of a plant. "Of course I do," she said. "But let me tell you something. I've watched Ishmael play with Sarah some evenings. I've listened to him. That kid has problems we know nothing about. He's being pulled several ways at the same time, and he doesn't know which way to go. The system tells him he's just like any child on the kibbutz; it tells him over and over again that no one is better than anyone else, that no one has any greater opportunity than anyone else, and so on. Then he comes here in the evening. He knows I am his mother, but as soon as he walks through that door he has two adults to contend with. I've tried to reinforce the system all these years while you've been away; I've tried to add to his concept of a communal life. I don't overwhelm him with a lot of emotional show; I don't want him to think he's someone special because he's *my* child. He might just as well be Martha's, or Miriam's, or even Sarah's. But Sarah, on the other hand, is a mixture of old-fashioned ghetto love, of the mamma complex, her half-understood ideas of what we're trying to do, and her dependence on the principles and prejudices of a religious fervour. Don't misunderstand me, Abraham. I'm not criticising Sarah *per se*—she's been wonderful to me and to Ishmael—I'm just being realistic about what she is. I wouldn't want to have to sort out what goes on in her mind. Do you realise, Abraham, that Sarah resents not being allowed to cook meals for you? She'd like to be able to make chicken soup, and have you read from the Bible, because she thinks it's a woman's *duty* to feed her husband and children. She'd like to quote endlessly from the Scripture, praising and flaying with the mighty rod of the Chosen Word!"

199

"You don't appear to like Sarah."

"I like her, Abraham. I love her as a sister, as a person who's been móre than kind to me and my child; but I don't *approve* of her or the fifty or so like her we've got in Guvena. Do you know that some of the new members were lighting fires on their back verandahs and cooking in the evening? They were taking food from the canteen, and cooking it!"

"You can't expect to change human nature overnight."

"That's a platitude, Abraham, and unworthy of you. People can change themselves instantly. They can see their error, and spit that instinct out every time it rises in their throats. But first they have to accept the *principles* of communal life."

She *had* changed. Now she was more mature, more sure of herself, and it showed in her bearing. Before she had been a pretty girl; now she had the poise of confident beauty.

"You've never thought of marriage, Hagar?" he asked.

"I'm trying to have a serious talk with you, Abraham, and you bring in these irrelevancies. No, I haven't thought about marriage, I've been too busy thinking about more important things. Don't I miss having a husband? Answer: no. Don't I get randy sometimes, long for a man on top of me? Answer: yes. Have I never been in love? Answer: frequently. Right now it's a man who runs the Haifa Histadrut. I may decide to let him climb on top of me, I may not. It's not important, Abraham! It's not *important*!"

"I came in here to ask you to put a matter before the committee on my behalf!" Abraham reminded her.

"You always change the subject when the going's rough. I have to be away when the next committee meeting takes place; why don't you go as my alternate, and raise the question yourself? If it's something you've set your heart on and you believe it's good for the kibbutz, good luck! They're very hard to persuade!"

"Will you be gone long?"

"Only a few days."

"I'll miss you!"

"Good old Abraham," she said. "Pop a coin in the slot,
200

and out comes a chocolate bar."

"Who's going to look after Ishmael in the evenings?" Sarah was preoccupied with Isaac. She couldn't wait for supper to end to go to the nursery to collect the crib. Many younger mothers spent the two hours in the nursery itself; Sarah insisted on lugging the heavy crib all the way back to their house. Abraham had volunteered to bring the baby for her, or to help her carry the crib, but each time Sarah refused. Now that she had Isaac, she was rapidly losing her interest in Ishmael. That was natural, of course, but not so natural was her objection to having Ishmael in the house when Isaac was there. "It's bad for Ishmael," she insisted. "When Isaac is there, Ishmael competes with him for everyone's attention." It was true; when they were there together, Ishmael would interrupt anyone playing with Isaac. "Look at me," he'd say, "watch this, watch this." His childish enthusiasm was so infectious that at first only Sarah had noticed what he was doing.

Hagar wanted to move out of the house when Abraham first returned. Perversely, Sarah would not let her do so. Perhaps, in those days before she had Isaac, she felt her link with Ishmael would be weakened. Abraham was happy to have his own house. Life as an officer had accustomed him to sleeping alone; he was restless in bed, and sensitive to other people. He was always pleased, therefore, when Sarah returned to her own bed after their intimate evenings together.

As soon as Isaac was born, however, Sarah suggested Abraham change houses with Hagar. Abraham demurred; he liked being in his own quarters, and he didn't want to have to decide which child to spend his evenings with. He realised that no matter how he divided his time one mother would be hurt. It was safer to keep the two children in one house. Sarah had striven increasingly to get him to sleep in her house; he had steadfastly refused to raise the matter with Hagar, who never volunteered to move, though she was certainly aware of the tension. Now Hagar and Ishmael often spent their time together out of doors.

201

"Misha and Miriam will have Ishmael while I'm away,"
she said. "Ishmael gets on very well with Reuven."

"But Miriam is a mamma."

"They're all mammas at heart," she said, "and that's
going to be our greatest problem!"

Abraham went to the next meeting as Hagar's alternate.
"Your arm ought to elect somebody who can be here all the
time," Chaim complained. "You're the third replacement
we've had!" In the past everyone would have been pleased
to have Abraham's counsel, but he welcomed his new
equality. How often he had hoped that people would run
their affairs without depending on him! He sat humbly while
the main business was transacted. He then asked for and
received permission to introduce new business.

At first they were sceptical. "Farming without soil? Growing vegetables in stones? It isn't possible!"

"At Eli-Dov," Abraham said, "we drained water from
ordinary soil into a trough filled with stones; we planted
crops in the stones—that's the trickiest part—and the crops
grew larger and sweeter than anything with roots embedded
in soil!"

It took some time to win them over. So many crack-pot
schemes had been suggested, so many people came to the
committees with ideas to make fortunes overnight and to
revolutionise kibbutz living, that they resisted automatically.
Most of the committee members were farmers from Central
Europe. They'd scratched an existence from the covering
of magical grains they called soil. But to plant crops in bare
stones? Hair-brained! Fantastic!

Abraham was prepared to compromise. "If I do the work
in my free time, if I can persuade people to help in their
spare time, can I have the tractor for one hour in the
evenings?"

"Well, Abraham, my *meshuga* Abraham, that's different,"

Chaim, the chief dissenter, said.

The meeting discussed other business for another half hour. Just before it closed, Abraham asked permission to raise another matter. The committee groaned; they'd been hoping to get away early. "It's personal," Abraham said, "and it won't take long." He laid a piece of paper on the table in front of Chaim. Chaim looked at it.

"Why didn't you give me this before?" he said. "I'd have approved your scheme like a shot!"

"That's why I waited. The one should have no influence on the other."

Chaim passed the paper round the meeting. It was a banker's draft, made out by Glyn Mills and Co. of London, England. It was for two thousand English pounds, in respect of the balance of gratuity, back pay, savings, and interest on the same, of Major Abraham Chaldean, M.C. Made payable to 'the duly authorised officer, for and on behalf of Kibbutz Guvena, to close account'. It was every penny Abraham owned.

"Welcome home, Major," Chaim said, as he shook Abraham's hand.

One evening, when she went to collect Isaac from the nursery, Sarah discovered long fingernail scratches on his face. Rowena, on nursery duty, said the scratches had appeared during the afternoon play session, when all the children were put on the floor to crawl about together. The larger children at this session took care of the younger babies and helped them get around. "It's necessary exercise in collective responsibility," Rowena explained. The scratches had been dressed, and Isaac was all right.

"Relax," she said, "every baby gets a few scratches from time to time! You can't wrap a baby in cotton wool."

Sarah showed him to Abraham. "That's what they do to

my baby!" she said. "I'd like to know what kind of a person could do that to a little baby! Who never harmed anyone in his little life, did you, baby?" She lifted Isaac from his cot and enfolded him in her arms. The baby squirmed in Sarah's tight grasp, but his feeble strength was no match for her smothering love. He started to cry. "There, are the naughty scratches hurting you?" she cooed. She spit on a handkerchief and wiped the scratches; the baby howled even more.

"That's unhygienic!" Abraham protested.

"What are you saying, that the mouth of the mother that gave him birth is bad to him?" There was nothing Abraham could say. Eventually the baby grew tired of crying, his eyes closed, and he went to sleep. This was the pinnacle of Sarah's happiness.

"I wonder how Ishmael likes the drum Misha has carved for him; Misha was going to give it to him this evening," Abraham said.

Sarah glared at him. "Ishmael," she said, "always Ishmael! You've no interest when somebody rakes the cheek of my Isaac with his fingernails, but when Misha breaks the rules and gives the other child a drum for himself to keep, much interest then, ha?"

Abraham didn't reply; he knew he'd been a fool to mention Ishmael in this charged atmosphere.

"Now that there are so many of us," Sarah said innocently, "people are thinking of establishing a religious kibbutz in the hills near Jerusalem. There's a lot of support for it. People are appalled by the loose living of the non-orthodox; they could get a hundred to start a new kibbutz and the Federation of the Hakibbutz Hadati would provide the funds. I thought *we* might help get it started. After all, you've had enormous experience of that sort of thing—few can equal you. And, what's more, Isaac could be brought up properly."

"We might think of it a little later," he said, as vaguely as possible. "I've just started this new scheme and I'd like to see it running. You know I don't like to start things and then abandon them!"

"If we are going to move on to a religious kibbutz, don't

you think it would be a good idea to talk with the rabbi? And to eat at the table?"

"Possibly later. I've got too much on my mind now."

"Shall I talk to the rabbi for you? He would come here to instruct you in the evenings. After all, you don't do anything while I have Isaac except sit and read!"

"I also try to save some of my time to see Ishmael!" he said firmly.

"Ishmael, Ishmael, always Ishmael!"

"He is my child, and you mustn't forget that!"

"How can I? You never let me forget it, always ramming the word down my throat!" The sound of her voice woke Isaac, who started to cry. She reached the cup of orange juice from the table top, and gave it, a sip at a time, to the baby. "I'll tell you this much," Sarah said. "These scratches didn't come on my baby's face by accident. They were put there by that devil, your Ishmael!"

How Abraham longed for Ya'akov when he started to grow his plants without soil. Ya'akov made light work of anything mechanical. Abraham's idea was to catch the water from the fertile woodlands in the hills, and carry it by culverts into his stone-filled troughs. He reasoned that water which had washed through the centuries-old leaf mould of the hills would have the goodness plants require. He had dug into the loam of the woodland after a heavy rain; the water in his hand was rich in minute particles of leaf mould and tasted bitter and chemical. He started by cutting long drains, a half metre deep, between the trees. During the rains the drains filled and the water leached the chemicals from the soil as it ran downhill. The drains ended above the rocky plain where he would build his stone-filled troughs and his reservoir. Honouring his gift of money the next meeting of the kibbutz committee granted him a labour force of six men, the use of the tractor for an hour a day, and the right

205

to work on the scheme during the day for an experimental period. The reservoir was watertight, built of stones and mud clay. A culvert led down the hill to the horizontal trough, a hundred metres long and two metres wide. It was filled with a ballast of small stones which had been crushed, sieved to remove the dust, and hand-graded.

When the last load of ballast had been tipped, he walked down the length of the trough, nervously smoothing it with his hands. The work team shared his anxiety. He looked along the length of the culvert. Everything seemed in order. He crossed his fingers, then nodded to Ezekiel. Ezekiel knocked the top board from the stack holding the reservoir water in check. It was thirty centimetres in breadth; the water it held back weighed 300,000,000 kilograms. The water spouted forward, hitting the culvert with an unimaginable destructive force. As the immense weight came hurtling down, it smashed everything in its path.

Abraham started to yell. "Divert the culvert," he shouted, as the juggernaut headed for the laboriously-built stone trough. He dashed to the end of the culvert, dragging stones like a madman, clawing at the mud clay that bound them.

Ezekiel yelled, "Get out of the way, Abraham, get out of the way fast!" The five of them ran as quickly as they could, guessing what would happen when the torrent of water hit the trough and its crushed stones. Now the water carried large rocks like weightless corks. There was a roar like thunder as it hit the trough. Water, rocks, mud clay and a billion carefully sifted stones were flung in the air in a towering column twenty metres high. The top of the column rolled lazily into a mushroom head, then fell like hail. Within seconds, the waters had parted, swilling shallow and loose like the foam-flecked lazy end of a tide; but the culvert and the trough, so many hours of thought and labour, had gone, scattered malevolently like grains of sand. The men stood stunned by the bareness of the land before them. Not a trace remained of their efforts of the past forty days; the rock was scoured as clean as when they first saw it.

"That's the first lesson learned," Ezekiel said. "We lower

the boom a millimetre at a time."

The klaxon sounded for the ending of the day's work.

"We have an hour before supper," Matthew said. "Let's make a start before we go down!"

They all knew that if they came back in the morning to bare rock, this task before them would seem insurmountable. The men devoted that evening to restoring some of the damage that had been done. The following day, the work began again. Abraham stopped coming back for supper; Matthew's wife would climb the hill with a pannier of food, and they would stop work for a few minutes, sitting on the stone trough which was rapidly taking shape again. This time Abraham altered the design so that if anything went wrong, the force of the water would shoot away from the trough. Sarah complained that he spent so much time away from Isaac; but Hagar often brought Ishmael to watch them in the evening. Abraham saw that her thoughts were not on Guvena and its small local problems. She had agreed to sit on the committee on the drainage of the Hulah Valley, co-ordinating plans obtained secretly from engineers from all over the world. Most of the engineers came to see the valley. They stayed at Guvena, and Hagar spent much of her time helping them.

Hagar was there the evening they next turned on the water. Ezekiel and Moshe had designed a system for lowering the boom by winch and rope. It was geared so that five full turns of the handle were necessary to lower the boom level by a millimetre. This time they were taking no chances. The water came out of the reservoir in drops; the drops became a trickle, the trickle a gentle flow. It took all night to fill the stone trough, so carefully did they control the water flow. At first light the water level had just reached the top stones. The trough was leaking all along its length, of course, since they could not hope to plug it watertight with mud. Gradually, as the water flowed, the silt of leaf mould it contained caulked the leaks. By evening, the exterior of the trough was dry.

They let the trough stand for several days, then emptied

the water and slowly filled it up again. One of Abraham's books pointed out the disadvantages of a limey soil, and Abraham guessed there'd be lime in the small stones they had crushed. They washed and drained the trough four times before he pronounced himself satisfied; the fourth time, the water ran from the trough clear as from a spring. They had created an overflow system, so that if a sudden flood came during a season of heavy rains the excess could be drained off. They also built a large stone chamber for manure from the beast-yard and residue from the cheese. Abraham remembered that Reuven had grown his cucumbers with the aid of manure at Eli-Dov.

Still Abraham had planted nothing, and the kibbutz, always sceptical of his scheme, was beginning to deride it openly. Aaron lost faith, and left him for work in the conventional fields. Abraham didn't replace him. All day long and most evenings he pottered about, examining the culvert, digging his hands deep into the ballast to pluck out a handful of stones. When the first manure pile was high, he ran it with water, then flushed the liquor into his trough. For three days and nights the trough stank intolerably, but then it ceased to smell, and when he plunged his hands into the ballast, the stones were brown, stained through with the colour of the manure liquor, and the water was sweet. "What are you waiting for, Abraham?" they asked; even Ezekiel, his strongest supporter, suggested it might be wise to start planting. But Abraham refused.

"We'll know when it's time," he said.

"Dammit, I wish I could see it all," Misha often said as he sat on the edge of the stone trough, listening to Abraham. Misha always carried his chisels in his pocket, and he carved as well as if he could see. He could run his hands over a man's face a few times, memorise his features, and reproduce them with uncanny accuracy. He'd sit carving, listening to the chink of stones. "That one doesn't ring very solid," he'd say, and Abraham would remove the stone. Ten to one it'd have a crack in it. "You don't sound very convinced about that," Misha would say, as Abraham explained his intentions, and
208

Abraham would pause, reappraise his theory, and often change his plans.

One evening Misha was sitting on the trough's edge when Hagar came up the hill with Ishmael.

"Hello Hagar," he said, "hello Ishmael!" It never failed to surprise them that he could identify them by the sound of their walk.

Hagar was angry. "Sarah's gone too far this time," she said. "Every time Isaac gets a bump on his head, or a scratch, she accuses Ishmael. To hear her talk, anybody would think that Ishmael didn't like Isaac!"

"What's happened now?" Abraham said.

"Let Ishmael tell it," Misha said, interrupting. Hagar looked at Ishmael, and at Abraham.

"Come on, Ishmael," Misha said, "what's happened?"

Ishmael looked up at Abraham; he stood there, his hands in the pockets of his shorts, kicking the stone at his feet.

"Isaac slipped during playtime this afternoon, and fell and bruised his head."

"How did it happen, Ishmael?" Misha asked.

"I was helping him sit up in his cot and suddenly he banged his forehead on the corner. It bled a bit, and now his eye's black."

"And you had nothing to do with it?" Misha asked, kindly.

"No, it was like I told you, it happened exactly like I told you, I was helping Isaac sit up and he banged himself!"

"All right, Ishmael," Misha said, "thank you for telling us."

Hagar burst in. "Of course, Sarah said he pushed him deliberately. She blames Ishmael for the bruise and the black eye. You've got to do something about it, Abraham; since Isaac was born, she's . . . well, sometimes, it seems to me, she's got a personal vendetta against Ishmael."

"How does she behave towards you?" Misha asked.

"Oh, I don't see much of her."

For the last month, Abraham had spent virtually all his time on the hill. He had supper and dinner there, and came down to the kibbutz only to sleep. He hadn't seen Isaac at all, and he suddenly realised that he hadn't spoken to Sarah for four or five days.

"Answer me once again, Ishmael," Misha said. "Did you push Isaac?"

"No, Misha, honestly!"

"Did you punch his eye?"

"No, I didn't! I didn't do anything to him." Now Ishmael was indignant, defending himself with vehemence.

Misha changed his tone and became more discussive, less inquisitorial. "You like Isaac, don't you, Ishmael?"

"He's all right, I suppose," Ishmael said.

"But you do *like* him?"

"Oh yes, I like him very much. . . ."

"What are you doing, Misha," Hagar burst in angrily, "interrogating him?"

"No, I'm just asking him a few questions, aren't I, Ishmael?" Ishmael was crying; he ran to his mother's side, and pressed his face into her stomach. She put her arm round him and looked at Abraham, a crease of worry across her brow. "I would take him down the hill, if I were you," Misha suggested. After she had gone, he turned to Abraham. "Why don't you and Hagar come round to the house later on?" he suggested. He jumped from the stone trough and set off down the hill, walking unerringly through the myriad sounds of evening as if they were lines on a map.

Abraham came in during Sarah's last five minutes with Isaac. "I thought you'd weaned him," he said.

She smiled, the baby at her breast. "There's no milk there, but he likes the comfort of it," she said complacently. He walked across the room, and before she could prevent him, he jerked Isaac away from her breast.

"Are you mad," he asked, "letting the kid suck at you that way! Fasten your shirt, woman!"

"There was a time when you tried to get my shirt open," she said. "But perhaps you spend your time opening somebody else's! I've seen the two of you up there, at your so-called water scheme. Plenty in there," she said, "and it isn't for the baby! Still, if it isn't you, it's all these engineers.

210

She's turning the guest house into a whore-house, that's what she's doing!"

The baby still in his arms, he slapped her across the face with his whole hand. The force of the blow knocked her sideways off the bed, and she sprawled on the floor, hatred in her eyes.

"Shut your filthy mouth, woman!" he said and put the baby into the crib.

She sprang from the floor as if to attack him, but leaped instead to the crib. She seized the baby and held him up.

"That's what her bastard has done to my Isaac," she said. "He's mad, he deliberately pushed Isaac!" She collapsed on to the bed, sobbing, the baby crying beside her. Abraham walked out of the house.

Miriam was at a play-reading when Abraham and Hagar arrived at Misha's. They looked at him as if he were a master of ceremonies; certainly he had that air about him. "Abraham," he said, "I want you to help me with an experiment. I want you to go back over your army career, and describe an incident in which you played the major part—and I'm not making a pun on your rank. Now this is the point; the thing you tell me can be either true or false!"

Abraham thought for a while, and then he coughed. "True or false," he said, "anything I like?"

"That's right . . . anything."

"I met a girl in Brussels," Abraham said, smiling at Hagar, "and she invited me back to her hotel room." Hagar made a sign, as if to tell him to take the matter seriously, but Misha interrupted.

"You think this is a joke," he said, "but that doesn't matter. It'll still work. Tell me, what was the name of the hotel?"

"The Albion."

"What floor was her room?"

"I don't remember," Abraham said. "I think it was the fourth floor. Yes, I remember now, we went up in the lift, it was the fourth floor; room, let me see, room 117, or was it fifteen? No, I can still see the seven. It had a piece broken along the top."

"Was she a prostitute?" Misha asked. Abraham didn't reply. "Come on," Misha said, "I'm sure Hagar won't be embarrassed."

"It's strange you should ask that," Abraham said. "I met this girl in the lounge of the hotel, just like you might meet any girl. The Albion's a decent hotel, after all. We spent all evening talking, and she suggested I go to her room with her. I hadn't a room for the night, and so I went. It turned out that she was a prostitute, but not the normal kind. She was available for the duration of normal army leave, seventy-two hours, and if you didn't want to make love to her, that was all right."

"And you didn't make love to her?"

"I'm afraid I did; she was just what a battle-weary old soldier needed at that moment, so, as someone I know would say, I climbed on top of her!"

Misha held up his hand. "Stop that!" he said. "We're not here so that you can score points off each other. You two have a serious problem, and I'm trying to make you realise it!"

"What is the problem?" Hagar asked.

"Ishmael blacked Isaac's eye today, and what's more, he did it deliberately. He knew quite well what he was doing."

"Oh my God!" Hagar said, her eyes wide open with horror. "How do you know this, Misha? Has he told you?"

"You could say he told me in a way, just as Abraham told me more than he meant to just now. Everyone knows that being blind develops all your other senses, but what most people don't realise is that it also makes you understand more. For example, Hagar, I knew that you were angry when you came up the hill today. And just now, when Abraham was telling me that story, he thought he was being clever by mixing fact with fiction. The *fact* is, Abraham, that you met a girl you liked somewhere in Europe. I'll make a

212

guess that it wasn't in Brussels, and certainly not in the Hotel Albion in that room with the conveniently broken number; possibly it was in England, in London; you started to think you might have an affair with her, and to your absolute horror she turned out to be a prostitute instead of the sweet young amateur you thought her. And in case you're wondering, Hagar, when he discovered what she was he got out of the room as fast as he could, and didn't—how did you put it—climb on top of her."

Abraham said, "How do you do it?"

Misha thought for a moment. "I suppose sincerity and in- sincerity are very hard to fake; I can detect insincerity, and I always know when someone is not telling me the truth. Ishmael was not telling me the truth when he said he didn't push Isaac into the corner post of the play-cot."

"The little monster!" Abraham said.

"We have to accept the fact that Ishmael hates Isaac," Misha said gravely.

"We can't blame him," Hagar said. "He's only what he's been made!"

Misha stopped her. "We can ignore the problem and hope he'll grow out of it; but I don't think that will happen before he does Isaac a serious injury. We can waste our time in recriminations and try to place the blame. But the only sensible thing is to work out a plan."

"You know more about Ishmael than anyone else," Abraham said. "What do you suggest?"

"I have to ask Hagar a couple of questions," Misha said.

"I wouldn't dare lie to you . . ."

"Which is more important: the work you're doing for the kibbutz movement, or the mental health of your own child?"

"I can't deny my work's important to me," she said. "If you'd asked me a week ago, I'd have said the problems of one individual are less important than the problems of the mass of the people. But I can't truly say that now. Of course, if this is a confession, I'd have to say I've thrown myself into the work because of Abraham. In my heart I always hoped that since he and Sarah had been together so many years

213

without bearing a child, he'd divorce her and marry me!"

Abraham looked away. He'd suspected this was true, but hadn't dared let himself think about it. Love's a curious game: he loved Sarah and wanted Hagar; he also loved Hagar, but every time he looked at her, Sarah came to his mind. He knew Sarah hadn't been herself since Isaac's birth: 'post-natal depression', Ari called it. Sometimes, Ari said, it could last many months. But his feelings for Sarah were not based on events since the birth; they were based on twenty-six years of being together, twenty-six years of sharing every human emotion. He and Sarah had been together too long, had come too far together. He knew he couldn't leave her, not now, not ever.

Hagar understood his silence as clearly as if he'd spoken. "A dozen people could take my place on the committee. I don't think anyone else could help Ishmael, except the professionals; perhaps they can help me at the same time, teach me to be a mother to the poor little bastard!"

"A mamma?" Abraham asked, but without malice.

The following morning, Hagar and Ishmael left the kibbutz to seek advice and treatment. Abraham talked to Ari about it, and Ari approved the decision. "The tensions here were far too strong. Ishmael knew you were his father, of course, and the mystery about it, the conspiracy of silence was just too difficult for him to handle. Now maybe you can work on your major problem."

"What's that?"

"Sarah. I'm very worried about her, and have been ever since she had the baby. This post-natal depression! It's very strong in some women and worse in older ones. You remember how she was the night Ishmael laughed at Isaac."

"I thought that was just a passing thing," Abraham said.

"It is normally. But it's taking Sarah a long time to pull

round; now you'll be able to give her more of your time, show her a bit more love!"

Rachel was waiting when Sarah went to collect Isaac from the nursery. "The nursery committee had a meeting today, Sarah, and we've decided to ask you not to take the baby to your house for a few days. He was sick again this morning, and we know you've been feeding him orange juice in the evenings. You can stay here with him for an hour, if you like, but the meeting decided—it wasn't just me, it was the full committee except for Doctor Ari—that we want to keep an eye on Isaac for a little while."

Sarah stumbled out of the nursery without even seeing the child.

When Miriam returned from the nursery, she told Misha what the committee had done to Sarah. He ran as quickly as he could to Sarah's house. He could smell the flowers blooming, the pungent odours of the foliage, all along the path. "Needs watering!" he thought. There was no sound in Sarah's room, and no reply to his tap. He opened the door and went inside, all his senses alert. There was no sound inside, none whatsoever. He walked forward, moving his hands before him in case furniture had been moved from the standard kibbutz arrangement. He stopped still when his fingertips touched her knee. When she swung from him, he heard the creak of the rope over the beam and smelled the odours of death.

After Sarah's funeral Abraham climbed the hill and stood by

his stone trough. "You can't grow plants without soil," they'd said.

Almost in the centre of the trough a seed had fallen, scattered by who knows what natural or divine agency, carried on what wind?

The water without soil had softened the seed, cracked it into life; the roots had formed and thrust themselves down into the sustenance hidden in the water. The stem of the plant was slowly uncurling; already it was a centimetre high.

BOOK THREE

OUT OF THE WILDERNESS

Headquarters of the Southern Command of the Israeli
Ground Forces gave the order to attack the Egyptians at
8:15 on the morning of Monday, 5 June 1967. Seven divisions
of Egyptians were deployed in the Sinai Desert in defensive
positions established over twenty years. The Israelis had
three divisions, under Generals Tal, Yoffe, and Sharon. Some
were regular soldiers, some trained reservists: shopkeepers
from Tel Aviv, taxi drivers from Haifa, housewives, school
boys and girls, kibbutzniks, *moshaviks*, workers on agricultural settlements, teachers, barmen and archaeologists.
They faced Russian-trained Egyptian soldiers, with sufficient
tanks, weapons and ammunition to be called one of the
richest armies in the world!

The township of Rafa at the southern end of the Gaza Strip
was selected for the initial breakthrough. Rafa is separated
from the Mediterranean by sand dunes. It was guarded by a
U-shaped minefield and three brigades of the Egyptian 7th
Division. To the rear of the position was a brigade of artillery
equipped with 122mm and long-range 100mm guns, and
another minefield extended south to sand dunes.

General Tal planned to avoid the minefields and the
artillery, and attacked via Khan Yunis, eight kilometres to
the north-east. One brigade was to be used for this attack.
General Yitzhak Rabin, Israeli Chief of Staff, said they'd use
armour "like a mailed fist thrusting with speed and massive
momentum deep into enemy territory; not to take his positions but to throw him off balance and make his positions
untenable".

At the same time another brigade pushed west along the

217

edge of the sand dunes to the south, past the tip of the mine-field. Once round the mines the brigade would circle north to silence the guns and assault the Egyptian forces, then attack Rafa from the south-east. One brigade coming down from the north-west, another up from the south-east, a classic pincer movement.

Before the battle, General Tal told his men, "If we are to win the war we must win this first battle. The battle must be fought with no retreats; every objective must be taken no matter what the cost in casualties. We must succeed, or die!"

Prior to the attacks on Khan Yunis and Rafa, the Israeli Air Force took off in its Mirages and Mystères, their target the entire Egyptian Air Force—the Tupolovs, Ilyushins, Sukhoys, and MIG fighters sitting on the ground at airports all over Egypt. The attacks were timed simultaneously for 0745 hours, when Egyptian generals and commanders were on their way to work, when sentries on guard and pilots on standby since before dawn had lost early alertness, when ground mist had dispersed, and visibility for placing bombs accurately on planes and runways was perfect. The attack came in waves at ten-minute intervals; each flight was per-mitted only minutes over its assigned target before racing back to Israel for refuelling and reloading.

In three hours the Israelis broke the Egyptian Air Force as an effective strike force.

The air above Khan Yunis was therefore free of enemy airplanes when General Tal ordered his advance.

As they saw the Israeli tanks coming, the defenders of Khan Yunis opened fire with everything they had—field artillery, anti-tank weapons, mortars, machine-guns and rifles. Six tanks in the first wave were knocked out by anti-tank fire, but the attack went on, the mailed fist continued to punch, and punch, and punch its way through the defence. The momentum was irresistible; the tanks broke through at one point and then another, guns biting, destroying field artillery positions and concrete entrenchments. The Israeli tanks rolled into Khan Yunis with turrets open. It was a matter of pride that commanders ride the tanks with their

218

heads outside the open turrets, the better to see the battle-field. Assault casualties included thirty-five Israeli tank commanders with head wounds, but the tanks slammed into the barbed wire and the soldiers it was meant to protect, bursting through the Egyptian positions into the town.

From Khan Yunis two battalions turned north and west along the dunes between the Egyptian positions and the Mediterranean. The rest of the troops went straight forward, riding the main highway south-west to Rafa, inside the soft belly of the enemy defence.

Simultaneously General Tal's southern force had raced along the edge of the dunes south of the minefield tip. When they were in range of the Egyptian lines, a battalion of tanks moved up and began shelling to provoke the Egyptians into retaliatory fire that would reveal their positions. The Israeli commander then flanked the positions to the south, came in from the rear, and the Egyptians were destroyed. The way was now clear for the advance; the Israelis moved north and east, heading for Rafa.

Without knowing it, they left an entire Egyptian brigade intact in a hollow in the ground. This brigade was behind them as they smashed north into Rafa's defences. It was a major tactical error.

Abraham left the command car and climbed on to the artillery half-track. "Can you manage, Pop?" asked the driver, an orthodox Jew from Bat Yam, his ear-curls hanging beneath his steel helmet. The half-track started with a jerk that snapped Abraham's head forward, then raced down the road. The six soldiers on board were front-line replacements for a knocked-out gun crew. They found the gun slewed to the side of the path, its right track buried in the loose sand. The dead crew was still aboard. Abraham climbed from the half-track and, though he felt his sixty-six years, he quickly organised the replacement. The bodies were dragged out and

219

placed beside the road in a neat line. Meanwhile the artificer inspected the gun. Its breech was open, but there seemed little damage to the mechanism. The damage had been done to the interior of the half-track, to the humans aboard it. The engine artificer sat in the driving seat, and turned the starter switch. There was no response, and he scrambled beneath the dash-board on his back.

"What do you think?" Abraham asked him.

"Won't take long, and if this is all the damage we'll have it back in the war within fifteen minutes." Already he'd started stripping the wires to make emergency joints. The bombardier opened the compartment beneath the long seats. The shells were there, all intact. They could only be ignited by a direct hit, or a raging fire. The machine-gunner inspected the gun. One look told him everything. He unfastened the locking clip, lifted the gun from its swivel mount, and flung it over the edge of the half-track. Uri, meanwhile, had unclipped the spare gun from the half-track that had brought them and staggered over with it. It took a few seconds to lock it into position in the swivel.

Centurion tanks were pouring past them now, heading for Rafa. The half-track gun carriage normally worked with the front line of tanks, its highly mobile extra firepower available all along the line, helping the tanks where necessary by knocking out gun emplacements the slower tanks couldn't reach in time. It was a job for a young crew.

The radio was useless, of course. The radio operator, a kibbutznik from Judea called Joseph, who also acted as second driver, unscrewed the radio from its mountings. Then he screwed the spare radio into position. Within a couple of minutes, he had installed the set and trimmed the aerial. He wound the microphone round his throat, opened the *send* switch, and began to speak. The radio had already been netted; he was immediately in touch with Misha, at command radio headquarters. "Tell Abraham to hurry it up," Misha said; "I have another one for him." Joseph gave Abraham the message. A Centurion running alongside them slewed its tracks suddenly, throwing a cloud of sand dust that made them cough. The tank commander gave them a hand sign; they returned a less respectable one through the dust. From all round came the sound of vehicles on the move and the chatter of radios. Planes flew overhead, awaiting the call to pounce with deadly accuracy on any specific target; an air strike about fifteen minutes ago had destroyed twenty-five Egyptian tanks commanding the road between Khan Yunis and Rafa. It was good to know they had an umbrella. The sounds of the battle—the crump of the enemy artillery, the high-pitched whee of anti-tank shells and the long drawn out swoosh of the Russian anti-tank missiles—were now at least two kilometres in front of them.

Abraham did a quick check. Gun okay, ammo okay, machine-gun okay, ammo okay, engine . . . "How much longer's it going to take you?" he asked the driver, still squatting beneath the dash-board.

The driver's curls trailed in the dirt. "Finished," he said. He leaped back into the driving seat, and pulled the starter. There was a clunk. He leaped off the half-track, yanked aside the metal sheet that covered the engine housing, and fiddled inside. "Pawl's stuck," he said. "It'll be all right once we've started it."

Abraham walked to the carrier they'd come in. He drove it forward, backed it in, and Uri hooked him to the second carrier which was now in gear. When Abraham drove forward its tracks screeched over the sanded road and suddenly caught; the engine pulled round disengaging the pawl on the starter motor, and fired. The driver let in the clutch, revved, and the carrier emitted a cloud of oily smoke.

A bus was passing, all its windows open. Along the side, in large chalked letters, someone had written CAIRO-NON-STOP. The bus still carried the number of the Tel Aviv-Be'ersheva line. The thick cloud of oily smoke was blown straight into the bus; the troops inside shouted catcalls and shook their fists before they were carried on. Uri took off the towing chain, and the men transferred all their equipment. They were a complete gun crew under the command of a sergeant.

"All correct?" Abraham asked. The sergeant, who had checked, nodded. "The radio okay? You on net?" The sergeant nodded again. "Okay, good luck," Abraham said. The sergeant climbed aboard; the radio operator called command headquarters on the radio's 'A' frequency, and was given a map reference. The sergeant checked his map; the machine-gunner worked the bolt to put his first round up the breech; the bombardier loaded the gun; the driver let in the clutch again, dropped the carrier into first gear, and away they went. Abraham watched them go, the seventh replacement crew he'd put into action that day. It was now one o'clock in the afternoon. He climbed aboard his carrier, got a tomato and half a cucumber from his knapsack, and started to eat as he turned back. Several busloads of troops pretended to jeer at him as he drove past.

"You're going the wrong way, Major," they said. "The enemy's the other way."

Abraham smiled. "See you in Cairo," he said, when he bothered to say anything. These fresh-faced kids in buses, or standing in tanks with their heads sticking out, they had pride; this was their war for the future. This time they'd trounce the Arabs and put an end to incidents, bombings, guns fired into border kibbutzim. This time the United Nations would have to take heed. Abraham had fought World War Two, the War of Independence in 1948, the 1956 Sinai campaign. In those days he held the rank of brigadier; in this Arab-Israeli war he was content to be graded major with a job of vehicle recovery. It had been his own idea to maintain a squad of well-equipped reserves; many knocked-out vehicles could quickly be brought back into operation with new men, guns, radios. It was a harrowing and dangerous job; many vehicles were burned, littered with charred corpses, and still in the fighting line; but every vehicle was precious. Blind Misha from Guvena manned the radio link, tirelessly calling fighting units for information. Commanders were naturally impatient at his insistent demands for map references and other details, especially in the midst of battle. Being blind inured him to protest; his ears and delicate fingers flipped from net to net, monitoring the progress of battles, anticipating a need of recovery. Twice he'd placed Abraham and his crew within a kilometre of a knock-out before the carrier had been damaged. He could tell merely by listening to the tone of the voice of the radio operators if the situation into which they were projecting themselves so forcefully but so willingly would be likely to prove fatal.

"You're too old for this war," they'd told Misha and Abraham; "stay at home and grow the food we need." But at sixty-six Abraham didn't feel too old; and even though he was fifty-nine and blind, Misha knew a way in which he could help. The first time he'd donned headphones and listened to the dying sound of a beat-frequency-oscillating tuner, he had known what he could do. Few young ones could beat him; he could listen to two separate headphones, one on each ear, two conversations simultaneously; he could talk into a microphone while he listened and all the time be writing messages in his meticulous but rapid handwriting. When Abraham needed someone to eavesdrop on battle frequencies, to intercept messages from commanders to their headquarters reporting casualties, Misha had been the natural choice.

Abraham pressed the key on the carrier radio. "Coming in to pick up another crew, Misha," he said, ignoring complicated signals call-up procedures. "I hope you have a good one for me."

Misha sounded excited. "I've got a beauty," he said. "What do you know about the T-54?"

"Enough!"

"I've got one for you, reported untouched, abandoned by its Egyptian crew, and Abraham . . ."

"Yes, Misha?"

". . . take a pot of paint with you. It's Russian!"

In the barracks Abraham found sufficient troops to man fifty tanks, all eager to go. He selected a young kibbutznik from Omsk to translate the signs in the tank for the rest of the crew. As Misha had said, the T-54 had been abandoned.

223

There were no signs of booby traps or enemy damage. Inside the tank Abraham found pairs of army boots, down at heel, cracked from excessive wear in hot sand. The Egyptians had fled in stocking feet at the first sign of the Israelis. The boy from Omsk painted a white Star of David on each side of the turret, and the vehicle was ready for action within ten minutes. Busloads of infantrymen racing to the front cheered when they saw the tank; the signals operator netted to the frequency of battalion headquarters, then sprinted across the foothills to a battle rendezvous.

By four o'clock Abraham and Misha had restored a score of vehicles to action, fourteen of which were Russian tanks abandoned intact by frightened Egyptian crews.

Abraham was back in the command car at headquarters when news came through that a tank battalion, aiming for the second Egyptian brigade position, had swung too far north before turning east towards El Arish. They were caught in a heavy engagement with a task force of Egyptian tanks. Meanwhile the southern brigade commander, attacking the Egyptian brigade with only one battalion of tanks, found himself encircled. The commander's voice came over the radio, loud and clear, not unnaturally annoyed at having lost half his force. General Tal immediately despatched the reserve battalion in the aid of the beleaguered tanks, and ordered the northern brigade commander to turn back southeast. The rescue came only just in time. When they got through, the encircled Israelis were down to their last rounds of ammunition. The battalions linked and fought their way out of the encirclement. When they pulled away after an hour they left a thousand Egyptians dead, and the tattered remnants of a mighty Egyptian armoured brigade. The radio was calling for first aid and medical orderlies: there were fifty Israeli casualties in need of urgent hospitalisation. The smoke from the blazing tanks hung low over the battlefield, then started to drift away. The Israeli tank squadrons reformed and continued the punch towards the next target, El Arish.

Misha listened excitedly. "Move your reserve down there,"

he said to Abraham. "There'll be lots of vehicles to salvage!"
Abraham collected as many men as he could carry on the
half-track and loaded the rest into a bus. "Follow me," he
said to the driver, and sent the half-track hurtling down the
road. After five kilometres he turned right towards the encircled tank battalion. The men in the half-track waved to
a helicopter airlifting wounded back to hospitals at base.
The half-track raced up a hill, the helicopter following low
behind them. Suddenly the helicopter banked steeply, turning
back towards the south. For a long second it stood still in
the sky; then it plummetted, its rotors buckled, 250 metres
behind them. The bus accelerated to the site of the crash;
three men disembarked and ran to the smoking ruin. They
broke open the plexiglass dome and dragged the men out of
the helicopter. When they'd gone a hundred metres, the helicopter burst into flames. The three men who'd been riding
it were dead.

Across the crest of the hill in a large saucer-shaped valley
protected from outside vision, an entire Egyptian brigade
had dug in, occupying formidable fortified positions. The
Israelis had bypassed them in their advance.

The radio on the half-track crackled into life; headquarters
had taken a hasty report from the helicopter before it
crashed; they were asking for a repeat. Abraham seized the
microphone and gave information about the crash and the
Egyptian brigade. The voice of the southern commander
came on. He would lead a tank battalion to attack. The
exhausted troops changed direction once again; Abraham
was ordered away from the battle zone. Grumbling, he drove
back a half a kilometre, parked the half-track and the bus
out of sight, and settled back to await the oncoming battle.
It was late evening; already the hill ahead was dark. Suddenly
they heard the sounds of hell as the mailed fist began to
punch into the battle. The night became a maelstrom of tracer
fire, mortars, tank and anti-tank guns, impossible to separate
in the dark. The battle ebbed and flowed across the valley
floor. Tank after tank was hit and caught fire, an eerie torch
of oil illuminating other tanks and guns, men cowering

225

behind tanks, men running in panic.

Suddenly a Stalin tank lumbered over the top of the crest, dipped, and started down the slope towards them. They estimated it would pass within fifty metres. Abraham and his men withdrew behind the rocks in absolute silence. The tank came cautiously on. "We could get a track off with this," one of Abraham's men said. It was an old army trick to throw an iron bar like a javelin between the sprockets of the track-driving wheel. With luck the track stripped off or the cogs broke.

"They only have forward or side vision. Nothing behind unless someone's looking out of the turret. Leave the bar. Let me have the tank!" the lieutenant artificer, Dov, pleaded.

Abraham nodded. He too wanted the tank intact. "If we divert him in front, can you get behind?"

"I could try!" Dov said, grinning.

Abraham started the engine of the half-track. Dov hurtled across the scree towards the tank, keeping under cover. Abraham let in the clutch and raced the half-track forward; he slewed it into a right turn about 250 metres in front of the Russian tank. The gun slowly began its traverse, a long finger pointing at Abraham. He glanced behind at the tank, noted the direction and point of traverse, then suddenly wheeled the half-track away. The gunner was caught napping. He had to stop the traverse, reverse it, traverse back again to aim at the carrier. Both vehicles were now running about ten kilometres an hour in a line over the terrain. Abraham watched behind him and again at the right moment, he whipped the carrier in a tight arc to the side. The gun stopped, started back again. Now the tank was level with Dov's position. Confident all eyes would be directed towards the carrier, he stood up and ran behind the tank. He grasped the metal pin ladder, swung himself on to the platform at the back, then slowly lifted his head until he was an arm's length below the top of the open turret. He took a grenade from his belt, pulled the pin, let the handle fly, then counted "one, two . . ."

On the count of three he tossed the grenade into the open

226

turret, dropped off the back of the tank, and ran.

The explosion came a second later. The tank stopped dead as a wisp of flame came through the turret top. There were a few curls of smoke, but nothing else.

Dov raced towards the tank. He scrambled up the back of the turret, then lowered himself inside. There were only two men in the tank. Both of them were dead, but curiously neither had any obvious lacerations. However, the concussive effect of a grenade explosion in a tank is insupportable. The pressure blows into the head, tears and destroys ear drums, windpipe and lungs. Dov pulled one of the men from the driving seat and pushed him into the turret. Abraham dragged him out of the tank. There was a pronounced smell of eau-de-cologne on the second man, an officer. Dov yanked him from the gunner's seat, and Abraham pulled him through the turret hole, toppled him off the tank, impatient to get inside. There appeared to be nothing wrong with the tank. The 'fail-safe' mechanism had operated without the pressure of the driver's feet, and the engine had cut out. Abraham ran his fingers over the controls, testing each one. Then he found the starter button. The motor turned over; the engine caught and fired. He drove the tank forward a pace or two, then turned it round and ran it to the bus.

He climbed out of the tank and stood on the side of the turret. "The Lieutenant and I, we want a crew," he said. "We're going over the hill to have a crack at the Egyptians." He selected two men, and the others groaned in disappointment. "Mark, in the extremely unlikely event I don't come back, you take over," Abraham said. Mark was a motor mechanic from Haifa, a captain by rank, an engineer by vocation. Dov meanwhile had painted the Star of David on the side of the turret, and they climbed back inside.

"Too old at sixty-six," Abraham snorted, "I'll show 'em." Dov was tuning the 'A' radio to the Israeli command frequency. The 'B' radio would be netted to the other tanks when they joined a squadron on the other side of the hill. Abraham clipped on the second headset and throat microphone and eased into the driving position. "Let's go," he nodded. He put his heel on the 'dead-man's handle', his feet on the driving fingers. The tank eased forward. "Misha," Abraham called, "Abraham here; over."

Misha's voice came over the air waves as clearly as if he were in the tank. "I know it's you, Abraham. I'd know that voice anywhere, even on a Russian microphone."

"We're going over the hill to have a crack at 'em," Abraham said. "Give me a frequency code!"

Misha chuckled. "You're too late," he said. "They surrendered five minutes ago."

Ishmael was working in the hospital in El Arish when news of the attack came over the portable radio in his office. After he had been round the wards, he went to his house on the hospital grounds and brought his mother into the hospital. There were two beds for observation of special patients in a tiny ward near his office. He often slept there himself when he needed to attend a patient during the night. "You'll be safer here," he told Hagar. She grumbled but went back to bed. Lately she'd been spending mornings in bed; there was a slight flutter, no more, in one of the valves of her heart. Ishmael was treating her with medicines that relaxed the arteries and eased the strain, but nothing he could do was as good for her as rest, horizontal, preferably in bed. He telephoned the hospital administrator, who was still at his home in Nahal Sinai. "We could take up to fifty wounded in here, you know, Hamid, if you could get me the cots."

Hamid laughed. "My dear Ishmael, where on earth are you going to find fifty wounded? The Israelis won't advance a foot into our territory. By this time tonight, we shall be in Tel Aviv. You really must stop panicking," he said as he put down the telephone. Hamid was listening to Radio Cairo, Ishmael to Radio Tol Israel. They were talking about different wars. His mother was already asleep again. He drew the cotton cover over her, and she stirred, but didn't awaken. Then he went back into the long ward. There were fifteen beds on either side and two tables in the centre. Mona, the American sister, had already put out day flowers. In America she had been trained to remove flowers from the ward each night; even though here the hospital windows were open all night, she clung to early teaching. She smiled when she saw him.

"Have you heard the radio?" he asked.

She shook her head. "I haven't had a moment since seven o'clock," she said. He followed her into the sister's room. It was a morning routine—rounds from nine o'clock until ten o'clock, then coffee in Mona's room. She imported it specially from America; she couldn't drink the Turkish coffee black and sweet the way it was drunk by the Arabs.

"They started the war at eight fifteen this morning," he said, his voice calm. "I heard it on Radio Tol Israel. Cairo's denying it, apparently, still plugging the line that they'll be in Tel Aviv before the Israelis get to the border."

Mona was an attractive girl of twenty-eight. She had qualified in the large Bellevue Hospital in New York City. Immediately afterwards, she had worked in hospitals in Casablanca, Tunis, and Cairo, where she met Ishmael. They had come together to the small specialised hospital he ran in El Arish. "There won't be much actual nursing," he warned her, "but you can guarantee that for every patient we send out cured, we save a life and, if there is such a thing, a soul!" El Arish was a hospital for drug addicts; its staff and its patients came from all over the world. After Ishmael had qualified in medicine in Guy's Hospital in London, England, he had specialised in the medical problems of drug addiction. His staff included a psychiatrist, Dr Klaus Vorberg, from Leipzig, and a resident physiotherapist, Ena Hamilton, from Australia. The hospital normally had about fifty patients and a waiting list of approximately a year. Most patients came in the advanced stages of heroin or morphine addiction. For every ten patients who left cured each year, at least ten died. Most of them were in the last stages of physical decay, and in any other hospital in the world they would have been put

229

on one side to die. Their hospital was financed by endow-
ment from an American family trust. The heir to an American
cereals fortune had died at twenty-five in advanced stages of
heroin addiction, and his father travelled the world looking
for someone who could cure his son. At that time Ishmael
was working in Cairo; he met the father too late. When his
son died, the father made his son's legacy over to the hospital
Ishmael had dreamed of founding. El Arish, in the Sinai, as
removed from civilisation's drugs and drug pedlars as possible,
was chosen as the site.

"You're going to have to decide which side you're on,"
Ishmael said. "Radio Cairo denies there's any danger. They
say they're confident of stopping the Israelis. But I don't
believe they will. I believe the Israelis will come past here,
and it won't take them very long."

"What will you do?" she asked.

"I'll stay, of course. I don't suppose they will interfere
with us. Not deliberately. There'll be fighting all around us,
but it isn't as if we were anywhere near a military target."

"That's not what I was thinking."

"I have an Irish passport."

"It's not a question of nationality. I have an American
passport, but I'm a Jew. I've never been in a synagogue, but
I'm a Jew. My father didn't go to synagogue once after he
left Spain for America, but on the day he died he was a
Jew. Just as you will be, on the day *you* die! You can't run
away from it, Ishmael; if you're Jewish it's in your blood
whether you have an Irish or an Israeli passport."

He put his coffee cup in the sink and held out his hand.
When he clenched it the vein jumped on his wrist. "Mona,
take a sample of my blood. If you can find any difference
between my blood, Eshkol's blood, and Nasser's blood, I'll
put your name forward for the Nobel prize. Mona, there's no
such thing as Jewish blood or Negro blood, Chinese blood or
Protestant blood. It's all blood of one chemical group or
another."

"In the heart, Ishmael? No difference there? If an Israeli
soldier and an Arab soldier came into this room fighting,
230

which one would you want to win?"

"You mustn't ask questions like that, Mona!"

"Why not? Are you afraid to say you'd want the Jewish boy to win, because the Jewish cause is right?"

Ishmael shook his head, smiling. "I'd want the man who was losing to win. You know me. I fight for the underdog. I'm always on the losing team, by instinct!"

"If the Arabs take Israel, they'll push the Jews into the sea."

"Then I'd be on the Israeli side! Why do you think I've chosen to work with drug addicts? Not because they're interesting medically. No, I work with drug addicts because they're underdogs—as you would say, all-time losers. They're self-inflicted; they *have* nothing, they *are* nothing. When we get them, what are they? Rotting, near corpses! They're so far under, and they've been under for so long, that no one pays them any regard. In an ordinary hospital—if they can get into a geriatric ward, and not many can—they're neglected, suffered, tolerated. Lots of doctors deliberately work out a treatment—though of course they don't talk about it—to guarantee speedy death! And they think they are making it easy on the relatives."

Mona looked at him. She knew he had this zeal, this dedication to his job at El Arish.

"I still say that when the first Israeli tank rolls down the road outside, you'll know you were born a Jew!"

"That's one advantage I have over you, Mona. I was born a *bastard*, and bastards are international. From my first recollections, bastardy took precedence over that mystical injection from the Talmud you say makes Jews."

"Then why did you get an Irish passport? Because you were ashamed of being a Jew?"

"For no other reason than that I wanted to be free to travel anywhere in the world. And being a Jew isn't a nationality, it's a religion."

When he'd qualified at Guy's, Ishmael had taken a resident's post in Dublin. His mother had travelled with him. She had a passport stamped Palestinian. His travel docu-

231

ments had been arranged by Dr Gervis, who had treated him when he left Kibbutz Guvena. It was Dr Gervis who had originally interested him in medicine. In Dublin Ishmael found an official from the Irish Passport Office as his patient in the hospital. Patients often develop an enormous debt of gratitude towards the doctors and nurses who cure them; Ishmael's Irish patient was pleased and relieved to be able to express his gratitude in a positive way. It had seemed an ideal opportunity to lose the stigma of being Palestinian, both for himself and his mother. He already knew what he intended to do with his life. Because so much drug addiction occurs in the Arab world, he would need freedom to travel. The three of them had a celebration supper the night the passports arrived; Hagar looked at the documents and sighed. "The only thing they can't do, Ishmael, is give you a new foreskin!" she said.

Two kilometres from El Arish, when the shells from the Egyptian guns started landing around them, Captain Isaac Chaldean and his men disembarked from the bus. They jumped as if they were leaping from a plane as they had been trained. There'd been some good-humoured grumbling at their continued use of the ground, but so far no parachute drops had been made. The fighting for El Arish was rising to a peak. An Israeli tank battalion had smashed its way into the outskirts of the town and was now hull down among the buildings, smashing the enemy's defensive perimeter. Tanks from the reserve brigade had effectively cut the link between the airport and the town itself, and already the call was out to bring up the sappers to prepare the airport for Israeli planes. The paratroopers had been on standby for an assault on the town. But when the High Command saw Tal's progress, the assault was cancelled and most of the paratroopers were pulled out. Rumour had it they would jump into Jerusalem. "Lucky sods," Zach, Isaac's lieutenant, had said, when the news leaked out.

They darted for cover, a hundred men spread out in company formation. Each platoon had a walkie-talkie set netted to the company radio. As soon as the three platoons reported themselves in position, Isaac ordered them forward at the double. The battlefield in front was a sea of fire. Tanks built into the outer perimeter of defence were proving almost impossible to dislodge. The anti-tank guns were located behind them, firing with the aid of spotters. Isaac saw four Israeli tanks knocked out as they rushed forward. The Egyptians were obviously panicking, firing loose bursts of machine-gun fire across the entire front. In company headquarters were Isaac; Yoram, his signaller; Zach, his lieutenant, second in command; David, his company sergeant-major, a veteran of the 1948 and 1956 campaigns; Uri; Frank; and Benjamin. They ran forward in spearhead formation, A platoon behind and to the left, B behind and to the right, C in column behind company headquarters. They used the Israeli system of 'leading from the front' since the front man of the entire company was Isaac himself. As they advanced, he looked to the sides, giving a quick instruction to Yoram to 'get A platoon up, get B platoon back, maintain formation'. Once at target, he'd need to know by instinct exactly where each of his platoons would be. Each man was equipped with an Israeli-made Uzi machine-gun. None wore steel helmets since they preferred to fight in paratroopers' berets. Now they were within range of the machine-guns and bullets whipped through the air. Ahead was a large flat-sided building with arcades along its length. Their target, a telephone exchange, was immediately behind it.

"A and B down for covering fire," Isaac said, "C platoon follow me into that arcade, but sideways left and right, because there's a machine-gun inside the third arch. Two sections left, one right, and wait for the machine-gun to be cleared before they come in. Got it?"

Yoram nodded, pressed down his *send* key, and passed the message to the platoon commanders. Isaac waited impatiently until each officer had confirmed. Then he nodded

233

and Yoram called the start signal. The fire from the two platoons spattered the buildings on each side of their target. C platoon aimed in particular for the arcade. After a few minutes of rapid fire, Isaac nodded to Yoram who passed the word, then headquarters and C platoon behind them each ran towards a corner of the building. Almost at once the machine-gun in the arcade opened fire. Frank was hit, and Benjamin went down. "Stop that machine-gun," Isaac yelled as he ran. Yoram pressed his switch and yelled into his radio; both A and B machine-gunners plastered the nest under the arcade. The machine-gun was suddenly silent. Isaac was twenty metres from the building. Suddenly a rifle spit from the second-storey window. The shot tore through Isaac's shirt. He lifted his Uzi and pressed the trigger, still running. The bullets squirted up the side of the building, spraying the window opening. The platoons had seen the sniper as well, and the fire from the machine-guns splashed into the window. Now Isaac was under the building at the corner of the arcade of shops. The machine-gun had been mounted over the mansard of a leather shop and heavily protected with sandbags. Although the gun had a wide arc of fire, the outer hole through which the barrel projected was less than twenty centimetres in diameter. The sandbags, however, ended a metre from the roof of the mansard. Isaac crouched in the doorway of the first shop watching the gun. Suddenly it began to stutter. He nodded to Yoram, who quietly spoke on his radio. Now the company fire was directed away from the arcade. One section of C platoon was waiting at the far end of the arcade; two sections were behind Isaac. He ran forward under the machine-gun, pulled the pin on two grenades and lobbed them one after the other.

The first hit the sandbags and fell back into the arcade; the second cleared them and went inside the machine-gun nest. Isaac turned and ran like hell to the end of the arcade, and the platoons rapidly faded into cover. Seeing a grenade come over the sandbags, an Arab in the machine-gun nest made the mistake of vaulting out into the arcade. It was a three-metre drop, and he landed almost on top of the other grenade with a broken leg. Both grenades went off at the same moment. The section at the far end swept through the arcade, firing into each shop they passed. Two soldiers ran up the steps inside the leather shop, into the chamber the machine-gunners had built inside the mansard. "Okay, Isaac," one of them shouted without formality. The machine-gunners were dead.

When the company reassembled they'd lost five men out of the hundred.

The post office was a well-fortified building in a tree-lined avenue. Arab gunners and tanks were grouped at the far corner. One Arab gun had been built into the ground floor of a nearby building which had been buttressed with concrete. The building itself had been hit by an Israeli air strike, but it had collapsed on to the bunker beneath without impeding the gun at all. There were two tanks, one on each corner, both Russian T-54s. What was left of an Israeli tank stood in front of the post office, still smoking. The Egyptian gunners had held their fire as it advanced forward of cover, then the two Egyptian tanks came round their respective corners, and the bunkered gun opened fire. Three shots hit the Israeli tank simultaneously; it exploded instantly. Isaac's assignment was to take that section of El Arish, clean out the post office (keeping the equipment in good working order), destroy the gun hidden in its bunker, and neutralise the two tanks.

Isaac studied the terrain. "Who knows how many snipers there'll be in that building," he said to Zach.

David was looking through his field glasses. "I've got one of the bastards," he said. "Permission to shoot?"

"Not from here. Get yourself into that basement and shoot from the grilled window. We'll see how many retaliate."

"Good luck," Zach said as David skittered into the building. It would be a question of shooting and ducking back immediately, since any sniper worth the name would find a target on that grill within seconds.

They were watching when the sergeant-major fired. There was a scream from the sniper he'd spotted through his glasses, and a hail of fire on to the grill. Isaac counted three snipers' positions. A section of A platoon advanced down the left side of the street, while the others poured a fusilade of fire into every window space they could see. One man from the section was killed outright by a shot through the head. That section held the small house they had occupied, fired from it, while another section raced down the street, leapfrogging them. Meanwhile another section was firing steadily at the bunkered gun, hoping to land that one-in-a-hundred shot through the sighting aperture. Isaac led A platoon to the ground floor of the post office building. They held it while B platoon came down the side of the avenue.

Isaac was examining the back wall of the building next to the post office. "It's worth a try," he thought. The front wall was protected from the street by closed wooden shutters, which, though they had been pierced many times by small calibre bullets, were still intact. Yoram sent a message to the C platoon signaller, who got in touch with the Israeli tank commander. The tank withdrew, circled the back of the arcade and the post office. The building with the wooden shutters was obviously a garage. They manoeuvred the Centurion slowly forward through its wide doors. The noise inside was deafening. They traversed the gun round until it was pointing at the wooden shutters. Isaac had his eye to one of the bullet holes; he pointed his finger forward, and the tank commander lined the gun barrel along the approximate direction of Isaac's finger. A huge grin split his face.

Isaac and Zach opened the wooden shutter. The gun was pointing more or less directly at the concrete gun emplacement. As soon as the shutters swung open, snipers started pouring in their fire, but the gunner in the tank sighted the gun on the concrete emplacement and fired three rounds rapidly into it. The first round cracked the concrete, the second round hit the breech of the anti-tank gun, the third round went smack into the centre of the bunker, hit stacked ammo and exploded the bunker. By now the tank at the corner of the square had traversed through forty-five degrees, got the target, and fired. The first shot must have come a

236

fraction too soon, and the round smacked into the wall to the right of the tank, carrying away a square metre of stones, and whamming through the garage. Before the tank could fire its second round, the Centurion gunner made the small correction to his arc to bring the gun from the bunker on to the Russian T-54. His shot hit the tank amidships and exploded it.

Isaac looked up at the ceiling. "Run," he shouted to Zach and Yoram. They ran like hell to the back of the garage, and got outside just as the ceiling came down. The force of the explosion of the three shots from the Centurion had cracked the concrete beam on which the first floor was built, and it caved in. Isaac could hear the tank revving as the crew tried to push their way out of the debris. Suddenly, the hull appeared in the garage doorway pushing a ton of broken concrete, roof plaster, and timbers.

Isaac's company took the post office intact except for one booby trap which damaged a bank of switch gear. All the electronic equipment had been mined, ready to blow; but the officer in charge of the fusing mechanism had fled from El Arish at the sight of the first tanks, and no one could get into the cupboard where it was kept. No Egyptian dared to force the door in case the sensitive mechanisms inside should explode. The operators fled from their boards and within a couple of hours, the post office was being used by the army to communicate with Tel Aviv.

Isaac and his company, however, had moved on.

"Your next target," the battalion commander said, "is at map reference 093.364.675."

"Got it," Isaac said. "What is it?"

"Something called the Hobart Trust Foundation Hospital!"

Hagar woke at 11:30 feeling refreshed; somehow morning sleep eased her more than the long night. During the night she usually dreamed she was suffocating. Usually she woke gasping for breath shortly after dawn, and could not get to sleep again until the day had begun. The heart flutter was a bore; nothing more. It meant she couldn't exert herself, but she had long passed an age when exertion meant anything. She smiled as she remembered the number of times she had taken a spade into the fields or lifted stones. She remembered the kibbutz in the Negev, and that boy, what was his name? she was so fond of. When he died they named the kibbutz after him, didn't they? Eli-Dov; Dov, that was his name. She slowly pushed back the sheets, and slid her feet to the edge of the bed. "Get up carefully," Ishmael had told her. She did as she had been told, took a long time to slide her feet across the sheet, to bend them down to the floor. If she exerted herself, she always felt a small nagging pain in her chest. For years she'd thought it was indigestion, heartburn. As a young girl, she'd often had heartburn, but for a different reason. No difficulty remembering Abraham's name! He'd be sixty-six now and, like her, probably taking things easy. Abraham had been a comet speeding across the sky; like all comets he'd burn out one day, just as she had burned out, and she was nowhere near as old as he was. He'd given her heartache, first at Eli-Dov and then Guvena. She'd been in love with him in Guvena, when she was big with Ishmael and he'd been married to Sarah. She left the kibbutz too soon; by the time she learned Sarah had killed herself, Ishmael had been committed to treatment. She asked the psychologist what effect it would have on Ishmael to see Abraham again knowing as he did that Abraham was his father. The psychologist talked it over with the doctor. Two words spelled death to her hopes. "Better not!" they said.

Had it been the right thing to do? Looking at Ishmael now, one couldn't doubt it. He was a fine son, a good doctor, and still young enough to become brilliant with experience. As long as he remembered to steer clear of women, not to ruin his life for that strange thing called love the way Hagar had done. She knew Ishmael had slept with the American, Mona, a time or two, but that didn't harm. Presumably both were smart enough not to get themselves into the sort of mess

Hagar had. If she lived to be a hundred she'd still remember the moment of Ishmael's conception; she'd always remember the look on Abraham's face, the depth of his eyes, as he released himself into her that night. She had known at that moment that his seed had fertilised her. The next morning she'd wanted to tell him. All night she'd lain in bed, sleeping but not sleeping, unconscious but not, aware of his force working inside her womb to start life within her. She wanted to hug him the next morning; she went to his house but already he'd gone for breakfast; she wanted to hug him and look into his eyes again and tell him he was alive inside her, that his years and years of anxiety with Sarah who couldn't produce a child for him had ended. How triumphant he would have been. But at breakfast that morning, he'd been cold and unresponsive and almost immediately the two men had come from Haganah and he and Ya'akov had left the kibbutz. Now her feet were touching the floor, and this morning there'd been no stab at her heart. She felt easy and relaxed. "Silly old cow," she thought to herself, "fancy remembering all that about Abraham!" He could be dead and buried by now.

Ishmael must have heard the slight creak of the bed; he came into the ward, bringing an armful of her clothing from the house.

"What's the news now?" she asked without much interest.

"Radio Tol Israel is claiming to have destroyed the Egyptian Air Force on the ground. Radio Cairo denies it, of course, and says the Egyptian troops are racing towards Tel Aviv."

"We'll know when they get near here," she said. He came and sat beside her on the bed. "You all right?" he asked. She nodded.

"Taken your pill?"

"Not yet!"

He reached for the pill box he'd placed beside the bed, and poured a glass of water from the thermos jug.

"If they come," he said, "what will you do?"

"Do? I shan't do anything!"

239

"What will you say?"

"I don't understand you. What *should* I say?"

"Will you tell them about us?"

"What is there to tell?"

"About our being Jewish."

"Who said we're Jewish? I was born in France; I lived in Palestine. You were born in Palestine, but now we're both Irish. It isn't important where we were born, is it?"

Ishmael laughed, and put his arm around her. "Funny thing! When they come, and I'm certain they *will* come, we may have to tell them we're Jewish to save our lives. If they think we're Arabs . . ."

He left her to get dressed. She slowly put on her clothes and looked at herself in the mirror. Where had it gone, the lean brown look of her youth, the rounded cheeks, high proud figure? She took her spectacles from the case and put them on. Her skin had started to wrinkle—too much sun in her youth; her shoulders were stooped—too much hard toil. When she came from Kibbutz Guvena with Ishmael, she worked as ward maid in the hospital where Ishmael was in treatment. The hospital had its own nursery for young children brought from Europe. Many had seen their mothers raped and their fathers slaughtered, many were in a state of medical and psychological shock; and though the Youth Aliyah set up special kibbutzim for them, a small percentage had to be detained in hospital. One boy would set fire to anything if he could get his hands on matches. Another, re-enacting the scene of his sister's slaughter at the hands of the Nazis, killed several girls on the boat coming over before he was detected. Of course, Ishmael was not as deranged as most of the patients; but as soon as he realised he was 'abnormal' and needed treatment he lapsed into silence. He didn't speak for an entire year, not even to Hagar. It was Dr Gervis who finally got him to start talking again. Over a period of months, he put the boy under hypnosis. He got Ishmael to draw and then gradually released him from hypnosis so that Ishmael would know what he had been doing. They looked at the drawings together. Dr Gervis talked about them and

240

about Ishmael, but he didn't attempt to get the boy to speak. This happened once a week for three months. By that time, he had not said a word for six months. During the next three months, Dr Gervis caused the boy to write the answers to questions under the influence of hypnosis. At first he was afraid the treatment would break down. Ishmael would sit for hours looking at the paper, and Dr Gervis sat patiently with him, keeping his subject in and out of hypnosis. Eventually Ishmael began to write. After nine months Ishmael was asked to draw and write at the same time. Sometimes Dr Gervis would read to him and ask him to draw an impression of the words he was using; sometimes he showed a picture and asked Ishmael to put his impressions of it into words. At the end of the twelve-month period, Dr Gervis put Ishmael under the influence of hypnosis, showed him a picture, and without providing pencil or paper, asked for his impressions. Without hesitation, Ishmael began to describe his feelings. Gradually Dr Gervis relaxed his hypnotic hold and gradually Ishmael began to realise who was speaking. The final test came when Dr Gervis put Ishmael under very light hypnosis and showed him a picture of a baby boy Isaac's age. Ishmael began to talk about Kibbutz Guvena, and all the things the other children had said to him about Abraham. When Ishmael left the hospital, he had admitted the existence of right and wrong, and he knew that what Abraham and his mother had done was wrong by one set of values and right by another; and he knew that what he had done to Isaac was wholly wrong.

Hagar could remember the day she realised how completely he had been cured. When he was ten, he went to school near the hospital. It was a normal state school which took the children of everyone in the neighbourhood. One day he came home with a black eye. She tended the bruise, bathing his face in warmed water.

"Why were you fighting?" she asked.

He looked shame-faced. "I was trying to help another kid in my class."

"You mustn't get into fights, Ishmael," she said.

241

"I wouldn't have, Mother, except they were calling him a bastard!"

Hagar went to the window and looked out over the tidy lawns of the hospital. The six-room house in which she and Ishmael lived was on the other side of the grass. Usually there were two gardeners working; she'd come out in the late morning and talk with them, looking at the flowers. Each day she made a simple lunch for Ishmael. There was a vegetable plot behind the house where they grew all the ingredients for salads. He ate just as they had always eaten, tomatoes, lettuce, and cucumbers, orange juice or the sweet beer from Cairo, but never, these days, the sour milk of her youth. The gardeners were missing today. She walked to the verandah and looked around the garden. Neither was to be seen. That was unusual. She went out into the garden and walked slowly round the paths. The desert roses were in full bloom. One had already blown and lost its petals, pale rose pink on the rich ochre earth. Strange, it wasn't like the gardeners to leave a spent flower on the bush. Absent-mindedly, she pulled the dead head, wondering where the gardeners could be. Suddenly, from the east, she heard the dull boom of gun-fire.

Abdul Mohammed el-Saboor was a tank driver with the armoured support battalion of the Egyptian 2nd Infantry Division, stationed at Abu Agheila, twenty kilometres west of the border with Israel. The defence of Abu Agheila had been planned in depth by the Russian advisers. Unfortunately Abdul's tank was in an exposed unit north of the defence, just off the road to El Arish. The Israelis crossed the border at nine o'clock on the morning of 5 June. By noon they were in the forward defences. At three o'clock, a reconnaissance group supported by tanks ran into the position occupied by Abdul's battalion. The battalion fought fiercely, and Abdul's

242

own tank immobilised two of the enemy. The Israelis counter-attacked, and by half-past three, what was left of the battalion was in full flight south, seeking the protection of the main Abu Agheila defensive system.

Abdul's tank was in the rear of the flight. It had travelled only a couple of hundred metres when a shot blew off the sprocket wheel and shattered the left track. The tank slewed round, digging further into the sand, and the engine stopped. The crew piled out instantly—a sitting tank is a perfect target—and ran across the desert. A sand-storm reduced visibility; one moment they could see for a kilometre, the next moment they were choking in dust, their vision restricted to fifty metres at most.

The rest of the crew ran south, following the line of the tanks. Abdul sat behind a rock until they had disappeared, then set off northwards. He'd had enough of war and deserts. The Mediterranean was forty kilometres to the north; the thought of the cool clear water hastened his feet away from the scene of flaming carnage he had just witnessed. Walking at a steady pace of five kilometres an hour, he would arrive at the ocean during the night. In a satchel he had snatched before leaving he had a bottle half full of water, a box of dates, and a tin of soup, more than sufficient to last him. A man could live for days on a box of dates alone. . . .

The sand-storm moved south, and after a few kilometres he was in blazing light and heat. He cursed himself for for-getting his hat; the sun was almost directly overhead, burning its way into his skull. Unaccustomed to marching after a couple of years of sitting in a tank, his feet began to swell in his tight boots, and his ankles became sore from scrambl-ing over the rocky surfaces and through sifting sand. It was almost impossible to navigate correctly; he cursed himself again for leaving the compass in the instrument panel. His shadow extended about three-quarters of a metre on the flat ground; if he kept that shadow about forty-five degrees to the right of his toe, he would be travelling approximately north. But did the sun travel in a straight line from east to west? Would the angle with his toe remain the same all afternoon and evening, with his shadow merely lengthening as the sun progressed? They'd had lessons in navigation at the tank school in El Qantara, but he had not paid much attention. There was always another tank to follow, always an officer to shout if he were going wrong. His sweat dried on his clothing in the intense heat, and his trousers were rimmed with salt crystals that rubbed against the soft inside of his legs like glass-paper. "Damn the Jews," he thought. Abdul had worked in the docks in Port Said before they pulled him into the army. He liked his job on a crane because half the time the crane was idle, and half the time it seemed to be broken. Then he just sat in the cab until the German engineer came to repair it. It was an easy life, and it paid good money regularly. Who could want anything more? It was certainly better than walking away from the blasted Jews through this blazing desert.

He saw a small oasis of palms about a half a kilometre in front of him. "I will not be made a victim," he said firmly to himself. He knew the oasis was a mirage compounded of his own desires and the shimmering heat of the desert. Like the time in the café in Port Said when the French girl winked at him, or so he thought. French girls don't wink at crane drivers, not even that type of French girl. That had been a mirage. Of course, she had every right to wink at him, for wasn't he a fine-looking man and big and strong. There weren't many like him around, and he'd show her a good time in bed, much better than anybody else could, for wasn't he a bull of a man when aroused, and he'd show her! Sand on his face! How could that be? Where was he? He was lying in sand, his face pressed in sand. He sat up and brushed it from his face, picking it carefully from inside his lip and his nostrils. His lip hurt as he brushed his fingers lightly over it. He brought his tongue forward to lick his lips, but his tongue was dry and swollen. He lifted his hand; there was a pain at the side of his head, and when he touched it, his fingers came away sticky with blood. He staggered to his feet. He'd stumbled over a rock, hit his head, fallen with his face in the sand. He must have been knocked unconscious. How
244

long had he lain there, unconscious? How did he get here from the café in Port Said? But then he remembered he was in the war at Abu Agheila, and he was walking north away from the war! Or was it west? Where was he going? Back to El Qantara, of course. No, somewhere else. The sea . . . the Mediterranean; that was it, he was heading for the sea, the Mediterranean Sea, which was due north. When he got to the sea he'd find a boat to take him back to Port Said and the café where that French girl was winking at him. "Stop that," he shouted. The sound of his voice was flat, without echo, on the desert floor. He knew he was a victim of hallucination. He had to get into the shade, but there was no shade. He'd been walking for six hours and the sun was still hot, still blazing down, burning his head and his skin. His eyes ached from being half-closed against the light; his lips were cracked, his mouth dry. He opened his satchel, took a date from the box and chewed it, then he put another in his mouth and held it there while he walked along. It was good to have a date on your tongue to roll around the inside of your mouth. As his saliva started to flow, confidence came back to him and he tried to smile at his own folly. "You've only been on the march for five minutes," he said to himself, "and already you're starting to panic. There's no call for panic. Walk north, walk north, and soon you'll find yourself by the shores of the Mediterranean. Walk north; soon the sun will go down and you can look for a star, and you can walk along that direction, and before this long night has ended, you'll be up to your waist in water."

He walked steadily forward, confident again, energy flowing from the date. The sun dried the blood of his wound, and drew out the pain. He was still walking when the sun set, but for the last half hour he had been walking in a circle. The stars came out, one by one, and one by one he looked at them, and rejected them. Finally he saw a star that seemed more attractive than the others. "You're a beauty," he said, thinking of the French girl. He walked towards it. He was heading due south-west, into 200 kilometres of arid desert.

Already he was talking to himself, asking questions that had no meaning, giving answers that made no sense.

Isaac and his men had been continuously on the move for thirty hours. He used his radio to ask four hours for 'rest and regrouping' before proceeding to his next target. To his surprise, the request was immediately granted. He withdrew his men east along the coast road which connects El Arish with Gaza. They found a stand of trees on the dunes overlooking the ocean, dispersed, and lay down to rest. Most of them fell asleep instantly. Isaac and Zach walked among them, seeing them settle down. The noises of the battle were several kilometres to the south, and though tanks and trucks rumbled along the road behind them, the encampment was an oasis of peace. When they had been round the camp, Isaac stared at Zach. "You look dead," he said.

"You don't look much better!"

They flopped to the ground. Zach smoked a cigarette with his back against a tree, looking out over the ocean. He fell asleep almost immediately. Isaac gently pulled the cigarette from his lips, took hold of his knees and dragged him forward so his head could rest on his pack. He walked to the water's edge to urinate into the sea, and then turned back to his men. So many men, so much responsibility. 'Lead from the front,' the Israeli army said, but that didn't reduce your task of keeping as many men alive as possible. They all said Isaac worried too much, and perhaps it was true; but he was more concerned with the survival of his men than with his military objectives, and that, he knew, was a bad trait in the commander of an attacking force. A do-or-die effort was required of him all the time, and though there were no limits to the extent he would push his men to achieve their targets, the whole effort seemed pointless if none of them survived.

He sat down on the top of the dunes. Sleep was out of the

question. They had started the campaign with a hundred men, and now they were down to eighty. Twenty per cent of his men dead! Was that his fault? Had he led them badly? Abraham would say, "Forget it, son. Do what you have to do in the best way you know how." Abraham was like that and always had been. As a young boy Isaac had listened to Abraham's stories of the early days in Eli-Dov and Guvena, tales of Ya'akov, and Shlomo and Shula, Alexander and Leiyla, and Reuven. And, of course, Misha and Miriam, who were still at Guvena, and Hagar and Ishmael, his own half-brother. Isaac still remembered the day his father had told him about Hagar and Ishmael and how he had driven them 'into the wilderness', as he put it. At the time, he and Isaac were living in a kibbutz in the foothills of Mount Gilboa. Isaac was thirteen. "If I believed in the orthodox Jewish way," Abraham said, "you'd have been *bar mitzvah*'d according to tradition; you'd have taken on your own religious duties, worn the phylacteries, been reckoned an adult in the synagogue when they were counting heads for a quorum. As it is, I give you a birthday present, and I want to talk to you." The birthday present was a precious leather knife and sheath Abraham had had for years, carefully tooled and carved, delicately inlaid with fine strips of shell and mother-of-pearl. Isaac still carried that knife on his waist belt. He drew it from the sheath. The blade had worn from constant resharpening, but the handle—of light and dark beaten leather—was still firm to the touch. Ya'akov had made the knife long long ago, Misha had made the sheath, and Abraham gave them both, his only possession, to his son Isaac.

Sitting by the pool with Mount Gilboa behind them, Abraham told Isaac of his mother Sarah, Hagar, Ishmael, and the feelings a man may hold for two different women. Abraham made no attempt to excuse himself. "A man can lie with a woman, as you will do when you grow older, and never be the same again. The woman is never the same again. A man lies with a woman so that she shall have children by him; sometimes it happens, sometimes it doesn't. When it

247

doesn't, a man begins to doubt himself. Having children becomes more important to a man than the food he eats, the air he breathes. If it doesn't happen a man begins to think himself worthless. It doesn't matter how successfully he may do everything else; it doesn't matter how many men may tell him how good and noble he is; if he can't make a child, everything else goes for nothing, all his other abilities rust away like an un-oiled knife blade. Hagar and I lay once together. I shouldn't have done it; it was wrong, and it's my responsibility. People blame the woman, but it isn't the woman's fault; the responsibility is with the man. And somewhere on the face of this earth is a woman called Hagar and a boy called Ishmael who is your half-brother."

"You never tried to find him?"

"I tried, but too late. When Hagar left Guvena, your mother had just ended her life in the way and for the reasons I've already told you. I stayed at the kibbutz, trying to . . . how can I put it, trying not to run away. Trying not to be a coward. I made the excuse I wanted to get the hydroponics scheme working; it did work, as you know, and the fish tanks for carp worked too. By the time all that was going, I felt I'd repaid my debt to your mother and the kibbutz. That's when you and I left to join the new kibbutz near Be'ersheva, before we came here. But now . . ."

"I know," Isaac said, "you've got itchy feet again!" Abraham had fought in the War of Independence, joined the Palmach, fought again in the war of 1956, and worked as no other man had worked at Guvena and Be'ersheva. Now he was anxious to move again.

"Does it show?" Abraham asked.

"It does to me, but then, I know you." He was old for his years; knocking about with Abraham and in kibbutzim without Abraham when he was away fighting had made him independent. "I've got something to ask you," he said in his boyish, serious way. "I like it here," he said, "and I've made a few friends. Do you think, I mean, this time when you go, will you mind if I stay here?" He'd been thinking of this for six months or more, waiting for the signs that his father was impatient to move again. Now the signs had come, and he had found the courage to ask his question.

Abraham thought about it for a while, then he ruffled his son's hair, thick, black and curly like his own. "If that's what you want, Isaac," he said, "but always remember one thing. Do what you have to do in the best way you know how!" Now he was nearly twenty, and had a captain's responsibilities; would Abraham think he was doing what he had to do in the best way he knew how? Abraham would be somewhere in this war, Isaac was certain of that. Not at the front, he imagined, but somewhere fighting. It had been a long time since they'd met and they'd never been good correspondents.

The wind blew in cold from the sea; the sounds of the battle had moved along the coast. Where would they end the day? In El Arish, at the Hobart Trust Foundation Hospital, whatever that may be, or jumping out of aeroplanes over Jerusalem? Yoram had left the radio with him. He could hear the voices of the commanders as they regrouped, calling for ammunition, reinforcements, discussing locations and places. Estimates of the Egyptian casualties were in thousands; their own dead were in tens. Thank discipline and training for that. They didn't salute much; and all his men called him Isaac; but when he gave them a command, obedience was instinctive.

Where would he end the day?

Sitting on the sand dunes looking out to sea, he suddenly had an intense yearning to see his father again.

It was six o'clock in the morning when Miriam awoke in Kibbutz Guvena, though shelling had kept her half awake most of the night. You don't break life-long habits easily. For a moment she wondered where she was. She knew she was awake, yet it was dark all around her. Habitually she slept with the shutters open and awoke to sunshine. She put out her hand and touched the wall. Feeling the rough concrete

249

brought the memory of the night back to her. They'd come into the bunkers when the night shelling started at nine o'clock. She climbed out of the berth and recited the *shacharith* morning prayer. Then she went to the end of the bunker, to the small closet protected by a blanket, and washed her hands and face in the ritual the Rabbi had taught her. The Rabbi said, "The human body is a sacred vessel containing the divine spark, the soul, and must be kept sound and clean: to bathe daily is a religious duty the Jew is bidden to perform to the Glory of his Creator." Miriam made her bed as other people were stirring. She climbed the steps out of the bunker and looked round the kibbutz. The synagogue had been hit again during the night, and they had all turned out to fight the fire; the ruins of the east wall were still smouldering. The dining hall and kitchen were still intact. There were several new craters in the centre of the meeting area. The bandstand tilted crazily. Smoke from the kitchen chimney spread lazily across the fields. She walked to the dining hall and several people called a greeting or commented on the bomb damage. They were making breakfast in the kitchen. She accepted a cup of coffee.

"How are you feeling?" Nimshi asked when he came in. Nimshi was permanent secretary of the secretariat. Most of the young men had gone from the kibbutz to fight, and many of the young girls were gone too. They were short of labour, and behind in the work. Nimshi was carrying a transistor radio. "Bombing was widespread last night," he said, listening to the news flashes.

"How are they in the Sinai?"

"Tal's taken El Arish, Sharon's in Abu Agheila, Yoffe's in Gebel Lifni."

"Tal, Sharon, Yoffe! I want to know where my Misha is with that hellion Abraham!"

"Abraham will see no harm comes to him."

"That wandering Jew! He's never in one place long enough to protect anyone!"

When Hagar left the kibbutz, it was Miriam who, surprisingly, took on most of Hagar's duties. Marriage to Misha
250

seemed to drive away all her uncertainties. Having children, too, had stabilised her. At first she worked with the water engineers on the Lake Hulah plans. When the project finally got under way after the 1948 Proclamation of Independence by David Ben Gurion, Miriam was already a regional representative of Ihud Hakevutzot Vehakibbutzim and a member of Mapai, the leading labour party. Since those days, she had expanded her interests to include the Histadrut trade union, and she spent most of her time away from Guvena. Once a year, however, she took a rest from her national duties and came back to Guvena to live for a month as an ordinary kibbutznik. Knowing the war was imminent, she sought parliamentary leave, and came to offer her help in the kibbutz. For the time she was there, no one would refer even obliquely to the life she led outside; she was Miriam, as she had always been, and welcome.

"I really wouldn't worry about Misha," Nimshi said.

"I'm not; whatever happens to him is God's will!"

There was no time for more talk. The Syrian bombardment started again. The first shell fell to the west of the kibbutz. Miriam was on gate duty that morning. She put on the tin hat she had brought from the bunker and ran to the post built into the gateway. The gate had been widened, and at each side was a concrete- and stone-bunkered gate-house which could be approached via a concrete-lined slit-trench. Miriam dashed into the bunker; Givona was already there. Ruth and Shulamit were in the other gate-house—everything in twos as Hagar had proposed all those years ago.

Miriam looked across the valley from the bunker; her task was to issue early warning should the Syrians advance. So far, there'd been no sign. The valley had been dried by the drainage and irrigations schemes she and Hagar had been concerned with in the early days. Now the land was firm and mosquito-free, and they grew the best crops in Israel. Several kibbutzim had been established in the valley overlooked by the Syrian heights. Israeli intelligence knew that the Syrians had spent the last twenty years fortifying their positions with Russian advice and assistance. Several infantry brigades with

251

armoured and mechanised battalions were poised to swoop into the Hulah Valley. The Syrian line was interconnected by underground bunkers, tank pits, and gun emplacements which dominated the valley and the plains and hills beyond. The Russians had placed vehicle-launched *katiyusha* missiles in the heights—twelve rockets to a launcher, each capable of firing twenty-four rockets a minute a distance of sixteen kilometres. Also in the heights were 130mm guns with a range of thirty kilometres, almost half-way to the Mediterranean.

"Oh, why won't they live and let live?" Givona asked Miriam in exasperation.

Miriam smiled grimly. "Look at the land," she said. "Look what we've done down there in the valley, how we've drained the swamp, and carried the water all over Israel, even as far as the deserts of the Negev. But what have they done during the last twenty years? They've built a Siegfried line of defences, poured money into weapons and armaments; and the people who live on the land are no better off."

"But that doesn't explain why they won't leave us alone!"

"Jealousy at our success? Greed, because we've made the barren land they once occupied into fertile fields? Fear, because we have the strength of our success, because we've made a strong country? They can't understand that our strength is directed into ourselves, not outwards towards aggression. They see us prospering, see our university, our schools and colleges, our farms producing goods on sale all over the world . . ."

"That still doesn't explain," Givona said, "why we're sitting here waiting for them to attack, when we should be working in the fields; why we've got soldiers squatting behind this hill out of sight of the Syrians, when they should be back on the farms or in their businesses, or even, some of them, in their schools!"

When the defensive troops of the Northern Command had filtered inconspicuously into the hills, they established a camp behind Kibbutz Guvena. The soldiers recognised Miriam, a national figure, when she went with other members
252

of the kibbutz to give them fresh fruit and vegetables. The soldiers swarmed all about the hollow; Miriam, Gisena, Givona and Shulamit set up a stall, and the men brought lorry-loads of gifts for the troops, plums and oranges, the produce of which they were so proud. The soldiers marched into the assembly area laughing gaily. Miriam ran among them, kissing them on the cheeks, pressing fruit into their hands, tears in her eyes at their young bravery. As they marched in, they sang the songs of the war of 1956, laughed and joked with her. Many were wearing the *tzitzis* fringe— "so thine eyes cast down may see it and be reminded of the Lord". Miriam went among them, touching the fringe and the *yarmulka*. "Lord bless thee, Lord bless thee," she said. Several times she heard the soldiers talking impatiently. "Why don't we go across and get them?" they asked. But the High Command ordered patience. The Syrians were too well ensconced to be moved by costly suicidal frontal assault; the planes would come from the Sinai and bomb the concrete emplacements, and then the Israelis could advance. Meanwhile they were patient! They sat concealed in the hollow, cleaning guns, testing the mechanisms of war for the moment of ultimate revenge when the long history of assault by the Syrians could be quenched in the blood bath of conquest. "Israel must extend to defensible borders," they said. That meant moving the line further east, pushing the Syrians over the edge of the heights from which, for years, they had observed and shelled the valleys and settlements below. It could cost them dearly, a life for every metre taken; but this time they were ready to pay the price, to draw on the surging capital of Jewish blood to end the steady attrition of a life of sporadic bombardment. When the Israeli army was successful, and no one doubted that it would be, the sabra children would emerge from the bunkers and, for the first time in their lives, they would sleep above ground free from the fears of sudden death by shelling.

*   *   *

Ishmael could hear fighting in El Arish, about four kilometres from the Foundation Hospital. The Israeli advance
had swept past them two kilometres to the south. They had
heard the rumble of tanks, the sharp crackle of machine-gun
fire as the infantry cleared enemy outposts. He had walked
the wards once again. All patients lay peaceful, few of them
in medical or mental condition to know about the war. Early
in the afternoon a patient died. He'd shivered on the brink of
death for days, and though Ishmael knew nothing could
preserve his life he still tried. Morphine addiction ravages
flesh structure, destroys living cells like acid. They buried the
patient in the cemetery hidden from the hospital by a grove
of cedar trees. But there was no point in sending the notifica-
tion to Cairo that would normally have brought them a
replacement within twenty-four hours. The telephone lines
were down, and there had been no sign of the hospital
administrator. Several of the ward staff had failed to come
to work, though most of them lived in the huts behind the
hospital, and only went into El Arish on days off. About five
o'clock in the afternoon, an Israeli half-track came up the
drive leading to the hospital. It stopped within sight of the
buildings for twenty minutes or so, its radio quacking. Then
it reversed and left them alone. Later one of the patients,
who was subject to frequent violent fits, went berserk and had
to be jacketed and taken into the isolation box, a padded
room without furniture where a patient could rant without
injuring himself or others. The irony didn't escape Ishmael.
"Out there," he said to Mona, "men are throwing death at
each other with all the violence they can command, fighting
for what each side thinks is an ideal. We try to save the life
of a man so far removed from ideals he would destroy himself!"

They came moving quietly through the belt of trees after
six o'clock. Hagar saw them. She had been reading; she put
down the book and stood at the window, looking across the
garden to the trees beyond, hearing the distant gun-fire. "Jew
against Arab," she thought, "but they're all blood brothers,
just as Ishmael and Isaac could have been! They destroy
254

each other in a mad war that can never end. Can the Jews conquer the might of all the Arab states, drive to Cairo, Amman, and Damascus and impose a peace? The Arabs could more easily penetrate to Tel Aviv and honour their promise to drive the Jews into the sea. They'd lost the War of Independence, the border skirmishing, even the Sinai campaign of 1956, but would they always lose? As they grew in strength, must they not also grow in valour and skill?" She took off her reading glasses and suddenly saw the flutter of limbs beneath the trees. Her mind flashed back to Eli-Dov and the instinct for danger of her youth.

She hastened along the corridor; Ishmael was in Mona's office mixing medicine.

"I saw soldiers in the trees," she said.

Ishmael went to the window. "Where? I can't see anyone."

"By the carob. I can feel them all around us!"

"Jews or Arabs?"

"What does that matter? By now they've surrounded the hospital with a dozen machine-guns pointing. What does it matter who pulls the trigger?"

He put an arm around her shoulders. "They mean us no harm, whoever they may be. This is a hospital, not a tank bunker! There's nothing around here, certainly nothing of strategic value. Why should they want to attack us?"

Soldiers advance by battering; they don't go round, they go through, smashing, stripping, slaying everything and everyone in their path. "I don't want you dead of a bullet, Ishmael. That's not why I conceived you," she said, "not so that a bullet fired by no one at no one could kill you!"

"There really is no cause for alarm. They may have come here for food or beds or medical attention. I'm a doctor, Mother, and it's my duty . . ."

"It's not your duty to die in this ridiculous war, Ishmael. These people have nothing to do with you; you've lived your entire life without them."

As a doctor he knew the symptoms. Her distress hurt him as her son, but as a doctor he knew how to diagnose and treat it. "You'd better lie down," he said. "There's nothing

255

we can do but wait. No point in getting all worked up. We don't want anything to happen to *you*, do we?"

"Don't use your bedside manner on me!" she said, and went back to her room. Her heart hurt but she wouldn't lie down.

Isaac had two machine-guns pointed at the building; his three platoons were set at the corners of a triangle, surrounding the buildings but out of one another's line of fire. Yoram was squatting on the ground behind him; Zach, by his side, chewed a wooden match and waited for the next order.

"Anything?" Isaac asked Yoram.

Yoram shook his head. "All negative. Nobody can see any trace."

Isaac was worried. The Foundation Hospital appeared completely undefended. Through his binoculars he could see people moving about the wards; a doctor, or someone who looked like a doctor; a nurse; several orderlies. There were no buildings to conceal guns or troops, no underground positions, bunkers, trenches, just a hospital alone among the trees.

"Shall I take a look?" Zach asked. He could see Isaac was puzzled. One thing was certain: they wouldn't discover anything more by sitting where they were. Zach was anxious to get back into the mainstream of the action. It was his personal ambition to be in the vanguard when they reached the Suez Canal; El Qantara, Ismailia, Port Taufik, Suez itself, these were his targets. He wanted to see the bastards swimming back across the canal in thousands.

"I'll go," Isaac said. "Cover me. Get Victor to take over the company net on his radio; I'll have Yoram with me. No firing unless I order it via Yoram."

"Or something happens to prevent the order?" Zach asked grinning.

"Cheerful sod!"

"If you come across any pretty nurses . . ."

"I know, save one for you."

Isaac started through the trees, walking slowly forward to draw fire. "If they're going to shoot, if anyone is in there, let them shoot while the range is long," he thought. A section of A platoon rose from the ground, fanned behind him at two-metre intervals. Two machine-gunners covering them from the flanks swivelled guns experimentally along the arc of fire. Each man on the ground had selected alternative targets; all windows, doorways, corners were covered. In front of them were the lawns of the hospital grounds, beautifully kept considering the arid wilderness. In the background was the thump of the diesel that supplied the electric power to pump water from the well into the high tank. In the tank? Snipers? Ideal vantage point!

Isaac looked at the hospital. He knew that other eyes would watch the water tank. Cowboys and Indians; when you come down to it, all wars degenerate to cowboys and Indians; man with hand on trigger walks towards man with hand on trigger and whoever holds his nerve the longest wins.

Hagar, Ishmael and Mona all saw the start of the advance. "Jews," Hagar said fearfully. "Jews," Mona said with relief. Ishmael said nothing but went to the linen cupboard at the end of the ward.

"Look," Yoram said, but already Isaac had seen a large white sheet draped out of a window; it hung still, picking out the sunlight against the ochre wall.

"A sheet doesn't necessarily mean anything," Isaac said. His eyes flicked along the front of the building. The hospital was still but for the diesel thump. Now he was close enough to see the faces of people standing away from the windows, looking back at him. There was a sudden movement at a window sill, but before anyone could fire, he realised it was the grizzled head of a man twisting himself in bed to watch. The man was old, his face almost a skull.

"Halt," Isaac softly called and raised his hand. The men advancing with him squatted on one knee prepared either to spring forward or to drop to the ground.

The main door of the hospital opened, and Ishmael stood there in a white lab coat. When he saw that the soldiers had stopped, he walked slowly forward. Only Isaac was stand-

257

ing; Ishmael came up to him.

"We have no weapons," he said mildly. "This is a hospital. We try to cure people, not to kill them."

"Then you have no objection to staying here with me while my men search the place?"

"None whatsoever, though I'd be grateful if you'd leave your men here, and come in to look around yourself. I assure you it's not a trap; I just don't want my patients disturbed more than is absolutely necessary."

"You an Arab?" Isaac asked, suspicious of Ishmael's dark skin, his thick black crisp hair.

Ishmael shook his head. "I'm not an Arab, whatever that may be," he said. "I have an Irish passport, but if you're asking my religious belief, I'm an agnostic."

"But you speak Hebrew . . ."

"I also speak Arabic, French, German and English."

"You're not Jewish?"

"I told you I'm an agnostic."

"That's not what I meant."

"I know what you meant; the answer's still the same. Now either come into the hospital and assure yourself we have no military weapons, or clear off and leave us in peace."

Isaac flushed with anger. "Don't you realise we're fighting a war? I could lift a finger and have you shot."

Ishmael made no attempt to disguise his contempt. "That doesn't trouble me. I have fifty patients, half of whom would be pleased to have you shoot them quickly. This is a hospital for drug addicts."

"We don't have drug addiction in Israel," Isaac said smugly.

"Then consider yourselves lucky! Anyway, regardless of what you have in Israel, those fifty patients are my only concern. I don't care what you childish bullies do to each other. Whether you're Jews, Christian or Moslems is all the same to me. Any man who shoots a gun at another man, for whatever reason, is an offensive killer, the antithesis of everything I believe in. I'm trying to *save* fifty lives. I shan't succeed, some are dying and nothing I can do will prevent
258

it; but you can start by putting that ridiculous thing down," he said, pointing to Isaac's Uzi machine-gun. "Come into the hospital if you must, but behave like a civilised human being and leave us in peace as quickly as possible!" He turned and walked back the way he had come.

Isaac watched him go, his finger itching on the trigger. He'd heard the phrase a million times but never experienced it; he *itched* to point his gun at this Irishman and to squeeze the trigger. Instead, avoiding Yoram's eyes, he placed the gun on the grass and walked into the hospital.

When he came out he waved his arms to platoon commanders, and they ran from defensive positions to meet him by the hospital gate.

"Get on to Battalion HQ," he instructed Yoram, who tuned his radio to the B frequency, elongated his aerial, and reported the hospital clear.

Yoram listened to the reply. Isaac was opening his map case, ready to locate the map reference of their next objective. Yoram turned to Isaac, his face grave. "They say 'keep listening watch and wait for further instructions'," he said.

"Listening watch? Hanging about here? What the hell are they playing at?"

"They seemed surprised to hear from us. It wasn't Schmuel on the frequency, some girl . . ."

"What did she say?"

"She sounded surprised . . . asked me repeatedly was I Ya'ariv Two."

"Oh God, they've gone without us . . ." Isaac said. Ya'ariv Two was the code name for the next operation, either Jerusalem or the Golan Heights.

While Isaac and his men were asleep, Tal's force had reached the Suez Canal. It wasn't possible for the battalion to wait for one company when paratroopers were so urgently needed. By now they'd be airborne or would already have dropped under new command. The frequency had passed back to Brigade, whose signal links were operated mostly by girls.

"Damn! Damn! Damn!" Isaac said. "Into the trees," he

ordered his platoon commanders. "Regrouping, perimeter defence, sharp about it!" There were groans, but the officers quickly dispersed. The men had had only four hours of sleep on the beaches; they'd be happy to get their heads down again.

The first chance of real action and they'd been left behind. They were supposed to have jumped into the Sinai. What's the use of training men as paras if you send them into action in buses? Isaac had been promised a drop into Jerusalem or the Golan Heights, and the bastards had left without him and his company, all because of a damned hospital for damned drug addicts run by some damned doctor. "Damn" is about the only thing you can say when you're two months short of twenty and have just been called a childish bully!

He felt dreadfully lonely. He sat beneath the trees while the evening drew about him, wondering where the rest of his kibbutz group could be. Most of them had stayed together to form an infantry unit. They all volunteered for paras of course, but only he and Joseph had been accepted. It had been difficult, deciding whether to stay with his group or to train for parachute jumping. Joseph now had his own company. "Lucky devil," Isaac thought, "I'll bet he's on his way north, the lucky devil!"

Isaac had stayed on the kibbutz beneath Mount Gilboa, Kibbutz Safona Gilboa, when his father left. His father often called in when he was passing. Isaac himself left the kibbutz frequently, as they all did, on organised hikes, visits to the towns, visits to historical sites throughout the land. He went to train with Haganah, to agricultural school, but always with the group; Safona Gilboa was always their home. At thirteen he lived in a communal dormitory with the group teacher and the *metapelet*, a vigorous woman of forty-one, and twenty-four other children, though the size of the group was reduced as new houses were built.

At seventeen Isaac was allowed to study kibbutz administration, even though he was receiving a general high school education. He'd acted as assistant kibbutz secretary or treasurer many times, and everyone seemed to agree that he had a head for that sort of thing. The subject had long fascinated him. Many of the older kibbutzim had diversified from straight agriculture. Safona Gilboa's furniture factory employed outside workers including Arabs who'd elected to stay in Israel. Isaac reorganised the accounting methods of the factory and devised labour- and time-saving schemes for stock control, tooling, and the supply of raw materials.

When he was seventeen and a half, he was permitted to go to the business school in Tel Aviv for three months; he returned to Safona Gilboa to a dormitory that had two girls, Ruth and Rachel, and two boys, himself and Joseph. All were seventeen, all were sabras now living away from their parents for one reason or another. They would be eligible for military service on their next birthday. Ruth, Rachel, Isaac and Joseph had known each other for nearly five years; they'd lived together, been educated together, eaten together and slept together during all that time. Each knew he could rely on the other members of the group, could expect their understanding and sympathy, their discipline and criticisms. Their characters had been moulded together, by their *metapelet*, by their teacher, and by the constant friction of young mind against young mind, exploring issues, developing group consciousness and responsibility, arousing individual awareness of life about them. They were the children of the free men and women of Israel, but unlike their parents they had no background of fixed social customs and attitudes. All their lives they had been freed of any economic or social differences; their motives were shaped by group considerations of equality, where each opinion contributed to the whole but had no individual importance. This mode of life had bound them inexorably together. Especially Ruth and Rachel, Isaac and Joseph.

"Why are they hanging about?" Mona asked. "What are they doing out there? Couldn't you get them to leave? They're bothering the patients."

"I know that," Ishmael said, "but I don't want to provoke them any more than I already have." Thinking of his anger, Ishmael was suddenly scared. "They'll go soon," he said.

"They'll get another order to kill Arabs and leave us in peace."

Mona looked at him. She'd never seen him so roused. He was a placid man normally. She took great comfort from his quiet authority and deep understanding. They were the same age, twenty-eight, but already he had the wisdom of a much older man. One of his strengths was that he could combine endless enthusiasm and energy with careful planning and mature authority.

"I'm afraid your day off is spoiled, Mona!" he said.

How like him to think of that! She had planned to take the car and drive the 150 kilometres to El Qantara. One of the patients was well enough to be discharged, and they would deliver him to El Qantara Hospital so that an ambulance would take him on to Cairo. "It doesn't matter," she said. "I wouldn't want to be away from the hospital!" She meant 'away from you' but didn't say so. Their wonderful relationship depended largely on her ability to separate their professional and personal lives, to recognise his moments of need. "Do you think the Israelis will be back?"

"You mean the main army, with the Arabs chasing them?"

"Yes."

He shook his head. "I wouldn't think the Arab army is much good in retreat," he said, thinking of the little he'd read of the Sinai campaign. They were sitting in the room set aside for staff, though only he and Mona used it. When the hospital opened he'd tried to get all the staff to use the room, even the Arab gardeners. He had hoped they could found their own community, break down some of the traditional barriers between doctors and nurses, orderlies and manual workers. It hadn't worked. The staff nurses clung together off duty; they had large airy dormitories at the ends of the administration building. The orderlies and manual workers lived together in a two-storied building beneath the water tower. The doctor had his own house, and there was a flat in it for the use of Klaus Vorberg, the psychiatrist, who was fortunately visiting Cairo at the moment. Fortunately, Ishmael thought, because Klaus would have panicked at the sight of the soldiers; he had little physical courage. Ena Hamilton, the Australian physiotherapist, was also on leave. She'd flown to Nicosia to spend a few days with her parents en route for England. She was due back in two days, but she'd have a difficult time getting in while the war lasted. Ishmael knew, however, she'd do her damnedest to get back by any means and any route possible. He wouldn't be surprised to see her come riding in on the back of a tank of either force. Klaus Vorberg, on the other hand, would stay in Cairo until the war had safely ended, unless Cairo was bombed, in which case he just might come back to the hospital as the lesser of two evils.

"I thought we might have supper on the lawn," Mona said.

"Anywhere, anywhere you say!"

She put her hand on his arm. "What were you thinking about? You looked a million miles away . . ."

"I wasn't actually. I was out there, in that wood. I know they carry food with them, and all that sort of thing, but I imagine an officer gets pretty lonely. Do you think we might invite that young chap to come and have a bite with us? It's only civilised, after all, and I'm afraid I *was* rude to him!"

She put her hand on the side of his cheek, reached down, kissed him lightly on his lips. "You can't be rude to people, can you? It gives you a conscience. Sometimes we have to be rude; it's the only way."

"I can't bring myself to believe that."

"Ask him to supper, and we'll all be extra charming to him. I hope he doesn't wear his boots, bring a gun and stay too late."

"Should I go and ask him?" He was worried by the protocol. When you've called a man a childish bully and a killer, how do you set about inviting him to supper? Apology before invitation?

"Send a message," she advised. "If he doesn't care to meet you again he can send a polite refusal and save you both embarrassment."

When Tewfik, the Arab orderly, returned, he was grinning

263

hugely. "The Jew-Captain will come," he said.

Isaac was glad of the invitation. Though each platoon had its officers, there was no one in whom he could confide. He'd just received a message from Brigade ordering him to place himself at the disposal of an infantry battalion doing ground defence duty in the desert. He'd called the battalion commander immediately on the radio. "Stay there," he'd been ordered, "you'll be as useful there as anywhere. I'll send a signal in the morning if I need you for anything."

What a way to end a campaign, guarding a patch of desert, while forward troops were at the Canal, perhaps even on the road to Cairo! Two years, training for *this*? He looked about him, at the static military position they occupied. If only he had someone he could talk to, someone with whom he could vent his anger. Dammit, he hadn't wanted the paras; but for Ruth and Rachel he would have served his time with *nahal* on a kibbutz. Instead he'd pushed himself forward just to prove his own individuality. The trouble had started when he returned to the kibbutz from business school in Tel Aviv. In the city he'd been alone for the first time since he was thirteen. He lived with a family in a street off the Rehov Hayarken. The father of the family, non-orthodox, had a thriving diamond business. He also had two daughters, and late one night after a dinner at a French-style restaurant in Old Jaffa, when Isaac had drunk an unaccustomed quantity of wine, the two girls had taken his virginity. Though he was too tipsy at the time to derive great emotional benefit from the experience, the unaccustomed touch of a girl's private parts had aroused deep sybaritic feelings. It was enormously pleasurable to have a girl stroke him, to stroke the soft hair between a girl's legs and even more intimate places. It was pleasurable to fondle a girl's breasts, even to kiss her nipples, sensations he'd never believed existed. In the kibbutz he had grown used to a girl's naked body—he'd seen them all his life. He was used to the sight of girls washing or sitting on the lavatory. He knew that girls bleed once a month. These intimacies had been exposed to him and the other boys of their group as natural functions of the human body. As they

264

grew older, of course, the boys occasionally had impulses they found it hard to control, but the group system helped; just as a boy learned at an early age to control outbursts of temper, so he learned to turn his thoughts to more positive outlets should lustful feelings grow strong in him. Many people said kibbutz children learned too much control too soon. Certainly in such a close society few children would touch other children, and spontaneous outbursts of affection were comparatively unknown. When the two girls had come into his bedroom and one had touched his penis, at first he had been repelled by the invasion of his person. He had wanted to hide himself from them. But soon it became apparent that he was enjoying what they were doing; soon he too was playing an active part that would have astounded any other member of his group. The girls were at the age of youth that enjoys experimentation, and his ecstasy knew no containment.

When he returned to Safona Gilboa, there were a million things he longed to tell them; for the first time, however, he could not unburden his thoughts. For the first time, too, he found it impossible to share the same bedroom, lavatory, and showers with girls of his own age without being sexually stirred. Every time he looked at the mouth of Ruth or Rachel, he imagined the lips of the girls in Tel Aviv; every time one of the girls bent over to straighten her bed, often naked, he remembered what he and the two girls in Tel Aviv had done together. But kibbutz doctrine insisted not only that he not touch the girls in those soft moist intimate parts he so desired, but also that he banish those desires from himself. When Isaac found he could not look at a girl's body, he discovered he could not bear a girl to see his own. Rachel flipped a towel off him one day after he had showered; for the fraction of a moment he tried to hold on to it but realised how extraordinary this would seem to her.

The greatest humiliation, however, came in a group meeting one evening. They were discussing a recent book which contained an attack on and a defence of the kibbutz system. At this particular meeting, they were to start a chapter called

265

'Sex in the Kibbutz'. There was a general hubbub of talk which Ruth, the discussion leader, effectively quelled. "Let's get on with it," she said.

There was one of those momentarily awkward silences in which the smallest noise sounds like a clap of thunder. Rachel's voice could plainly be heard by all. Later she denied that she had meant everyone to hear; her remarks were for Joseph's ears alone, as a joke in not very good taste. When Ruth called for order, Joseph had said, "How can we discuss sex in kibbutzim when there is none?" and Rachel had replied, "If there's no sex in kibbutzim, why does Isaac masturbate every night?"

It was true of course. Every night, watching Ruth and Rachel prepare for bed, watching them get into bed, his overheated imagination stimulated by what he had experienced in Tel Aviv, Isaac got an erection, and masturbated.

From the moment the group knew about this, Isaac's life in the kibbutz became unbearable. He wouldn't have minded if everyone had ignored it, if he could have been left in peace. But the minute he walked into the shower room, everyone there, even the boys, covered himself. Every time they had a group discussion, someone would raise the question of 'Isaac's difficulty'. Even the most innocent conversation suddenly became charged with innuendo, phrases like 'make it hard for you', even in the most innocuous context, suddenly became taboo, since they could be guaranteed to cause universal giggles. Isaac suffered a month of this before he left to join the army. "I'll show them," he said. Such was his enormous enthusiasm, his eager willingness and his natural ability to organise his thoughts and actions, that he was an officer within a year, and a captain by the time the war started. "Now they can damn well giggle," he said, the day he pinned on his third pip and adjusted the red beret.

"Abdul Mohammed el-Saboor," he said out loud, "your
266

name is Abdul Mohammed el-Saboor. Remember that, Abdul, for that is your name . . ." He walked forward, keeping the rising sun to his right hand. "I will not be made a victim," he said. He reached to get a date from his satchel, momentarily forgetting he had lost his satchel. How many days ago had he lost his satchel? He was walking towards the Mediterranean Sea. If he was walking why was the sand so close to his face? No, he was not walking; he was lying down. He stood up. The sun was high above his head. "Abdul Mohammed el-Saboor, that is your name," he said, and then he shouted, "I WILL NOT BE A VICTIM." The words uttered from his lips in a thin croak that wouldn't have frightened a sandpiper. He saw the oasis before him, date palms, cool water; it was the hundredth he had seen. "I'll play a game with them. I'll walk towards them, and see if I can get to them before they disappear." He walked forward. The oasis moved further away as he walked. Now the sun was overhead, but in front of him. "My name is Abdul Mohammed el- . . ." he said, as he turned round to put the sun behind him. All about him the sand rolled like waves. He had passed no one, seen no one for, how long was it? When had he lost his satchel? He raised his hand to his face, to rub an irritation of his cheek. The skin was cracked, and rough, and sandy. Now he could see an oasis and an armoured car. He'd walk forward and see how near he could get before the armoured car disappeared. He walked forward; no, you can't walk on your knees, he thought, and he must be on his knees since the sand was so close to his face, and his hands were buried in the sand. He stood up, put the sun behind him, and reached for his satchel. No, he'd lost his satchel. The armoured car was coming towards him. That's strange. The oasis went away, armoured cars came towards. "My name," he said, "is Abdul Mohammed . . ." The armoured car stopped in front of the oasis. Soon it would go away. He walked forward. The sky and the sun cartwheeled in his eyes, and now he was looking up at the sun, staring straight at it. A shadow appeared between him and the sun. He couldn't be walking forward, with his back on

267

the sand, and his hands on the leather boot, on the leather boot, on the leather . . .

"My name is Abdul . . ." he said.

Abraham bent down and put his hands beneath the Arab's arms, picked him up, slung him over his shoulder and took him back to the half-track. He placed the Arab gently along the bench at the back of the vehicle beneath the canvas roof. He unscrewed the stopper of his water bottle, and poured a spoonful of water into the Arab's open mouth. He wet his handkerchief, grimy though it was, and used it to wipe the Arab's face and lips. The Arab tried to suck the handkerchief when he felt the moisture on his lips, but he had no control of the muscles of his mouth. Abraham poured another spoonful of water into the Arab's mouth. He'd never seen a man's face in such condition, burned black by the sun, the lips swollen, cracked through into the flesh, and now bleeding into the water. The man's ears were puffed, and deep ridges full of sand ran across his sunken cheeks. All the skin of his face and neck looked like cracked black parchment, old as a scroll.

"What's your name, you poor bastard?" Abraham asked.

"Abdul." The Arab had heard and understood him. That was a miracle. How long had he been wandering in the desert? His boots were gone, his feet were covered in blisters which had burst, and new blisters had formed beneath them. His hands had been banged raw; dried blood was caked on top of the skin and in cracks deep down to the flesh. The heel of each hand was completely stripped of skin, revealing only bare flesh. The poor devil had fallen so many times, had scraped the palms of his hands in the sand so many times, it was a wonder the flesh wasn't torn away to the bone.

Abraham took the map from the map case. The Israeli front spread all along the Canal from El Qantara east to Port Taufik; the auxiliary arms were dotted throughout the Sinai. Yoffe had linked with Sharon in the Mitla Pass, and was now streaking down to Sharm El Sheikh through the Negev, while a naval assault force and troops in helicopters embarked from Eilat at the tip of the Gulf of Akaba. Abraham had travelled fifty kilometres from Abu Agheila to where he found the Arab. He was on his way to Nahal Yam. Now that the main battle had swept on, there was little for him to do. The main job of vehicle recovery belonged to the Corps of Engineers, with their heavy vehicles and workshops. They were already in operation ten kilometres behind the troops who sat impatiently on the Canal, waiting the order to cross. At Nahal Yam they had overrun a detachment of the latest T-55 Russian tanks, and Abraham was to supervise their recovery. The Corps of Engineers already had its own officers. Abraham fought the knowledge that his presence wasn't really necessary.

He switched his radio to *send*. "Misha," he called. "Misha from Abraham, over . . ."

"You can't be in Nahal Yam already," he heard Misha's voice saying. "Where are you, and what's happened?"

"Look, I've found an Arab. He's been wandering about in the sun and got himself badly burned. Where's the nearest hospital? I reckon my map reference is about 227.549, along a straight bearing from Abu Agheila to Nahal Yam."

He waited several minutes while Misha checked. The frequency was dead, with only a carrier hum. He longed to be switched into the main frequency, hearing the crackle of the action.

"Abraham," Misha's voice came over again, "you're out of luck. All the casualty receiving units have gone forward a hundred kilometres west of your position and the seriously wounded are being helicoptered back to Be'ersheva. You haven't a hope of getting a chopper to stop for one Arab; be reasonable, Abraham!" As usual, Misha had anticipated Abraham's request. It wasn't reasonable to expect a helicopter with an urgent cargo of their own badly wounded troops to locate Abraham, drop down, and pick up one enemy soldier.

"I don't want to leave him," Abraham said. "Poor bastard's been out here for days to judge from the look of him."

Misha had been working. "Hang on, Abraham, there is

one chance, a hospital just outside El Arish. It's only thirty kilometres or so from where you are now. Apparently it's been cleared by infantry and there's a doctor."

"Thanks, Misha. I didn't fancy putting a bullet into this poor bastard . . . over and out!"

It was nine o'clock in the morning when Abraham arrived at the hospital with Abdul. The Arab was unconscious; Abraham had had to decide whether to go like hell to get him to a doctor, or to travel more slowly to avoid bumping him. Luckily he had decided in favour of speed. He noted signs of military occupation all the way along the road from El Arish, the remnants of fighting units left to patch their wounds before launching themselves back into the victory drive. Several times he was stopped, but Misha had obtained a direct authority for the carrier's movement from Headquarters, Southern Command, and the password got him rapidly through despite the Arab in the back.

He ran the half-track up the hospital drive. Ishmael's anger at what he thought was another invasion disappeared at the sight of the Arab. One of his two remaining orderlies helped Abraham bring the Arab inside, and they placed him in a bed in the small emergency ward. He asked Abraham to stay while he stripped Abdul and examined him.

"Where did you find him?"

"Thirty kilometres south-west, in the desert. I got him here as fast as I could. I hope I did right!"

"Thank God you hurried. Another half an hour and you'd have been too late. As it is, there may be a hope. What do you know about him?"

"Nothing. I found him wandering."

"Unfortunately we don't have all the equipment we need, but I'll manage. There don't seem to be any breakages. All these lacerations are caused by falls, I would say. We don't know if there's any internal damage, of course; if he was in a bomb blast there might be internal haemorrhage, but we'll soon find that. His heart seems sound, well, sound enough. His pulse has gone wild, of course, but that's caused by dehydration. You can't tell me anything at all about him?"
270

"I'm afraid not . . ."

"In that case, perhaps you'd like some food or coffee? I'll need the sister to help me when she's finished in the wards, but one of the orderlies will get you something. You *can* stay, can't you? You look as if you could do with a rest."

Abraham had not slept since the battle began. "At my age, you don't need much sleep," he said.

"At your age, you ought to be taking it easy."

"After the war . . ."

Ishmael had pressed the bell, and Tewfik came into the ward. "Take the officer and show him my sitting room. Make him coffee, food, anything he needs. Understand?"

"Yes, Doctor," Tewfik said and bowed Abraham from the ward.

When he brought the thick black Turkish coffee he stood before Abraham, his hands clasped together before him. Abraham was already three parts asleep. "You are a good man," Tewfik said. "You brought my brother from the cruel desert."

"We're all brothers, if we only knew it," Abraham said as he fell asleep. Tewfik brought a bowl and carefully washed Abraham's hands and neck and face; he then took off Abraham's boots and washed his feet.

When Abraham awoke after four hours of deep dreamless sleep, Hagar was standing before him, Ishmael at her side. She knelt, her hands on Abraham's knees. "I've been in to look at you a hundred times, and still can't believe it's you."

"Hello, Hagar," he said. He looked at Ishmael, standing behind her. "You must be Ishmael," he said as he held out his hand. Ishmael gripped it.

"That Arab . . .?" Abraham asked, struggling to his feet, holding Ishmael's hand. "He's going to all right?"

Ishmael nodded. Abraham looked at Hagar, put his hand on her cheek. Her skin, soft and smooth, brought back instant memories of the last time he had touched her. "I'm old now, Abraham," she said.

"We're both old now!"

Ishmael looked at his father. Abraham was a rock of a

man, strong still despite his age, his body firm. His skin was the colour of antique leather, free from blemish; his teeth were white, his jaw hard. Abraham shifted his grasp and put his arm round Ishmael's shoulder. Ishmael touched his father's hair, crisp like his own. The years between them dropped away as if they'd never been; a void Ishmael had never known existed was suddenly filled.

"Twenty years!" Hagar said. "And if it hadn't been for one Arab, wandering in the wilderness!" She put her hand on Abraham's chest where his shirt was open at the throat, taking pleasure from the touch but unable yet to liberate the myriad thoughts of their lives apart.

Abraham held them both close.

Isaac sat on the seat of the half-track and switched on the radio. When the ammeter needle registered, he pressed the *send* key on the microphone and identified himself.

"What on earth are *you* doing there?" a voice asked.

Isaac was mystified. He identified himself again, and the voice came back to him, "All right, Isaac, I heard all that. Now tell me what you're doing there." Misha was having his fun. He knew the half-track had arrived at the hospital and delivered the Arab safely to a doctor. Since there was no urgency about Abraham's going to Nahal Yam, he'd let Misha know he was obeying the 'doctor's' instructions to have a 'little breakfast' and would call later. Misha guessed the 'little breakfast' would doubtless became a 'little sleep'; he'd taken the opportunity himself to doze in his chair, headphones clamped to his ears. He had been wakened by the carrier wave preceding a voice he recognised, even before the identification, as that of Isaac.

"Some officer came to this hospital near my company position with a wounded Arab. The officer's still inside the hospital. We've brought his vehicle to our company position, and I thought I ought to find out who he is, and if there's

272

anything we can do to help. I went to the hospital, but the doctor tells me the officer is sleeping and must not be disturbed unless there's a real emergency. I thought I'd better call on his radio link to make certain the officer's not needed elsewhere. Over."

"You haven't seen the officer?" Misha asked.

"No, why do you ask?"

"And you don't know who I am?"

"Your voice is vaguely familiar, but I'm afraid I don't quite recognise it."

"If your unit moves on, Isaac, don't leave the hospital without seeing the officer, understood?"

"Understood, but why the mystery?"

"In times of war, Isaac, we don't ask too many questions. Over and out."

Isaac put down the microphone, switched off the radio, and climbed from the half-track. "Did you see the officer who brought this in?" he asked.

Zach shook his head. "He went up the drive as if the entire Arab army was waiting and he was taking 'em single-handed!"

"Keep a watch on that front door, and when the officer reappears, bring me at once."

"Understood!"

There was no need for the watch, or for Isaac to be notified. Soon after Abraham met Hagar and Ishmael, he came looking for his half-track to radio headquarters and clear himself of duty for an hour or two. He also wanted to give Misha the news.

Isaac was sitting at the edge of the trees, brooding over his arbitrary withdrawal from the war, and wondering who the officer and the Arab could be. As soon as the door opened he recognised his father and dashed across the lawn to greet him. The pleasure of reunion was nothing compared with his feelings when he learned the identity of the doctor and his mother.

"Fancy all of you eating dinner together, and not finding out who you were. Surely somebody must have mentioned

Guvena, or even my name?" Abraham asked.

There was another surprise in store for Hagar and Ishmael before the evening ended. Just as they started dinner, they heard a commotion in the drive. A large pantechnicon had driven to the front door of the hospital, bristling with aerials. The side door opened, revealing the radio operators sitting at the eight radios the command signals centre contained. With a roar, Abraham dashed out of the front door. He touched Misha's arm and drew him into the hospital and the command car drove away to rejoin the war.

"Or what's left of it," Misha said. "The war's practically over. We've beaten the daylights out of the Arabs this time. We've overrun the whole of the Sinai, and, what's more, we've taken Jerusalem!"

They were all stirred by the news. At last, at last, Jews were back in Jerusalem, the hope of centuries.

Isaac was furious. To think the Jews had been in Jerusalem for nearly twenty-four hours, and he hadn't even known!

Ena Hamilton, the Australian physiotherapist, arrived at the hospital at midday on Friday, riding an Israeli scout car. When she heard the news of the outbreak of war, she packed a rucksack, had herself driven to the Nicosia airport, and badgered her way on to an aeroplane flying to Tel Aviv within the hour. From there she hitch-hiked to Be'ersheva, Abu Agheila and El Arish by posing as a journalist. As soon as she arrived she took a bath, changed into her white coat and toured the wards. When she returned to the doctor's office, she pronounced the place "in absolute bloody chaos!" Ishmael smiled; he was used to her outbursts. He had met her in Tunis, where she was working with patients recovering from bone diseases and disorders. The effects of drug addiction, wasting tissue and muscle and severe emaciation, required similar skills and patience. Beneath her bludgeoning manner Ishmael had perceived an immense dedication.

274

"I left a programme of activities which the wretched nurses have completely neglected."

"We've been short of nurses this week!"

"The ones left should have worked all the harder. It's all very well to mend bodies, Doctor, but unless we strengthen muscles and work at co-ordination, we shall turn out cripples."

"We have had a bit of a war to cope with . . ."

"What do we care about wars, Doctor? That Indian lady in bed seventeen—her spine's like a question mark. She should have been strengthening her back all this week; we could have had her practically straight by now." She led her patients behind her like a flock of ducks. On the way to the physiotherapy lab she looked at Abdul Mohammed el-Saboor, who had been awake all morning. His eyes glittered at her from among the bandages. She clicked her teeth in disappointment when it was apparent he wasn't yet ready for her ministrations.

On the floor of the physiotherapy lab, she had drawn the footprints used in Fraenkel's method for assisting and re-learning co-ordination. Two footprints were drawn side by side. There was another set outside the first, and a third in front. Patient 15 in the chair had been a British prominent personality but such styles were forgotten here. Ena placed her patient's feet in the first set of footprints. "I want you to lift your left foot, move it to the side, and place it exactly in this outside footprint. Then lift it again, and put it back where it was." Ena lifted the patient's foot and drew chalk marks the exact shape of the patient's slipper. "Right, away you go!" The patient lifted her foot, carried it across, set it down again. On the way across, however, her foot twisted slightly and though her heel was in the chalk mark, the toe was several centimetres out. "You twisted your leg, love, did you see that? You mustn't twist your leg; just lift your foot, and carry it across." Ena took the patient through the sequence of movements to lift each foot in turn and place it accurately in the other footprints. Though the method was devised more for osteomyelitis and sclerosis victims it had already worked

275

wonders for patients whose musculature was wasted by drug addiction.

"I'll never get it right," the patient said, beginning quickly to despair.

"Yes, you will," Ena said. "I'll help you. We'll take it slowly!" The other patients were dotted round the physiotherapy lab, doing general strengthening exercises to give power back to emaciated muscles. Every so often, Ena looked up and corrected a patient. She seemed to have a built-in radar that allowed her to know what each patient was doing.

"Tuck your chin further down on to your chest, Hamid, and then lift and press further back! No slacking!" Hamid, grinning at her, rolled his head in an exaggerated gesture. "That's right," she said. "Why don't you do it like that every time?"

Mona was sitting by Abdul's bed. She could tell he was awake since his eyes followed her every movement, but he did not reply when she spoke to him in her careful, book-learned Arabic. "Ishmael really is a miracle worker," she thought, "to take a cadaver like this and fan the flicker of life into flame!" Mona was worried, however, by the patient's lack of response. "You might look at Abdul, the new man," she said to Ena, when they were drinking coffee together in the late afternoon. "With so many people away, I don't have time to sit with him as I'd like, and the poor doctor's run off his feet. Luckily his father Abraham is helping, and that marvellous man Misha—you'd never realise he was blind, would you?—but I do wish you'd have a look at Abdul . . ."

Abraham's part in the war had ended. So had Misha's. Isaac and his company hung around, waiting. A cease-fire during the night of Thursday/Friday had been broken. The Syrians had resumed artillery fire from the Golan Heights and the Israeli Air Force was out again, destroying the concrete bunkers the Syrians had so laboriously built over a period of years. Several soldiers of Isaac's company asked and got permission to tend the hospital garden to while away the time. Several also helped inside the buildings as orderlies, though Ishmael insisted there be no contact between uniformed soldiers and the patients, many of whom were still mentally disturbed. Abraham, wearing white trousers and a white shirt of Ishmael's—a perfect fit—helped Mona on medicine-administering rounds, and made beds. For such a solid man, used to the rough life of kibbutz agriculture, he had a curiously delicate touch. Misha walked the wards as if he had full vision. He seemed able to sense not only the position but also the condition of the patient in each bed he passed. He sensed those who wanted to be left alone, those who would appreciate a little conversation. He'd make his way round the side of the bed, feel for the chair, sit down. "English, français, Deutsch, espagnol, italiano . . ." Eventually he'd get to a language they could understand. Often he'd sit by a bed, talk to a patient for thirty minutes, and leave without the patient's realising he was blind.

Only Isaac did nothing active to help. His intense disappointment at being abandoned by the military High Command would not leave him. Coupled with it was a jealousy that stabbed every time he saw Ishmael and Abraham's obvious pride in Ishmael's achievements. "Fancy a lunk like me being a father of a brilliant doctor," Abraham had said one evening at dinner. Hagar looked at Isaac and rapidly changed the subject. Ishmael himself was embarrassed by his father's attitude. Though he had achieved authority in medicine, at heart he was modest.

"You ought to give a hand in there," Abraham said on Friday afternoon, when he saw Isaac sitting on a bench looking over the desert, brooding.

"That an order, Major?" Isaac asked.

Abraham sat down beside him. "Don't be bloody silly. I'm not a major, any more than you're a captain. The war's over."

"The war to end all wars? Fat lot of good I did in it."

"You took the post office in El Arish. That's an achievement you can be proud of."

"But not like being a doctor saving lives! Though why he

277

bothers with drug addicts I'll never know. I'd let the lot die . . ."

"Drug addiction's a symptom and a disease, Isaac, of a disordered society and a deranged people. There are more widespread addictions that kill more people. We came here to fight a war, and perhaps it's appropriate we ended in a hospital for drug addicts. Sometimes I ask myself if war hasn't become a more general addiction than we admit. Look at the decimation of Israel's national resources by our addiction to war! The flesh of Israel is certainly being wasted here in the desert. When I look back over the years I spent with Ya'akov, and Alexander, and Reuven, and Misha, trying to make a country healthy and strong, and now I see the weakness, almost the emaciation of the body of the country by all this fighting and war . . . This is not what we wanted all those years ago at Eli-Dov and Guvena."

"We've got to fight the Arabs for survival!"

"Is it the only way, Isaac? Must we become addicted? We started off with the marijuana of skirmishes on our kibbutzim. I know, I had a whiff of that. Then we went into the hard stuff, the raids into their territory."

"You've got to go out there to teach them a lesson."

"That's what we're doing now, is it, here in the Sinai? Teaching poor buggers like Abdul a lesson? I think it's time we realised we're the ones who need to be taught how to pick up our feet and where to put them down again! When I see you youngsters pumping the heroin of aggression into your veins I ask myself if you're hooked on war just as these poor bastards were hooked on their kind of poison."

"Kind of a twist, isn't it, Father?" Isaac said, a sneer on his lips. "The kids are supposed to be the pacifists, the oldies the war-mongers! If you'd given us defensible borders when you established the country, we wouldn't be at war right now."

Abraham stood up and looked down at his son. "I'm going to take a look at that diesel engine," he said. "Misha thinks it sounds a bit off, and you know how sensitive his hearing can be. You wouldn't care to give me a hand, I suppose?"

"No, Major, I wouldn't. I'm awaiting the orders of my battalion commander, like a good soldier should; fixing a diesel engine for a bunch of druggies who'd be better off dead is no part of my duty!"

Abraham abruptly left him. The diesel engine *was* sounding a bit off; he stripped and cleaned it. A small speck of dirt in the fuel line impeded the flow of fuel. The tank still held 35,000 litres of diesel oil, certainly enough to last until after the cease-fire. Where would they buy diesel in the future? From Israel? Would the Israelis occupy the Sinai? Would this become a Jewish hospital? Would Ishmael, and Hagar, who had spent most of their lives outside Israel, consent to stay here under the new regime? Abraham finished his work on the diesel, then went back into the hospital. Not one of them spoke of the future. They listened to the latest battle news on the radio, but the purpose of the war seemed as far away as its location. Abraham felt released from war since he had come to El Arish; he could understand the feelings of patients when Ishmael told them they had kicked the habit and could now go into remedial physiotherapy. Misha obviously felt it too, and avidly spent his time among the patients. "He's a lot more useful around here than our professional psychiatrist," Ena thought. Without saying so, they were all waiting for the cease-fire to take effect. They listened to radio accounts of the United Nations sessions as fanatics pulled helplessly at the fixed chains of national attitudes and international political expedience, releasing a seemingly endless flow of words. The war wounded died in Be'ersheva; the cries of the dispossessed in Jerusalem were stifled by the sound of the *shofar* blown at the Western Wall; Israeli troops, their hands stained with Arab blood, took out the prayer-books they had carried into battle; Arabs wandered without officers, food, water, hope or a sense of direction, beneath the broiling sun of the Sinai Desert.

Abraham and Hagar sat on the hospital verandah. Ishmael and Mona were making the last rounds of the day; Misha was helping the lonely ones compose themselves for sleep. Hagar produced a packet of rich Egyptian cigarettes from the pocket of her dress and handed one to Abraham. Then she held a match for him. He nodded his thanks and sat back in the chair exhaling smoke. Both were thinking of Ya'akov, big, burly, laughing, gay, go-anywhere, do-anything Ya'akov, who always had a cigarette for Abraham. Abraham reached out and grasped Hagar's hand. "He would have hated it here," he said.

"Not enough doing for Ya'akov!"

"He'd have wanted to be at the front, fighting. On the Canal, in Jerusalem, at Guvena, he'd have wanted to be everywhere!"

"Perhaps he too might have reached the age of discretion . . . ?" she said, looking at Abraham. It was all still there, the heat and the authority, but now the fires were banked. His hair was as crisp as ever but touched with grey above his ears; his eyes had sunk into his head as the skin aged and drew tighter on his bones. "What's to become of us?" she asked. Both accepted that now they had come together again they could not part.

"They'll establish new settlements on all this land. It'll be a hard life here in the Sinai and in the Negev. Another Eli-Dov. I may be too old."

She didn't argue with him. He knew his own strength and weakness. He was as active as ever, a little slower perhaps, but his stamina remained. She knew he was not thinking of physical things. Someone must stand in front and carry the burden of other people's doubts no matter how heavy his own may be. Above all that person must have the courage and enthusiasm to persuade others that what he says is right or can be made to be right.

"This heart condition of yours, how serious is it?"

She thought for a moment. "It exists and eventually I'll die of it, Ishmael says. But I don't propose to sit back and wait for that to happen."

"You'll take it easy?"

"I'll do the few things I still want to do!" Then she laughed. "I shan't drive tractors, or carry stones."

"What would you like to do?"

280

She squeezed his hand. "Grow young again and start all over with you."

"Have we wasted a lot of time, Hagar?"

"I don't think so. We've been apart for a long time, but I don't think of that as waste. You've helped make Israel grow, I've watched Ishmael grow. He'll make a life for himself, with Mona or somebody like her. Israel no longer needs men like you, and Ishmael no longer needs me, and so . . ."

"We can do what we want, instead of what we think we ought to."

"Is that what you were thinking when you said you were too old?"

"Too old for Israel. The land belongs to Isaac and boys like him. Captains of the paras, falling like manna from the heavens above. It's a country for young men and women. Of course our generation still holds the Histadrut and the Knesset and the Mapai, but we're on the way out, almost caricatures of the fighting heroes of the past. There won't be any more Eli-Dovs. The whole kibbutz idea will slowly die a natural death like all experiments in communal living."

"It was a good idea."

"Yes, when we were young. But it ignored one thing. Man is still a beast, Hagar; he must be to continue to believe that the way to get what you want is to stick in a knife. Beasts can't live together; they belong in the caves of lonely housing developments, isolated city apartments."

"They had to get to Jerusalem, Abraham. Two thousand years . . . promising a tomorrow in Jerusalem . . ."

"Chasing a mirage . . . like Abdul, looking for an oasis that's a figment of his own imagination. Hagar, there is no Jerusalem; it doesn't exist."

"They had to get there, to find that out for themselves."

It was evening, and the sun, a dull red ball, hovered over the ochre landscape. Only the trees and bushes of the hospital grounds, the few remaining flowers, relieved the monotonous colour of sand. Evening dew had started to condense from the humid atmosphere, and the timber of the verandah sweated, cold. Behind them the hospital was silent but for the

281

quiet thump of the diesel engine.

Abraham, restless, shuffled in his chair. "What about us, Hagar?" he finally asked.

She turned from the soul-expanding landscape and looked inwards at him, at them. "You're too old to change," she said. "I know that. But whatever happens, now that I know you want me, we'll stay together. I'll be a burden to you eventually, but you've taken other people's burdens all your life so I'll be in good hands."

"People grow old, and places change, and yet, Hagar, things somehow have a habit of staying the same," he said, with an air of profound wisdom.

She laughed out loud as she got up. "Stick to mending diesel engines, Abraham, and leave the philosophy to wise men!" she said, but there was no malice in her laughter.

At half past two on Saturday morning the wards were quiet. Ena had volunteered to take night duty in order to relieve the overworked nurses. She sat in a chair in the main ward, beneath the pale glimmer of a blue night light. The tension at dinner had been unbearable. They had listened to the news of the latest fighting in the Golan Heights, and to the ineffectual bleatings of international politicians trying to secure a cease-fire that would work. Isaac still took supper with them; he was silent and moody at table. After dinner, she had been pleased to escape to duty. Misha came with her, walked the wards saying goodnight to some of the patients. Later Ishmael and Mona administered sedatives to patients still in need. Some patients were unable to take food in the normal manner and had to be fed by liquid every four hours. She glanced at her watch. The next feed-time was four o'clock. She turned her attention back to her book.

She didn't hear Abdul enter the ward.

Her back was to the door, which she had propped open to help provide a through draught of air in the hot night. An air-conditioning unit was waiting for pick-up at Port Said. She wondered if they would ever see it. The thump of the diesel engine, a persistent almost companionable sound, was the last she heard.

Abdul, standing behind her chair, brought his arm quickly across in front of her and slit her throat with a scalpel from the tray left in his ward. Blood from her severed artery splashed the book, the chair, and the table beside her. Strange cells of comprehension are unlocked with the return of sanity; though Abdul knew his army had been defeated and his officers had fled before the Israelis leaving the men trapped in tanks to fight it out, he saw clearly he had committed the ultimate military crime: he had deserted. He looked about him, heard Hebrew, and wrongly believed this was an Israeli military hospital. Deep inside himself he felt the time-old Arab hatred of the Jews, the ingrained lust to destroy them, and resolved to become a soldier once again.

Misha and Abraham had discussed the diesel plant by Abdul's bed. He found the hosepipe and tank stopcock where they said they would be. He dragged the hosepipe to the main corridor of the hospital. It never occurred to him that he was incapable of walking; the strength of his intention pumped the adrenalin he needed. He went back to the storage tank and opened the valve. Diesel oil gushed over the floor. He poked the end of the pipe into each ward where drugged patients lay sleeping; when the tank was empty and diesel oil swilled along the corridors, the engine, starved of fuel, stopped.

The sudden silence woke Misha instantly. Abraham awoke. The sentry on duty at Isaac's encampment noticed the silence. "The engine's stopped," he thought, but it was no concern of his.

Abraham cursed and got out of bed. "That damned fuel line's blocked again," he thought. Ishmael awoke when Mona's hand touched his shoulder. "The diesel's stopped," she said.

"The emergency'll come on," he said sleepily, his head nestling in her shoulder. A small emergency engine fired automatically should the main diesel stop. It had its own starter box, its own tank of 2000 litres.

Abraham cursed when he remembered he'd switched off the emergency engine after he had mended the big engine. He must have left the switch in the *off* position.

Misha started to dress, so strong was his premonition of danger.

"It hasn't fired," Mona said.

"Oh, damn!" Ishmael was awake. He got out of bed and put on his lab coat as a dressing gown.

Abraham was walking towards the main corridor. When he paused at the top of the step, he thought the corridor was flooded. That step saved his life; no diesel had seeped along the corridor to the staff quarters. "What a stink," he said, lifting his hands to his face. The smell of diesel oil lingers on skin even after repeated washings, and he thought the smell was coming from his hands. He saw a figure in the centre of the corridor, some way along it. It looked like Ena. She seemed to strike a match and hold it to a piece of paper. "Damn silly thing for Ena to do," he thought. Why didn't she use one of the electric torches? The figure threw the paper into the water. The paper flared as it ignited the diesel oil, and the fire, engulfing the figure, filling the corridor, travelled slowly towards Abraham, rumbling, pushing with explosive pressure. Abraham flung himself sideways through the open door at the top of the steps. He banged the glass sprinkler system and alarm on the wall with his hand. The sprinklers were operated by a pump which relied on the diesel engine but the battery-fed bell started clanging immediately.

Then the hospital exploded. It took only a brief minute for the ignited diesel oil to generate sufficient pressure to explode the windows; the roof was lifted on a stump of blazing fire with a short punch that stunned ears in Isaac's camp. The woodwork of the hospital building caught fire instantly, and the explosion was replaced by the hard crackle of dry wood burning. The area for a kilometre around was lighted. Isaac rushed from his tent. He saw a small procession

284

come through the blazing hospital door: Ishmael in his lab coat, Mona wrapped in a sheet, Abraham carrying Hagar and leading Misha. There were no heroics, no attempts to dash back into the blazing building. It was apparent to them all that only those in the administrative quarters at the end of the main building could have a hope of survival.

EPILOGUE

Ishmael now works in a hospital in Tours, France, studying techniques of transplantation, with particular reference to problems of rejection.

Mona works in a children's hospital in Jerusalem, has become an orthodox Jewess, and hopes to be accepted on a kibbutz as a *metapelet*.

Isaac has done very well for himself. He lives in Tel Aviv, owns a Mercedes, and is married to Rachel. They have no children.

Miriam has been re-elected to the Knesset.

Misha lives in the artists' colony in Safad, and whenever Miriam passes through on her way to and from Guvena, she stops and visits him and the young Swedish sculptress who takes care of his day-to-day needs.

Abraham and Hagar now live on a kibbutz they helped to establish on the site of what had been the Hobart Trust Foundation Hospital. When they had time, in 1969, they were married. The kibbutz is called, in honour of the man responsible for Abraham's being there—though somewhat sentimentally, Hagar thinks—Kibbutz Abdul Saboor. Not a day goes by that Abraham doesn't bless the Arab he brought out of the wilderness.